THE
TRUTH ABOUT
SASCHA KNISCH

THE
TRUTH ABOUT
SASCHA KNISCH

—o⊘o—

TRANSLATED FROM THE SWEDISH BY THE AUTHOR

ARIS FIORETOS

Overlook/Rookery
New York, New York

THE TRUTH ABOUT SASCHA KNISCH

This edition first published in The United States of America in 2008 by
The Rookery Press, Tracy Carns Ltd.
in association with The Overlook Press
141 Wooster Street
New York, NY 10012
www.therookerypress.com

Cataloging-in-Publication Data is on file at the Library of Congress

Printed in the United States of America
FIRST EDITION

ISBN 978-1-58567-957-7
ISBN 10 1-58567-957-7

1 3 5 7 9 8 6 4 2

For Sophie

In questions of sex, nobody sticks to the truth.
Magnus Hirschfeld

THE
TRUTH ABOUT
SASCHA KNISCH

Chapter One

My name is Knisch, Sascha Knisch, and six days ago my life was in perfect order. I earned a few reichsmark here, a few there, I had a place to live that could be called home, and a sex life in which nobody interfered. Certainly, sometimes I was behind with the rent, and no doubt there were moments when I wasn't the only one to wonder when I'd get the kind of job the ads in the *8-Uhr Abendblatt* describe as 'German' and 'honest'. But I'm not the complaining type. I had what I needed, and all the time I could wish for at my disposal. Now my sex is the only thing that remains – which is, of course, what puts me in this situation. The story I'm about to tell concerns the so-called 'sexual question'. Believe me, I've done what I can to avoid having to answer it. But there's no longer any point. While I wait for Manetti – yes, *that* Manetti, 'mastermind' Manetti – to knock on the door, I had better recount what happened. And what didn't happen. Because the truth lies in what didn't happen, and only that can save me now.

Even if most of all this has its origin a few years back, nothing occurred until the last Friday of June. Some days earlier, Dora Wilms had suddenly appeared in the foyer at the cinema where I work part-time as a projectionist – alone as always, beautiful

1

as always, her movements full of hunger and risk. And six days ago, three days before Hindenburg's Germany officially entered summer, I visited her. At the Apollo, she had said it would be nice to meet again 'under different circumstances' – adding, after a pause pregnant with suggestion, 'your true self'. My true self, I wondered and rubbed the palms of my hands against my trousers. Dora's eyes were calm as deep water, but when she shot glances to the sides, as if she felt observed, I understood that she, too, could feel nervous. Presumably it was because of what had happened the last time we had met, a few months earlier. If I wanted to, she continued, fixing my eyes again, I could visit her the coming Friday. She still lived in the Otto-Ludwig-Straße, in the old flat overlooking the *Stadtbahn* tracks. And two days later, I cycled there in the heat of the afternoon, on asphalt soft as syrup, across the city to the part known as 'the west'. Not only did I arrive an hour too early, but I also misunderstood her. In no small way, either.

I should have doffed my cap and turned on my heels. But chivalry isn't my strongest trait, and as always Dora's face gave nothing away. Instead, I tried to make fun of my mistake. When she had spoken about meeting 'under different circumstances', I had thought that, well . . . I made an embarrassed gesture. She understood what I meant, didn't she? Although I felt ill at ease because of my mistake, all prick and palpitation, I have to admit I was no more than half sincere. Truth to tell, I was delighted that Friday suddenly seemed to mean what it once had: thumping heart, hot hands, eager thoughts tripping over each other. In short: itchy, delicious nervousness.

It was on Fridays that I used to knock on the door of room 202, a couple of flights up at Hotel Kreuzer in the centre of town, on a quiet side street, with a Russian porter who always wanted help with the crossword puzzle in the paper. The person who lived there weekdays between midday and seven in the evening used neither title nor last name. The first few times we met we tried 'Mrs' and 'aunt'; I felt her first name wasn't enough. Once, indulging a British whim, we even used 'lady'. However, with its soft *m* at the beginning and the end, long as pleasure doubled, and its two expectant *a*'s opening up on either side of the tongue's erect *d*, *'madame'* clearly was the right term. Even the silent *e* at the end was fitting, for it gave the word a touch of ornate Frenchness – like a frill of frozen air. 'Madame Dora', then, was what I called the woman in room 202, or preferably just 'Madame', for more than six months – before one thing led to another, and eventually ended in this unfortunate scene at the beginning of what the newspapers already have dubbed the 'spectacular' summer of 1928.

Dora waited until I had exhausted my excuses, then she stood up and suggested a suitable sum. Astonished, I looked at her. Holding her empty cigarette case between her hands, consciously or unconsciously she had assumed the same pose as the mythical woman in red holding her mysterious box in the reproduction on the wall behind her. Having pondered the resemblance – head tilted, hands horizontal, lips softly pursed – I realised not only that she forgave me my mistake, but also that friendship made no difference. Slowly I laid the bills on the table, one after another, in the hope that she would stop me before I went too far. But by the time she packed away the case and asked me to follow her, I had put a month's rent down. She paid not the slightest attention to the money. Unfortunately, we hardly had time to make ourselves comfortable in the bedroom before the doorbell rang. I looked at Dora queryingly, or perhaps pleadingly, but she just pressed the yellow blouse into my hands and said: 'Take this and hide in here. We'll continue in a little while.' Then she opened the large closet and drummed her fingernails, polished and impatient, against the oak panel.

I pushed apart a couple of hangers and stepped inside. To make sure, we checked whether the door could be opened from the inside. But by now the doorbell was ringing so insistently that Dora, who didn't deem explanations necessary, patted my cheek and said, gaze lowered and voice equivocal: 'Be a good girl and don't come out until I call.' I nodded and swallowed and the lock latched shut with a compliant click. For a few confusing moments, I actually thought I could *hear* her looking at herself in the closet mirror. First she pulled her forefingers along her lower eyelashes, then she softly smacked her painted lips and pushed, quite unnecessarily, her newly cut hair behind her ears. (Perhaps she didn't possess what *Filmwoche* would call 'classic' features, but her bony appearance was oddly attractive, at least in my eyes, and her hair always perfect.) It wasn't until I thought I could also hear the evening sun glow in her earrings, like wisps of light, that I knew imagination had got the better of me.

I stretched my neck – the high crêpe collar caused some difficulty – and strained my ears. As I couldn't discern the click of her heels, I assumed she was walking on the wicker mat in the hallway. A few seconds later, however, I made out their sound, vague and distant, like hard, solitary raindrops. She must have reached the parquet floor in the hall. Perhaps she was looking for signs that she already had a visitor? But it was summer, whatever the calendar purported, and I had brought neither raincoat nor umbrella. Then the visitor retracted his impatient forefinger – and it was at that moment, just after Dora had turned the key in the lock, that fate began to string together its obscure threads.

If I'm speaking in veiled terms, I beg your indulgence. As so often with the sexual question, the story is improper and embarrassing – improper perhaps for many, but embarrassing for me alone – and I need a little time if the words aren't to stick in my throat. Should the story offend all the same, I'd like to point out there's plenty of dirtier linen that ought to be washed. Also, not all truths are naked.

Of course, last Friday I didn't know that the threads were coming together, nor did I know that it would be the last time I'd meet Dora. We hadn't seen each other for several months, and there I was, surrounded by her clothes, with my pulse pounding softly and plushly – as if suddenly, ripe with rapture, I existed in all parts of my body. Fate probably was the last thing I thought of. The darkness in the closet was at once narrow and infinite, and while my hands groped around, I tried to remember what Dora used to wear when we were still seeing each other. Next to me were blouses with stiff stand-up collars, flowing shark-fin collars, and no collars at all. I remembered that some had pleated breasts, others had hems or bows. After the blouses came sweaters, a jumper I didn't recognise, ditto a cardigan, and a couple of British slipovers, which, I recalled, were custard yellow with striped borders in made-up college colours. On one hanger were five or six wide silk cravats, on another a flimsy nightdress that I pulled, fingers trembling, towards my face. The soft mixture of perfume and cigarette smoke made me think of what was going to happen once the visitor had left. In a few minutes, Dora would light one of her American cigarettes, put away the case in which she kept them, and prolong the sweet agony a few moments more – smoking in one of the chairs by the window, one leg folded over the other, so that the evening sun could glide along her shin and the leather shoe, as black and glistening as motor oil. Then she'd roll the tip of the cigarette against the edge of an ashtray and slowly utter my name.

Was I holding the violet nightdress that I had once slipped over her arms, raised so matter-of-factly that I'd been able to see first the bent elbows, then the steep slope of the nose, and finally the chill-stiffened nipples outlined through the material? Or was it the shiny white negligee, usually thrown across the foot of the bed alongside the kimono in artificial silk? It was impossible to tell the colours in the dark, so instead I continued my fumbling exploration. Further in were skirts, dresses, and evening gowns of silk. Some garments hung almost down to the floor, because when I moved my hand their hems rustled with a smooth sound, almost like seaweed. Imagination aflame, it wasn't hard to picture myself as one of a troupe of elegant dancers lined up, one after the other, waiting for the doors to be flung open so we could sail out onto the wide, shimmering parquet, where we would be met by gentlemen in tails, with pomade in their hair and cigarettes burning between sinewy fingers, next to signet rings in matt silver or mellow gold.

Suddenly, I made out muted voices, as if they were talking into pillows. Then a laugh rang out, surprisingly loud, almost provocative, and someone broke into song:

Drive, obscure, I'm in your wicked hands,
all shrewd ache and furtive glance.

It sounded like the great Rigoberto. Dora must have invited her visitor into the living room and put a record on the gramophone. Carefully I resumed my groping. Presently I came upon what could have been an old-fashioned petticoat, lined and padded, with frills of the kind my mother had also used. Then there were a few jackets, one of them from Berchtesgaden as I could tell from the typical cut, the thick seams, and the heavy material, after which followed a complicated leather ensemble, and finally Dora's 'Amazon' outfit. I remembered the stylish tweed jacket over an asymmetrically cut skirt, which in turn partly covered a pair of jodhpurs. Ever so patiently, without making the hangers click or clatter, I groped until I found the skirt's high slit and could insert my trembling fingers between the trouser legs so as to feel the leathery crotch in the glowing palm of my hand.

Slowly, however, the heat of the closet began to make me impatient. When would we finally be alone? How long would it be before she uttered my name? Dora must have been expecting a visitor. Why hadn't she asked me to come back an hour later, as originally agreed? Cautiously I put on the blouse. Then I turned my head and laid my ear against the door, collar cutting into chin. Was that a man speaking just now? The voices seemed to be coming from the living room, because now I heard Dora say, loud and clear: 'I hope it will pass. Perhaps we should . . .' Then the door to the bedroom was pulled shut.

In the distance a *Stadtbahn* train went by, all rattle and routine, after which I only heard my short, scant, not particularly dignified breathing. My pulse throbbed hotly at my temples, the clothes chafed provocatively. I've already said that mine is an improper story, so I might as well admit that the stuffy heat, no, the stiff waiting, made me feel aroused. Without thinking, I let my hand glide down my stomach and the covered buttons, which arched softly across my midsection, like bumpy sow's teats. The waist curved inwards and when I flexed my abdomen, the corset ribs pressed against my trunk in rigid rows. It was as if I'd become . . . No, this is difficult. I didn't know that some words really *are* harder than others to get across one's lips. It was as . . . As if I . . . One more time. It was as if I'd become a flower.

From the ribs down I was a moist stalk, from the chest up a glowing bud about to burst. While I imagined what I looked like, flushed and myopic, my hand continued to make its way down the ribbing and the sleek silk, towards the elastic suspenders which had been tightened and ended in metal clasps that held the stockings in place. To delay the wild, wondrous torment I felt welling up inside me like a fabulous cloud, I avoided my trembling sex and instead travelled up the other thigh, past the hip and the stiff curve of the waist, until I reached my majestic bust and burning armpit.

Racked by lust, racked by dread, I waited to hear, at long last, the creaking of the wicker chair and Dora striking a match with that fatal smoothness of hers. Calmly she would drag on the cigarette and utter my name, smoke wafting in the late afternoon sun. Again I made out voices in the hallway. Now they spoke more mutely than before. But was her visitor man or woman? Surprised, I realised it was impossible to determine the identity of a person solely on the basis of the sounds they made with their body. Finally, I decided that if they went left, back into the living room, it was a man; if they turned right, into the kitchen, a woman. Soon . . . Wait. The living room. Dora had male company. In that case, I wasn't going to sneak out and sit on the bed. Not in this get-up.

Suddenly I heard a shrill shout, followed by a muffled sound, and I understood I had been wrong: they had gone into the kitchen – and thus the visitor was a woman. Had Dora called my name? I pressed my ear against the door, but couldn't make out any further sounds. I was certain she'd call again if she needed help. Carefully I shifted my weight from one foot to the other; blood was swelling my legs. But space was scarce and every time the hangers hit each other with a ripple of titters, I stopped. Slowly impatience mounted. Why did it take so long? Would the visitor really stay for ever? Dora must have been reading my thoughts, for just as I stretched my toes, I heard the handle come down and the door to the bedroom open. The uninvited guest had left. We were alone at last.

I made out a dull, shuffling sort of sound and a scatter of spry steps. Odd, it sounded as if she was pulling something. Again a *Stadtbahn* train went by, this time with a thunderous hullabaloo that reluctantly lost itself in the distance, then Dora sat down on the bed. That much I understood because the springs in the bed moaned. After a short pause, she checked the drawer on the bedside table – probably for the extra cigarettes she used to keep there. Evidently they were elsewhere, for she rose and went over to the other side of the room. First she pulled out the drawers of the chest with muted chalk-on-blackboard shrieks, then she searched behind the curtains, and finally – wait – finally she checked behind the chair on which my clothes were. I was about to whisper through the closet doors that my Moslems were still on the table in the living room, when it struck me that perhaps she wasn't looking for something to smoke. Rather, she might be preparing herself. Of course, *that*'s why she had wanted me to hide: not in order to shelter me from the unknown eyes of the visitor, as I had thought initially, but so as to prevent me from seeing, in advance, what she had planned to do once we were alone.

Dora pushed back the chair and approached the closet. Immediately, my heart pounded hard and wild, and not only the hair on my arms stood erect. But instead of saying something, she seemed to hesitate in front of the mirror doors. Perhaps she was checking her makeup? My body melted into hot, bubbly expectancy. Any moment now, Dora would utter my name. I had promised to be a good girl, so the best thing was to remain calm. Conscientiously, I pushed my legs together, straightening my back, and let my hands hang with elbows pressed to my sides. Then an uncomfortable thought occurred to me: what if it wasn't Dora who stood on the other side, but the visitor who hadn't yet left? Were the steps I had made out not heavier, the breathing not hoarser and deep? No, no, imagination. Of course it was Dora. She'd never have let the visitor into the bedroom alone; she just wanted to test my endurance. Now I could hear her returning to the hallway – presumably to get my cigarettes from the living room. Apparently, she was out of her own. Soon she would be back, and then, at long last, it would be my turn.

But time passed and nothing happened. Gradually, silence descended on the flat. One might almost have thought somebody had passed away. Should I leave the closet and check? Or did I merely imagine things? I almost burst out laughing when I realised the simple truth: Dora had tiptoed back, shoes in hand, to see how long I'd last before I broke my promise! I clenched my fists and shut my eyes, and in this way I managed to remain steadfast for another few minutes. But then I couldn't take it any longer. Although the pricking agony was delicious, it suddenly felt as if my bladder was about to burst. The alarm clock on the bedside table showed 6.25 when I threw open the doors and emerged from my involuntary paradise – with the yellow blouse straining across a brassiere stuffed stiff with napkins, my hair in plaits, and my hands carefully on my hips, tottering bravely on high heels, with a red satin bow tied around my mad sex.

After that, nothing was the same again.

Chapter Two

When, an hour later, I entered the projection room at the Apollo, One-legged Else was about to mount the last newsreel. That's what everyone calls her, although she's missing both legs. My colleague didn't deign to acknowledge me with even her standard hello. Usually, she talks quite a bit, but this time her silence was so dense it had become palpable. Although I had just had the worst experience of my life, clearly there was only one thing to do: to lie low, very low. So I sat down on a stool and groped in my pockets. After a few miserable attempts, I managed to light a cigarette.

Immediately One-legged Else rolled over to the projector, carrying tonight's main feature in her lap. It was still *Refuge*, which we'd be showing for another week. Silently she deployed the brakes (they look like diminutive ski sticks), silently she raised her gaze, and silently she followed the dusty light beam out of the projection room, over the dark heads in the theatre. I recognised the images recreated on the screen. They were from the German Prize in Nürnberg last year, when Mercedes had taken all medals and Elizabeth Junek ended fourth in the two-litre class with her Bugatti. The organisers hoped for a similar sensation in a few weeks.

As usual, Otto molested the piano in the theatre. Personally I believe he is not just mute but also deaf, though that's just a private theory. According to Else, his proud mother, he has a perfect ear, yet lives in his own world, where harmonies are different from those of Busoni, but just as heavenly. Now Otto shivered with the keys the way I taught him last autumn – showers of fine, nervous rain – and as I looked out I saw the drivers slide into their cars. Soon thereafter, they adjusted their glasses and drove away in jerky but surprisingly reliable movements, to the wild consent of an almost invisible crowd. The latter one could tell from the eager flags and hands that protruded from the lower part of the screen. A cap flew up in the air – and never returned to its owner.

I put out my cigarette and pocketed the matches. I haven't been told why, but Otto likes to play with fire and One-legged Else has asked me never to let any lie around. If only she knew what had happened! Yet stubbornly my colleague kept her eyes glued to the screen, her unusually big hands resting on the rubber wheels, unimpressionable. Else had pulled her hair back behind her ears, so that in the penumbra, it looked as if she, too, had donned a helmet. Her slanted eyes blinked only rarely in the light from the projector, her bosom heaved and sank slowly. A Polish sphinx.

On the screen, the race cars vanished in a cloud of sun-studded dust and profuse black exhaust in the upper right corner – only to return a few seconds later, this time from the lower left corner of the screen, as if they had circled the cinema, where they were waved across the finishing line, one after the other, by a man in knickerbockers and chequered flag in hand. In the theatre, Otto hammered out the finale while the winner strolled over to Junek and embraced her according to all rules in the book. (The result? Two fractured ribs and a number of sore toes. I'm not joking.) Then the last chords could be heard – always the same when Otto interprets a 'heroic victory' characterised by 'German dignity' – and soon thereafter, the screen shone, empty and amazed, over the nonplussed audience.

The theatre was only half full. Some men removed the arms they had placed along the back of the chairs in which their company was sitting – most of them nurses from the Miséricorde, the big hospital which is usually referred to, simply, as the Misery. One woman adjusted her hair under her bell-shaped hat, another began to dig for something in her handbag. Immediately, her companion held up a lighter. The slick sliver of fire danced silently, a diminutive god of gas, but she just wanted to powder . . . Wait. Did someone say something?

'I said scientifically proven human thoughts generate beams and waves. Emissions received by radio scopes. Soon everybody read thoughts. President Hindenburg, Lilian Harvey, Justus Stegemann . . . Only matter of years.' Although she has spent considerable time in this country, One-legged Else doesn't speak perfect German. I usually try to imagine that what she's attempting to say is a film in which every eighth or tenth frame is missing. Then it's easier to get the drift. 'Not expensive.'

Still, sometimes you don't follow. Did she refer to the thoughts or the years?

'The radio scopes naturally.' My colleague turned around, eyes more benevolent than I had dared hope. 'Mass production five years. Everyone can afford. Nurses, bricklayers, war veterans. Even Sascha. Democracy in pocket size. No larger than pack of cigarettes.' She pointed to my Moslems and loosened the brakes.

Aha. Oh, Else. Cross because she had to take care of the news-reels alone. I was just about to explain myself when my colleague raised her hand: 'Excuses later. First realise race cars belong to history.' She rolled over to the tiny window and looked out on the white screen on which the projector lavished such unnecessary attention. 'May as well run backwards. People of future travel in thought. A see B thinking, think question. B see thought, think answer. Wordless understanding.' She raised one eyebrow. 'But problem keep thought to oneself. For example, difficult to cheat on wife. Win race at Nürburgring. Lie to colleague. Or what Sascha think?' Gripping the wheels, Else rolled backwards to the projector.

I nodded helplessly. Certainly, if she said so. With radio scopes, imagination might well be put out of play. Now the first whistles could be heard from the theatre.

'Some don't understand silver screen is paradise. Like inside of eyelids. Everything possible, everything projection. At least according to Dr Froehlich.' She must be referring to Martin Froehlich, the famous *Sanitätsrat* and the brain behind the Foundation for Sexual Research. But what did he have to do with film projectors? I hummed uncertainly, with an encouraging pitch added at the end. 'News show Froehlich at station with Gielke. On their way to Copenhagen. Found international league for sexual reform. Train leave platform. "Our century belong to grey sex! One day world understand man can be anything: brother, monster, mixture. Everything question of projection!"' Philosophically, she adjusted the camera lens. In an earlier incarnation, One-legged Else must have been a teacher back in Poland, or possibly a governess. She has opinions about most things and explanations for all. 'But not even Froehlich will count sisters . . .' Before I had had time to ask her what she meant, she continued: 'Just as train depart he declare: "Road to salvation long. We need reform. And peace between bed sheets." Gielke lean out and wave. First hand, then kerchief. Thereafter both: *"Fraternité!"* Compelling tableau. Now Sascha help?' She turned off the projector. Apparently, her account of the portion of the news I had missed was over.

After some difficulty, we managed to get the first reel in place. It was new and new ones are often awkward. I threaded the shiny celluloid through the levers and controls, attaching the end to the empty back wheel. Then I turned the receiving spool a few times and thought what I always think when I do this: the spools were just like bicycle wheels, the film a well-oiled chain. I nodded to my colleague, who switched on the electricity again. The theatre turned silent. A woman laughed, whereupon Otto began to play on nervous keys. The main feature could begin.

'Ice tea?' Having rolled over to the sink, One-legged Else clattered with glasses and china. 'Earlier today, Stegemann install refrigerator in foyer.' (While my colleague has her back turned to me, I hasten to insert that Justus Stegemann is the owner of the Apollo. As a type, he's pure Prussian: punctual and stingy, with a shrill voice that often breaks, a clipped little moustache, and something hectic but unfinished in his movements – as if he didn't know how to end and resented the fact. According to my colleague, it's because he is all skin and no spine. I've been meaning to ask her how she knows, but this was hardly the opportune moment. Besides, she was just turning towards me again.) 'Boss claim he make more money on thirst than imagination. Beer good for people. "Germany says Schultheiss!" But people poor morale. Russian Dabor come with pockets full of bottles. As soon as lights go out, he open. Not good business for boss. Boss angry. Tell Else. Then Else Otto.' She rolled over and put the glasses on the table. 'And Otto finally stop.' The ice clinked calmly, the tea leaves rotated and sank to rest.

There we sat, Else in her wheelchair, I on my stool, and everything seemed as usual. My colleague philosophised, I hummed in assent, and now and then we listened to her son's interpretation of the main feature. The ice tea tasted of peppermint. The only difference was that, this time, chaos ruled my thoughts. After a few reels, I slowly began to get it under control. Finally, I even managed to tap a Moslem against the table, put it in my mouth, take it out, put it back, and light it, and was just about to present an edited version of what had happened at Dora's place when Else interrupted me: 'But perhaps Stegemann right. People don't like screen. If radio scopes cheap, only matter of time before Apollo retire. End of film, end of freedom, end of projection.'

If only she knew how unreliable my personal projector had been a few hours earlier! Had I considered reality a little more, imagination a little less, nothing would have happened. Did Else remember Dora? Although my colleague prefers monologues, she had actually chatted with Dora the week before. Perhaps if I refreshed her memory? Bony face; short, dark-blonde hair as

14

of late; 'Nordic' looks. Not as tall as one might think. Slow, fatal movements, narrow, sinful hips, strong ankles. A bit like . . . I tried to think of a suitable actress. Like Dary Holm, perhaps. But with smaller bust, heavenly fingers, and perfectly straight shoulders. As well as a front tooth of which one corner had been chipped off.

'New reel.' Silent and synchronised, we made the change. For a few moments, the film shivered, then it found its rhythm and continued to tell the story of an upper-class youth who returns to Berlin after nine years in the Soviet Union. 'What Sascha do?' One-legged Else looked at me in tranquillity.

What I did? The same thing as the fop on the screen. My best not to lose my nerve, of course. And to retire honourably. What else?

'Almost hour too late.' Her oval eyes glittered in the light from the projector – one part interest, three parts anticipation. 'If Else not tell boss that Sascha, not Otto, take care of Dabor . . . No, wait. Not Lakritz!' She eyed me with contempt. 'Pah, not even try. Else understand without radio scope, too.' My colleague turned away, and although she had read me wrong – my best friend had nothing to do with the matter – I realised, gratefully, that protests were futile.

Was it for the same reason that I hadn't said a word when, finally, a few hours earlier, I had flung open the closet doors and emerged from my private Eden? As soon as I realised there was nothing I could do, I pulled off my blouse, wiped off the makeup, and tried to steady my nerves. A while later, I picked up the phonebook on the shelf in the hallway, under Dora's address book, and dialled the number of the nearest police station. I heard the signals peter out in the distance, but the officer in charge had barely answered before I slammed the phone back in its cradle. Abruptly, I realised the seriousness of the situation. Who would believe me if I claimed I was innocent? If I maintained I had neither seen nor heard anything – at least no more than a few footsteps with matching breath on the other side of the closet doors – the inspector in charge would shake his head and, index finger pointing towards bed, declare the obvious: the woman there must have died in *some* way, no? Did I really mean to say I didn't know how? Was I arguing, in all earnestness, that she had crawled into the bedroom on her own and fallen asleep for ever, lying on the bed with hands peacefully clasped? Clearly it was wiser to wait. As long as I kept my mouth shut, at least I couldn't compromise myself. In the meantime, before the police got interested, I better check whether my poetic licence was still valid.

In the theatre, Otto continued his maltreatment of the piano. I lit another cigarette and contemplated what I had realised during my furious ride to the Apollo: without an alibi, I'd never make it. The crooked match twisted, turned, and died in the ashtray. After a few fortifying puffs, I finally pulled myself together. 'Else,' I said and saw the smoke whirl in the light from the projector. (Nobody would dream of addressing her as 'One-legged Else'.) 'Something has come up and I need your help. But you have to promise me not to tell anyone.'

Having rearranged a few things, I then proceeded to inform my colleague roughly of what had occurred.

Chapter Three

We closed just before midnight. Except for the confiscated beer bottles, the evening had unfolded without incident. Now we waited for Otto to turn off the big neon letters that Stegemann mounted on the façade last autumn, then there would be a change of scenery, at least for me. I had to find Lakritz as soon as possible. Only my best friend would know what ought to be done. We saw a white *A* disappear, thereafter a red *P*, followed by a yellow *O*. After another couple of letters, the final glossy black *O*, too, vanished without trace. Now Otto could lock the doors, pull down the creaking shutters, look for the padlocks, receive them from Else, in whose lap they had been lying, and bend down to lock the shutters also. Since it was too dark to see properly, his mother gave him a box of matches. Otto struck a sulphurous light, locked the blinds with a few deft movements, blew out the match, and straightened his back. Wordlessly, he bid goodnight. His beautiful face – clean, what some would call 'Nordic' features, solid chin, steel-grey gaze – was devoid of expression. For a moment, he seemed to hesitate, then he returned both keys and matches to his mother. Having crossed the street, he disappeared at the corner. For a few seconds longer, his drawn-out shadow could be seen, then it, too, pulled its head in and vanished.

'Sascha's secret in safe hands. Compared to Else, grave is chatterbox.' Stoically, my colleague put her hands on the rubber wheels.

'Thanks, I appreciate it.' I already had mine on the wooden handles of my black Torpedo. 'See you tomorrow.'

'In time this time,' she replied as she rolled towards the gutter. 'Not provoke fate. But Sunday stay home. Stegemann new show for private patrons.' With admirable skill Else made it down from the high kerb and followed Otto. They live north of the Misery. I swung myself up on the leather saddle and began to pedal east.

For the last few weeks, the weather had been tremendous, with big, booming skies during the day and warm nights full of promise and secrecy. But this night, the streets felt narrow and threatening. Without warning, the city officials seemed to have increased the distance between the lamps. When I found myself between a couple of them, I could hear only the taut creaking of my saddle, as if darkness were about to capsize. To make sure – suddenly, I felt inexplicably jostled – I stood up and gave the pedals an extra push, to the next lamp. As soon as I had slid out of its luminous circumference, however, humid darkness took over anew. Again I stood up, pushed the pedals down their elastic kind of nothingness, and reached the next quivering lamp. And again squeaking darkness swallowed me. Things continued in this manner for a good while, fairly predictably, while sweat glossed my forehead and my mouth filled with the twinge of iron – until the bell began to rattle. Finally, a cobbled street. Now my pedalling echoed securely between the houses. No reason to panic.

As I reached the big intersection a few blocks further on, a tram eked by, the rhomboids on its roof swaying with sullen resilience. In the last car, illuminated by yellowish light, were two passengers: a middle-aged man with his head tilted so far back his mouth stood open like that of a Christmas pig (only the waxed apple between his teeth was missing) and a younger woman with too much makeup, who sat next to him and just turned to the window with a muscular grimace. When she saw her own reflection, she stifled her yawn with a surprisingly swift hand. Farther up the street, the tram jerked to the left, where it was met by a companion containing the same cargo of worn-out light. The latter stopped right in front of me, releasing six people. Two of them, both men, hurried into a restaurant from the Rhineland known mainly for Jolly, a half-naked hunger artist who lives on mineral water and cigarettes, sitting in a glass box doing nothing.

I turned into the street and noticed the pleading gaze of the driver. Then I understood he was merely looking in the mirror in front of him, waiting for a sign from the conductor. A bell tolled, the driver lowered his gaze, and the train continued through the windless night. As I reached the next crossing, I jumped off my bicycle, pulled it onto the pavement, and locked it next to a wall. The Blue Cellar is some hundred metres down one of the side streets, behind a synagogue, and hardly the kind of place at which one arrives on two wheels.

As usual, Konrad sat on the chopping block outside the entrance. He's easy to describe: open vest, rolled-up sleeves, tattooed arms poised on an ex-boxer's knees. Between the index and middle finger, a short but fat cigar glowed. When he saw me he stood up, put the well-chewed butt in his mouth, and extended a hand big enough for two. 'Knisch, haven't seen you in ages!' His forehead glittered in the light from the bulb above the door. Noctuids performed a wild dance in the naked light.

'What's happening?' At the Blue Cellar, things rarely happen, and if, occasionally, they nonetheless do, they're never any good.

'Rigoberto's performing. And Gertie and Ludmila show their breasts. But you probably know them already.'

'Is Anton here?' I ignored the suggestion.

Konrad looked over my shoulder. New guests were just arriving. As I turned around, I realised it was the couple I had seen in the tram a few minutes earlier. The man was short, chubby, and fifty. Considering his overcorrect clothing – not even the golden chain connecting buttonhole with waistcoat pocket was missing – he might be a notary, or perhaps a diplomat. He whispered something in the ear of his companion, who laughed an affected but charming laugh. 'Madam, sir. Good evening.' Shifting his cigar from one corner of his mouth to the other, Konrad narrowed his eyes queryingly.

'Is this the Blue Cellar?' The man's voice was so hoarse it hurt to listen. To make matters even worse, he spoke with a French accent. Konrad looked at him as if he had not understood a single word. When the newcomer didn't receive the reply he had expected, he pulled the tall woman towards himself; stooping, she removed a strand of hair from her ear. I noticed that she held her handbag pressed to her chest and wore high brown boots with red laces. Once he had finished, the man clicked his heels, folded his fingers around the sleeves of his jacket, and – entirely unnecessarily – pushed out his already starched shirt-front. '*Alors?*' he commanded. His companion said nothing, but straightened her back and eyed me with a look both silken and sullen.

Instead of answering, Konrad turned to the woman. 'Dominique,' he said, placidly removing the cigar from his mouth, 'it's always good to see you.' Dominique pulled closer to the man with sandpaper for vocal chords. 'But this is no place for your friend. May I suggest' – Konrad looked at the man, who had taken off his hat and was now thumbing the rim – 'the Stork's Nest?' Again he scrutinised the newcomer's hands. 'No, The Cuckold would be better. Just around the corner. Surely the lady knows it.' He nodded to the woman, then turned to me. 'Lakritz? Haven't seen him. But he'll probably show up. Sooner or later, he always does.' Konrad sat down, extinguished his cigar by twisting his foot first this way, then that, and began to whistle melodiously. Irked, the woman called Dominique turned on her heels and left with her companion who suddenly seemed deflated.

I walked down the stairs and remained for a while just inside the door. Everything was bathed in blue, cocktail-coloured light. The great Rigoberto was just finishing his last number with a theatrical fist clenched to his chest:

They found nothing in the flat, o Lord,
nobody saw her other part.
So they thought: 'Why not take the reward,
and make of blindness an art?'

It was quarter past midnight, the applause scattered and distracted. In one corner, I discovered Molly. Dressed in a thin blouse that did much of her justice, she was conversing with a tanned man in flawed but fantastic German. Probably she hails from South-west Africa, but nobody seems to know. Not even herself. Molly smiled and I noticed she hadn't had time to visit the dentist. One night last December, the police raided the Blue Cellar. In the chaos that ensued, someone punched out her front teeth – apparently a token of affection compared to what Konrad did when he had sorted out the bedlam and invited the person responsible into the courtyard. Molly swears, however, her dental difficulties have certain advantages.

There were only ten or so guests present. Rigoberto just sat down at the bar. As he saw me, he turned away and began to talk to Gertie, who was buttoning her blouse with bored fingers. I passed two pimpled youths, who hardly looked of legal age, sitting with half-empty glasses in front of them. They stopped talking until I had found a table in a corner. I thought I felt their gazes in my back, but realised I was probably oversensitive after what had happened earlier in the afternoon. Behind the counter, Helmut polished glasses with economical gestures. Holding one up to the light, he scrutinised it as if it were made of Bohemian crystal, then proceeded to pour beer before I had time, or wits, to order.

On the chair next to me was a newspaper. With thoughts chasing each other in loops and circles, however, I found it difficult to concentrate on the headlines. Perhaps I shouldn't have called from the Apollo? Else had forced me to do so between the first and second screening. 'Nobody should be left alone until dead officially,' she said and advised me to call the police. Worried about the consequences, I finally gave in, hoping it wasn't possible to trace a call in the few seconds it took to utter words such as 'dead', 'help', and an address. To be on the safe side, I used my lightest voice. Even if the police officer who answered didn't take my call seriously, he must follow regulations. I assumed that meant he had sent out a couple of colleagues, who probably had left the headquarters down at the big square only reluctantly. An hour or so later, they must have called for backup: the city had another corpse on its hands.

Presumably the body was carried downstairs, into an ambulance, and transported to the morgue. Presumably the inspector in charge had interviewed the inhabitants of the building to find out if they'd noticed anything unusual, before he asked them to disperse. And presumably he'd gone through the flat, looking for signs of what might have happened. Having sealed the front door – a proper search could wait until later – he returned to headquarters with his assistants, where a first report presumably was just being typed on a typewriter thundering in the empty corridors. Tomorrow they'd begin to look into Dora's past for clues. Sooner or later, they'd presumably, no, definitely, encounter me.

I surveyed the guests, wondering if I should have given my name. Almost immediately, I rejected the idea. As long as I couldn't prove my innocence, safe was better than sorry. After all, there were things I preferred not to have to account for – among them, habits which are still punishable according to paragraph 168 that allows people to wear the clothes of the opposite sex only in private. Considering what had happened at Dora's, and also that she had asked for money for her services, her closet surely would be deemed public space. Intuition told me it wouldn't take long before the case was in the papers, and then it was only a question of time before I ended up in a house of correction.

I was in a fix, a damn dangerous fix. In all likelihood, it could be proven I had been to Dora's place. If it came to the worst and the police suspected me, they'd wonder why I hadn't contacted them. Traces of my visit must be all over. Certainly I could explain most of them by saying that we had been partners once.

But what about the clothes Dora had given me? No, they had been folded and put back in the drawers, the shoes were now in the closet, the makeup box had been tucked away, and the napkins were again in the kitchen. Why would the police wonder if somebody other than the owner of the flat had the habit of dressing as a big, sweet schoolgirl?

My eyes fell on a photo in the paper, showing an elderly man with a laurel on his head, sitting in front of long rows of vessels mounted on shelves. In each of the containers, a grey scrap of cloud seemed to hover. Distracted, I began to read the article. Halfway through what turned out to be a surprisingly interesting account of a Swedish craniologue, whose 'soul biological' collection had recently been put up for sale, Helmut placed a bigger and a smaller glass in front of me. I must have looked dejected, because when I discovered the schnapps he whispered reassuringly: 'An attempt at resurrection.' Shimmering in the alcohol, his little silvery copy nodded with a beatific smile – standing on its head. I raised my gaze and thanked the original, then returned, none too thrilled, to the merry-go-round installed in my head.

The woman I had visited a few hours earlier was no more. Although we never got to know each other as well as I would have liked, I had reason to mourn her. Before I did so, however, I must save my own skin. At the moment, neither she nor I would gain anything from missed opportunities. Arousing the police's suspicion was the last thing I needed – which meant I had to find out, as quietly as possible, what Dora had been up to since we stopped seeing each other. Obviously, she had been in danger.

I thought back to the day in August 1926, when I had seen her name for the first time. It had been in an ad in the *8-Uhr Abendblatt*, which had talked about 'the eternally feminine' in ways that hadn't given me much rest. Repeatedly, I leafed through the paper to ponder the text with its hidden promise. ('Become a woman with that little extra! Dora, experienced sister, reveals the eternal feminine in you, too!') Did the words really mean what I read into them? Finally, deciding to find out, I went down to Heino's coal cellar at the corner and used his phone to dial the number given in the ad. My resolve surprised me, but I suppose there are times when one's drives remain obscure even to oneself. Luckily, the neighbourhood florist was standing up on the pavement, so although my heart was stuck in my throat, in a manner of speaking, I could talk freely. The number turned out to be that of a hotel. When I had been connected, however, the woman at the other end tactfully refused to answer any questions. Instead she merely replied she didn't think I'd be disappointed by her use of words if I came by. She accepted visitors weekdays between midday and seven in the evening. In room 202. What? Yes, it was all right to come by this very afternoon. Having jotted down the address on my palm, I returned home. As my heart made itself comfortable in my chest again, I washed carefully, sitting in the zinc tub with my left hand raised in the air. One half of me had already capitulated to my drives.

Yet the closer I got to Hotel Kreuzer a few hours later, the more uncertain I became. Shouldn't I return home? Or at least have something strong while considering what I seemed about to do? I read the feeble trace of the address left on my palm and realised that, in any event, I must invent an alter ego. You never knew what might happen. Recently, the papers had begun to carry odd reports of men who had committed suicide after having been blackmailed. Was there anything more undignified for a German gentleman than to make up his face and dress in the clothes of the opposite sex? As a gesture of protest, a highly placed person – a commercial counsellor, I think – had had a Turkish orange in his mouth when he was found hanging in stockings from the chandelier, dressed in a tunic he had once bought for his wife at the bazaar in Constantinople. His painted toenails, colour-coordinated with the orange, had touched a pair of high-heeled mules, which, neat to the last, he had put aside on the floor. The orange was interpreted, by the liberal press, as an 'eloquent disapproval' of the self-inflicted silence suffered by men of the counsellor's complicated nature.

Having pondered different pseudonyms (healthy German names such as Ingolf, Lothar and Wolfram), I settled for the alter ego closest at hand, then continued to pedal with increased speed. Again my pulse began to beat, wildly and willingly. It didn't quiet down until I pushed open the hotel doors and entered the foyer – as if I had crossed a threshold and, unexpectedly, found myself on the safe side. Now, steadying my feral heart, I made an amazing discovery: a difference of only a few metres sufficed to separate two beings. A minute earlier, I had been Sascha Knisch cycling through the city. Presently, I was not only anonymous, but reduced – no, 'reduced' is the wrong word: *concentrated* – to my drives. Having been a person with biography, I had become a sex without history.

Behind the hotel desk sat a man so emaciated that, when undressed, he was bound to appear as a coat hanger mounted on a broom. His skull was as polished as a bedknob, but generous amounts of hair grew out of nasal and other openings. I assumed it wasn't the first time he had enacted the little comedy to which I gathered we now had to devote ourselves. At first, he pretended not to notice me. Personally, I did my best to seem dreamy and distracted. But then I thought my counterpart exaggerated his role a bit. Immersed in his crossword, he didn't look up during several long minutes, until, indignantly, I was forced to bring my palm down on the bell. At that, the porter raised his gaze, still half absent, carefully folded his glasses, and put them in his shirt pocket – where they disappeared as if the inside had been lined with oblivion.

I cleared my throat and explained that, well, actually, I was looking for an acquaintance of mine. In room 202, I thought. The man looked at me as if he hadn't registered my voice. Or perhaps he was busy committing the new visitor to memory? If so, it can't have been very difficult: red hair and green eyes, the latter flickering and glassy, a pair of flushed earlobes, and freckles blown across nose and chin.

In order to seize the initiative, I wondered with big, elastic mouth If He Somehow Suffered From Impaired Hearing. No, his hearing was excellent, the porter replied in broken German, inserting a wriggling index finger into one of his furry ears. But there was a wasp in my hair. It took me a while before I realised what he had said. 'Ah, wasp,' he repeated, pensively this time, pulling out of his ear. Again he unfolded his glasses; again he put them on; again he leaned over his crossword. 'Five letters, *s* in middle. "*Wespe*", naturally.' He looked up. 'That's how you pronounce word, no? *Wespe*?'

I had better things to do than correct his pronunciation. When, finally, I had shaken off the insect, I proceeded to remind the porter of room 202. Apparently it was located a couple of flights up, to the left. I left the desk at the same moment that he brought down his paper on the unwelcome guest, who was just trotting across a calendar hanging on the wall. (The wasp died on Monday, August 23 – three days later than in reality.) Again, my pulse began to beat. When, at last, I stood in front of the door to the room for which I had been yearning with such a bewildering mixture of ardour and irritation, I counted the beats, waited until they no longer sounded like snooker balls colliding, and knocked. Now there was no return. I'd become one with my sex.

'Anton?' The woman who opened had short, jet-black hair and knee-high boots. The golden shoelaces were threaded through hundreds of tiny, metallic loops. Under the foot-long *déshabillé* in a material thin and grey as pencil shading, a honey-yellow nightdress shone through. Her movements were at once strict and relaxed, and although we had just met, I thought her, simply, captivating. 'Dora,' she added, not waiting for an answer. I smiled in what I believed to be a becoming fashion, touching her extended fingernails with my lips. They were glossy and hard, like beetles' backs. When the woman had closed the door – finally here, finally inside – she pointed to a frayed velvet couch and sat down in a matching chair. The curtains were lined with shivering summer light. Behind them, a window must have been open. 'You called because of the ad, and now you thought . . .' Expertly, she allowed the question to hover in the air, a shimmering bubble of suggestion, while she poured water from a carafe. On the table was a vase with flowers about to blossom.

Having emptied my glass and fumbled with my cuffs for a while, I found words for some of the things I had thought of during my ride to the hotel. I fear certain wishes still seemed a trifle cryptic, but a feeling of timidity, or perhaps it was shame, still impeded me. Was there by chance anything more to drink? Dora smiled – ambiguously, I thought – and patted her abdomen with a distracted hand. 'Sorry, no champagne. Today, at least. How long did you want to stay?' I stuttered something, I no longer remember what, whereupon she mentioned a price. While she extinguished her cigarette, she explained that she didn't deal in '*K. u. K.*' When she saw my puzzlement, she added: '*Küssen und Körperkontakt*, sweetheart. "Kissing and body contact." If you're looking for the standard stuff, you'll have to visit another girl.' In case I wanted, however, she might help me at the end – but only 'under cover'. She leaned forward to pick up the gloves I just realised lay across the armrest of the couch. Bothered, I moved so she could take them, wondering what she might mean. Having rolled the leather sheathings up to her elbows with pliant, professional motions, Dora extended her fingers and made a rhythmic gesture with one hand – like when one can't get a grip on the thick end of a rope despite repeated attempts. Suddenly, I felt hungry and tired and wanted to leave. The carpets on the floor were stained and the big bed didn't look exactly unused. But Dora anticipated me. With that fatal calm of hers with which I'd soon fall in love, she pointed to a washstand behind a Chinese frame with elaborate dragons and roses on it. I turned crimson and thought perhaps we could play whist instead.

'And you, Anton?' Three minutes later, I stepped out from the painted frame – naked and curious, but no longer nervous. Somehow, I must have had a difficult time speaking, because Dora continued: 'Surely you want to put something on, I mean?' Probably I replied. At least she gave me some unexpected items of clothing and I disappeared again. Now desire returned and eagerness gave me hot, fumbling hands. A few moments later, a different person emerged.

'Why, if it isn't Sascha Knisch.' Confused, I put out my cigarette, although I had just lit it. Anton put a pair of boots on the table, then settled into the chair next to mine. 'For you. It took some time, but here they are.' He held up two fingers for Helmut and answered a question he hadn't been asked: 'Much to do tonight.' Surveying the establishment, he snorted as he discovered the two youths sitting a few tables away. 'Dangerous for your health.' He coughed hollowly, holding up my cigarettes. 'Yours?' I struck a match. 'Damned if I know what Hauptstein's boys are doing here. Or why they listen to that bastard.'

Inspecting the new footwear he had brought me, I assumed the latter referred to Rigoberto, who was just preparing the second act of his show by filling, repeatedly, his lungs with air and then exhaling it in short bursts, making a curious sort of flapping motion with his elbows. Anton rose to take the glasses crowned with froth that Helmut had placed on the counter. Returning, he gave the entertainer a shove in the side (who lost his composure and began to cough), then stopped and addressed the two youths. Suddenly, one of them stood up so forcefully his chair toppled to the ground. He groped for something in his pocket, and had his friend not put a hand on his arm, the evening probably would have ended the way it does when, occasionally, things do indeed happen at the Blue Cellar.

'Had to teach them a lesson,' Anton excused himself as he put down the beer. 'They're like Maier,' he added, drying his hands against his trousers. 'Only interested in corrections.' I wasn't sure what our old athletics teacher had to do with the matter, but thought it best to keep a low profile. The youths shot hostile glances towards us and my friend doesn't have much of a head for alcohol. If he feels provoked, the worse thing to do is to pressure him. He handles knives like an evil god.

'And yourself?' After a few silent minutes, Anton put down his glass, wiping the froth off his lips. His hand shivered and I realised how worn-out he looked, with a yellow complexion and bleary eyes. 'How are things going, I mean. With Love? Work? One-legged Elsbieta?'

'Else,' I replied, irritated. My colleague may come from Poland, but after decades spent in Germany she prefers to be addressed as a native woman. Inhaling deeply, I then proceeded to tell Anton what I thought he needed to know.

Chapter Four

As we left, close to three o'clock in the morning – I in my new boots and Anton with his collar loosened – my friend buttoned his shirt and promised to do what he could. 'Don't worry, Sascha. I . . . I . . . I'll fix it. A . . . A . . . What's it called? A cover-up!'

'Alibi,' I sighed.

Anton swears less when he is drunk. The drawback is that instead he exaggerates so much he has difficulties getting out a sentence. Adjusting his tie, he kicked the front wheel of my bicycle and whistled silently. 'Air, eh?' After which he stumbled into the street and managed, to the surprise of both of us, to hail a cab.

Anton and I have known each other since we went to school – in Vienna's seventh *Bezirk*, should anyone be interested. When I started first grade, he was two years ahead of me; when I finished high school twelve years later, three years behind. And never finished. At that point, he was already building what he called his 'love empire' and managed rather well, thank you, without *amo*, *amas*, *amat*. When we met it was by chance and always late at night – my day being about to end, his about to begin. I was still living in the Neubaugasse, with my mother and Agnes, while Anton, having made himself independent, was on his way to become the uncrowned king of the Viennese underbelly. He used to hang out in the 'black box', a *chambre séparée* at a café further down my street, in the same place that once had belonged to Willy Fischl's father, and I doubt my talent for Latin was welcome there.

During our years in school, however, we were like brothers. With his pimply face, eyebrows that met, and bad teeth, Anton didn't exactly look like Valentino. But there wasn't a girl around whom he didn't try to get into bed, and surprisingly often, he succeeded. In principle, the fair sex was never uninteresting, not even if it sat in a wheelchair and didn't have legs. My friend must have learned some very special tricks from his father, the cobbler with the beautiful voice and fluffy sideburns, or else he simply exuded a particular Anton smell that nobody was able to resist in the long run. Even our choleric athletics and drawing teacher, Herr Maier (moist forehead, nervous hands), let him come and go as he pleased. My friend still got the highest grade, which made it possible for him to sweeten the bitter pill when he had to explain to his father why he wouldn't move up next year.

During my first year in high school, we still met regularly, and on occasion Anton ate at our place. Mr Lakritz's culinary skills couldn't be mentioned on the same day as my mother's, much less in the same breath, he stage-whispered just loud enough for her to hear from the stove. Then he got up from the table and courteously inquired about another helping. Never had he had such 'luscious' dumplings, he would claim, never such 'darling' lentils. Hardly a week went by without my mother saying it surely was a long time since she last saw my friend . . . You didn't have to be Einstein in order to interpret the three dots.

At times, Anton would join me as I went to the baker's or butcher's. While he leaned against the doorpost – match in mouth, film star's smile on his lips – I bought the bread or lamb chops my mother had asked for. When I put my hand in my pocket to pay, however, the baker's wife or butcher's daughter would look up from the price she had scribbled on the wrapping, first at me, then at Anton, and realise we were together. With a mischievous look in her eyes, she'd tuck the pencil behind her ear and declare that it was all right – even before I had managed to wriggle money out of my pocket. 'What was that all about?' I'd ask as we returned home.

'Only for the ladies,' Anton would reply. Noting my irritation, he'd add: 'Sorry, Sascha. But only they are allowed to know. And the Great Whoever, of course.' Smoothing over matters, he'd continue: 'You ought to be happy you got some unexpected pocket money,' and change the topic to something he considered more important – such as bicycle races, in which we were both interested at the time.

'Not many know it, but the best way to advance in life is not vertical, but horizontal.' A year after Anton had finally given up on school, we celebrated my birthday. He had offered me a pair of bicycle clips with my name engraved in German type on the inside. Now we stood outside the bar where I had just had my first glass of absinthe. As a goodbye gesture, Anton wanted to initiate me into some of life's mysteries. He had had more to drink than I, downing his glasses with a routine that surprised me, but now he cleared his throat and explained, in a voice both plain and steady, that the engraver was a tattoo artist as well. If I wanted to, I could join him the next time he visited him. At my age, it was a 'must' to get a tattoo. 'Women like men with class, you see. But you have to find a design of your own. Any wishes? It shouldn't be a heart or an anchor. That's cheap. Everybody has that.' I wondered whether he had any tattoos himself. Anton smiled enigmatically. 'Maybe, maybe not . . .'

'What's that supposed to mean?'

'You have to find the right design,' he merely reiterated. 'After all, you have to live with it for the rest of your life – like a motto, you know.' He pulled his fingers through his thick hair, combed backwards in the manner of Conrad Veidt. 'This shows true class.' From his pocket he brought out a flat tin case and read the script printed on the side: '*Brilliantine par Olivier Glissant*, *pour le gentleman.* The ladies swoon right away.' Carefully he nudged the case open with his stiletto, and put some of the sticky paste along the jagged side of a comb he extended to me. But my hair was too curly and the result left a lot to be desired. I asked for more pomade, determined to succeed, then some more. Finally, I resigned and returned the comb with a shrug. 'Seaweed,' was Anton's only comment. 'It's wiser if you leave these matters to us gentlemen. It looks as if you just emerged from the oil harbour in Le Havre.' He pronounced the city's name in French.

'Which you would know, of course.' Irritated, I tried to flatten out the curls across my skull, but they kept unfurling like wet wire wool.

'Who knows, who knows.' Worldly-wise, Anton pocketed his *brilliantine* and explained what went on in our neighbourhood. If I didn't know it – 'and you don't, Sascha, only gentlemen do' – the baker had problems with impotence and put money aside for therapeutic visits to Helga's massage parlour up by the Westbahnhof. Without telling him, however, his wife would borrow a bill or two to pay for the children's school uniforms. The butcher, a staunch believer in discipline, spanked his five daughters with his belt as often and religiously as he could. And old Simon Klein in the Lerchenfelderstraße, who repaired everything from alarm clocks, gas meters and box cameras, to water pumps and mechanical pianos, had a daughter who worked at a pension run by the same person who had sold him the French pomade. Anton twinkled. 'She's as beautiful as Mary Magdalene – and just as generous with her charms. If you want to, I could take you there. That is, if you change vehicle, of course.' He made a movement with his hand, along the crossbar of my bicycle. 'Your means of transportation, Sascha . . . It's a matter of class, you know.' Then, extending his hand, he bid a puzzling goodbye.

During my last year in high school, Anton advanced horizontally, lying on cushy down with piggy-pink cherubim floating in the air. At least that's what he wanted one to believe. Naturally, I couldn't be certain; not yet a gentleman, I had no experiences of my own for comparison. Moreover, he always spoke in veiled terms – as if he were unable to tell the truth no matter how much he wanted to. His attitude angered me, but when I pressed him, Anton would only reply: 'Who knows, who knows.' As always, without question mark.

In just a few years, my friend stamped out an entire love empire of a few worn-down pavements in west Vienna. Considering his hints, the ladies of the neighbourhood probably helped him. By way of the bed, he must have charted what was to become his own turf – a territory, more or less triangular in shape, between the train station, the beginning of the Burggasse, and what would soon become the Shanghai Bar halfway down the Neubaugasse, three buildings from where I lived. The district comprised some twenty blocks, including the church, and long before I realised there was only one thing I wanted to do in life (that, too, a horizontal undertaking, but not Anton's sort of thing), he knew his mission. I assume he financed the first years with criminal activities of different kinds: pocket picking, break-ins, and fraud, sham and extortion – what do I know? But I'm fairly certain his true area of competence was another, one that was spelled, simply, *l-o-v-e* . . .

Yes, well-dressed, well-greased, well-spoken – no, not well-spoken; cross that out – Anton Josef Lakritz was a pimp. Or as he preferred to put it: 'a trader in love'. When I asked him how big a region he covered, he just laughed, forming thumbs and index fingers into a triangle, and explained: 'That's what it looks like, Sascha. That's the only thing that matters.' The eternal feminine was his mission in life, and just as thoroughly as cunningly, Anton organised the sex trade in our neighbourhood. He and his companions (Teddie Levin, Mendel Gold, Karl Seidl and some others) offered the neighbourhood's pensions the possibility of helping them with rooms on a twenty-four-hour basis. They saw to it that knife-sharpeners, blacksmiths and grocers closed and opened again a few months later, this time as massage parlours with 'diplomas in body care'. They controlled what happened in the parks, under the railway bridges and in the urinals. And they converted at least three clubrooms to night bars with song and striptease numbers, poor but pricey champagne, and stalls in the back for 'hand and mouth service'. Finally, a couple of years after the dissolution of the double monarchy, Anton opened the Shanghai Bar, the jewel of his empire, on the same premises where earlier old Friedrich Fischl had served stale beer to nationalists with revanchist fantasies and holes in their wallet.

Thanks to its genuine Chinese lamps, red velvet couches, erotic drawings on the walls, and the cherry tree of papier mâché that was poised in the middle of the room and always blossomed pink confetti, the café attracted guests from all cardinal points not just in Vienna. The only time I visited the place, an evening the same autumn I left the city, it was filled with Asian tourists who sat, paralysed and sweating profusely, with tall Viennese women in their lap. The ladies had chalk-white faces and mouths as big as ripe strawberries, with millimetre-thin black arches over the eyes, drawn as if with sooty matches. Their hair was black, yellow or red, but always bobbed, and their absurdly short skirts were open at the side. The blouses were almost completely unbuttoned. Distractedly, the women played with the pearls they wore in several loops around their neck, or they pulled their fingers through the hair of the gentlemen, whispering soft promises that made the men's cheeks turn crimson. The latter invariably led to another bottle of champagne. When the number of corks, lined up in a row on the counter, was sufficient, the women slithered down from the guests' laps, smiled as the gentlemen shifted their legs with a pained expression, and walked, sinful hips extending their promise, towards an obese figure who sat at a table in the darkest corner of the place, a monocle tucked into one of her podgy eyes. From inscrutable Mrs Buddha they received a key with a coloured tuft attached, which corresponded to one of the doors behind her. Then, with index fingers curled upwards, the ladies enticed their company to follow them, like cats, whereupon the gentlemen in the high celluloid collars stood up, put down small heaps of unfolded bills on the table, and followed them. The pearl drapery clattered with corrupt promise.

Why Anton was forced to leave the 'black box' behind that drapery he never told me. Perhaps it was nothing for my chaste ears. But one day a couple of years after I had arrived in this city, he emerged from the entrance of a building not far from where I used to live back then, threw his cigarette in the gutter, and put his arm around me – with an ease that seemed to suggest we had met as late as last night. 'Sascha, my man, you know all about the movie theatres in this town . . .' My friend was thin and rumpled. His jacket was big enough to get lost in, his hand-shake soft and wet like a galosh. Gone was his ruddy complex-ion, gone his natural heft. Anton seemed stressed, and of the glamorous presence he wielded in Vienna, only a few traces were left: the kerchief in his breast pocket, the boots still polished with military precision, the eternally pomaded hair. He had begun to look like a weasel.

Of course he moved in with me, slept in my bed during the days, and was out at night. After a few weeks, however, Frau Andersen discovered our arrangement. My hostess had observed the bottles her secret lodger put aside but forgot when, around six in the morning, he managed to open the lock. Now she forced me to pay two months' rent and to move out at the end of the week. Instead of fighting her, I began to look for a flat of my own. It had to be something in the east of the city, as I could pay no more than I had for my rented room. At last, Anton found a place in a dilapidated building with a cemetery in one direc-tion and a modest but charming square in the other.

'What more could you ask for?' he wondered as I, still suspi-cious, inspected a broken window which had been fixed with newspapers. 'Life in one direction, death in the other.'

When I arrived, a few days into October 1925, after a trip to southern France on which, surprisingly, he had invited me, Anton sat on the stairs with a bottle of slivovitz between his polished feet. He smiled, pointing with his thumb over his shoulder. Against the wall, his house-warming present was propped: a stained mattress that had been sorted out of Pension Andersen, where *he* now lived.

'So you want people to believe you went out to buy cigarettes? And when you returned the door was open and the lady with the slippery fingers and the oh-so-soft mouth lay dead on the bed? Tsss . . .' Anton emptied his glass. 'Maybe One-legged Else will buy such a story. But she's hardly the trader in love, is she? Everyone will smell that you're lying, Sascha. You better come up with a smarter cover-up. Trust me: I know everything about sin's ec–, ec–'

'Ecumenicalism?'

'Damn it, you know what I mean. Economy! If you've already paid her, she'd lock the door and you may bid farewell to your dalliance. And if you haven't, she'd never even let you cross the doormat.' I looked at my friend, who was well on his way to getting drunk. His movements were sweeping, his words grand, getting grander. 'For heaven's sake, Sascha, you have to lie with talent. At least you should say that you had an appointment and that you knocked on the door, but nobody answered. When you pulled down the handle, the door turned out to be unlocked, so you called and entered. Still no answer. Yes, and then, well, then you found her unconscious on the kitchen floor. Now, you couldn't leave her there, could you? So you carried her into the bedroom and put her in bed. That's the least one can do for a friend, isn't it? You thought she'd sort herself out after some rest. Well, and then you left.' Anton nodded, jaded. 'Believe me: every gentleman knows that, when you cover things up, the best thing's to stay as close to the truth as possible.' He tried to fasten his watery eyes on me. 'And now you have to tell me what you were *really* doing at that lady's place.'

'We met a few years ago,' I began reluctantly, lowering my voice. But then I realised it didn't really matter. Given the lousy circumstances, I might as well tell Anton about the background. 'At a hotel, actually,' I added, raising my voice. 'Dora was a bit special. For a long time, I just called her "Madame".'

'One of those with a rod in their hand? Phew, I didn't know that about you.' I turned around, but nobody seemed to have heard what he said. 'Good for your *Sitzfleisch*, I suppose. A bit red perhaps, but not so bad that you can't sit here a few hours later.' Anton leaned back. As far as he was concerned, the topic was exhausted.

'No, it's not that. Dora was no' – I searched for the right word – 'no metatropic lady. Rather . . . Well, you know, a *minette*,' I said, using the French term that had become popular recently. It indicated women equipped with soft and not hard hands, empathy and not rod, as they helped men turn themselves into lamps or footstools, poodles, ash trays or, well, what do I know – schoolgirls, perhaps.

At least it was as a minette I got to know Dora. Only a few weeks after my first visit in August 1926, I called again. It had been impossible to forget the shameful things we had done. Although a new visit would cost me more than I could afford, I thought it worth the sacrifice. After all, it's not every day you discover new aspects of yourself. Having breathed 'Kreuzer' into my ear, the Russian porter promised to connect me. Instead he put down the receiver, however, mumbling: '"Sweet, divine substance, made by diligent insect." Five letters.' Tolerantly, I waited for him to figure out the solution. Yet after a minute, I shouted the answer. First there was silence, then, as a gesture of gratitude, the porter switched some cables. A few rattling signals made it through the chords, after which another receiver was lifted.

'Madame?'

'Depends on who's asking.'

'This is . . . Anton. I was at your place a while ago.'

'Not that I remember.'

'But I. And it would . . . I mean, it would be nice to see you again, I mean. Could I . . .'

Yes, I could. Next day, at five in the afternoon. Henceforth that became our time: Fridays between five and seven, Dora's last session of the week. Typically, several blocks before I saw the neon sign of the hotel, my clothes began to itch, my thoughts turned slippery. For each street I crossed, it felt as if I became more and more transparent. Finally, I was convinced people on the pavement could read me like an open book. Should I hold both hands on the handle or let one of them dangle by my side? Was I going too fast or too slow? Did I seem nervous? As each minute passed, my heart thumped harder. Surely the only gentlemanly thing to do was to turn around? Almost by accident, I increased the speed. Although the chain creaked tautly, the wheels rolled on with willing ease. A few minutes later, I braked, got up on the pavement, and leaned the bicycle against the wall. Now my pulse, already swollen, raised itself like a wave and broke at the same moment I entered the lobby. Soundlessly I was washed up on a beach of worn carpets, dead plants and a lifeguard who wasn't likely to prove the perfect swimmer.

After a few visits, I was able to manage my heart with greater skill, until, finally, I went straight up the stairs. But that initial wave of emotion remained my threshold. It marked the beginning and end of some one hundred and twenty minutes, during which I wasn't Sascha Knisch, and perhaps didn't want to be, either. I experienced it on my way to the hotel, and I experienced it when, a couple of hours later, I went down again, nodded to the manager who now deferred to me as 'Herr Honig', and emerged on the street. Oddly enough, I forgot almost immediately what I had just experienced. Again, I was one among many bicyclists on their way home, to a bar, or to a cabaret. Inscrutable.

A few blocks farther, I had difficulties remembering even what Dora looked like. If I conjured forth a lone limb or an unexpected gesture, I succeeded more or less. But as soon as I tried to develop the image into an action, my thoughts scattered with depressing grace. Not until around midnight did memory begin to function properly again. As I lay in bed, our time together returned with undiminished power, lovely and lewd, and I was able to recall what had happened in every shameful detail: Dora's lax, sinuous movements, our smooth, coordinated sounds, a vague but unmistakable blush, then her determined glove and hot breath next to my powdered face. I reconstructed the entire chain of events with the same precision an engineer will fill a film projector with tiny screws, taut springs, and chock-full of whirring cogs – until I couldn't stand the machinery any longer, so oily, so rhythmical, but did what an engineer, too, might have done in my situation.

> On the bed lay Alex, an engineer,
> and agile Minette, love's proven dear.

Anton's beautiful voice brought me out of my reverie. He's inherited it from his father and often sings when drunk. At the bar, Rigoberto pulled a face. 'Minette sounds better. Frankly, I find it hard to imagine you with bit between your teeth and tail stuck in your rear. While madam breaks in her . . . Hell, what's the word? Pony. Or, as governess, asks you to lie across a chair and count out loud, while she holds a sheet of paper towards your bottom in which she's cut out "25", keeping the pace with a strap. The least mistake and you have to begin anew. Damn, Sascha! I know everything about corrections.' He slapped his palms on the table and cleared his throat. 'What do you think Maier did with all those who couldn't get across the vaulting-horse?'

I replied that the pedagogical zeal of our old athletics teacher hardly had anything to do with it. Besides, did it matter what we devoted ourselves to?

'But you did play roles.'

I suppose he could say that. Yet one day, or rather night, I uttered the wrong lines and our wonderful drama came to an abrupt end. Time went by – until one day, without warning, Dora stood in the foyer. Only last week, as a matter of fact. At first, I hadn't recognised her. Again she had changed her appearance. Now she cut her hair short as a man's and made up her face in a matter-of-fact way. No nail polish, flat shoes. Merely her dress, thin as a summer wind, showed she still paid attention to her appearance. With one arm hanging by her side and grasping, with her other hand, the bend of it from behind her back, she stood in line, waiting to be let in. It was at that moment I realised who Dora was. Quickly I pulled down the kiosk shutter – with surprisingly feeble muscles – and replaced Otto at the entrance. Halfway down the ticket line, I distinguished her voice. 'Sascha,' she said, shifting keys and cigarette case between her hands (as usual, she didn't use a handbag), 'still in the services of Apollo?' I pretended to be surprised and buttoned my jacket, embarrassed but delighted to see her again. We exchanged a few meaningless phrases; most of them credited to my already over-charged account. Then I asked if she might want to see the film from the projection room. Considering what had happened between us, it was a daring suggestion, and Dora eyed me ambiguously. It was impossible to tell whether she tried to contain her laughter or was embarrassed on my behalf. But instead of saying anything, she shot a few glances to the side, nodded quietly, and went up to One-legged Else while I let the remaining guests in.

I looked at my friend. 'When I had punched a hole in the last ticket and joined them in the projection room a quarter of an hour later, Dora said she'd leave us in peace. I was surprised, but she claimed she had forgotten something and had to go right away. She extended her ticket, saying that it had been interesting to see what it looked like "inside the head of Apollo". Naturally, I was disappointed. But before she went she whispered that she wouldn't mind meeting again "under different circumstances". Nor would I, I discovered. So two days later, I cycled across the city, to the west part of town. Unfortunately, we barely had time to adjust to the new circumstances before the bell rang and I had to check into the closet.'

'Bad boy, you.'

'Boy? Not exactly.'

Anton waited for Helmut to replace our empty glasses. Once the bartender had left, he downed his beer in one routine sweep, concluding behind the hand with which he wiped his mouth: 'I'll be damned: Sascha as a hat-check girl . . .'

I shrugged. He could call me whatever he liked. Now that I thought about Dora leaving as unexpectedly as she had turned up, I realised she had seemed a bit anxious. Regrettably, I didn't know why, and now, even more regrettably, it was too late to ask. Anton looked at me quizzically. I explained the police had probably already been to the flat. In the intermission between first and second screenings, One-legged Else had urged me to sneak into Stegemann's office and dial the authorities. 'An officer answered with his mouth full of food. In my lightest voice, I told him something terrible had happened and put down the receiver before he had time to swallow.'

'You didn't find anything that might explain what had happened? Other than . . .'

The body in the bedroom? I thought back. Someone had carried it into the bedroom and put it on the bed – probably so that it would look as if the cause of death was natural. After having groped in vain for a pulse, I tore off my clothes. Then I searched the flat, panic growing inside me. In the living room, a record scraped by on the gramophone underneath the kitschy drawing of a secretive woman in a red dress, executed by an English master, to which Dora had been so attached. The chairs were arranged in the positions I remembered, the decorative items on the bookshelves were untouched, and except for the cigarette stubs in the ashtray and the money on the table, I found nothing that indicated she had entertained a visitor – and *that* visitor had been me: the bills corresponded to one month's rent and the cigarettes were all stubbed out by yours truly.

On the kitchen counter had been a pie so raised it must have been baked by a baker in his sleep. Dora had put out plates and crystal glasses. Next to the napkins lay some spoons as well as a flat metal object I couldn't identify, but took to be a cake-slice. On the table was her cigarette case, on the floor a tilted chair. Why I put the case in my pocket I can't tell, but the chair I raised because it disturbed my sense of order. Then I looked around. My nerve, I mustn't lose my nerve. One last time I went into the bedroom. Unperturbed, the alarm clock continued to tick – 7.07, 7.08 . . . – and the body was still lying on the bed.

Carefully I clasped the hands on the belly, pushing in the tip of the tongue that had protruded through the lips. I tried a few more times, but each time it slid out like an indolent, unknown animal. With the side of my hand I wiped away some froth that had gathered in one corner of the mouth. Finally, having turned off the light, I went into the hall. On the table below the mirror, next to a paper, were Dora's keys, long and slightly obscene. I pushed open the door, heard a *Stadtbahn* train thunder by, and decided to descend as if walking down the path at a cemetery. 'Fortunately, I didn't meet anyone. As soon as I came out on the street, I unlocked my bicycle and pedalled . . .' Wait. Damn. Could it really be? I checked. 'Hell, Anton. I may have forgotten something.'

'Great.'

'Do you remember the clips you gave me?'

'The ones which looked like armbands with your name engraved on the inside?' He stretched out for my beer glass. 'Sure. Back then you wanted to be the king of bicycling – like Binda or whatever his name was. But that's a long time ago. Do you still have them?' Untroubled, he took some deep swallows, believing I wouldn't notice.

'Yes. Sorry.' Christ, how could I have forgotten them? Probably the clips were still in the bedroom, where I had put my clothes.

'If you're lucky, the police won't think about them until next week – when they've looked up your friend and realised she may have been hiding something in the closet. If they're unsure about the cause of death, probably they've just done a first superficial check.' Rigoberto began to sing again, so Anton had to raise his voice: 'Take it easy, Sascha. You've just found yourself a guardian angel. The great Lakritz will descend and come to your help.' Theatrically he leaned forward, arms extended. 'Just give me the address, and I'll take care of the cover-up. Who knows, perhaps I won't just retrieve your bicycle clips, but also find out why she seemed so anxious?' He leaned back as if he had just uttered a key line, then quietly added, before shutting his eyes: 'Meanwhile, be smart: act stupid.'

Startled, I watched him doze off while the great Rigoberto poured his heart out over the harsh conditions of urban life:

> *Noise, riot and turmoil, bounce, bob and ball:*
> *in today's city, there's space for all.*
> *Suddenly, you hear screaming – shy or bold?*
> *Oh, who can tell if it's warm or cold?*

What did he mean? Didn't he realise what a fix I was in? For Anton, it might be all right to take it easy. For me, it was merely a matter of time before the police would come. Perhaps even tomorrow. And even if, with the help of my friend, I managed to prove my innocence, how could I do so without revealing aspects of a life the authorities had no business inspecting? I studied the dandruff on Anton's shoulders and wondered how often he washed his hair. Under one armpit, the seam had cracked. His nails looked like black slivers of moon. Not much of a guardian angel, exactly.

Around three in the morning, Konrad came down the stairs. By this time I had twisted and turned paragraph 168 so many times it had begun to look like a pair of handcuffs. The Blue Cellar was almost empty. Rigoberto had left; the two men Anton had fought with, too. In one corner, Molly was still entertaining her companion, who had ventured a tanned hand under her airy blouse. Helmut emptied the ashtrays in a bucket, Gertie and Ludmila collected beer glasses. It was time to leave.

'Sorry to bother you, comrade . . .' Reluctantly, I prodded Anton in the side. He moaned alcoholically, making some complicated movements with his hands. 'Do you need help?'

Eventually, he managed to unbutton the top of his shirt. But scratching the back of his head, he misunderstood me: 'Hell, no. It's best to work solo. Although, if there's someone she trusted – not like this . . .' Anton rubbed his two index fingers along each other. 'But more like this . . .' Now he hooked them into one another. 'It wouldn't hurt to speak to her. Perhaps she knows something? Personally, I believe your madam had something precious that her visitor was after. And if it wasn't the gal in the closet, only a girlfriend could . . .' The rest disappeared with the smooth, coordinated sound of Konrad sweeping the floor.

A girlfriend? The sole person I could think of was Karp, Felix Karp at the Foundation for Sexual Research.

Chapter Five

I had done what I could: Else would vouch for me and Anton had promised to visit the flat. Further investigations into Dora's past would have to wait until tomorrow. Having left the Blue Cellar, I cycled, not altogether straight, home through the night. The trees were big, bloated shadows against an ever lighter sky, the streets deserted. The bell on my bicycle shivered as I ran over cobblestones, clattering like teeth, while the rubber tyres hummed warmly and soothingly as soon as the ground shifted to asphalt. Reaching the square where I live, I discovered Heino, who has the coal cellar on the corner, next to the kiosk, but sells flowers in the summer. He wore a *faux* Chinese dressing gown and stood with one arm outstretched. Presumably, he was waiting for Chérie, who seemed to have made common cause with the darkness by the wall. Heino waved soundlessly as I went by, then the ugliest dog in our neighbourhood pulled the leash, and the two disappeared into the night.

I locked my Torpedo outside the gate and sneaked up the stairs. Since a clumsy craniologue was just testing the inside of my skull with his careless hammer, my concentration wasn't optimal. But I was lucky: Frau Britz wasn't fussing about in the courtyard. It must be one of those nights when she wasn't forced to prepare for the hard work at the market hall down by the big square. Moved or drunk, possibly both, I thanked the higher powers who had abandoned me earlier in the day. At least I didn't have to discuss financial matters with my landlady.

Finally, after the fifth or sixth attempt, the shapeless stump in my hand transformed itself into a smart key, and I managed to open the door. The nameplate swung with a raspy sound reminiscent of Dora's gramophone (it hangs on only one screw). Kicking the door shut, I extricated myself from my clingy clothes and fell headlong into the bed, sleep welcoming me with endless arms.

Somewhere in its compliant depths, Heino disentangled himself with his rumpled poodle. Now I could hear him say: 'I hope it will pass,' pointing indignantly into the dark – but not at his dog, which I had assumed as I followed the extension of his finger, but towards a boy who stood on a desk floating freely in the night. To my surprise, I discovered it was I. A spotlight came on, and now I realised I was back home in Vienna. Balancing on the dinner table, I asked my mother what our last name meant. 'Be happy you have one,' she answered with clenched teeth from her chair, not bothering to look up, 'so that you can stand still when asked to.' Gripping my feet, she jerked them straight and added: 'There you go.' I looked down and saw she had attached shackles to my ankles. The fetters glittered with an evil sheen, the balls were big and heavy. In order to prove that I could play the role of a chained seamstress's dummy if I had to, I straightened my back and pretended, bravely, to be made of tin.

My mother continued her work, silent and determined. Only once in a while the chair creaked. Her glasses were poised at the tip of her nose, needles stuck between her lips. With one hand she stretched the hem of my dress, while with the other she made short, precise motions. It was impossible to tell whether she was sewing something on or removing it. Although the latter seemed unlikely, even for a dream, I suspected she was in the process of lowering the hem of the school uniform Dora had thrown across her bed just before the doorbell rang.

Before long, my mother would be done and I'd finally be able to go to sleep. When a shorter stretch of eternity had passed, she bit off the thread and pushed back her glasses. Now. Soon. Meanwhile, however, something seemed to have happened. Suddenly, there were at least fifty metres' distance between us. As I gazed down, I could barely make her out; if I hadn't known what my own mother looked like, I might even have considered her a stranger. Instead of smiling and saying I had been brave, now I could go to bed, she took off her diminutive glasses and put them next to the diminutive scissors, which lay on the diminutive table. 'What's the matter?' she shouted, hands formed into a cone. On one finger, a thimble gleamed tautly.

'Peppercorn,' I shouted back, 'or apple tree, tailor, jug . . .' I had used the silence to contemplate what was written in block letters across my striped chest.

'I'm sorry?'

'In my class,' I explained, pointing indignantly to my name, 'there's one peppercorn, two apple trees, one tailor, one flower, one jug, one angle, one cobbler, two dukes, one merchant, twelve who don't mean anything, but all end with an *l* – and then me, Knisch. And what's that supposed to mean?' My mother sighed the way all Weisses do (she was a Weiss before she married), and immediately shrunk to the size of a screw head. Filled with inexplicable pity, I squatted, stroking her across her round head with its straight part down the middle. Tears welled up, fat and oily, as I assured her I hadn't meant to shout. But she understood my situation, didn't she? I needed to clear my name and she'd been so far away.

'So you think distance means anything?' Again my mother swelled to normal size. Promptly and primly, she asked me to stop crying and take off the skirt – which turned out to be one of my sister's nightdresses. Discreetly I nodded towards my feet; amazed, my mother wondered why I was in shackles. When she had freed me, kicking away the balls that bounced off as if made of cork, I removed the dress. Pinning needle to cardigan, my mother carefully folded the garment. Then, looking tired, she removed her thimble. 'About names we shall speak another time.' That was all. Nothing about Pfefferkorn, Apfelbaum, or Schneider, I thought bothered. Nothing about Blume, Krug, or Winkler. Nothing about Fischl, Krankl, Seidl, or any of the other boys in school. And nothing about Knisch.

I realised I ought to have used a different tactic. For example, I could have pretended to know already what my last name meant. Or better still: I could have said that somebody in my class had claimed Knisch stood for a line of work that no longer existed – and as a matter of fact, neither should I. Once in a while, schoolmates entrusted me with wisdom of this order, and now I figured that if only I had told my mother what they said, she would have responded. Perhaps I ought to tell her the truth: that Willy Fischl had said the thing about not existing? And that Erwin Winkler had added, purely for my edification, as he was quick to point out, that the name designated a hunched figure with wet lips and meaty nose, who was imprisoned in a closet and took care of the court jester when he had the day off, poured himself a schnapps, and was German again – 'only a little short, you know . . .'

'My knisch,' the jester would say as he leaned over the wash-bowl, rinsing the soap off his fingers, 'at least you lead the comfortable life of a louse. You're lucky not to have to shoulder responsibilities of my kind.' That last bit I used to invent myself, as I tried to understand what my schoolmates told me. The jester would hold up his hands in the air, while the knisch put the water jug aside. 'Towel, please.' Since my great-grandfather held hood, tricots and shoes in one hand, and hadn't yet released his grip on the water jug with the other, he was forced to bend forward so that the jester could take the towel slung across his shoulder – at which point you'd hear the golden rattle of the bells attached to the hood. A knisch was a servant then, Winkler claimed, who should know (his father subscribed to Brockhaus), 'or more properly: a serf.' But only until the Turkish siege in 1683. Thereafter, they disappeared from history – 'until one day they resurfaced,' Fischl added pedagogically, snapping away an invisible piece of dust from his sleeve, 'like lice in a closet.'

But, of course, a knisch could also be an edible dish, I thought to myself, a tool, or a bicycle brand. Or it might be a particular way of looking cross or amazed: 'Don't be so knisch', 'Go knisch yourself', 'Are you knisch today?' . . . As a little boy, I often made up such explanations. Somehow, it felt as if I re-invented my father. But my mother had heard all variants – many times, too many times. 'Your father', she now said, as tight-lipped as ever, and looked down at the floor (was he residing below the boards?), 'had nothing, did nothing, and gave us nothing. Other than trouble. May his memory not be blessed.' Quickly she gazed up at the ceiling, adding in a whisper: 'I'm sorry, God. But that's the truth.'

According to my mother, that's all I had inherited from my father: the ability to make trouble and a last name. If you believed her, one thing could not be separated from the other. Naturally, I had my own theories about that, but in the particular phase of the dream in which I presently found myself, I understood with a sort of clear-eyed madness that it was better to inherit too little than too much. Pleased I thought of Winkler, who was the class leader. Being of 'good' stock, his family even had a painting by Polster hanging in their living room. From his father, Winkler had inherited the eyes of a fish, legs short as clogs, and remarkably active pores. Not once did one see him without a shiny forehead and rings under his arms which, before orthography was over and the school day had come to an end, reached his belt. At night, Winkler wasn't so much undressed as wrung out. As if his father's genes weren't enough, from his mother he had inherited a voice capable of cutting through crystal and a repertory of expressions that all contained the words 'suppose' and 'shit'. I forgot the sausages: those, too, he had inherited from his mother – ten fat ones serving as fingers. But even if his father was a pharmacist and his mother too good for anything but nervous breakdowns, everyone saw that, in type and breed, Erwin Winkler was a butcher's son.

The latter made me think of Greta Harassowitz, since her father really was a butcher. Greta was the beauty of our neighbourhood, with braids blonde as bread and eyes as white and blue as Prussian china. Already in third grade she was careful to smooth out her dress over her belly – not always to look proper. We boys used to nudge each other in the side and nod in rhythm while she was jumping rope, supremely alone in the world. Only her teeth weren't beautiful. Small, yellow, and unevenly spaced, they were placed as if at random, with gums going so far down it looked as if Greta's teeth had suddenly stopped growing. As a result, Harassowitz's youngest daughter kept her mouth shut and dreamed about becoming a movie star. Then she wouldn't have to talk.

At least that's what she told me one day when we were playing. As soon as she had made this confession, Greta lowered her voice and added, lips pursed, that if I wanted to, she could show me what she looked like – 'and I know you do, Sascha. All boys do. But you have to promise not to say a word to my sisters.' (She had four, all of them older.) I nodded solemnly, unsure what she meant, but delighted by a buoyant kind of confusion stirring inside me. Hand in hand, we went down the stairs, to the basement. There, Greta quickly and expertly pulled down her panties, adorned with a red ribbon, and loosened her stockings. Then she raised her school uniform, tucking the hem under her chin. So that I would see better, she balanced on a wooden block – surprisingly long, I thought, before I realised she wanted me to admire the tiny blonde hairs curling here and there between her legs. I was just about to extend my hand when Greta wavered, dropping the hem and curtly pronouncing the feature to be over. While she rehooked her stockings and pulled up her underwear, she explained that she had changed her mind. After all, I wouldn't be allowed to kiss her on the mouth; she was a decent girl and not one like me. I had hardly time to explain that the thought hadn't even occurred to me, when she ran up the stairs with clattering soles, yelling: 'Iii, iii, a knisch, a kniiisch!'

Before I met Anton, I never thought about my friends' behaviour. If you're named after a serf and have red hair, you learn to take life in your stride. Freckles don't exactly improve the situation. 'Have you washed yourself with shit again?' Fischl used to wonder as I emerged from the locker room and lined up, waiting to be the last person picked for the basketball teams. 'Let's suppose: some *eau-de-merde*?' Winkler added. (Lord knows where he got that from. Perhaps his father had begun to subscribe to Larousse?) Then they held their noses and asked Mr Maier if they could please change places, please. Once the game had begun, I wasn't allowed to touch the ball even once – until at the very end, that is, when Fischl, with unexpected kindness, passed it to me. Unfortunately, it was such a sorry throw that Winkler, who played on the other team, happened to push his elbow into my stomach, taking the ball from me. 'Like stealing candy from a girl,' he reflected, looking over to Greta Harassowitz, who continued to jump ropes with grim face and bouncing braids.

Immediately, Fischl rushed forward. 'Maybe you're a girl, Knisch? Or a hooker? One might think so, seeing how loose you are. I suppose it's the perfume,' he added more philosophically, holding his nose while Winkler, who had just netted the ball, performed a war dance around the post. 'I guess anyone who passes to you has to count on losing.' After which he joined his friend. Together, they began to whirl around the post that creaked like mother's working chair, beating sticks against the back of a bench – chanting in my honour: 'Knirsch, knarsch, arsch, arsch . . . Knirsch, knarsch, arsch, arsch . . .'

That did it: I awoke. At last, I realised someone was pounding on the door, repeating my name. Confused, I pushed away the pillow on top of my head. (In the morning, the sun shines into my flat and I have no curtains.) Then I got up and tried, hopping on one leg, to get into my uncooperative trousers, to pull on my undershirt, and to open the door – all at the same time.

'Please, you may close the door,' a correct, middle-aged man declared, walking straight into my flat and placing an elegant briefcase on the table. 'My name is Wickert, Doctor G. Wickert, deputy inspector at the Vice Squad. And we are investigating a mysterious . . . May I?' He dusted off the chair and sat down. 'Death.'

The inspector smiled a prosthetic smile – all glossy dentures. Adjusting his gold-rimmed glasses, he politely waited for me to catch up. But I lagged at least half a waking life behind, so I wondered whether I could . . . Perhaps he understood? He understood and I could. I did what I needed to in the designated space in the stairway I share with my neighbour. The last fragments of dream and confusion vanished as, subsequently, I held my head under the running kitchen tap. When I had dried myself, the coffee water was already boiling. Unfortunately, I was out of both sugar and milk. I asked my unexpected visitor whether he'd like a cup of black coffee, but he merely began to drum against the lock on his briefcase, his manicured nails shining in the bright morning sun. I went to fetch a chair in the kitchen and realised an alibi wouldn't hurt, exactly.

'You're Alexander Knisch, born 1899 in Vienna, registered at Tresckowstraße 39 for the last two and a half years, since October 5, 1925, to be precise, and working as "projectionist" . . .' Wickert ran his tongue across his teeth. 'I suppose that means you're in the movie business.' He raised his gaze. 'And not of the Protestant faith?' He had consulted a small spiral writing pad, which he now closed. The kind eyes behind the glasses were coffee brown, the dentures continued to shine. I shrugged and acknowledged that my name was, indeed, Alexander, but usually I went by Sascha. While I stirred my coffee with a piece of bread, Wickert continued: 'According to our files, you've even published a book. *Deranged Esther*? *Disturbed Ether*? Something of that order. I haven't read it, I'm sorry to say. There weren't many books in Hannover when I grew up.' Apologetic, he cleared his throat. 'But your line of work is of no importance to us. Important is only where you were yesterday.'

His hair was brown and a bit too well-groomed, his facial features even, his lips full. Wickert wore his shirt open; white collars on top of brown jacket. Disregarding the perfect teeth, he resembled an older version of a comedian whose name I couldn't recall. Where had I seen this kind yet sombre look, these tilting shoulders, that melancholy patience? Wait, now I knew: Wickert reminded me of the American who had just toured Germany with his two sons. But what was his name? Keats or Carlton; something like that. When, despite repeated attempts, I couldn't remember the name, I began to ponder what the inspector's initial might stand for. Gerhard? Georg? Perhaps Günther? Wickert calmly waited for me to finish. 'Yesterday night?' I finally asked, suitably distracted, while looking for my cigarettes. I stuck my hands in the pockets of my jacket that hung on the doorknob, found first Dora's case, then my own Moslems. 'Has something happened?' I put the case on one of the bookshelves, before sitting down again.

'Mr Knisch, we can make it easy . . . Thank you, I don't smoke. And we can make it harder. But since you're a thinking person and I don't possess a radio scope, I suggest we make it easier. Otherwise, you'll have to come with me to the headquarters, and that would mean . . . Let me put it this way: it would be best if it didn't happen. In contrast to us at the Vice Squad, Karla Manetti over at Homicide thinks we may have a murder on our hands and might like a word with you.' Delicately, he waved away the smoke. 'Let's trust it's just a regular death, shall we? Unusual – why, bizarre even, but nonetheless. It's best that way, wouldn't you agree? So let me ask again: where were you yesterday?'

I explained that I had tried to finish a text. But since my thoughts had been sluggish, I had hoped some fresh air might prove inspirational. 'And it did. I went downstairs, to the square, where I was able to write quite well – despite the fact that Ivan Britz was busy teaching our neighbourhood's bakeresses how to care for their bodies. You know: sun, eurhythmics, and all the other things that Adolf Koch preaches. From the scaffolding where they're constructing the new building,' I nodded towards the window, across the square, 'the workers whistled. Next to me, Mr Vogelsang sat. Yes, that's his name. No, I didn't invent it. Annoyed, he ordered me to put an end to the spectacle.' I explained that Ivan Britz was the son of my landlady, a Spartakist and ardent supporter of nudism, while the construction workers, to judge from their invectives, were more nationalistically inclined. During the last months, the two parties had been engaged in a dispute that seemed to get more heated, the farther summer progressed. As for Siegfried Vogelsang, he was a retired sergeant with clear views on law and vice, but sparse control over his bodily functions. 'Of course, I did as Mr Vogelsang asked me, trying to busy Chérie by throwing sticks as far towards the tanned body worshippers as possible.'

Who was Chérie? Heino's poodle, who usually ran around unleashed. Who was Heino? The person with the coal cellar at the corner. Who was Adolf Koch? But . . . 'Unfortunately, it didn't turn out too well. First, Chérie ran in a wide arch, then, tiring of it, she tried to take the sticks straight out of my hand. After a while, I had enough. Sergeant Vogelsang could solve his problems on his own. Personally, I planned to cycle to the restaurant down by the river and finish what I was working on. But when, on my way, I passed by a construction worker who was putting sewage pipes into the ground outside the Stock Exchange, and asked him what time it was, I realised it was getting late. So I continued straight to the Apollo. I arrived in time for the first newsreel. It can't have been more than a few minutes past seven. And as usual, I stayed there until midnight, when we closed.'

My account sounded haplessly cluttered, hopelessly confused, and least of all convincing. But Wickert didn't seem to notice. Perhaps he realised not only that I had just gotten up, but also that I was suffering from a royal hangover? 'I see: Britz, Vogelsang, Chérie, construction workers both here and there . . . Many names, many witnesses. That's good.' He put aside his spiral notepad. It looked as if I were off the hook, at least for the time being. Click-clicking his golden pencil against his dentures, the inspector seemed to ponder the alternatives. A minute went by, then another. At last, straightening his back, he opened his briefcase and pulled out a file. 'Yes, we do understand each other, don't we, Mr Knisch? You have a . . . How shall I put it? A good attitude to the cultural life of our times. Perhaps we could use you at the Vice Squad?' He smiled at the thought. 'Surely you could tell me who you see in this photograph?'

I studied the picture as if never having seen the woman before. But it was Dora. She couldn't have been more than sixteen or seventeen at most. Her hair was blonde and lank, her cheeks high and bony, the mouth thin as a blade of grass. Although the irises sat unusually high and were partly covered by the eyelids, as if clouded over, her gaze was challenging. Shoulders pulled up, Dora seemed guarded, almost suspicious. The impression created was of a person who didn't feel free, but was prepared to pay the price to become so.

'Passport photo,' Wickert explained. 'Enlarged.'

The Dora whose grainy eyes met mine was more girl than woman. Probably she had limbs like broken twigs, hips like those of a boy. I couldn't discern any makeup – or perhaps a little around the eyes. It was difficult to say, as her face had turned grainy. Neither was it possible to distinguish the chipped-off front tooth behind her lips. Of the clothes, only an open fox boa and the collar of a flowery blouse could be seen. The photograph must have been taken in the winter. Of course, she was beautiful. At least in my eyes. And I recognised the boa.

'You'd be wise to choose your words,' Wickert said as I returned the picture. 'The truth must out.'

I wondered what he expected me to say. That I had hidden in the closet of the same person (twenty years older) and not seen a thing? That I had had other things on my mind than to think about an unknown murderer moving about in the flat? Anxiously, I stubbed out my cigarette. I must be careful. Finally I decided to do the only wise thing I could think of: act stupid, I reminded myself, and remarked that the woman on the picture did seem familiar in a peculiar sort of way. But today, my head wasn't working properly. It had been rather late last night, as perhaps the inspector might understand? Yet if I could keep the photograph, I was sure I'd be able to develop . . .

'A shadow from the past? Why, of course, Mr Knisch.' Faultlessly smiling, Wickert turned the photograph over and wrote a number on the back. He pushed the picture across the table. 'Let's hope you do, for both our sakes. But time is short. Each minute this woman bathes in the liquids of your memory may cost us dearly. Also, my colleague over at Homicide may want to interrogate you. You'd be wise to contact me as soon as you're done.' He pointed his pencil at the photo. 'But only at that number, Mr Knisch. It's the direct number to the Vice Squad. We'll arrange a meeting.'

Wickert stood up and smiled. I stood up and smiled. Wickert took his briefcase and went towards the door. I took my cup and followed him. Wickert said: 'We must find out what this woman really did,' as he pulled down the door handle and stepped out in the stairway. 'It's about time we did something to the rot that's spreading in this city.' I said nothing and remained where I was. Wickert glanced at his hand, then added kindly: 'I'm already looking forward to your exposure.'

'Looking forward?' it echoed from the stairs. The inspector turned around and nodded to a woman with a heap of filthy skirts tugged up on her wide hips. I swore silently: Mrs Britz – landlady, one-woman market hall cleaning patrol, and debt-collecting agency, all rolled into one person. 'As for myself, I'd look forward to your paying the rent,' she huffed and puffed as she reached my floor. Smiling, she inserted one felt slipper in the door. (I must confess those slippers have never persuaded me aesthetically.) Having followed Wickert until he had disappeared down the stairs, she turned to me and added, beatifically out of breath: 'Problems – with – the – police – eh – Knisch?'

Chapter Six

The grainy photograph brought memories forth. Although I had never met the girl who looked at the world with both dare and dullness in her eyes, as if she'd already seen too much of it, we had things in common. After Wickert had left, I began to leaf through these mutual recollections, images coloured in bright, nervous colours, but then I stopped. Did we? What had Dora and I truly shared, apart from some items of clothing and ways of conduct? No, truly?

Since I woke up this morning, six days after having emerged from her wardrobe, I've tried to ignore a growing unease over not knowing what Dora was up to. Now, I profess I can't any longer. I'm beginning to understand she never let me get close. Although she showed me the practical delights of intimacy, she kept all her personal affairs a secret. I'm starting to realise that, if I'm to find out what has happened, I might have to re-screen everything Dora said and did in my presence. I can only hope imagination will function a little better than it did as I dwelled in her closet last Friday. Perhaps there are details I haven't thought of, details that, seen in a sober light, will reveal what she got herself involved in? For that to happen, however, I must begin with what brought me to Dora in the first place. In short: it's time to focus on the album pages chronicling my visits to Hotel Kreuzer.

Our following meetings were like the first. Although I was co-operation embodied, Dora's hands remained matter-of-fact. Frankly, I had the impression they might as well have plucked eyebrows or cleaned teeth. I understood she meant what she said: if it was 'K. u. K.' I was after, I'd have to turn elsewhere. At regular intervals, Dora, distracted in her oddly factual manner, asked if things were good in this way or that. But she always kept her breath when doing whatever she was up to, which created an impression of restrained unease. I nodded of course, enthusiastic in my tense way, since I hadn't yet learned to state what I wanted. Still, I must admit it was difficult to believe there was true interest in her queries. Probably they amounted to curiosity. Matters would be simplified if she understood how I – no, how my sex – worked. And I . . . Well, I wanted to know what it might be.

As time went by, I began to experience the person into which I was transformed during the drawn-out hours in room 202 as second nature – a twin figure who slid in and out of me, and occasionally possibly was more true to me than I myself. Visiting Dora, time went slower than normal, and I discovered aspects of myself I hadn't noticed before. In her presence, I tested gestures and attitudes with an eagerness that surprised me, borrowing attributes and playing roles, one more shameful than the next. Whatever she asked me to do I did, although I wouldn't have been able to foresee it even in my wilder fantasies. For the protocol, then, I'd like to make clear that, normally, I have no trouble with either eyesight or time – or decency, for that matter. But when I visited Hotel Kreuzer, it was as if I dilated. My body shivered full of foreign motion, and if I wished to ascertain which actions were performed by Sascha Knisch, I had to rely on organs other than my eyes.

Regrettably, I needed no clear vision to realise Dora merely traded services for money. Even a blind person could have told she didn't rent room 202 for my sake. It was I who forced her to do everything, although I rarely did anything but follow instructions. 'Pride' probably isn't the first word to use in this context. After a few weeks, however, I found delight in the practical anonymity that characterised our meetings; slowly, I learned to intensify their impersonality – and to my surprise, things went rather well.

Until one Friday, that is, when I heard Dora's stomach rumble. By this time, a few months had passed, and we had gotten as acquainted with one another as one may reasonably expect under circumstances such as ours. Naturally, there was nothing unusual about the sound emitted from underneath the violet nightdress in which she had just let me clothe her, and I still feel uneasy mentioning it. But as Dora lowered her arms, whispering wayward words in my ear while fastening my narrow blouse, pearl button upon pearl button, all the way up to the throat, I felt the smell of . . . Garlic. I must have seemed surprised, because slowly she realised something had happened. Courageously, I shook my head at her questions, unable to put into words what might have been amazement, perhaps something else. But I didn't fool her. Dora looked at me, then shrugged. Obviously it was my business if I didn't want to say what was wrong. However, instead of continuing with one of the base marvels to which we devoted ourselves, she lit a cigarette and pointed with leather-clad finger towards the high heels by the mirror. If I wanted to, I could put them on and be a catwalk model for a while. Surely I didn't want to remain a naughty schoolgirl for ever, but eventually would like to become a 'lady of the world'? Sooner or later, I, too, had to grow up, didn't I? The irony was unmistakable, and I felt like an impostor. Accordingly, my show was both embarrassing and uncomfortable. Next week, I didn't get in touch. Or the ones following, either.

The garlic settled the matter. I should've known better and confessed. To my defence, I can only say that an intimate part of me really did feel surprised Dora wasn't lust and disguise only, wet, glossy teeth and thin, untouchable lips. She, too, had an interior; she, too, needed to eat. And frankly, I didn't know how to handle this knowledge. The shoddy veil of the old proverb had been torn away, and perhaps it doesn't count in my favour that it took me the rest of the autumn to come to terms with what was behind.

When, shortly after New Year 1927, I visited Hotel Kreuzer again, having spent a few weeks back in Vienna, I told myself it would be the last time. The visits cost too much, not only in terms of money, and I wanted to assure myself they weren't as important for my self-esteem as I'd come to believe. To my surprise, however, the meeting brought us closer. The moment Dora opened the door, I realised the climate had shifted – not much, just a few degrees, but enough to make a new, crisper edge felt. Perhaps it had to do with my absence, perhaps it was due to my just having cut my hair. But for the first time I could see clearly, and what I saw made me want to see more.

From the moment Dora kissed me on the cheek, I was no longer merely a sex. Suddenly I perceived aspects that were . . . I suppose 'genuine' is the word I'm looking for. I'm no experienced gentleman, like Anton, so perhaps I should be more careful. But once we got to know one another, I identified several of the traits I now discerned as Dora's own. There was the way she had of not looking me in the eyes but on the mouth when she said something important; there was the muffled laughter in the middle of nothing, full of glee or rebellion; there was her biting her lower lip, pensive, about to make up her mind, so that the chipped tooth became visible; and there was, of course, the manner in which she put one hand on her back and, with it, grabbed the other arm's fold.

After a while, I discovered we were talking about things that belonged to the world outside room 202. Since that had never happened before, understandably, it made me giddy but nervous. Dora was just telling me about a documentary she had seen, entitled *Prometheus Unbound*, which had been shot shortly after the war. I had heard about the film, because it had been a bit of a scandal in its time. Made on the initiative of a scientific–humanitarian committee, it chronicled the so-called 'male' relation to the body. The aim was pedagogical, or so it was claimed, yet evil tongues suggested that, for some, it might fill the function of pornography. According to Dora, a great hulk of a doctor had guided the spectators through the history of masculinity, going from one tableau to the next while big cardboard posters mounted on the wall explained the different roles assumed by men over the years. There was the god, the titan, and the warrior, the father, the son, and the brother; but also the peasant, the worker, and the teacher, the idler, the lover, and the artist. The scenes predicting 'the man of the future' had especially interested her, even if she thought, she said, biting her lip, that it might take another century before he began to look like I did.

'Is it true that some scenes were pornographic?' I smoothed out my skirt.

'Pornographic? Not likely.' Sure, one scene was filmed in a fake gym. In it, an instructor, short and slim like a pencil, with goatee and high collar, had stressed the importance of man regaining his potency, while a shy teenager in a tight-fitting jumper, with sad eyes and bundles of muscle he didn't know how to handle, had demonstrated suitable exercises. Perhaps that scene could be termed pornographic, Dora mused, or rather, come to think of it, obscene. But the ones that followed, showing Adolf Koch, a well-known Socialist, with his disciples during various outdoor activities, had been precisely what people ought to see. Nobody had done more to raise people's consciousness of their body than the city's famous 'apostle of nakedness'. The only possible exception would be Health Chancellor Froehlich, who apparently had been a member of the humanitarian committee backing the film. At Koch's nudist camp on the outskirts of town, Dora informed me, people shed their social attributes and returned to being themselves. It didn't matter if you were baron, secretary or seamstress. In the eyes of this Adolf, all people were equal. Together, they ate nutritious meals, read edifying literature, and celebrated the healing powers of the sun. If, one day, society would be revolutionised, from the bottom up, it could happen only in this glorious way.

After a quarter of an hour of this sort of propaganda, I coughed and said something about why I considered French movies more interesting (less nature, more clothes). And besides, surely it couldn't be considered a problem if men wished to increase their potency? After all, not only their own sex would stand to benefit from regained strength. Extending her arms along her sides, Dora began to move the elbows in birdlike fashion. Slowly the movements became wider, until it looked like her elbows had evolved into bellows meant to pump up the entire body. Finally, exhaling a loud, pleasant sigh and raising her arms in a triumphant gesture, she laughed: 'But you should have seen the exercises! That poor boy had to pump until he was blue in the face, while the pedantic gentleman, all limp wrist and extended index, pointed out different muscular groups which needed to be activated for a "biological elevation" to become possible. Had the boy been mine, I'd wonder about such zeal.'

Apparently, the sad youth had been asked to imitate the function performed by the testicles, since 'true' masculine power was alleged to reside in the scrotum. Only by tightening the sexual muscles would man be able to meet the requirements of the future. With a powerful gesture, he'd throw off the fetters of decadent society and again become potent – 'like Prometheus. It seems there are censored scenes,' Dora continued, 'shot on the sly, that circulate at select movie theatres. In them, the instructor demonstrates precisely what kind of "elevation" he's hoping for. But I've never seen them. It might well be just rumours. In any event, I thought it quite enough with what I did see.'

As I wasn't particularly interested in the mythical aspects of modern gymnastics, I took the opportunity to change the topic, and asked Dora whether she often went to see films. With curious calm, she returned my gaze. 'I don't live here, if that's what you mean.' Flustered, I stuttered something and began to study the pattern on the Chinese frame, suddenly aware of where I was. Some moments went by, then Dora looked at her watch and slowly inched on her gloves. 'It's quarter past six already. We have to hurry if you're going to make it.' But her body spoke a different language. Calmly she went over to her makeup box and added, with surprising dreaminess in her voice: 'Come to think of it, Anton, I wouldn't mind a counter-demonstration.' Adjusting one of the straps on her bustier, she then proposed something different, and considerably more attractive.

The details are not important, but for the sake of the sexual question, I ought to mention that, after a while, Dora asked me to dig my heels into the pillow on the chair. By this time she had removed not only her dress and petticoat, but her stockings, too. Luckily, I had managed to persuade her to keep bustier and footwear on. Now she gripped my ankles and pushed my feet back, then she slid her warm, leather-clad palms along my calves, gently parting my shivering knees. From her makeup box, she removed a rope and what I think may have been a shoelace. The latter she tied so that what she wanted to emphasize separated like two fat almonds. Satisfied but not yet ready, she took the rope, tied a knot, and began to pull what she referred to as my 'appendix'. 'My appendix?' I wondered. I could hear her breathing, but because of the hem I was lifting, I remained in the dark as to what, precisely, she was speaking about. Slowly, however, things got tighter and started to smart. Each time Dora pulled the rope, it got tighter. Then, finally, she straightened out and put her hands on her hips, considering the result with head tilted to the side: 'A rope maker wouldn't have done a better job.'

I didn't follow, but as I tried to straighten my back, I realised an important part of me had been tied to the bed-post. With some difficulty, I managed to step over the two cords and put my wobbly heels on the floor. Dora asked me to walk over to the mirror and raise my skirt – which at this point was no longer perfectly smooth. Of course, I did as told, all totter and want, despite the fact that, for each step, I felt the two parts of me still tied up straining backward and to the sides. When, eventually, I reached the mirror, my pride pointed in the direction it usually does on grand occasions, whereas what Dora had referred to as my 'appendix' had disappeared entirely. I can confirm it did look peculiar.

Smiling, Dora removed her gloves, finger after artful finger. From her box, she took a red satin bow and applied it skilfully. 'There; good girl. Now you, too, have a clitoris. And how sweet it is.' At first I wanted to protest, as the body part of which she had spoken seemed bigger than that of most girls, and I couldn't discover the corresponding opening. Also, the more I groped towards the mirror, the clearer I realised how difficult it is for a man to liberate himself from his appendage. But as I glanced at the girl in the mirror, I understood that Dora might be right. When we both had admired her for a while – with her blossoming cheeks and stylish bow she really did resemble a work of art – Dora asked me to perform certain actions. 'And now it's my turn,' she added a while later, shortly before urging me to assume a position that normally wouldn't have been conspicuous, but in this situation acquired a new meaning. 'Don't move until I tell you.'

The unexpected turn that my visit was taking had the same ridiculous character as so many other things in my life. Again, I could merely hear what was happening. It sounded as if Dora fidgeted in the chair. Her shoes fell to the floor, then there was silence. I tried to catch a glimpse of her in the mirror, but from my perspective, all I could see were the gloves on the floor, matt and sinuous like shed snakeskin – as well as the diligent girl, of course, with that big, red bow so prominently displayed. Standing with my legs bent and parted, I placed my hands on my knees. Since it is a demanding position even for a lady, I did my utmost to breathe in a calm and dignified fashion. A while went by before I was able to make out sounds behind me. At first, I distinguished a movement repeated with a certain stubbornness, then came a slithery and wet, almost rubbing sort of noise, whereupon Dora to my surprise, but not misery, began to whimper. 'Move,' she whispered with muddled voice.

When I had overcome my fluster, I thought I should try to do my part, too. So I began not only to move, but to form some of the delicious sounds Dora now emitted with ever shorter intervals. But she just said – breathless and definitive: 'Be quiet.

No, quiet. Move. Yes. Faster. Faster, I said. Faster.' And good girl that I was, I did as I was told.

After that Friday, frankly, it became impossible to give up room 202. When Dora and I now met, we always kissed. She no longer wore any gloves, and we talked about what everybody does – films, restaurants, even picnics and politics. At times she commented on other visitors, their manner and preferences, and I didn't discourage her, as these confidences made me feel ever so slightly an exception. Perhaps our acquaintance would have continued in this manner, with meetings on Fridays and the art of intimacy they conveyed – if it weren't for Elizabeth Junek, who one day declared she'd participate as the first woman in the hardest car race of all: the Targa Florio on Sicily. It was a grey and damp Friday at the end of January last year. When I told Dora the news she proclaimed such 'emancipation' ought to be celebrated – 'Don't you think?'

I was fiddling with my tie and hadn't understood what she said. As I tucked down my shirt, I thus repeated distractedly: 'Yes, don't you think?' When I continued to put on my jacket, however, I noticed Dora looked at me in the mirror, as if in my turn, I'd said something of which she hadn't understood the significance until now. Gradually meaning dawned on me, or perhaps on us, and uncertain as to how to act, I chose to put on my overcoat. I might as well continue being distracted, I decided, winding my scarf around my neck before saying something about double-sided cylinders. Yet as I was about to leave, Dora gave me her hand in a motion at once calm and challenging. Silently she looked at my mouth; I lowered my gaze and kissed her fingers.

That was all. No greeting, no goodbye. Nonetheless, I was convinced we had formed a pact. During the seven days and nights that followed, the words we uttered rang – at least in my mind. It took me three days to trust my intuition, another three to persuade myself, but not until the seventh day did I realise it didn't matter who had made the invitation. That Friday I had to force myself to stay home until four-thirty in the afternoon. I counted the hours, then the minutes, and finally the seconds – the last standing in front of a café opposite the hotel. Dusk settled, the cold was cracking. For a moment, I considered whether to go inside and buy something, then I realised it would seem exaggerated. I was delighted to see Dora, but what if I had misunderstood her? To be frank, I might also have been nervous at the prospect of celebrating Junek and her Bugatti, type 35. Among other things, it might mean I'd have to show who I was outside room 202. What if Dora had no interest in an Austrian, ten years her junior, who worked part-time as a film projectionist? A middle-aged man with damp hair and flushed face came out on the pavement, turned up his collar, and went with inverted steps away from Hotel Kreuzer. A visitor? My predecessor? I turned around and crossed the street.

The visit was less lax than ever, with impractical movements and forced ardour. It felt as if a window was open and neither one of us could ignore the cold. Not until I got ready to leave – as usual with pain lumped in my groin, yet this time my body remained without thrill or resonance – was the pattern broken. Standing at the door, holding one arm behind her back, with the hand in the other arm's bend, Dora waited for me to get ready. Lightly, almost carelessly, she said: 'There was that business of emancipation, wasn't there?' And a few days later, we became persons with history.

We met at the Paris Bar, a French restaurant not far from where, I later learned, Dora lived. The time was my suggestion; the choice of place hers. Apprehensively, I gave her a present I had found in a junk shop the day before.

'For me?' I nodded quietly, studying Dora's chipped tooth while she opened the gift. 'But . . .' She looked at me. 'What is *this*?'

'A cigarette case.'

'Doesn't look like it.' Sceptically, she turned the object in her hand. It was as big as her palm, and because of its false silver looked more expensive than it really was. Still, the case was unusual, and I assumed she'd never seen one quite like it. Two shell-formed halves were held together by an oblong spring at the back and a small lock at the front. Across the surface, thin, welted patterns criss-crossed, and the edges of the two halves were shaped to look like . . . 'Labia?' There was disbelief in Dora's voice.

'Look here.' Embarrassed, I held up the tiny key to the lock and opened the case. Inside, it was lined in burgundy velvet, with space for two lines of eight cigarettes. I pointed to the ornate script in gold embossed on the elastics that kept the cigarettes in place.

'*Pandora's Box*,' Dora read. '*Made in England by H. E. Faist & Bros.*'

'I couldn't help thinking of you when I saw it.' I extended the key. 'That's what the case is called. "Pandora's Box."' Quietly, I wondered why I hadn't chosen a more tasteful gift. 'The name's probably supposed to hint at the misfortune that awaits the person who opens the case. But you only need to worry, I think, if you're a big smoker. It wasn't expensive,' I added. 'If you don't like the case, you could give it away. I wouldn't object.'

'No, no, I *do* like it,' There was a pensive lilt to Dora's reply. 'At least I think so. Could we check if they fit?' She proceeded to fill the case with her American cigarettes, then closed it with a delicate click, letting the tiny key sit in the lock. Having placed the one remaining cigarette on the table, she crumpled up the empty packet. 'Neat.'

For the rest of the dinner, we spoke about ourselves. Or rather: Dora talked about herself, while I speculated about somebody who still called himself 'Anton'. In either case, the scenes presented were carefully taken out of context – which made me think of the drawings in the weekend newspaper supplements: swarming across a nondescript background, a series of numbered dots have to be connected. The result may yield a landscape with a stranded boat, a homey interior with reading chair and fireplace, or a spectacular playground with whirling swings, roundabouts, and stoic wooden horses mounted on giant springs. The tableaux have only one thing in common: they're all curiously devoid of human beings. Neither Dora nor I connected any of the dots we described, and I suspect neither of us observed the proper numerical order. Yet I'm convinced that, at least in her case, the moments described were dots of a genuine past, whereas mine . . . Well, I admit they were either borrowed or invented.

Everyday life created the greatest difficulties, since we both had to move back in time and become what we were not yet: people with history. As for me, I was circumspect and only asked things I was prepared to answer myself. But by the time we ordered shots of chilled, slinky absinthe, I could no longer resist wondering why Dora had moved to the city. From my accent, she had figured out that I came from Vienna, and having been asked why I had moved here, I had answered that I felt too confined at home. In this city, existence was a little looser, life a lot freer. Perhaps you might call it 'emancipation'? Dora raised one eyebrow, black and supreme, but instead of replying with her usual mixture of irony and directness, she explained that she had fallen in love with the wrong person. 'Your "wicked, little secret?"' I asked as she finished. The waiter had taken our plates and I hadn't caught her last words.

'I just meant to say I was eighteen years old and pregnant.' Suddenly, she seemed almost impatient. 'There was no other reason to move here, you know. If it interests you, I arrived the same weekend as a balloon competition was arranged in the northern part of the city. I remember that much, because I felt as if I, too, was swollen up – with nerves and blood and future.' On a piece of paper Dora had clutched in her hand and never let go of, not even during the ten-hour train trip, had been the address of a doctor who hailed from the same city as she. When she had knocked on his door the following morning, having spent the grey hours in the park opposite his private clinic, the doctor had served her hot broth and nudged her to tell him what had happened. Occasionally, he performed abortions on 'sisters', but never without first inquiring about their means of support. Satisfied with Dora's account, the doctor had urged her to sleep on the matter for one more night. If, after that, she decided not to have an abortion, he'd see to it that the child was placed in a home 'full of love and without sorrow'.

'Apart from the six months left of the pregnancy, there'd be no burden involved. He told me I could help out at the clinic if I wanted. Once the day grew near, he'd prepare the departure of my "wicked, little secret". Nobody needed to know about it.' When Dora had replied she might want to have an abortion anyway, the doctor had reminded her she was in a phase that wasn't without its dangers. Besides, she could count on compensation.

That night, Dora didn't fall asleep until shortly after the vegetable merchants put up their stands. She had loved the father of her child, she explained, a man who waited at the same restaurant where she had worked. But they had been too young and their mutual future anything but certain. Since the restaurant was owned by the boy's father, and the son risked losing his inheritance, Dora had done the only right thing and had, despite a heavy heart, left him. The money her friend had stolen from the cash register ('It was the last thing I thought Jupp Walther would give me') covered the abortion, but neither her living expenses nor the trip back. And if complications arose . . . Slowly Dora realised she didn't have much of an alternative. When she had returned to the clinic towards lunch the next day, she and the doctor had agreed on a sum of money – 'More than I expected' – and already the same afternoon, she had started to sweep floors.

'You never regretted it?'

Dora lit the cigarette she had put aside, then began to study the darkness outside. A long time went by before she turned to me and explained it had been a boy. 'Once they had tied the umbilical chord, they held him up. He screamed and screamed and screamed. I thought he'd never stop! But he did – abruptly, the instant I showed him the wooden toy animal I had bought for him. At last, the doctor could tie the ribbon around his wrist that newborns get. Since I wouldn't keep him, there was no name on the tag. Surprised, he looked at it, as if realising what the absence of a name meant. Then he shook his tiny fists and peed on the doctor. I remember I thought he should be called something heroic. Like Parsifal. Or do you think Eros would have been better?' She exhaled calmly. 'I've often thought I should give the boy the tag if ever I were to see him again. So that he might fill in his name himself, I mean. Wouldn't you?' The smoke ring Dora had made lost itself in the air like an errant halo, and I was just about to reply when she added in a small voice: 'No, I never regretted it. The doctor promised me the baby would be placed in a good family. Only he and the parents would know he was adopted. That suited me well. It made it a lot easier to begin a new life.'

Dora had decided not to return home – wherever *that* was: Kolberg, Breslau, Königsberg? Perhaps farther east? Lemberg? Instead, she had rented a room with a nurse who worked at the clinic. The rest of the money from the 'sale', as she termed it, she had used to fund her way through evening school. 'I managed three advertisement agencies which all folded, one repair shop which first blossomed and then was mismanaged, and half a year at a firm whose line of business I never quite figured out. After that, I gave up. There were other ways of making money – "faster" money. And now I think it's time to change the topic.' Dora scrutinised my mouth. 'Your name isn't Anton, is it?'

'It is,' I replied, perhaps a bit too hastily. 'It really is. Anton may not be my whole name, but . . .' I made an embarrassed gesture, while silently cursing myself. Why did I continue to use my best friend's name? Was it just because, as a child, I had heard that spies were told to construct biographies – 'legends' – which were as close to their real lives as possible, since it lowered the risk for fatal mistakes? 'And yours?'

'Dora,' Dora replied, gauging me with cloudy eyes. 'Frankly, I thought you had invented the name. Most of my guests do. I can't understand why. It's not that I wish to get to know them, exactly. Good of you to use your own name. I can't bear people who don't stand up for who they are. Anton . . .' Smiling, she pocketed her cigarette case. 'Yes, that'll do. You may be my Anton from Vienna.'

There was no way back.

Chapter Seven

It was already past two on Saturday afternoon when I unlocked my bicycle. Frau Britz had been so unyielding that I had agreed to settle my debt no later than by Monday. For each month I managed to cover, I could stay an additional night. But if I hadn't settled the entire debt next Thursday, July 5, I'd be thrown out before midnight – 'without pardon', she had added, investigating what was up with my nameplate. Her son was looking for a place to live, and my flat would do just nicely. Raising her hand, Mrs Britz began to count on her fingers. When one hand wasn't enough (I was not five but six months behind), she engaged her second thumb, remarking, surprised: 'I had hoped it'd be Thursday, but it's really Friday.' With both her palms in the air, she added that, no, no, it didn't matter what I retorted. 'Your word's no longer worth a reichspfennig, Mr Knisch. Ivan will have to wait until Friday.' Gratefully, I realised her mad mathematics had given me an extra night's respite.

I rolled down the slope that leads to the Stock Exchange and the river running through the city. The Foundation for Sexual Research is on the other side of the water, in a remote corner of a lush, verdant park. Because of its founder's interests, the place is surrounded by many rumours, not all of which could possibly be true. When I pass by on my bicycle, I happen to see people standing on the pavement outside the gates, pointing to the building with embarrassed faces. Once in a while, a covered car will pull up and a person known from the illustrated press hurries in, all brilliant smile and dark glasses. At other times, student organisations will unfold banners and sing with full throats and erect backs turned to the Foundation. But worst are the brownshirts, who have begun to patrol the street in order to scare away timorous patients.

Apparently, there are sixty-five rooms on the palatial premises. In the part that once belonged to Prince Radziwill, the basement accommodates kitchen, offices and staff quarters. The ground floor includes the reception and a hall with dusty memorabilia. One flight up the wide marble staircase – stucco figures to the side and a chandelier suspended in midair like a giant snowflake – the museum shares space with the private quarters of Health Chancellor Martin Froehlich. In an adjacent building, donated by the former director of war materials, Adam Hatz, are clinics, archives and the scientific library of the Foundation that supposedly contains Europe's largest collection of 'forbidden literature'. Above the entrance, facing the park, is written 'Amori et dolori sacrum' – proud words which embody the spirit in which Froehlich and his staff have chosen to work.

The Foundation opened its gates almost ten years ago, in July 1919. Within a few years, it had won international acclaim and has even become a tourist attraction listed in every guide devoted to 'what is not in Baedeker'. When I moved here in 1923, during the worst months of the Inflation, not many days passed before I heard of the Health Chancellor. 'It's cheaper only at Froehlich's,' the ladies said, positioned under the streetlamps around the railway station, close to the hotel where I had found lodgings but no sleep.

In my old hometown, people aren't wildly happy with the Chancellor's reputation. As a strict science, his sexual biology is still stuck in its 'infantile' phase, they argue, unable to understand how a colossus as unruly as Froehlich's may claim to be an organic body of scientifically proven truths. Is his research object not more monster than man? What do masturbation machines from Augsburg have in common with hysteria, hirsutism with penis envy? I don't know if it's true, but according to the papers, the Health Chancellor laughed when he first heard about the criticism. 'The Viennese delegation must be patient. One day the truth will dawn on them, too,' he told a reporter dispatched from the *Tageblatt*, while a photographer tried to place him so that the advantageous light that had just made an African sculpture in ebony come alive would reflect in his eyeglasses, thick as the bottom of beer jugs. 'What my Austrian colleagues term the subconscious, I call the endocrine system,' he continued, repeating his famous slogan. Then he added, putting his arm around the brown stele: 'And I can assure your readers: *that*'s the same for monsters as for men!'

Still, Froehlich has already been championed as the 'Einstein of Sex'. The designation isn't as unfitting as it may seem. Since the turn of the century, he has devoted himself to a theory of sexual relativity, dreaming of doing, one day, for our intimate life what the technical expert at the Bern patent office has done for our world view. According to the father of sexual biology, it's unreasonable to speak of merely two sexes. 'Three billion people and only two sexes? Over my dead body!' Between the hundred per cent male and the hundred per cent female – 'two wild abstractions' – there's an entire spectrum of possibilities. Every endocrine system produces the hormones andrine (abbreviated to A) and gynecine (abbreviated to O), in varying amounts and with different concentration. Hence, depending on the mixture, each individual is only more or less man, only more or less woman. 'Love is quite literally the effect of hormones.'

Basing his theories of man on hormonal percentages, Froehlich argues for the so-called 'grey sex'. In order to explain this notion, he takes recourse to a simile that has already become famous. If a round disc is painted in all the colours of the rainbow and then spun around, only one colour will be visible: grey. Accordingly, the task of the sexual biologist is to lower 'the psychological speed' in order for all nuances of a person's love life to emerge. The grey sex contains every aspect between *A* and *O*; it's merely a matter of establishing the exact distribution in each individual – which is done most efficiently by filling out the questionnaire that Froehlich has developed.

The interview appeared under the header 'MEN OF A NEW ERA'. Next to the picture of the Health Chancellor with his arm wrapped around the African phallus, was one of the 'founding father of the institute surrounded by his family'. In this group portrait, taken at the inauguration of the Foundation, one could see the white-clothed Chancellor standing together with colleagues and patients on the stairs of the main entrance. The shot carried no legend, but the heading was easily explained by Froehlich's concluding remarks: 'Although the new century has taken only a few stumbling steps, it has already witnessed more cruelty than anyone had imagined man capable of. Our meagre luck is that the war has turned nations into brothers. "No more!" the proud call sounds which now resonates in parliaments all across the globe. Confronted with such truth, we all stand as naked as on the first day of creation. We must mature into an adult community, in which every person is respected regardless of his or her orientation. My institute would like to contribute to this honourable mission. It espouses the same principle on the terrain of sex, as the statesmen plead for on that of politics: *fraternité*. Trust me: this century will see new men!'

One morning in April last year, I read aloud from this article. After our dinner at the Paris Bar, Dora and I had begun to see each other – sporadically but with pleasure, and only when she wanted to. In this manner, late winter turned into a glittering array of days, and nights, when we met in secret. My friends knew nothing about our liaison, and I doubt Dora had said anything to hers. Although we didn't break the law, it felt as if we'd become comrades in crime. Every night we saw each other, we committed new sins – and I, at least, devoted the days in between to coming to terms with the delectable loot.

Now that we no longer met at Hotel Kreuzer, paragraph 168 had lost its meaning. Still, it was hard to ask Dora for the kind of things to which we had devoted ourselves in room 202. The only time I hinted at my wishes, she interrupted me by saying that these were two different worlds, and I had to decide to which one I wanted to belong. There was that of 'purchase' and there was that of 'partnership'. She wasn't ashamed of the way she made a living, but work was work, private life private. When, the next night, Dora exclaimed: 'Naked at last!' I realised her preferred form of meeting, and discovered I had nothing against it – at least not to the extent that it bothered me.

In February, she floated in the warm, soapy water in the bath-tub, while I, sitting on the floor with one arm under the sudsy surface, played English submarine. 'There, our proud fleet lost another battle ship,' Dora would sigh as the last shivers ebbed out and her kneecaps sank below the surface. If we happened to find ourselves in bed, which was the case in March, she preferred to position herself snugly on my palms, bareback as an Indian on his horse, and asked me with an impatient twist of her head to insert one finger in the place that wasn't occupied, so that she could 'rejoin Old Shatterhand'. April began with tests of my endurance, for which Dora assumed different roles – extraordinary water pump inspector, certified snake charmer, sausage measurer – and refused to budge before she had concrete proof of my riches. And one night towards the middle of the same month, sitting naked in my lap, she rested her head on my chest and fidgeted as if she were twenty years younger, while whispering with a voice both light and wondrous: 'Please, don't. No, please, please, don't . . .'

Increasingly, Dora exhibited more of herself, and I became more and more enchanted. 'I like being with you,' she remarked one evening, pushing a strand of hair from her face. 'You make no demands, but everything's possible. It's like being at sea: by turn ebb and flood. First you decide, then I. It's all very stimulating.' And another evening, or rather night, she confessed that, already early on, she had wondered who I was. 'When you visited Hotel

Kreuzer shortly after New Year – you had just cut your hair, remember? – I thought it might be nice to have you as a brother, and almost wanted to suggest we skip the visit and go to the café across the street. But you seemed so serious, and I didn't want to disappoint you.'

I suppose we fell in love – she in her way, I in mine. Yet like siblings, we also realised we'd never be a proper couple. For that, Dora's past seemed too complicated and my present living situation too volatile. 'I like getting to know you,' she whispered one morning as I lay behind her, one arm slung across her hip, the other extended under her warm neck. 'And to be known. But I don't want to be possessed, Anton. You can understand that, can't you? Love's so unpredictable.' I fell asleep with her hair in my face.

When, later the same morning, I put the newspaper aside, Dora pointed to one of the persons in the group portrait and claimed he was her oldest childhood friend. 'Felix runs the museum at the Foundation. He also gives advice. If you have no money, you don't have to pay. It's not like at the Misery, where they amputate limbs left and right, and patients who can't afford to convalesce properly have to make money on the neighbouring streets. The Foundation stands for the most important thing there is: each person's right to decide about his or her own sexual life. What we're born with is one thing, what we'd like to be another.'

I hadn't known Dora was so engaged in the sexual question and tried to make light of the 'professors of love'. Not replying, she groped for the cigarette case, which she kept in the drawer of her nightstand. Having lit a cigarette and fastened the kimono around her waist, Dora brushed herself in front of the closet mirrors. Finally, picking the hair out of the brush, she replied with the cigarette quivering in her mouth: 'Anton, I think it's about time you considered the sexual question soberly.' Noticing my discomfiture, she lowered her voice and continued wryly, like a gangster: 'Well, partner, it's like this: you've cracked the safe, now face the loot.' Assuming the posture of the red-robed woman on the reproduction behind her, she added: 'Trust this Dora: she knows everything about corruption.'

That must have been shortly before Easter, because I remember the coloured bows and paper eggs that hung on the gates as we approached the Foundation. We ascended the same stairs on which the group portrait in the paper, which Dora had crammed into my coat pocket ('Just a memento, darling, for when you've sobered up'), had been taken a decade earlier. As we entered the reception hall, we discovered a man with red braces and horn-rimmed glasses sitting behind the counter. Dora asked if Dr Karp was in, to which the receptionist replied with a mild nod. If we'd be so kind as to enter our names in the register, he'd be happy to call him. 'For the sake of statistics,' he added and made an ornate note of '*Museum*' next to our signatures (Dora's genuine, mine still fake).

While we leafed through some of the prints lying on the counter – among them copies of the famous *Psycho-biologischer Fragebogen* – the receptionist walked over to a telephone mounted on the wall. He dialled a few times with a ring-adorned index finger, then turned to us while waiting for the signals to make it through the cords: 'There's more for sale upstairs, in the museum, you know – also pills, accessories and such things.' Adjusting the receiver, he proceeded to inform the invisible doctor that visitors were waiting.

A few minutes later, a man in his late thirties, early forties, with pale features and circumspect mien, descended the stairs. I recognised him vaguely from the group portrait. He had short, dirty blond hair and was impeccably dressed. Still, there was something stiff and correct about him, as if he had been cut out of cardboard. When he noticed us, he turned his palms out and increased his pace. Dora met him at the base of the stairs, whirling around with her friend on the marble floor. Since she was dressed in trousers and the jacket from Berchtesgaden, for a few seconds I actually had difficulties telling them apart. 'And this is your companion?'

'Anton,' Dora replied, beaming.

'Delighted. Felix, Felix Karp.' The doctor shook my hand with genuine care. Whispering something to my friend, he put what looked like a spatula in his pocket, then wondered if we'd like to meet the Health Chancellor before inspecting the premises.

I looked at Dora to see her reaction. 'That would be an honour, wouldn't it?' She had to speak for the two of us.

Froehlich turned out to be a squat man with big, glossy lips hidden behind a massive nineteenth-century moustache. He had myopic yet attentive eyes and a sturdy frame he carried with surprising delicacy. We found him in an oriental-inspired parlour one flight up, sunk in a voluminous velvet chair with his legs crossed like a Turk, sipping coffee from a gilded cup. On his big, naked feet were worn-down patent leather shoes. Next to him sat Kurt Gielke, his striking assistant and partner, as I later understood. The Health Chancellor extended a ruddy hand with curly black hair covering the back, while Gielke contented himself with a discreet nod, stirring his cup with ceremonial fingers.

Once we had sat down, Froehlich poured us coffee, Karp having declined with a courteous gesture. Then he asked Dora if she and I were '"partners", as the Americans like to say'. Expectant, he munched on his moustache (tiny, wet, insect-like sounds). First we looked at each other, then at him, after which Dora shook her head, smiling. 'Not quite . . .' Eagerly, Froehlich thrust himself forward and asked if, in that case, I happened to carry a knife in my pocket. Now I felt not only speechless, but also taut and rolled up, like an umbrella. Self-consciously I fidgeted with the cup in my hands. Dora placed a calming hand on my arm and said, in order to shift the attention, something about having seen a documentary about an unbound Prometheus.

'Let's not talk about that ill-fated film, Miss Wilms.' Shaking his head, the Health Chancellor seemed more sad than angry. 'Perhaps you could tell me whether your mute friend carries a knife in his pocket?' Again, he regarded her expectantly. 'The importance of silence for the sexual question hasn't been stud- ied closely enough. What you hear is not always what you get, you know. In the case of silence, we may truly speak of covering one's sex. If we were able to establish its proper relevance, we might make a pioneering contribution – and at the same time correct some of the hypotheses proposed by my vociferous opponents.' Not until later, when Karp asked us to fill out the 'psycho-biological questionnaire', did I realise what Froehlich alluded to.

The father of the Foundation represents what liberal journalists term the 'regenerated', but their nationalist colleagues prefer to call the 'degenerate' Germany. As early as 1897, merely thirty years old, Froehlich founded a committee with the purpose of protecting the rights of homosexuals. Ever since, he has fought to abolish the infamous paragraph 175, which criminalises their 'activities'. As a young doctor, Karp continued as he took us upstairs, Froehlich studied the effect of alcohol on accidental pregnancies in the impoverished areas of the capital. Today he's the energetic defender 'of all minorities', is often consulted as legal authority, and frequently acts behind the political scene – 'with a certain success,' our guide informed us quietly, 'albeit not always to the delight of the people.'

In 1907, for example, Froehlich was called on as an expert in the 'Hatz Case', as the director of war materials as well as high-ranking officers were charged with 'criminal activities'. 'Rumour had it the generals in Potsdam had a particular eye for the white cuirassiers – stately male specimens, who bowed only to higher command.' The journalist who promulgated these 'lies' was taken to court, where, after a second process, he received a minor sentence. Froehlich's report had settled the matter. In it, he succeeded in demonstrating that the main culprit, Adam Hatz, who was charged with having seduced two generals, suffered from a grave shortage of andrine, which explained his 'endocrine tendency'. After a series of test treatments, mainly with a drug later patented as 'Testifortan', the situation was alleviated, and the director could even give his wife a much longed-for child – thus settling the case in his, and the generals', favour.

'Whatever the truth was,' Karp continued, 'the case was used for nationalistic purposes. Gradually, the rightwing press undermined Hatz's position. In order to protect the integrity of the military, he took an honourable discharge. He and Froehlich kept in touch, however. After the tragic death of the Hatz family in arson in the summer of 1918, it turned out that Martin would inherit the building to which we are now heading – as a token of gratitude for having saved the director's honour. But not even the death of Hatz could put an end to the accusations,' Karp added. 'Ever since the Potsdam case, the tabloids speak of organised Hebrews attacking what some claim to be the noblest thing championed by Germans: the "ideal" friendship between men. When the Foundation opened, Martin's opponents found the target they had been looking for. "Humanity from behind", the allegation runs. Since then, our critics haven't tired of propagating that "the nest must be fumigated from which stems the weak stench of perfume and Vaseline".'

Apparently, the most vocal opponent was a former colleague who had been working with Froehlich before the Foundation opened, and authored a study of athletic clubs considered as an erotic phenomenon. Shortly before the inauguration in 1919, however, it was discovered that he had falsified his doctor's degree and that, in reality, he merely wanted to pave the way for what he termed 'the future German': an athletic male, with a strong sense of brotherhood, who'd re-establish the honour lost so humiliatingly in the Great War.

'Today he runs a club for "titanic body culture", open only to men, and takes every opportunity to criticise us. It seems "gymnastics cannot be performed in skirt or caftan" . . .' According to Froehlich's former colleague, German men were alone responsible for today's crisis. Evidently, their crime consisted in no longer being a hundred per cent male. 'German women, too, have ceased to be only women. On one hand, like Amazons, they try to claim the rudder of the state; on the other, as emancipated beings, they demand erotic liberation. In both cases, they betray the honour of their sex. Hence, traditional gender roles must be restored. If a biological elevation doesn't occur soon, we may all expect a new Sodom and Gomorrah.'

Karp chuckled, then opened the door to the library and knocked on a counter. From a door left ajar in the corridor behind, we could hear a chair creak. 'Osram Röser,' said the person who soon emerged, tore a napkin from his collar, and made a solemn bow. I sensed Dora stiffen, presumably because of the man's appearance. He was both big and bulky, and across his bare skull liver spots scattered profusely. Most remarkable, however, was the man's face, which was too wide for the cranium. His mouth went down on either side of the chin and his eyes, black and unmoving, sat so far apart they no longer seemed connected. As I studied them, I realised they looked as if made of porcelain. 'This is Miss Wilms and her friend. With your permission, Doctor Röser, I'd like to show them our holdings.'

'As you wish, Doctor Karp.' Clicking his heels, Röser eyed his watch. 'Alf should be back any minute now. He can show you round. If you'd be so kind as to wait here.' Palm flattened and extended, the librarian pointed to a table with periodicals neatly arranged at the far end.

'Thank you, that won't be necessary.'

'But I think . . .' Röser thought, then changed his mind. 'Of course, Doctor Karp. I shall inform Kinkel when he returns from his lunch hour. Are you feeling better today?' Smiling at his colleague, he reinserted the napkin in his generous collar, and returned to his lunch.

Our guide shrugged his shoulders. Alf Kinkel, we were later told, had once been a homeless boy who had belonged to one of the street gangs roaming the city. Now he worked as an assistant to the librarian. Adjusting his cuffs, Karp began to show us round. Since the turn of the century, the Health Chancellor has collected literature about man's sexual life in all major and several minor languages, so that today, the Foundation can boast a unique collection of tales from Sacramento in the west to Kupang in the east, from Kiruna in the north to the Sahara in the south.

On the top shelf of one bookcase, I noticed several copies of *Transvestites* from 1910, as well as the proofs of what Karp claimed would become Froehlich's masterpiece, a *Geschlechtskunde* in five volumes. In this sexual atlas, the director of the Foundation planned to gather his entire doctrine, 'based on thirty years' worth of evaluated questionnaires,' as our guide pointed out, having stepped up a ladder and taken down the typescript. Presenting the material, he explained that Froehlich was determined to treat statistically facts from all fields of sexuality in a 'useful text intended for each and everyone – male, female, and all those in between. For the first time, man, seen as a sexual being, will feature in full figure.'

'And what about literature,' I coughed, 'fiction, I mean?' I handed Dora the stack of paper.

'Ah, you *can* talk. This way, if you will.' We passed some desks cluttered with archival documents, and came to rows of books ordered alphabetically, according to language. 'Welcome,' our guide announced, drawing his finger along the shelf closest to us. 'Our forbidden literature.'

Looking slyly at me, Dora asked if Karp could recommend 'something really, really illegal'.

He smiled a scholarly smile. 'That won't be particularly difficult.' At first Karp stopped at *B*, leaned forward and pulled out a print entitled *The Gymnasium of Pleasure*. But changing his mind, he put it back and held his chin. After closer thought, he explained, he wasn't looking 'for athletic fantasies or pedagogical measures of correction, but for a more appropriate image of today's society, characterised by inflation, disarmament, and an emerging sense of sisterhood.' Pausing, he added: 'Although that's easier said than done . . .'

'What do you mean, Felix?'

Karp straightened up. 'What we term forbidden literature is almost always written by men, for men. Women are merely used to make the stronger sex look better. When, I wonder, will one of these gentleman scribes try to step into the shoes of the opposite sex?' Noticing my look, he pointed to the shelves. 'Well, if you don't believe me, try any of these books. Chances are, you won't see things from the fair side.'

The fair side? I glanced at Dora, but she just raised one eyebrow and regarded me neutrally – as if she wanted me to listen and only then make up my mind whether Karp was being ironic. It took our guide a while, then he seemed to have thought of a suitable piece of writing, because now he slid his finger along the spines on the opposite shelf. Almost immediately, he stopped at *R*, where he pulled out a slim volume. Placing it in his open palm, he leafed through the pages, stopping each time he came to an illustration. 'This is an extreme piece of writing. By a young poet, later turned arms merchant. Just published. The manuscript was found among the papers he left behind when he disappeared in Africa. I managed to get hold of a copy in Paris last month. A real *trouvaille*. Very evocative.'

Apparently, Karp often travelled to France. He considered the cover: *Les Stupra* it said in embroidered letters. 'Many people don't want to accept that their cherished genius wrote these sonnets. That's why they've been banished to the libraries' poison cabinet. Here, look.' He showed us an illustration. 'Pure dynamite for Hauptstein and his ilk. Consider these testicles, consider this elevation. Yet the size of the gigantic phallus unrightfully makes us astonished,' he declared sombrely, then began to recite:

> *Obscur et froncé comme un œillet violet,*
> *il respire, humblement tapi parmi la mousse.*

From his inner pocket, Karp produced his metal object, which he placed along the fold of the book. Having closed the volume, he explained the contents of the poem. 'A sodomitic scene. "Dark and puckered like a violet carnation / he breathes, humbly shrunk in the moss." No German would write in this way. Not even Blei. And certainly no woman. Still, at least the poem makes an attempt to show things from a less bellicose side. *Obscur et froncé*: that's what you term a "retreat", no?'

Karp considered the suggestion, then added, tapping his finger against the cover: 'As long as *fraternité* serves as our model for a fair society, I fear this is what we'll have to content ourselves with.' Removing his spatula, he put the book back. 'Let's end our tour in the museum.'

Chapter Eight

Having returned to the first building, we entered a room at the end of which hung a fat, white *A* that corresponded to the black *O* we now discovered above our heads – more bathing ring than halo.

'Which side would you prefer?'

Dora nodded towards the *A*, then turned to Karp. 'Could we start from the beginning?'

'If you say so.' Our guide walked over to a poster of what, at a distance, looked like a plant or a butterfly. 'Perhaps you recognise this organ? The apostle of semen. The very model for our Foundation.' He smiled apologetically. 'Martin considers our work as sexologists a mission. And what model could serve better for our task of spreading the message of Amor than this blossoming angel? Naturally, we preach all sexual gospels. No orientation is too irrelevant, no deviation too trivial!' As we approached, we could see Karp was right: drawn to look like it revealed its interior, the organ did, indeed, resemble a flower crossed with an angel. The stalk was thick and protruding, with pointy, leaf-shaped wings, while the bud proper had a glossy sheen and a pleated collar reminiscent of a crooked corona. 'Drawn after one of Toldt's preparations. Only in the third month do the testicles slide through the groin channel here into the scrotum. Until then, they reside in the abdominal cavities on either side of the spine, here and here, where incidentally we believe the hormones andrine and gynecine are produced – the male ones mainly to the right, the female largely to the left.'

Karp pointed. 'All embryos contain both hormones in different amounts and concentration. Originally, no human being is a hundred per cent male or female. During the first years of life, however, one's sexual tendency gradually becomes clear. Puberty is the last critical phase. During this period, biological needs encounter the cultural demands imposed by the individual's surroundings. Generally, from the age of fourteen or fifteen, we believe the sexual profile of a person is clear.' Tapping against the drawing, he added: 'These small parts here, suspension devices, really, are called cremaster muscles. When the scrotum curls up – from fear or lust – they raise the testicles. There are those who deplore the Versailles treaty and believe this elevation may be translated into other areas than those of biology.' Karp laughed dryly, as if crumbling a biscuit. 'But a nation is no body, a people no biological organism.'

Realising we didn't quite follow, he leaned towards the poster. 'The seminal fluid travels along this path, ultimately issuing forth through the ejaculation channel here. Those colleagues who believe in testicular elevation as a social principle consider this drive "titanic". Perhaps you recall the mythical figure Prometheus?' Karp didn't notice Dora's quiet nod. 'Well, together with his brooding brother Epimetheus, this upwardly mobile Titan is said to have created human beings out of clay and water. Or man, I should say – for woman was created much later, by Hephaestus on the order of Zeus, as a revenge for the brothers' hubris. When Epimetheus had provided the different animals with all available attributes, Prometheus realised none had been left for man, so he felt obliged to steal the fire from the gods. His plan was to raise man to a higher level of civilisation than other living beings. This fraternal instinct reminds certain colleagues of the function performed by the cremaster muscle.

Well, it's clear, isn't it? Raising the testicles, they elevate man's consciousness of himself.'

Karp noted our consternation. 'The claim is that the male's position has been diminished ever since Zeus sent the first woman to earth. Today, anybody may dress in whatever way he prefers. Therefore, the undiluted power that man possessed before the covered sex appeared on the scene has to be regained, so that he may become a titan once more.' Karp paused, then added: 'In primitive cultures, the testicles are considered the beginning of all things. The semen is a holy message, a mission white and pristine. Hence, a boy's first ejaculation is deemed free from sin. Similar ideas can be found to this day. For example, it's believed that, through athletic exercises, a kind of ur-semen may be conjured forth, whereby others, too, can take part in the essence of which the world once was made. The scientists opposing Martin's research maintain that a boy who is potentialised before his first ejaculation preserves his andrine in an untouched state.'

'Potentialised?' Dora rubbed her forearms. Perhaps she was cold.

'It's a method to turn today's male into a modern titan. Gymnastics doesn't improve one's potency enough. That's why they've turned to clinical techniques conducted on boys who haven't yet reached puberty. Through surgery, further production of gynecine is prevented – with the result that the boys' semen is maintained in an "ideal" state.' Karp sighed. 'Many years ago, Martin devoted considerable time to the question and found the theoretical solution to the problem. But he refused to correct biology in order to optimise man's essence. Not all scientific discoveries further the fate of mankind. His notes are kept in our poison cupboard in the library. It'd be quite unfortunate if they ended up in the wrong hands.' Karp walked over to a door. 'Instead, Martin developed Testifortan, a drug that strengthens artificially the amount of andrine in men troubled by their gynecine. Its effect on potency is quite illusory. But as long as people believe in the drug, it has proven to have positive effects on the sexual drive. We sell considerable quantities every year.'

Our guide smiled palely. 'Surely Prometheus and his brother had something in mind when they equipped man's endocrine system with andrine *and* gynecine.' He placed his hand on the door-handle. 'Every person contains both hormones. If you want to purify either one, it can be done only at the expense of the other. Those who advocate "biological elevation" deliberately choose to ignore one pole of our biology. In this case, woman is purged from man. That's why Martin prefers to talk about "the grey sex" – out of respect for an endocrine system in which the difference between male and female is rarely clear and never definitive.'

He opened the door. A sign announced that we were now entering the section for 'Deformations of the Sexual Instinct'. A young couple were studying a counter that contained what looked like instruments, while two elderly men scrutinised tablets, made of wood, which hung from the ceiling. We went over to a third tablet that told the story of 'Bertha D.', an entertainer of German–Latvian origin, who apparently, as a child, had been teased for her low voice. Once facial hair began to grow and she tired of shaving, she dressed in men's clothes and assumed the identity of a boy. Thereafter she could sing in deeper registers, too. At the age of eighteen, 'Bert', as she now referred to herself, had sexual encounters with teenage girls. At twenty, her sexual orientation included boys as well. Although she was unable to maintain an erection during these encounters, her considerable clitoris issued a shiny fluid reminiscent of sewing oil. 'D.' had confessed that her desire for women was at its peak right after menstruation, but that she usually got 'more' out of male companions. Was she 'a true bisexual', the tablet asked rhetorically, 'a lesbian with male homosexual tendencies', or 'something third, hitherto unknown'? A final answer pending, Bert or Bertha was, simply, 'Grey Sex No. 1,982'.

The many forms this sex could take were charted in photographic series mounted on the wall. In one, we could see six men lined up shoulder to shoulder, with black stripes across eyes, nose and mouth. All wore dark suits, not unlike Karp's, with white shirt, starched collar and cravat, some had kerchiefs in their breast pockets, others gold watches in their waistcoats, everyone had a hat on his head, and about half of them carried a walking stick. Immediately, I identified the men as persons from the lower rungs of the middle class, anxious to reveal the signs that indicated their rank in society. 'Ah, an "attributive" interpretation,' Karp said, 'based on secondary characteristics. If only more people would see things your way, sir.' He pulled his cuffs, then pointed to the next photograph in the series. In it, the men had removed their clothes – save for an Indian-like wrap covering their sex. Now, it wasn't difficult to see that, at least biologically, they were in fact women with wide hips, small breasts, and poor growth of hair.

On a shelf next to Dora were rows of miniature phalli from the ancient cultures around the Mediterranean Sea. I couldn't help thinking of the spatula that Karp had pocketed: as far as its contour was concerned, it could claim a place among the oblong objects on the shelf. 'The things we love have many names,' our guide remarked solemnly, informing us that, at the Foundation, they had chosen the general designation *olisbos* – 'after the virile idol made of boiled leather, which the women at Miletos, but also widows, lesbians and other depraved women, used to make matters more exciting.'

Karp looked like a lecturer and spoke like a book. Now he pointed to a shelf displaying a woman's shoe with a big, fat heel – 'the Cobbler's Olisbos,' he declared. Evidently, it was a rare item in gutta-percha, made in Vienna. 'I managed to acquire it from one of our regular visitors. He has an entire stock of shoes he parts with piece by piece, in exchange for therapeutic favours. With this particular item, you sit on the side and bend your knee, so that the heel points up between – well, I'm sure you know what I mean.'

We went over to the other side and studied some slithery rubber envelopes arranged on a piece of velvet cloth. 'Our *vulves pneumatiques*. A car mechanic I met during my studies in Strasbourg manufactures them to order. The point is to attach the contraptions to a little engine – the so-called *"vibreur"* – that makes the rubber bladder contract and expand. The appendix-like pouch here', Karp directed our attention to a tumescent shape at one end, 'gathers the result. Earlier, cow udders were used, but it's easier to work with artificial materials. These are quite unusual.' He pointed to a series of cases. 'Manual vaginas. As you can see, they are, in fact, mittens. There are no fingers, and the area between index and thumb has been converted into a pocket, not unlike a web, lined with hair and painted in natural colours. Something for those who grow tired of their unimaginative hand.'

Stifling a smile, Karp opened a display case and took out some stamp-sized photo books. If one leafed through them fast enough, different scenes were performed. Dora laughed as she made a man with wild eyes come alive, as he pressed his face to the pudenda of a woman whose legs went up and down, ceaselessly, like train semaphores. I let a pale woman roll a long glove up and down her extended arm, while she performed a couple of elegant dance steps, her bare feet on a minimal Persian rug. The scene was almost indecently matter-of-fact. Dora tugged my jacket and smiled. 'Why do certain items of clothing exert greater attraction than others?' She pointed to the glove sliding up and down the lily-white arm.

'Fetishes,' Karp answered. 'It's the technical designation for a body part or an item of clothing that fascinates us in inexplicable ways. Our fixation on such lust objects occurs early in childhood, long before we're able to give word to our enchantment. As we get older, these experiences are repressed, but they remain lodged in our subconscious and may cause conflicts. In pathological states of mind, the person in question thinks he can gain satisfaction only by way of his lust object. Unwilling to reveal the truth behind the fetish, he does everything in his power to prevent what we term the denouement – or "unwinding", if you will. Personally, I suspect fetishes may be considered stories disguised as objects.'

'Stories disguised as objects?'

'Yes, the fetishist experiences a partial attraction. The main role in his sexual drama is enacted by an arbitrary but privileged detail. The complete sexual object is uninteresting; it may, in fact, even repulse him. Thus he's forced to develop strategies to prevent the object from losing its power. If the banal context is revealed, he risks impotence. That's why the fetishist prefers obscure spaces, veiled circumstances, hazy demarcations. It's a little like in a detective story: tension is maintained only as long as the lights don't go on and the solution is revealed.'

'You mean to say the sexologist's a detective?' Dora sounded ironic.

'Perhaps.' Karp smiled at the thought. 'But remember, we don't want to tear away the veil and ruin the fun for people. Those who prefer to keep their secrets to themselves may do so. We only try to help those who suffer. And they're plenty enough.'

The room we now entered was full of objects, instruments and items of clothing. I tugged Dora's sleeve; something had attracted my attention. Mounted on a pedestal in the middle of the room was a bicycle wheel without tyre and inner tube. As we went over to it, a young couple moved to the side. Next to the wheel, the hub of which looked like an eye, were a pair of wooden spools, three worn-down women's shoes, a few leather straps, and a cog wheel. 'Bauer's masturbation machine,' Karp proudly announced. As a boy, the inventor had been a passionate 'velocipedist', who soon discovered 'the easiest way for him to find release was to sit on his *membrum virile* while bicycling.' Since it had been both difficult and painful, he had begun to experiment with methods that didn't require him to keep an eye on the road at the same time. At first, he had used old rubber tubes, which he had tied around his member and attached to his ankles. Each push with the pedal had increased his excitement. But the tubes had an unfortunate tendency to get tangled up in the chain, and at one point the arrangement had almost led to castration. Thereafter, Bauer began to experiment with organic materials and stationary solutions. 'In short: he rubbed himself against the udders of the cows in the barn. When he was satisfied, he inserted himself into one of the calves, thus reaching orgasm. Despite the happy outcome, however, Bauer missed his bicycle, and pondered what might be done in order to obtain the thing he cherished most in the world: release in motion.'

A few years later, his 72-year-old mother was found unconscious, with her legs parted in an unnatural manner. As the authorities took the forty-year-old son into custody, they discovered how he had solved his problem. Standing by the machine, Karp explained: 'These leather straps were put across the waist. The thread spools you see here were used to regulate the tension. Bauer tugged the shoes he had stolen from his mother under the straps, so that the soles pressed against his abdomen. He claimed the leather reminded him of the family's cows. First he inserted himself in the middle shoe, having coated the inside with shoe fat. Then he wrapped himself around the wheel in this manner' – Karp made a motion, as if to somersault – 'and rolled back and forth. The movement would create the same friction as once the bicycle saddle had. Unfortunately, before reaching the longed-for denouement, Bauer's mother stepped in, and he lost his poise.' Karp placed his hand on the wheel. 'An instructive case of fetishism. As far as the human orgasm is concerned, no route is too winding, no road too long. Everything for *l'objet désiré*.'

Nodding to the young couple contemplating Bauer's invention, he continued to the next room. 'If you peruse forbidden literature, you soon discover a favourite motif: the stern teacher punishing his unruly student. But the reverse applies, too: young ladies disciplining older gentlemen. If the roles conditioned by culture are reversed, we call it "metatropism".' Discreetly Karp consulted his wristwatch. 'As you may notice,' he pointed to one of the walls, 'the English vice is no British exclusivity. But this', now he nodded towards a drawing in watercolour mounted on the adjacent wall, 'is a German specialty.' Leaning forward, we no longer saw crops but syringes, not bundles of twig but pitchers of water. Entitled *Delicate Manipulation*, the drawing showed a girl kneeling on all fours on a towel placed atop a table. A maid in a short skirt, with a white apron and lace in her bobbed hair, sat on a chair in front of her, holding up the girl's dress so that a lady with distinguished looks and waistcoat over her elegant, but too pliable dress – perhaps mother, perhaps teacher – could place one hand on the girl's back and with the other, slowly and lovingly, insert what looked like a nozzle. The scene had been painted in the at once exact and diluted manner so fashionable in the illustrated weeklies.

'She has pressed her chin to the maid's hairline,' Dora pointed out, 'and is gazing into the mirror here in the foreground. Look, it's even turned so that she can follow what happens behind her back!'

'A doubling which is common in pornography,' Karp declared. 'In this manner, the victim may see herself the way the observer sees her. The mirror assumes our presence in the picture. In a way, the onlooker is as much partaker as outsider. According to connoisseurs, this kind of ambiguous projection creates a certain *frisson*. Incidentally, we find similar techniques in forbidden literature.'

Politely, our guide placed his hands on his back. A couple next to us turned and twisted. The man seemed embarrassed, the woman rather baffled. 'Martin maintains that the central position of the anus in German culture may be traced back to medicinal practices of the last 150 years, primarily conducted with the aim of fighting infant maladies. But naturally, the border to pedagogical forms of punishment isn't easy to draw. Essentially, sexual research is "interdisciplinary" in nature. Its banner carries all colours of the rainbow. It's merely a matter of diminishing the psychological speed; soon enough, the individual nuances will begin to emerge. The key to a rich sexual life is in the details.' Our guide made an artful pause. 'Regrettably, however, this says little about the environment in which we live, which often enough is depressingly monochrome.' He pulled his cuffs. 'I believe the anus must be considered Germany's sun. *Obscur et froncé* . . . Indeed, we live in a brown culture.'

Courteously, Karp pointed towards the last room. 'We now come to my favourites.' As we entered the room, we could see rows of pictures on the walls, executed in different techniques. '*Mes sœurs*.' Again Karp consulted his watch with a diplomatic twist of the wrist. 'Well, only this lady here is medically trained, of course.' He indicated a drawing of a nurse dressed in a minimal black uniform, busy putting a female patient to bed. Apparently, everyone at the Foundation had his or her specialty. Froehlich preferred the male version of the ladies we were just observing, not necessarily dressed in trousers and jacket; Röser had his preferences of which he did not like to speak, but which, considering his interest in athletic youth, were no secret to his colleagues – 'and I, well, I devote myself to the sisters.' Karp spread his hands, and now we could see that all pictures portrayed scenes of women together with other women – in bars, under railway bridges, or below the hazy, almost dissolved shine from gaslights. He walked over to an aquarelle depicting two ladies turned towards each other. In the background, a man with stick and sunglasses groped in eternal darkness. The women seemed just as lost, although their close-fitting coats that made the hips emerge, their fluffy fur collars, and the shiny boots with thousands of tiny eyelets along the shins, all the way to the kneecaps, indicated they were hardly lost in the same sense as the blind man.

Karp leaned forward. 'There are cobblers who will manufacture boots in every shape and form, with high or low heels, embroideries, intricate patterns, and metal clasps. Depending on the colour, you can tell in what the ladies specialise. Look here: green boots and golden shoelaces. That means a night's worth of drudgery but champagne to top it off. Or here: red on chestnut – flagellation and caviar. And now,' Karp said, having realised it was getting late, 'I must bid goodbye. My supplier of shoes is waiting for me. You'll find the way out on your own, won't you?' Dora nodded quietly.

Karp bowed solemnly. 'But before you leave, please do fill out a copy of our psycho-biological questionnaire. It'll help us better understand the multifarious life of the sexes. Or as Martin puts it: "a happy marriage is made not in heaven, but in the laboratory."' Feeling uncomfortable, I wondered whether it would be all right to answer the questions at home. 'Naturally,' Karp replied, faultlessly smiling, and extended a copy of the form to each of us.

*

As we emerged from the building, Dora took my arm. 'She's quite something, isn't she?' We walked to the nearest *Stadtbahn* station, our breath smoke in the cold air.

'Who do you mean?'

'Felix, of course.'

'Who?'

Laughing, Dora extracted her arm from mine. 'You didn't realise he was a she?'

I fumbled for my cigarettes in my coat pocket, knowing they were somewhere under the paper and questionnaire I had crammed into it. 'Of course I did. Even as he arrived. That correct manner. That cultivated maleness.' There. Stiff-fingered, I lit up. 'The cuffs, the waistcoat, the cravat. As if it were all a uniform.' I inhaled deeply. 'And then that absurd spatula. A fetish, no?'

'Don't be silly, Anton. Felix is ill.' Dora took my arm again. 'He suffers from epilepsy, you know, and must carry it with him at all times. Otherwise, he might swallow his tongue during a seizure. Didn't you notice how pale he was?'

I released the smoke. 'No, frankly, I didn't have a clue. Now that you mention it, perhaps I can imagine he's a woman. When we arrived and the two of you whirled around, I did have difficulties telling you apart. But later – with that voice, those gestures? Not a chance.'

'Well, it doesn't matter, does it?' Dora took my cigarette. 'What you have between your legs, I mean. Felix considers himself male. That settles the matter. He claims it doesn't bother him if he lacks what some seem to consider the only thing to make him a worthy brother of Adam. As if ten centimetres of muscular tissue would make any difference.'

'Ten centimetres?'

'Ten, eight, twenty: size really doesn't matter. And as for the rest, it's merely an appendix, wouldn't you agree?' Dora returned the cigarette. Then she explained that, should she ever have reason to become a man, she'd like to be like Karp: calm, reliable, matter-of-fact. 'Trust me, I'd be an excellent doctor.'

'Perhaps you'd care to hone your skills on me?' I put my hand in my pocket. 'I seem to have developed . . .'

'Don't be silly. Felix claims only the breasts bother him. Not that he doesn't like them, though he prefers to see them on others. He tries to get rid of his own by using bandages. But penis envy? Only you Viennese believe in such things.' Again Dora took my cigarette. 'The bone structure's the sole thing you can't alter. Look at the shoulders, hips or wrists. That's where you may detect it.' She released a cloud. 'All right, then. What's wrong with you?'

Chapter Nine

The sun shone gloriously as I bicycled past the Stock Exchange. Had it not been for the dull thoughts that preoccupied me, I would have relished the weather in full. My shirt breezed in the air; the wooden handles fitted as if moulded in my palms; the pedals gave way with precisely the right degree of resilience. With the wheels spinning perfect circles, the chain doing its eternal loop, it felt as if I was travelling on a mobile infinity sign. One perfect day, I promised myself, I'd write an ode to the bicycle – a celebration of humming rubber tyres and the smooth rattle of the bell.

On my way through the city, I encountered only a handful of cars and nearly empty buses. In their own dignified manner, the vehicles whirled up dust and greenness and that particular light-heartedness that belongs to summer alone. For the few inhabitants who hadn't already decamped to the lakes on the outskirts of town, there didn't seem to be a single worry in the world. Personally, I'd be accused of murder if I didn't act quickly. As I rolled across the river, a *Stadtbahn* train rattled across on an adjacent bridge. Automatically, I increased my speed. Ten minutes later, I locked my bicycle outside the Foundation and hurried up the stairs. To my surprise, the receptionist just waved me through.

Perhaps it was too hot for him to open the ledger and make a note of my visit.

Speaking of my visit . . . If I hadn't made it myself, I'd be inclined to think I dreamed it up. The reason is simple but embarrassing: I had had too much to drink at the Blue Cellar. Since I suffered from quite a headache, my recollections aren't much to trust. But the worries caused by Inspector Wickert's words may also have played a role. In any event, I must use my imagination to recreate the visit I simply presume I paid to Doctor Karp on Saturday afternoon.

As I walked up the stairs to the museum, I encountered a man in his early twenties, who, with the lax movements of the naturally athletic, sauntered down – as if he owned the place or at the very least was the heir. His hair was shaved at the back and on the sides, but a biscuit-yellow fringe had been left that now was plastered to his forehead in the manner so popular lately. As he noticed me, he clasped his hands, turned the palms outward, and cracked his knuckles in a muscular gesture. His lips were glossy, his face full of acne. For some reason, he didn't release me with his gaze, which rather unsettled me. Did he mean to imply I wasn't welcome at the Foundation? Or was there something wrong with the way I dressed? Quickly I rolled down my right trouser leg. As I finally reached the second floor, I saw that the man, who by now had made it to the reception, had put his elbow on the counter. Turned towards me, he was leafing through the ledger, probably to look for my name. At the same moment as I pushed open the door to the museum, I could hear him berate the receptionist.

Shaking off my unease, I cut through the fetishes and olisbi, towards Karp's office located behind the room with the pictures of his 'sisters'. A couple of minutes later, I was safely installed in a chair opposite Dora's oldest friend, pondering whether his wrists might be considered unusually thin for a man. But if so, could they be deemed feminine just because of that? Karp's hips weren't particularly prominent, that much was true, and I couldn't distinguish any bust as he sat down behind his well-ordered desk (pens to the left; paper to the right; clips, spatula and blotting-paper in front). Still . . .

The doctor interrupted me. 'That doesn't bode well.' He pulled his waistcoat and I realised he was considerably more buttoned up than last time we had met – as if the nozzle of a revolver was pressed between his shoulder blades. 'If Dora's dead, I mean, the police ought to be informed.'

'They already are.' I told him an inspector from the Vice Squad had visited me earlier the same morning.

'He didn't say anything else?' Karp's face was pale, his movements stiff. 'That doesn't bode well, not well at all. Let's hope Manetti . . .'

'Manetti,' I broke in. 'Who *is* that?'

'Karla Manetti? Why, a recluse, rarely leaves the police headquarters, is never seen in public – for which, of course, there might be reasons . . .' Karp offered none. Instead he leaned forward. 'But make no mistake: she's aware of everything that happens. A real *éminence grise*. Manetti's mother was the daughter of a *Junker* who married an Italian from the northern part of the country – Lombardy, I think. They raised their child as a true Prussian with Latin blood. This mixture of German discipline and Italian cunning helped her capture the werewolf at the Leine, for example.' When the doctor saw my quizzical face, he added: 'Fritz Haarmann, you know. Executed a few years ago.'

Apparently, Manetti had solved the case that had enthralled and revolted the entire nation, assisted by a sceptical colleague. Soon she suspected what the local authorities didn't seem willing to believe: that one of the police's informers, the deranged person who had toured the mental asylums for twenty years, was the notorious werewolf of Hannover. Out of twisted lust, Haarmann murdered boys, whom he picked up in the streets around the train station. Having bitten into their carotid artery, he cut their bodies in pieces. The genitalia were conserved, since he thought they possessed magic powers. When Haarmann felt weak, he merely had to open a jar and make himself a fortifying meal. The rest of the meat was sold at the local market and the clothes distributed among acquaintances. As there wasn't much animal protein to be had, nobody could afford to suspect him. Apart from Manetti, that is. Her local colleague had greater difficulties accepting the notion, perhaps because he was trained as a doctor – or not a vegetarian, as Karp dryly suggested.

'Because of this prime capture, Manetti was promoted to the rank of inspector and placed at the Homicide Squad here in town. The sceptical colleague was also promoted, but placed in another squad. Doctor Froehlich, who wrote the forensic report, noted that Manetti's colleague, although a trained physician, might gain from acquainting himself with the true nature of man.' Karp regarded me closely, almost as if he had said too much. 'But tell me, when do you plan to . . .'

Contact Manetti? Well, first I needed to speak to somebody close to Dora, and I knew no one else but Karp. If I were to visit the police headquarters not knowing what she had been up to since we stopped seeing each other, nobody would believe me. 'Besides, why should I trust that mastermind?'

'What do you prefer?'

I pretended to contemplate the query. 'The truth, of course.'

'I see . . .' Karp thought for a minute, then two. Finally, making sure the door was locked, he closed the windows. A fly had lost itself between the frames. Irritated, it hit the glass, the captive of its own freedom, until Karp opened again and the fly disappeared into the day with patent ingratitude. Having closed the window once more, he drew the curtains – adding over his shoulder: 'There's no reason why others should hear what I'm about to tell you.'

Once reinstalled behind his desk, Karp thumbed his spatula. Registering my discomfort, he explained: 'I haven't felt well in the last few weeks. Yesterday, I was really ill.' I tried to imagine what could have happened. Karp in convulsions? Karp with foam lodged in the corners of his mouth? Karp, pale and lifeless, lying supine on a bed? After the night at the Blue Cellar, however, my imagination was of limited use, so I soon ran out of projections.

'But let's discuss more important matters, shall we? Do you see this obscurity?' My host pointed to the dimness that filled his office. 'In the same way, we are surrounded by the past . . .'

Suddenly I felt as if I were sitting in a cinema where the lights had just gone out. Soon the projector would be turned on, and I'd finally hear, no, I'd *see* the truth about Dora. For a brief moment, there were only shadows and silence. Then a light beam shuddered in the dark and a young, flimsy girl emerged out of nowhere. Apparently, she hailed from Kolberg on the Pomeranian coast. Thin and without front teeth, with pigtails and something careless in her movements, she stood hand in hand with an older boy. But Karp wasn't looking for this girl, for almost immediately he turned the beam to the side. The image shivered, then the same girl emerged, now a few years older. Her braids were full, her movements confident. Smiling with her entire face – even teeth; mischievous glance – she hurried through a corridor with plates stacked in her hands, towards what I supposed was a throng of voices behind a door. I imagined her clogs clattering against the wooden floor, then the door was opened by the boy, now older and dressed as a waiter.

'Dora once told me she had worked at a restaurant,' I offered. 'For somebody named Walther. And that she had had a boyfriend who . . .'

Instead of answering, Karp slid the imaginary beam through the mute darkness. The light shivered, then a young woman emerged, dressed in a winter coat with a fox boa around her neck, sitting on a park bench. Her eyes were swollen. When she wiped her nose, I noticed that one front tooth lacked a corner. 'Ah, there she is.' Karp seemed relieved. His earlier stiffness disappeared. 'I thought we might begin here. With Dora turning up in our city.'

I knew the beginning of the story already. Dora had arrived as a teenager, pregnant, and with only an address scribbled on a piece of paper. But I hadn't known that almost nobody in her hometown was aware of her pregnancy. 'Probably only two people: the person whose child she was carrying and the one who gave her the address.' Karp didn't deem it inconceivable that the two persons were one and the same. 'At least we must assume that none of the involved wanted others to know about Dora's state.' Now the light beam rested on what seemed to be an envelope, lying next to a vase on a table. 'This is the letter Dora left behind. She wanted to find her own way, she wrote, and wished that her decision would be respected. Still, she was afraid that her parents, the Walthers, would look for her. Thus the change of names. That was one of the things we helped her with during her pregnancy.'

'You mean to say . . .' Slowly I began to realise what Karp was trying to show me.

'At first, Dora often spoke about her pregnancy. Later, less so. Oddly, she began to ask questions again only a few weeks ago. Partly they were the old ones; partly they were new. Should she have acted differently? Could she be certain the child was in safe hands? Was it possible to file a report even though twenty years had passed? All of this we had discussed many times before. But now she also wanted to know what would happen if the authorities were told about the matter – to the boy, to herself, to those back home. Apparently, Dora still felt a strong link to her family – yes, even to Jupp . . .' Karp eyed me carefully; I gather I had difficulties sitting still. 'Indeed, I'm speaking of her brother. I wasn't told until recently, after many years of friendship. It may sound odd in your ears, but it happens that siblings are closer to one another than to others. There is much love, also feelings of a sexual nature that can be difficult to ignore and impossible to recount to others.'

Pensively, Karp formed his fingertips into a tent. If siblings showed interest in each other, it was almost always due to the parents withholding love from them. The least bothersome aspect of this was the neurotic tendencies to which it gave rise. Originally, a child's love was a natural state of being. Many sexologists even maintained that, during the first years, it was wholly sexual in character. 'The concerns of the endocrine system and of the heart haven't yet been sorted out. The child accepts every person who treats it well. That is to say: who does it favours. It hasn't yet incorporated rules for good and bad; it loves egotistically, without regard for blood ties. If such acts are frequent enough, they may lead to regressive traits in the child's development.'

Again the light beam swept across the darkness. Now I could see an abandoned park bench, snow-covered fields flitting by. Although I couldn't quite put my finger on it, there was something peculiar about the images. Then the light rested on a lonely figure in a shaking train compartment – and suddenly I understood what it was: the images retreated backwards. Abruptly the train stopped, and presently the woman put on her coat and hat with awkward movements, buttoning her coat from the bottom up, lifting down her suitcase, and walking backwards out of the compartment. Just before the beam was extinguished and then lit up again, this time directed towards a couple of hazy forms closely entwined on a small cot in a room with tilted ceiling, the boy I had seen earlier embraced the girl, standing at a gate on a grey and chilly morning. Karp turned to me. 'These regressive traits may explain why certain children prefer their nanny to their mother, others their brother to their father. At least we have to accept the possibility that exaggerated tenderness may result in an ill-fated fixation.'

It felt as if Karp's plea for understanding was the preamble to an insight we had yet to share. Uncertain as to the reaction expected, I retreated to what might pass for contemplation. While the sun filled the curtains with amber light, glassily conscious, I followed a buzzing fly with my eyes. Not until after a while did I realise that, despite the doctor's efforts, it hadn't left through the window – or it was a different fly. Boldly but jerkily, it strutted along the oblong metal object, passed a paper clip, and moved towards the fountain pen. It managed to inspect some blotting paper, too, before I understood that Karp had been speaking for a while.

'Responsibility rests on the older person, despite the fact that the courts prefer to see things differently, even in our day and age. That's one of the things Martin would like to change. A sixteen-year-old girl . . .'

'Sixteen? To me, Dora said she was eighteen.'

'. . . is a victim. Besides, her name wasn't Dora. But you already knew that, didn't you? She took the name. "Henceforth, I wish to be a woman without heritage. No family, no past. Emancipated." Her baptismal name was Dorothea.'

I couldn't help laughing. One night a few weeks after our visit to the Foundation, Dora and I had spoken about names. As usual, we had met at the café across the street from Hotel Kreuzer. As usual, we had had a few schnapps and cigarettes. And as usual, we had walked home through the city, to Dora's place in the west. But this time, as we entered the doorway, the lights didn't work. A *Stadtbahn* train went by, followed by a smooth stream of rectangles, luminous and askew, moving in the opposite direction across the wall. As soon as darkness had recuperated, we groped our way through the doorway. Then Dora, who knew where the staircase began, whispered teasingly: 'Anton can't catch me.' Releasing my hand, she added in a voice surprisingly light, almost glittering: 'Each time I touch you, you have to take something off.'

'Are you mad? What about you?'

Although I couldn't see it, I knew her eyes were on my mouth. 'For each time you touch me – but I promise: it won't be many – I'll take off . . . I'll take off . . . Two. No, one. No, two pieces of clothing.'

Reluctantly, I agreed. Dora probably wore twice as many items of clothing as I did, and surely could find her way blindly up the stairs. Fortunately, the game turned out to be too interesting for competition. Instead we groped around in the dark, advanced and withdrew. Each time we touched each other we kissed, then one of us extricated him- or herself, helping the other to shed a piece – which he or she received in return. Knowing that the neighbours might open a door at any time and we would stand there, half-naked in the incredulous light from an alien hallway, only increased the thrill. When, finally, we arrived at Dora's flat, I realised she was almost naked, whereas I still had most of my clothes on: trousers and underwear, socks, shoes and hat.

'Why didn't you take your brassiere off instead?'

'Because.' Shutting the door, Dora turned off the light. 'And now you have to rid yourself of the rest. Freedom, equality and all that.'

I placed her clothes on a chair. Dora had on a college-inspired ensemble, including one of the vanilla-coloured slipovers with striped borders I had felt in my hand as late as last Friday. While I undressed, she disappeared into the bedroom. I could hear her pull out drawers, but I was in no rush. The flat was warm – spring had finally arrived – and I experienced a wondrous kind of happiness, full of mute thunder, as I stood naked in the secretive dark. The wicker mat in the hallway scratched delightfully under my feet; someone walked with heavy heels in the flat above. As I reached the bedroom, which faces the courtyard and rested in glossy but not disadvantageous moonlight, I discovered Dora had dressed again. Sitting on the bed in her kimono of artificial silk, she adjusted a scarf around her shoulders.

'Why . . .'

'Because now it's your turn to be naked and mine to be dressed. It's about time you learned something.' Impatient finger extended, she pointed to my hat. 'Off, off, off.' Then she asked me to come to bed. 'Ssh, Anton. Be a bit cooperative. It's no fun if you're always so serious. Here, lie down.' She smoothed out the bedspread. 'I'll teach you something about men and women and other things.'

Clumsily but not unwillingly, I lay down – partly on the bed, partly in Dora's lap. Caressing me with her electric hand, she moved first across my chest, then down my shivering belly. Although she barely touched me, it felt as if her palm had been charged with moonlight. I have never felt so naked. Naked, not exposed. Because in its own way, Dora's hand dressed me as it caressed my hips, thighs and knees. The intimacy was overwhelming, and I immediately forgave her for no longer wanting to do what we had once done in room 202. Slowly, it dawned on me that this was I, only I – this whole, naked, enraptured body, elated by caresses. Nevermore did I want to make love with only one part of me, in only one manner, but always only with my whole body, with the whole world. Nothing less than the whole world! I felt a rainbow unfurl inside me, and realised what I never again wished to forget: Sascha Knisch contained all possibilities, all madness and all wonder.

Dora whispered, almost inaudibly, but her caresses spoke volumes. Reaching my extremities, she leaned across my face and said, hair tickling and voice humid, that I had feet like a bicycle champion, veined and strong. Then she stretched further down, held first one foot, then the other, slid across the heel, up the tendon, then down the wrist with a soft tickle, and out towards each of my toes. Suddenly, I felt her lips against my left big toe. She would happily anoint my feet, she mumbled, but in lieu of an appropriate vessel, 'my mouth will have to do'. She closed her wet lips around three of my toes. I sensed the sleek tongue inserting itself between two of them, my body transforming itself into thrilling warmth and glorious dampness. Quickly, I tried to remember whether I had washed myself that morning.

Much later, Dora lay with her mouth against my ear. From the living room floated the last chords of 'Obscure Drive' (a song by the great Rigoberto she had bought on a gramophone disc as soon as she had discovered he was identical with the hermaphrodite we had read about at the Foundation). As the last chord ebbed, she declared: 'If you want to know, your name has nothing to do with moon, minarets and other mumbo-jumbo. No, wait. Lie still. It's like . . . Like . . . No, ssh. Not like a pasha, if that's what you think. But clear and steady, almost like a mountain. Yes. That's it. Your name is an Alp top. With a deep, round spring in the middle, full of translucent water.' She shaped her lips into a circle, adding: 'Can't you hear it, Anton? Tranquil, but not mute. That's because of the vowels. The *A* is hard and taut like a mountain top, whereas the *o* is soft and pliable and opens the mouth.' Again she leaned over me. Perhaps she was embarrassed by the poetry; perhaps her thirst had yet to be quenched.

'And what about "Dora"?' Before she had time to answer, I pulled her down and turned around. 'The same vowels are in your name, you know.'

'Matter of fact,' she said. Her face was hot and pale and utterly present. '"Dora" is the name of someone who looks after herself. And maybe has a secret or two.'

'What's the difference between "Dora" and "Dorothée", then?' My arms yielded and I collapsed in a kind of happy vertigo. Perhaps, indeed, I was someone with the name of 'Anton'.

'Can't you hear that?' she said, investigating my ear with her stunning mouth. 'The two *e*'s at the end make the name mannered, you know.' Kissing, she continued down my neck. 'Or not mannered. Affected. "Dorothée" sounds like a woman, you know, who tries to meet others' expectations, you know, of what she should be like. Nothing for an emancipated woman, you know. Lacks, you know, independence.'

'Some names sound better with an *i* or an *e* at the end,' I admitted, adjusting myself. 'Some with an *a*. Wait, that tickles. "Lene" and "Leni" might do, I suppose, but "Lena" sounds like a maid. "Grete", of course, is pure . . . No, that really tickles. Pure film star,' I explained, parting my legs. 'Whereas "Gretchen" is silly. All things German concentrated into two syllables, don't you think?' Dora didn't answer. '"Dorothée" is the same thing, only in French. While . . . While "Dorothea" has something . . . Something noble and well-proportioned. Like a . . . Wait. Why do you stop?'

'Let's change the topic,' Dora said, undoing her kimono.

'Why?' I echoed a year later, shifting my gaze from the fly on the table to the doctor behind it. 'Why did she choose to keep the child?'

Apparently, it hadn't been proven conclusively that incest had negative consequences. One could assume the child would suffer, not least from a psychic perspective. But the almost universal prohibition against it might also be explained psychologically or sociologically. A radical biologist such as Froehlich refused to believe so, but fortunately he was a convinced pluralist and welcomed discussions. Personally, Karp imagined that the prohibition expressed a disinclination towards sexual relations between persons growing up together. 'Exogamy constitutes the basis for exchange, and hence what we term culture. Also, it often brings with it considerable gains in terms of dowry and social prestige.'

'Taboos will hardly answer the question,' I muttered, irritated by the scholarly explanation. 'Why did Dora give birth to a child she knew might suffer?'

Karp avoided my eyes. 'Perhaps she never told anyone that the father was her brother? Perhaps the doctor she contacted misjudged the situation? Perhaps she had no other choice?' He took his spatula; the fly vanished as if by magic.

The first questions I couldn't answer, but the last one seemed to me absurd. 'No choice? Dora left Kolberg of her own volition! As a sixteen-year-old. Surely that demonstrates initiative?'

'That's not what I meant.' Karp smiled stiffly. 'Perhaps the unsuspecting doctor had explained she couldn't count on help if she chose abortion? If at the same time, he assured her there would be no loss – I mean: for either mother or child . . .'

'Hardly a Hippocratic way of conduct.'

'Nothing says the person who has sworn the doctor's oath also manages to keep it, especially not if he labours under false assumptions. That's one of the untold tragedies of our time.' Awkwardly, Karp switched on the projector again. I had the impression he wanted to show me something he had saved until last. Yet only dusty light and boundless darkness could be seen. 'A sixteen-year-old doesn't know much about the world. If the gain is great enough, probably she could be persuaded, even against better judgment. A white coat carries considerable authority, you know.' He looked at me pensively, then added: 'In some cases, you don't even have to be a doctor. Just think of Hauptstein. Although he has no medical degree, people believe in his talk about potentialisation. As if we needed to show scientific respect for someone who claims that skirts and caftans belong to the lower realms of society.' Instead of explaining himself, Karp took off his glasses and leaned forward, fingers pressed against eyelids: 'What do you plan to do about the police?'

The police? They wanted to talk to me. As soon as possible. Probably I was their prime suspect. The inspector who had visited me had indicated an investigation was under way, making it clear that I ought to cooperate unless I wanted to get into trouble. Besides . . . I fell silent. Karp, motionless, didn't seem to listen. Should I repeat what I had just said? Gradually, the room grew so quiet I could hear his wristwatch tick. 'Say it as it is,' he finally suggested from behind his cupped hands.

As it was? And how was *that*? Again, I studied his wrists, and this time I realised I was in a greater hurry than I had thought. 'Sorry, Doctor. I'm afraid I must leave. Apollo's waiting.'

Smiling sadly, Karp looked at his watch. 'Believe me, sir: it's best not to be at odds with Karla Manetti.'

'Are you suggesting I should confess to something I haven't done?' The doctor's tranquillity annoyed me. 'Or that I should tell her about my – my – obscure drives?' I tried to calm myself. 'Frankly, there are aspects of my life which are nobody's business but my own.'

'I'm only suggesting you should tell the truth.' Karp seemed weary. 'Of course you don't have to play the inspector the entire film of your life. She understands hints, too, you know. Just be careful with what you say about Dora. The police needn't know every aspect of her past. For certain segments, it might be best to remain in the dark – or perhaps I should say: on the floor of your cutting room? Dorothea Walther died a long time ago.' Switching off the projector, Karp extended his hand. 'I hope I may rely on your silence.'

Chapter Ten

After my visit to Karp, I stopped at a restaurant by the water, not far from the Stock Exchange. Gradually, my hangover vanished, and a little later I was again in full possession of my powers – which is why, henceforth, I need no longer rely on poetic licence to account for what happened, or didn't happen, at the Foundation.

Around six in the evening, I bicycled to the Apollo, where I spent the hours until midnight. One-legged Else still discussed the blessings – or perhaps the curses – of radio scopes, while her son fulfilled his obligations at the piano with his usual brutal enthusiasm. As the lights were turned off in the foyer and the blinds pulled, my colleague reminded me there would be no feature the next day. I nodded absentmindedly; I had just discovered I had a flat back tyre. Irritated, I decided to take the tram to the Blue Cellar. There I spent a few hours with Ludmila, who lent me money to cover two months' rent. But Anton never showed up, so when Rigoberto prepared his last act, I left a message with Helmut and took the tram east. Lakritz could reach me at home the next day.

It was Dora who had said the thing about 'obscure drives' – on a summer night at the Paris Bar last year, when we had got

112

on to the musical merits of the great Rigoberto. After we had begun to see each other, she had avoided all talk of what had happened in room 202, but now that we were sitting in the restaurant where things had begun – or rather ended – Dora, dabbing her lips with her napkin, asked why I had replied to her ad. This time her hair was jet-black and severe, with kiss-curls reminiscent of sea horses. Her face was pale and powdered, and on one cheekbone she had placed a *mouche*. Her eyes sparkled like dry, grey ice. She wore a thin cardigan over a thin blouse, a narrow skirt, and silk stockings with wide stripes. Around her neck she had tied a dramatic scarf, and her petal-like shoes were adorned with big, bright buckles. She seemed to combine the fashions of piracy and tango – half buccaneer of the seven seas, half Argentine dancer with a rose between her lips. Quietly I thought my partner could be pretty strange at times.

Keeping one hand behind her back, Dora bit her lower lip in the manner she confessed she had learned from Ossi Oswalda in *The Girl with Protection*, then checked whether the sideburns were as they should be. When she discovered my look, she wondered what was the matter. Didn't I know she had the right to be anyone she liked? If people couldn't accept that, the problem was theirs. She was not merely a woman, but an entire world. If Froehlich had taught her anything, that was it. 'And now it's about time we sorted out your obscure drives, wouldn't you agree?'

I wore a new shirt that tugged at the collar and had too-short sleeves. Carefully, I loosed the cuffs underneath the table, promising myself never again to be tempted by street peddlers. Then I leaned across the table and whispered, pretending we were about to have a scholarly conversation. In the beginning there had been no lust, no longing, only curiosity. In an abstract sort of way, it felt as if I were looking for a secret – perhaps a new toy my mother had hidden, perhaps some sweets. The important thing was not *what*, but *that*. I didn't only poke around in my mother's closet, but a bit everywhere: in the escritoire in the living room, in my father's desk that still occupied half the hallway, underneath the beds, and behind the books in the bookcase. Didn't all children? I was attracted by things veiled and disguised. Sometimes, I found money my mother had put aside or flat boxes of the kind Mrs Witting used to give us for Christmas that contained brittle and dusty chocolates; at others, I discovered passports or insurance policies, parched and boring. And already at the age of seven or eight, I knew that the secret drawer in the writing desk (which wasn't much of a secret, everyone could see the tear in the varnish) contained yellowed letters from my father and sepia-coloured photographs mounted on cardboard.

But one day I became interested in my sister's diary. 'Agnes is five years older and used to hide it under her pillow.' When she suspected I had found it, she changed its place. Yet sooner or later, I always managed to discover where it was – usually underneath the sweaters in the drawer or under the mattress. The cover of the diary was burgundy red, adorned with a bright blue, spectacular butterfly, and locked with a flat, pink heart that hung in a metal loop one was supposed to press through a slit-like opening. It didn't take me long to figure out that my sister's secrets could be accessed without a key. If I twisted the heart to the side and pressed hard enough, it slid through the opening. I was never really interested in what my sister wrote, however. Sometimes she accounted for what she and her friend Lore had done; at others, she confided that she missed our father; and one time, she even drew a tree with his name hidden among the leaves. But most often, she discussed 'K' or 'G' or 'A' – boys at school in whom she was interested. And at the very back, on the inside cover, she noted different dates in front of which she put tiny red dots. It took me many years to realise this was her way of remembering when she had her days.

'Why wasn't she allowed to keep her secrets to herself?' Dora seemed genuinely surprised.

'But that's just it: I wasn't interested in her secrets. I never teased my sister for what she wrote, never once gave away that I had read her diary. I don't think I was attracted to the information as such.'

'Rather?'

I let the absinthe we had ordered fill my mouth, cold and oily. Perhaps it had to do with the transgression, I reflected, the feeling of being on the other side – behind enemy lines, so to speak. Yes, that probably attracted me. In a certain way, it felt as if I were disguising myself. Maybe that was what Froehlich meant by 'drives': the compulsion to do things one failed to justify rationally? Soon enough, however, I discovered that my mother's closets held greater interest. It sufficed to open the doors and inhale the smell of sandalwood, to pull out the drawers and feel the fabrics slide through my fingers, to open the wardrobe and fill my nose with the smell of greased leather from the shoes which had been stuck into the cloth pockets hanging on the inside of the door – it sufficed with any of these harmless actions, and at times even with the mere recollection of them, for me to experience the telltale tingle along the spine, a shiver as delicious as evident, from the foot soles hot as irons to the neck hairs raised like the bristles on a toothbrush.

'It was exciting . . .' Dora looked at me with curiosity.

Exciting? Yes, perhaps there was no better word. It was 'exciting'. With my head tilted so that I could better hear if someone was approaching the bedroom, I used to run my hands across clothes that didn't resemble any of those I was used to. My mother's garments were so supple and slithery, so wonderfully self-confident, that I was convinced they came from a finer, infinitely more variegated world. When, for example, I pulled out a couple of silk stockings – they could become fantastically long before they let go, with a soft shudder, and flew through the air like the fins of goldfish – I inserted my hand into them, extended my fingers, clenched my fist, then extended my fingers again. I had been given a second skin, pliable and wondrous. 'It must have been at that moment that my drives awoke.'

I told Dora I had seen my mother or Agnes put their feet into these magical covers, always with the ankle and toes pointing downwards and the arms extended along each side of their pulled-up knees. One curious time a few years after my father died, I even saw my mother paint her toenails in a blood-orangey colour. I surmised it had to do with her decision that Agnes and I would sleep at Frau Witting's that night. 'Mrs Witting was our neighbour a flight down,' I explained. She wore her hair "coiffed" and always smelled of violet lozenges.' I didn't say anything. Instead I observed, enraptured, how my mother pulled the stockings up her legs, smoothed out the seams by pulling her palms along her thighs, and clasped the top to the garters with a light twist of her foot, first to one side, then to the other – enchanted by the thought that she had put five ripe cherries each in two silken pouches.

'The older I got, the more often I tried on my mother's clothes. She's a seamstress, so I had some experience already. Off and on, I had to act as her dummy and dress in half-done clothes on which she cut, chalked or stitched something. Of course she knew nothing about my private moments.' These occurred during the precious hour when Agnes hadn't yet returned from school and our mother took the opportunity to run some errands after having put rhubarb cream and milk on the kitchen table. I always waited for the door to snap shut and her to appear on the street. Quickly spooning up the cream, I poured out the rest of the milk in the sink and rinsed my plate. Then, having dried my hands, I ran into my mother's bedroom, collected myself for a few seconds, almost as if in prayer, before I flung the closet doors open. 'In my mind, the taste of warm rhubarb and cold milk will always be linked to the happiness I felt as the hidden treasures were revealed.'

Dora turned the little key and took a cigarette from her case. I struck a match, then she nodded: I could proceed. The first few times, I tried only evening dresses, since I liked the self-conscious way in which they rustled. Yet these items were mostly too big and never looked like proper clothes, but rather like flowery potato sacks or Indian tents in lace. After a while, the turn came to the blouses; with them, I was luckier. Although they were difficult to tie and button, if I slit my eyes, at least they seemed sewn for me – until I stood in profile and inspected, disappointed, the result in the mirror. No protrusions! It wasn't until I had reached the underwear that I realised my mother's closet could give pleasure. No, that's not the right word. There was no 'pleasure', not yet, but rather comfort – round and warm and balanced, a feeling of satisfaction so reassuring that, in spite of the shame coursing through my body, I knew I wasn't prepared to give it up.

Dora looked at me inquiringly. I explained that without prohibitions, surely there was no attraction? She exposed the tip of her tongue, removing a flake of tobacco with thumb and index finger. 'I don't think so. A person can do very well without shame. Sure, a child might experience the first confusion as shameful – but only if it has already been taught to connect it with prohibitions. Otherwise, I should think it's prepared to do pretty much anything.'

'I might be Austrian, but I'm no Catholic.'

'That doesn't matter. What I dislike is that shame presupposes bad conscience. But why would a child have that? As time goes by, it grows older, and then timidity would be more appropriate. That's shame minus morals. If you're timid, you have no censor snugly seated behind your forehead. It's like moving naked in darkness. A timid person would do so as long as the lights weren't turned on; one who feels shame, never in life.'

The waiter arrived and we ordered another round of drinks. I didn't know what to answer. Instead I told Dora that Agnes's clothes fitted me better than my mother's. But they felt boring and didn't cause any of the shivering attraction that my mother's had. 'For a few years, my sister and I were roughly the same height and had roughly the same frame. Still, it wasn't until a year or so after she stopped undressing in my presence that I became interested in her clothes.'

'No longer the older sister, but a young woman.'

I considered the proposition. Perhaps she was right. In particular, I recalled one night when Agnes had fallen asleep and I had borrowed a nightdress from the drawer. 'My sister had her clothes in the three top drawers; I had mine in the three lower ones.

For a long while, I lay awake and moved in the moonlight. The slinky cloth slid across my body like a new skin, and for the first time, I got . . . Well, you know. Which wasn't caused by my having a full bladder or being afraid. When I awoke the next morning, my blanket was by my feet and I understood I must have been found out. The door to the kitchen was open and my sister already at the table. But nobody said anything. Just before I left for school, I put the nightie back in the drawer.'

It must have been around the same time that Agnes and I began to dress up. In mother's 'storage' – that's what we called the space between kitchen and hall, where she kept her dummy and the old sewing machine – we found a ball of yarn. Using scissors and safety pins, we manufactured a couple of braids, as thick and brown as my sister's. Then I dressed up in one of her skirts and school jacket, while she put on a cardigan over her uniform. We compared in the mirror, turned off the light, and compared again. Finally, placing ourselves in front of each of the two sliding doors to the living room, we whispered through the milky glass: 'Here I am', 'Here I am' – and then in chorus: 'And who's who?' Of course my mother made the wrong guess. As we slid the doors open, she laughed and said that with such twin daughters, she no longer needed a son. I became furious and tore my clothes off. But when my sister and I dressed up as me, it was never as much fun.

'Still, it wasn't until later I realised my interest wasn't innocent. By that time I must have been eleven or twelve. Perhaps thirteen. Even though I'm no Catholic, I'm not . . .' (whispering, I filled in the word), 'and I touched myself countless times every day. Whenever, wherever: in the bedroom, on the toilet, in the kitchen if nobody was at home. Until I turned all red and ached, and I thought a precious part of my body might fall off.'

'Boys . . .'

'As if girls don't rub themselves blue between the legs.'

'Blue? Never thought of the colour. Perhaps.'

Now I entered mother's bedroom on defined missions. I was the flat's one-person army and had to make sure our defence fortifications worked properly. First, I turned the alarm clock on the nightstand so that I could see it from where I stood. Only as long as the long finger had not ticked past a certain point was I able to do what I had in mind. I considered these circumscribed periods of time my 'safe' minutes. Naturally, as any good soldier, I pricked my ears anyway. If someone pulled out a chair in the flat above or footsteps could be heard on the stairs, I pretended to be furiously preoccupied – running through the flat, for example. I was still training to become a competitive cyclist. But after a while, danger getting the better of me, I grew more daring. Conscientiously, I pulled open one drawer after another, or unlocked the closet and considered the alternatives at my leisure. Would it be the salmon-pink negligee this time? Or the brassiere with all the complicated straps? No, no time to rearrange it once I was done. Six minutes left. What about the elastic breast flattener? But it wouldn't alter me the way I wanted. Perhaps a *combination*, then? Mother had one in an apple green hue I was particularly attached to. Or the garter belt, brownish black like coffee grinds? No, same thing as with the brassiere. What then? Three safe minutes left. Yes, it would have to be the pantalets, despite the fact that I had put them on the day before. At least they were open in the groin, which hardly hurt. Two safe minutes left – first in profile, then in full figure – and the other side – one and a half minutes left – if I squeezed my legs together – I had no – presto – as a – one minute left – but if I turned around and bent over – now there were only thirty seconds left – I could see – no, quick, off with the pantalets – damn – why wouldn't – the stockings – they had got into – twenty seconds left – so – but where – ten – there, underneath the nightie – five seconds – shut the door –

'And time was up.'

'Still, I always managed to put my clothes back on and move into the kitchen before I heard my mother close the door in the hall and ask me to help her with the groceries. She never noticed what happened in her absence.'

'Don't underestimate a woman's intuition.' Despite her tone, at once mild and mocking, Dora was serious. 'Personally, I'd realise immediately if somebody had gone through my drawers. Life is governed by rules. Stockings are rolled up this way and put to the left in the drawer. Panties are folded this way, with the crotch to the left, but if they have stains that weren't removed in the last wash, they go at the bottom. Nighties are hung so that the tailor's label points to the left, but the other way if they've already been used. You don't realise you follow rules until the pattern is broken. At first, you may not believe it. But if the mistakes are repeated often enough, I'd notice something wasn't right.' I thought about how my mother used to arrange her clothes; oddly, I didn't remember it. 'And now,' Dora added, 'I want to know everything about your red and aching thing.'

My red and aching thing? On the trembling tram home, I considered my answer. At times, it had been so present it felt as if it didn't belong to my body, but rather as if my body belonged to it. Muscles, nerves and blood were just depots supplying a finger-long, thumb-thick stalk with power. In particular, I liked to hold my sex so that it rested above the wreath of my clenched fist. It didn't take long to stiffen, and then it looked as if I held a fat, fantastical flower in my hand.

Like most boys, I played with my sex – pulled, kneaded and squeezed it, felt it stiffen from fear or excitement, or shrink in the bathtub and shrivel like a prune. If my hands had nothing better to do, one could usually be found between my legs. When, for some reason, I felt irritated, I squeezed my sex through my trousers, as if it were a handle. When I was worried or uncertain, I tugged at it until Agnes glared, annoyed, and expressed the hope that I didn't plan to eat with the same horrible hands. No part of my body was so elastic, none so compliant, as my finger-thick stalk. And no part gained a life of its own in such a short time, in less than a dozen years. Hands, feet, nose, ears and mouth were merely extensions of the brain. They executed its commands, both conscious and unconscious, but never explored the world of the senses on their own. The only organ to do so, although it might while away an entire day seemingly non-existent, only to begin stirring towards night, slowly but unmistakably to stiffen, and to demand attention, more attention, embarrassingly more attention, until every bodily function had been subordinated to its dubious whims and wishes – that organ was my red and aching thing.

The first time I tried to find out why people's intimate life was surrounded by so many secrets, I was in fifth or sixth grade. At school, Anton had told me that girls, too, had what I had. It was much smaller, however, never cut, and called a 'clitoris'. I wasn't sure I understood what he meant. But when I returned home, I shut myself in the bathroom, pulled down my trousers, and had a look at the situation. If girls had what I had between my legs, albeit a few sizes smaller, surely it wasn't impossible that I, in my turn, had what they did? Yet no matter how I twisted in front of the mirror, I couldn't discover even the hint of an opening. Anton must have meant something else. If the only difference was that boys had sticks and girls slits, then the clitoris must be something other than a smaller-sized penis. In which case I, too, had one.

After careful investigations, I concluded it must be lodged between scrotum and anus. Anton had told me girls liked it if you tickled their clitoris. 'I know,' I had replied, doing my best to appear the expert, 'you can hear it in the name: "clitoris", "tickloris" . . . It's all rather obvious.' And now I was poised to see if it applied to me, too. Having locked myself in the bathroom, I pressed my hand to my groin and began to tickle myself. But whatever I did, and I did one or two things, nothing happened. It itched of course, though only in the normal way, and finally I had to scratch myself to get rid of all the tickle.

Anton couldn't have meant the muscle below the scrotum. Carefully, I began to palpate the testicles to see if what I was looking for perhaps sat there. But my investigations yielded no result. It only hurt, and after a while I stopped. Something was wrong. Yet what? Anton had seemed so confident. If you tickled the girls between their legs, their faces would flush and they would go damp in your hand. That was the sign that indicated you had succeeded, and if you were lucky, you could now insert a finger. But not many allowed you to do that, and only those who were a bit older. 'Sorry, my friend. You'll have to wait with Greta.'

More by coincidence than cunning, I began to pull myself. Not downwards or sideways, as hitherto, but back and forth. I realised the feeling was not disagreeable, though I was more astonished than excited. Perhaps what I felt at the very tip, around the head, might be considered tickles? It was impossible to tell. Soon enough, however, I realised I must be on the right track, because when I formed thumb and index finger into a wreath, my scrotum rolled up into a ball. Almost like a hedgehog, I thought, while running my other hand across the skin, all wrinkles and fine hair.

Unfortunately, it began to hurt. My foreskin was dry and I barely dared to continue. What if the part at the end, the one that had turned tense and begun to itch, were pulled? There were bicyclists who had 'pulled' muscles during particularly strenuous stretches of the Giro d'Italia, and I was just about to stop when a big, translucent drop slid through the opening at the very top. Before I had time to consider the situation, the skin turned warm and slithery in my mad fist. I continued a little longer, but nothing more happened. Perhaps I had just 'come' the way the girls did, whom Anton claimed 'came' if you just tickled them long enough? Proudly, I put my aching thing back into my trousers and did a triumphant gesture in the mirror. After twelve years, I had finally made it across the finishing line!

The soundless applause followed me all the way into the living room. As usual, my mother had spread out cloth on the dining table. Her big scissors crunched authoritatively along a chalked line. I lay down on my belly and continued, uncomfortable, to read an article about a young Italian by the name of Alfredo Binda, who one day might become 'something truly great' in bicycling. Only a week later, after having spent the afternoons in the bathroom, I suddenly felt how I shivered, sickly and uncontrollably, as if in cramp. Inadvertently, I let out a scream and cursed myself. I had just pulled my most important muscle! I needed immediate help! From the living room, my mother wondered whether everything was all right. With tears welling up, I slapped my hands over my groin and answered that I . . . I just . . . No, nothing was the matter. (Damn.) I had just . . . (Oh, God.) Squeezed myself. (Heavens, heavens.) There was nothing. Nothing at all.

Fearfully I lifted my hands, prepared for the worst, and discovered that I had fluid on my fingers, more like water than milk. Amazed, I realised I had just found my tickloris.

I got off by the cemetery. At night the gates are closed, so I couldn't walk home through the graves as I usually do. Hardly had I turned the corner and reached the gravel path that leads across waste ground to the square where I live, when I heard crunches ahead of me. We had been four people to get off, and I assumed it was the older man with the hose in his hand. The rubber loops had swung rhythmically as he, with quick, springy steps, made it off into the darkness ahead of me. The other men – my age; lunch boxes in hand – had crossed the street in the opposite direction, towards the brewery, where darkness had swallowed them. Probably they worked the night shift.

With my eyes on the gravel path shimmering white and ghostlike, I thought about the liquid that had issued from me – and suddenly felt a pain so intense I folded over. Immediately, someone punched me in the back. I stumbled forward and, without thinking, straightened up, which led to another punch, this time in the stomach. Gagging swelled my throat. I coughed, gasped, and tried, I think, to scream. But not a single word crossed my lips, only wretched pants and hissing. New punches landed on my back, and this time I fell to the ground like a clubbed animal, with red, painful fog for consciousness. Instinctively, I pulled my knees up to my chest, coughed, wheezed, and twisted. I could feel the gravel against my temple and thought, confused, that perhaps it might suffice to fall asleep for the pain to disappear.

But the punches continued, now aiming for spine, hips and legs, shoulders and hands. Burying my head in my arms, I clenched my fists behind my neck. Each attempt to protect one part of the body exposed another, however, and sick from pain I realised I had to get up – the sooner, the better. Otherwise, I'd fall asleep for good.

I can't say how long the beating lasted. In a moment of absurd clarity, I discovered I was on all fours, like a dog, then a kick landed against my ribs so hard I was lifted off the ground. Again I fell to the side, and had it not been for the fact that my unknown tormenters (they had to be more than one, but were they two? twenty? a hundred and seven?) leaned over me to look for money, watch, valuables, it wouldn't have taken long before it'd all have been over. In a cloud of snot and tears, I heard them discuss what they found, but my body screamed so loudly I couldn't distinguish the words. Aching, I pulled my legs up to my chest, rolled around on my knees, and at the same moment as I felt a new kick, this time towards my caudal vertebra, I got up like a drugged sprinter and began to run, or however one would like to characterise what I did, straight into the infinite darkness in front of me – not knowing where to, only away.

Chapter Eleven

The first time I awoke from the enigmatic darkness that saved me it was ten o'clock, the second, half past one. When, finally, I had rubbed sleep from my eyes, I noticed I was lying upside down in bed. I had placed my feet on the pillow, as cover I was using my shirt (torn), and what until then I had taken to be a cushion, turned out, on closer inspection, to be a bed-sheet (bloodied) that I had wrapped around my head (aching). The light was so strong, and I was still so surprised to wake up, that I stumbled out of the flat, into the stairway, with one hand placed on my makeshift turban and the other holding a decent flap to my face – a derailed sheikh from the dominion of sleep. Usually, I have a hard time sleeping with even a sliver of light slipping underneath my door. But obviously, this time, the sun hadn't bothered me. Nor the fact that the flat was hot as a sauna or that all the limbs of my body were aching, even those I hadn't known I possessed.

Having returned from the toilet, which incidentally I share with Sergeant Vogelsang, I scalded myself on the water from the kitchen tap. At least on this, the first official summer Sunday 1928, I didn't have to heat my bath water on the stove. Crouching in the zinc tub, I scrutinised my body blemish by blemish. No bones broken; abrasions on elbows and knees. A sizeable extravasation at the back of my head; a smaller one on the left thigh. Thick lips. Black eye. Having dried myself, I found a bottle of slivovitz and a tin can of frayed plasters. The plasters I placed on my body, wherever it felt suitable, the bottle I put on the desk. From the wardrobe in the hallway, I retrieved the last pair of clean underwear and the stiff, almost unused shirt I had bought for the dinner with Dora. Pressed under the mattress were the trousers of my extra suit. With new clothes on my body, it gradually felt possible to become human again. I returned to the kitchen, where the coffee water was now boiling loudly but loyally. I fished up my cigarettes from the torn jacket, ascertained that three remained, and again stumbled into my combined sleeping, working and living quarters.

I placed the pack of cigarettes on the windowsill and gazed out. Anton was right: in one direction lived the dead, in the other, the living. While I limped towards my desk to pour schnapps into my coffee, I thought that, this day, I found myself more than ever between the two groups. From the cemetery there was not a sound, which perhaps was to be expected, but I couldn't even make out the vagrants who usually hung out next to the long brick wall. No rattle from tin pots over illegal fires, no Galician profanities, no brutal kicks or whimpering dogs. In contrast, there was all the more noise coming from the other direction: the window towards the square was open and all things alive – fowl, children and cars, even a Russian musician – vied for attention.

The Russian, by the way, is an interesting figure. He calls himself Dabor, and it was he who smuggled his own beer into the Apollo the other night. There's something noble in his manner, for instance the way in which he'll click his heels and bow if you throw a coin in his cap on the pavement. Since I have no Russian, however, and Dabor a handful of German at most, I haven't been able to establish whether he really was a captain in Wrangel's army and gambled away the entire capital he brought with him as he escaped – by way of Feodosiya, Sebastopol and

Salonica. But Ivan Britz and Heino swear to it. The former sounded condescending as he told me the story; the latter demonstrated greater understanding. Off and on, our flower and coal merchant is allied with Boris, a bow-legged grenadier in Kornilov's troops, who deserted early in 1918 and now makes a living at the Moustache Bar not far from the Stock Exchange. Only so-called 'bears' visit the place – not just Russians, but any male with a weakness for men with facial hair. Apparently, Dabor visited the bar one night. Pointing to the moustache which Boris still waxes in Tsarist fashion, he supposedly said in Russian: 'Mine is bigger than yours!'

Personally, I find it difficult to believe that one of Wrangel's captains would deign to speak to one of Kornilov's grenadiers. But as usual, Heino swears by his mother's thick head. Something must have happened, however. It's easy to see that Dabor hasn't been blessed by fortune lately. When he doesn't try to sell the beer he steals from the brewery on the way to the Stock Exchange, he plays Russian folk songs on a worn-out accordion. The moustache flags considerably, his watery eyes never rest. Actually, he looks a bit like a shabby Dobermann, so that's what I call him to myself: Dabermann.

Sitting at my desk, I tried to sort out the last insights I remembered before hard-knuckled shadows beat the soul out of me. Yet Dabermann's attempts to move an indifferent neighbourhood to tears had an unsettling way of getting into my thoughts. Frankly, I may have become a bit sentimental. This bruised Sunday, I found it impossible not to feel a little sorry for myself. After a while, my feelings began to take on colour, and new thoughts emerged. Suddenly, the shadows that had attacked me spoke Russian and the blond man who had descended the stairs as I visited Karp at the Foundation was transformed into bowlegged Boris. When, subsequently, Inspector Wickert appeared with Soviet insignia on his collar and a downy moustache mounted above his splendiferous dentures, I felt compelled to close the window, although within a few minutes, the temperature rose to gastronomical levels.

That's also the first thing Anton noticed when he came by: 'Hell, Knisch, are you baking?' I had pretended not to be home. But when he shouted from the other side of the door: 'Sascha, where the devil would you be otherwise?' I hadn't much choice. Now Anton hung his jacket on my desk chair and opened the window, believing he might create a draught. He held his shirt between two buttons and shook it. Then, leaning out, he cupped his hand behind his ear and listened. 'Menshevik battle songs. Will that protect us against the terror of the sun?'

I shrugged and asked if things had gone well at Dora's. Only now did he notice what I looked like. Showing him my injuries, I explained. 'And they didn't take anything?'

'Only pallet and wen,' I replied as I sat down behind the desk. My swollen lip made it difficult to talk. I tried to press it aside with my tongue, and discovered that made talking a little easier. 'I wouldn't mind getting my wallet back. It was brand-new. But they can keep the pen. This one's more reliable.' I held up the fountain pen with which I'm writing these lines. Then I explained I had hidden the money Ludmila had been kind enough to lend me in my underwear, and asked again if things had gone well.

'Not so fast.' Holding my chin, Anton turned my jaw this way and that. In particular, he seemed worried about the black eye. 'With that, you can't have seen who it was.'

'Ouch. No, not a chance.' I pulled my face away and told him it had been pitch dark. 'How did it go?'

'Very well,' he said and sat down on the kitchen chair. 'You should see a doctor, even though the damage is already done.' I asked him what he meant. 'A doctor, damn it. Someone in a white coat, who . . .'

'You know what I mean. The other thing.'

'Blemishes must be . . .'

'All right. The first.'

'Ah.' Demonstratively, Anton held up his hands. 'Simple. With methods that shall remain secret, I visited madam's flat last night. You were right: the police had been there. On the door hung a notice in German type and a hell of a lot of paragraphs

I couldn't be bothered to read. The flat was locked, but not even that will deter Lakritz. Nice place, by the way: Jugend furniture, English prints, tiled kitchen. Gas heating in the bathroom, knick-knacks on the shelves, carpets on the floor.'

'And?'

Anton considered. 'And a big closet. Clothes for most occasions and persons, for all times of the day. Some items were rather daring, I thought – like that ensemble in leather. Do you think she used it when she rode? Must have been damn uncomfortable with that high collar and nothing with which to cover the upper part of the body. Just a thin strap between the breasts. Or take the trousers! Covered at the front, but open at the back, like two cake tins. I suppose she wanted to feel the saddle on her bare bottom.' He held his hands in front of him, while making an obscene motion with his abdomen. I guess it was supposed to look like the kitchen chair was trotting.

'Save your digressions for another time.' I made a movement with my jaw I should have avoided. 'Ouch.'

'What did I tell you? A doctor . . . Now, look there!' Lighting up, Anton took the bottle I had put on the table as if it belonged to him. When, for the third or fourth time, I asked him if he had found what I had asked for, he pulled the cork out with his teeth and spat it into his palm. Pleased with himself, he pointed the bottle towards his bag. 'Hell, yes. It's all there.' Taking a couple of swigs, he dried his lips and looked around. 'Ah, Miss Pandora.' He went over to the bookcase. 'I could use a smoke.'

'Sorry, it's locked,' I explained, limping over to the windowsill. My aching body still felt as if made up of limbs put together helter-skelter. I threw my pack of Moslems on the table. 'The matches are over there.' I pointed, limping back again.

When Anton had lit up, he told me he had gone through the entire flat. At last he had found my bicycle clips in the hall, under a newspaper on the table in front of the mirror. I didn't recall having put them there, but when he fished them out of the bag, I realised my memory wasn't the most pressing issue at the moment. The keys, however, that I claimed had been on the table must have been confiscated by the police. The address book by the telephone, too. Perhaps Dora had a calendar? I tried to think. Maybe. For a while, she used to keep a little book in black leather on the writing desk in the living room. In it, she noted meetings and things she thought worth pondering. 'Happiness is good health and bad memory.' 'Secrets are meant to be kept.' 'Knowledge is dressed, wisdom naked.' The sayings reminded me of the embroidered tapestries at Mrs Witting's place, and I realised I still squirmed at the thought that Dora cherished them.

'At least she knew how to keep a secret.'

'What's that supposed to mean?'

Anton hadn't found the leather-bound booklet or the address book. If the police had gone through the flat, they must have taken both. Probably that was the way they had managed to locate me. I would have to continue to play stupid. Just because my name was in one of Dora's notebooks didn't mean I had visited her. But her unknown visitor had to have been looking for something. And if he hadn't found it, perhaps the police hadn't either? Anton told me he had looked everywhere – even in the kitchen. Regrettably, he had only noticed a few crystal glasses, a deflated pie, as well as something which had looked like a spatula.

'Cake-slice,' I corrected him, perturbed.

'So finally I told myself: "Hell, if this were the centre of your world, where would you hide something you didn't want anyone to find – no customer, no friend, no murderer, not even master-mind Manetti?"'

'As openly as possible,' I suggested, still distracted by what he had said. 'Where it's so obvious you don't . . .'

'Notice it. Right. In front of your nose. That's what I thought, too. So I went through the flat one last time. And this time, I was rewarded.' Pulling his bag closer, Anton rummaged through it. 'Perhaps you could explain this?' He held up the yellow blouse I had worn last Friday.

'That's . . .'

'No, wait.' Now I saw he had wrapped the garment around

an object. Having freed the content, he placed it on the desk. It was a horse – around twenty centimetres high to its withers, made of wood, and painted white. Black, stubby horsehair had been used to create a mane, but the tail was missing.

Vaguely I recognised it. 'Didn't it stand on the shelf in the living room?'

'It sure did. Underneath the reproduction of that femme fatale, next to the record player.' I explained that, if he was referring to the red-robed woman on the wall, she was, in fact, a mythical figure. Dora had acquired the picture after I had given her the cigarette case he had just tried to open – for which, regrettably, I lacked a key. 'Well, whatever you say.' Anton's eyes glowed. 'The question is: do you know what *this* is?'

I looked at the object. 'Seems to be a four-legged animal. Warm-blooded. Called *equus* in Latin.'

'Maybe you were best in school, Sascha, but this time you stand corrected. Wait, you'll see.' He pushed the muzzle and the belly fell down. 'A Croatian horse, damn it!'

'Trojan,' I sighed.

But Anton didn't listen. 'Room enough for a false passport, some high-denomination bills, a compromising correspondence.' With fingers inserted into the innards of the animal, he informed me he had discovered the animal among Dora's knick-knacks. Apparently, his father had once received a similar gem as payment. 'From Harassowitz – the butcher with the five daughters, remember? Probably the horse wasn't worth ten soles of finest Hungarian leather. But father never could say no.' He pulled out a pale ribbon. 'Looks like the kind you tie around the wrist of a baby. Why the hell hide it? Might as well have been lying where you could see it, no?'

'And then you left?' I avoided the question.

Anton nodded. 'No more secrets to discover. Why she died for this piece of ribbon is incomprehensible. There's not even a name on the damn thing. But if I'm not mistaken, as I came out, someone was sitting in a car on the other side of the street, under the *Stadtbahn* tracks, and I don't think he was waiting for amorous company.' Startled, I asked whether Anton had seen who it was. No, having emerged from Dora's, he had strolled in the opposite direction, as if leaving his mistress. 'But don't worry, Sascha. I took the *Stadtbahn*. He couldn't follow me.'

I thumbed the ribbon. It was pale and worn-down; probably it hadn't been particularly expensive even when new. I realised I knew whose wrist it had once adorned. But instead of confiding in Anton, I pulled up the horse's belly and wondered what he thought I should do. Ride to the police and say I knew whom the woman in the photograph was? Now they could stop watching the flat. Instead they ought to send a patrol car to my neighbourhood, so that I could walk home from the tram without being mugged. I placed the horse on the nightstand.

Anton had had enough, however. 'Sascha, it's hot as an oven in here. Let's go out and have a drink of decent vodka. Not this rubbish.' He pushed the cork into the bottle. Contemplating our options, I proposed a restaurant down by the river.

When we came out on the street, the wind seemed out of sorts. Not a leaf moved, nor hardly a person. In the square, two men half rested on a bench, shirts unbuttoned and chins in the air. I assumed they were sleeping off their inebriation or had no place to go. Dirty and dishevelled, they looked like the workers who usually cling to the scaffolding outside the house that is being built next to Heino's. I told Anton they quarrelled with my landlady's son, who believed he could make them change their political views. The other day, I had even witnessed how Ivan, having just finished his eurhythmic exercises, had pointed to his shoes in order to explain that, after the war fiasco, the German people ought to keep their feet on the ground. Clenching his fists, he had added that it was only there, in the lowest level of society, that revolutionary powers might be found. To which the men had replied by raising their arms in typical greeting, saying that for the true German there was only one way: he had to rise. Then, as usual, the parties had lunged into one another.

As we turned the corner, we could see children playing by the water pump. Anton threw a coin in Dabor's cap, whereupon the Russian clicked his heels and gave a melancholy nod. When two men came towards us carrying a couch, we stepped into the street. The tarmac was clean and black, with an oily sheen that turned thinner and more glittering the farther one's eyes followed it. In an incline just before the street reached the entrance to the big brewery, it shrivelled like tinfoil. Presently a truck left the beer factory with wooden crates tightly secured on the platform – unnaturally quiet, almost weightless, with an even, shivering sound from the bottles. On the side was written in big block letters: 'GERMANY SAYS SCHULTHEISS.'

I showed Anton where I had been mugged, then we turned towards the Stock Exchange and continued to walk on the shadowy side. My friend rolled up his sleeves – and stopped abruptly. 'Damn, Sascha! I must have forgotten my jacket at your place. No cigarettes, no money. Hell.' Irritated, he patted his breast and hips. 'Come. Let's go back.'

'Take it easy.' I threw my jacket over my shoulder. In one pocket, I had put some of the money Ludmila had lent me. 'I'll pay – as a token of my appreciation. You'll get your jacket next time we see each other, how's that?' Considering the weather and my ailing body, I didn't feel like exerting myself. Although he didn't seem happy, Anton gave in. After a few metres, I sensed the first droplets of sweat crawl down my sides, like fat insects with myriads of tripping feet. My hips were stiff, my legs leaden. I was just about to confess I might not be able to make it down to the restaurant after all, when I distinguished a familiar ticking sound behind me – and a girl around ten rolled by on perfect, spinning wheels. The air stream gave her a flowery hunchback. Balancing on her pedals, she turned around at the same instant as Anton and I stepped aside. Hair blew in her face, the hunchback was flattened out. 'And now?' From behind came the reply: 'To the right.' Soon thereafter, a boy whizzed by. He was the girl's age and had the same kind of Torpedo I have, only red and a few sizes smaller. I cursed silently: my own bicycle was still at the cinema.

'And now?' I reiterated once we had sat down at the restaurant ten strenuous minutes later. I had just bought two packs of Moslem from the waiter. Pensively, I removed the cellophane cover from one of them. Following a tourist boat with his eyes, Anton didn't answer. A woman stood on the deck, with a hat made of newspaper and a tin megaphone pressed to her mouth. First she spoke in English, then in French, and finally in German. In each language, her thin, metallic voice explained what the tourists were just seeing. Everyone held their hand to their forehead, as if saluting the sun, and many had binoculars slung around their necks. As if on a given command, they all turned their heads to the left and looked at us. The guide's voice, which was probably perfectly natural under normal circumstances, hovered in the warm air, padded with heat. Placidly the boat passed by, sootily puffing.

'She looked like your old girlfriend.' Anton pointed, but I had already noticed he was wrong and didn't bother to reply. He stretched for the unopened pack of Moslems, smiling. 'Perhaps I should forget my jacket more often.' Removing the wrapping, he shook out a cigarette and added: 'And now? Hell, do what you've always done and leave me out of it. Just one piece of advice: don't confess to anything unnecessarily.'

I followed the boat until it disappeared behind the museums, thinking it had been a long time since I had last seen the woman Anton mentioned. We had broken up the year before I began to visit Hotel Kreuzer, for reasons never properly sorted out. I wondered what she might be doing these days, and weighed the pros and cons of contacting her. During a few smokes and sips, I lost myself in melancholy thought. Time went by, and just before the sun vanished behind the rooftops, a breeze began to waft with tepid care. As the waitress gave us the bill, Anton pointed out that his wallet 'in finest German leather' was still at my place. 'But my colleague here has plenty of money, don't you, Mr Knisch?' I managed to dig out a few wrinkled bills, which I smoothed out with my palm and placed on the table. Soon thereafter we said goodbye. Anton needed to find Molly, with whom he had unfinished business. As for me, I felt fortified enough to walk over to the Apollo and retrieve my bicycle.

The distance from the restaurant to the cinema is no greater than fifteen minutes or so by foot – depending on your watch and muscles. I've never carried a watch, but I'm a fast walker, so if it hadn't been for my aching limbs and the fact that the evening was like balm on my thoughts, with languorous, salmon-pink veils drifting across the sky, it would have taken no longer than usual. This time, it took me half an hour.

As I turned into the side street where the Apollo is located, I could see the neon letters glittering across the tarmac. The white *A* seemed unnaturally extended: half the letter was on the pavement, the other in the gutter, as if decapitated. The middle letters had slid together to form an unreadable rainbow, whereas the black *O* at the end was so gleaming and precise it seemed positively mathematical. I was about to unlock my bicycle when I discovered that one of the doors was open – probably so that scientists running late might be able to sneak in. Between the window and the blinds, Stegemann had hung a sign: *'Private Scientific Session!'* Perhaps I ought to have a talk with One-legged Else before leaving? I planned to contact Inspector Wickert the next day. If the police contacted her in the meantime, it might not be a bad idea to make certain we still agreed on the preferred chronology of events.

Having glided in sideways – the blinds clattered complacently against the windowpane – I walked through the foyer, past the ticket counter and our serving area. Behind the counter with wilting chocolate sticks and sticky candy, was a crate filled with assorted bottles gleaming in the red light from the lamp outside the projection room. I noticed the plug to the refrigerator on top of the big, bulky piece, next to a towel that usually hangs by the sink. Perhaps Stegemann had already pulled the plug on his latest financial scheme? I returned the towel to its hanger and continued.

The theatre was mouse quiet. Perhaps a row of benches creaked, but it may as well have been the soles on my new boots.

Although I tried to walk as naturally as possible, instinct made me avoid any noise. Probably part of me was afraid of being discovered. I don't get along with Stegemann very well, in particular not since last Easter, when I managed to spill hot coffee over a stack of film reels – unfortunately, not only of that night's main feature, but also of some of the boss's private reels. Had it not been for One-legged Else, who took the blame for the spill, I'm fairly convinced he would have fired me. With diabolical skill, the liquid trickled down the celluloid strips. Although I used reams of toilet paper to dry things up, the top reel got stuck in the projector, costing a minor fortune. Stegemann's own films were probably completely ruined. At the end, he turned on the lights in the theatre and announced that the audience would miss the conclusion. If I remember correctly, we were showing *Madame Dubarry* that night. Stegemann promised the audience half of the entrance fee back at the ticket counter. 'Against a valid ticket, naturally. After all, we're in Germany.' At least for the later remark, I was grateful: not until I had recovered the money lost would I be paid again – which is, of course, the reason for the current trouble with my landlady.

As I walked up to the projection room, I could hear the celluloid whirling through the controls with a wet, fluttering sound reminiscent of thousands of trembling insect wings. I took the stairs two at a time and pushed open the door. Empty. Else must have gone home – or perhaps she sat in the theatre together with the scientists? The glasses we had used for ice tea were still on the table. Someone had smoked, but not bothered to empty the ashtray. On the shelves in the corner lay the metal canisters that contained next week's newsreels and Thursday's main feature. The film running seemed to be roughly halfway through, because on the stool on which I usually sit lay an empty, an open, and a closed cardboard box. I emptied the ashtray, put away the glasses, and pocketed a box of matches forgotten by the unknown smoker. Occasionally, Otto gets to the cinema before his mother, and I didn't want him to feel tempted unnecessarily. Then I peeked through the window, hoping to see my friends in the theatre.

I didn't. Instead my gaze fell on the silver screen, where two persons shuffled in and out of the picture with the same inscrutable ease as people seen through an open door. The camera was stationary and the two figures dressed in white didn't seem to take any notice of it. I understood they must be involved in some kind of surgery, because almost immediately, I discovered a third person strapped to a bench – probably so that the operation about to be performed could be made with the required precision. The patient had a black hood over his head, while curiously, the figures dressed in white wore masks covering their faces. Holding up a syringe, one of the doctors snapped his fingers against it. Four, five colourless droplets squirted from the tip. Then he rubbed a pad against the patient's upper arm and injected what probably was anaesthetic, whereupon his partner exposed the spot where the operation would be performed. Soon enough, all one could see were their white, bent-over backs. One was thin and short, the other tall and bulky.

A moment went by, then suddenly the film turned black and nothing could be seen. When the screen lit up again, the image was hazy, but focus was gradually restored. Stepping in front of the camera, the person I assumed was the assistant walked over to his colleague. The angle had been changed roughly ninety degrees. Having altered the position of the camera, he had been forced to refocus it. Instead of seeing the patient from the side, the spectator now saw him frontally. No question: it was a man, naked from the hips down, with his legs wide apart. The sight wasn't particularly flattering. His sex was pale and flabby, the pubic hair shabby and blond. Presently, the bulkier of the two scientists placed a piece of cloth on the man's belly, on which his partner put a kidney-shaped metal platter with a pair of scissors, a pair of pliers, something that looked like a probe, as well as . . . Wait. Again the picture turned black.

When the film continued, a fuzzy form turned light and vanished. Then, suddenly, one saw the patient's sex in close-up. A pair of spotted hands lifted the penis by the foreskin, while another pair tied a taut knot around the scrotum. Thereafter, they proceeded to wrap gauze – perhaps a bandage – around the middle of the organ, tied a softer knot, and pulled it backwards. The ends of the weave were pushed to the sides. I assumed the men wanted to prevent the penis from covering the testicles, which the man with the spotted hands now pensively weighed in his palm, like ripe plums in a sack of skin. The scrotum seemed shaven; at least I couldn't distinguish any hair. Its contents were bigger than almonds but smaller than eggs. If I hadn't known better, I might have guessed I was seeing some rare African musical instrument.

Slowly the man with the spotted hands began to pull the foreskin back and forth between thumb and index finger, dreamily, almost as if meditating, so that the patient gradually stiffened. Meanwhile, his colleague investigated the shrunken area between the testicles. When he had located the spot he seemed to be looking for, he took an elongated, slightly bent instrument with two loops instead of a handle. They must be surgical pliers, I realised, because when he inserted his fingers into the loops, the tip parted in two. Pushing the instrument together, he put the tip to the scrotum. It pierced the skin with surprising ease. Carefully, he now pushed the tip upwards and to the side. When three, four centimetres had disappeared underneath the skin, he held the instrument perfectly still while palpating the left testicle with his free hand. Once he had made certain he had found the ailing spot, he inserted the instrument an additional few millimetres, then controlled where, exactly, the tip was and squeezed the two loops. It looked like he was fixing whatever had caused the illness. Once the doctor was sure the surgical incision had been successful, he pulled out the pliers and repeated the procedure on the second testicle. During the whole time, his assistant kept pulling back and forth. His fat pinkie pointed up in the air, rather obscenely, I thought, in the manner of the finger old ladies raise when bringing a cup of tea to their lips.

Once both testicles had been taken care of, the pliers were pulled out. As the surgeon cleaned the instrument with a towel stuck into his waistband, however, I realised he hadn't used pliers, but a pair of scissors. The diminutive blades at the tip glistened sticky with blood . . . Once the scissors were clean, the doctor placed a metal nozzle in the punctured hole, and carefully introduced a bipartite probe. He pointed the ends upward and to either side. Clearly it must be painful, because suddenly the patient began to move. Immediately the assistant let go of what he was holding. Soon thereafter, the image faded.

When the film continued again, the patient appeared to have calmed down. Now only the penis was moving, fat and heavy, to the beat of a thickening pulse. Once the probe had been safely attached, the doctor fixed it with the help of wide rubber bands, connecting an udder-like container to the end. Thereafter his assistant began to pull again, this time faster, up and down, until . . .

I had seen enough. I'm not squeamish, but after the previous night, I felt a bit sensitive. I was just about to leave when the screen went black again, this time with a glowing lustre to its edges. Suddenly, my boss's shrill voice could be heard from the theatre. 'Gentlemen, gentlemen, I beg your pardon! The film has become stuck. A few minutes' patience, please, then the last reel will be in the projector.' I turned around and discovered he was right: with a taut sound, the end of the film tugged in the projector. It was only a matter of seconds before the bulb would burn through the celluloid. Instinctively, I turned off the projector. Not until it heaved a sick sigh of relief did I realise the audience must have understood there was an uninvited guest in the projection room.

At least Stegemann seemed to do so, because suddenly, a wooden seat smacked against the back and someone moved quickly through the row. Just before the lights went up in the theatre and I saw my boss blinking towards the little window in the projection room – standing next to a person who, to my surprise, I recognised – a nasal voice sounded in the dark. 'Brothers, without a willing specimen, it won't work. Once the patient has been anaesthetised, however, the operation may be performed with utter precision. We've done it countless times and there's no shortage of candidates. Yet never before have we been so close to a breakthrough! The potentialisation you just witnessed makes it clear that the testicle is Columbus's egg. As you know, I've always followed the principles of that able Italian: show greatest ambition and daring, but also patience and cunning. The scrotum is our holy grail, the ideal semen our goal! As soon as Mr Stegemann has put the last reel in his projector, brothers, you'll be able to see that I've managed to solve our last difficulties. Now I'm proud to announce the discovery of a new and reliable method of extracting pure andrine from German glands! In the future, anyone who meets our requirements may be virilised. A state of a hundred per cent maleness is no longer an empty promise. We only have to verify our method. Then we'll witness the triumph of testicles!'

Stegemann turned on the lights and I understood it might be opportune to leave. I took the stairs three at a time, and was just about to slide through the open door, when the boss's voice sounded. 'Hello there . . . Wait!' Pretending not to hear, I quickly closed the door, leaned over my bicycle, and feigned tremendous preoccupation. 'But Mr Knisch . . . What are *you* doing here?' Stegemann attempted a smile – and failed.

'Oh, good evening, sir. Last night', I improvised, 'I had trouble with my bicycle and left it here. I just went inside to wash my hands.' I showed him my clean palms. 'The chain, you know.'

'I see. I understand.' My boss didn't seem persuaded, however. Again he attempted a smile, this time a little more successful. 'You didn't see . . .' He turned around and lost his thread.

Quickly I unlocked my bicycle, and pedalled off with the back wheel rattling furiously across the cobblestones. The person I noticed next to Mr Stegemann just before I turned around the corner was the same person I had recognised in the cinema: the young man from the Foundation for Sexual Research, the one with the bad skin and biscuit-yellow hair.

Chapter Twelve

The next morning, I tried to slide three months' rent under Mrs Britz's door, but rags were jamming the thin slot. For a confused moment, I thought my landlady had relieved me of further obligations. Then I recalled her letterbox next to the front door, the one with the red exclamation point. I had been able to cover two of the months owed with the money I borrowed from Ludmila; the third was Anton's contribution. When I returned home on my incapacitated bicycle, I had investigated his jacket. His wallet carried more money than I had expected, considerably more, and I assumed he wouldn't mind sharing some of his funds in a brotherly fashion. Now, only another three months' rent remained.

Reluctantly I dropped the envelope in the letterbox, pushed open the door – and walked straight into a wall. It seemed impossible, but the heat had increased. Now it was cooler indoors than outdoors. I stepped aside for a woman with a face flushed and furious, pushing a twin pram. At the bakery, I bought half a litre of milk and some sandwiches, at the kiosk the latest issue of the *Tageblatt*. Crossing the street, I sat down on the bench where the construction workers had sprawled the day before and enjoyed my breakfast. At one point, Dabor walked by with a long, pitiful face and a bandage wrapped around his noble head. I waved, quietly wondering what he had been up to, and returned to my paper. Spread in fat letters across the entire front page was written: 'SPECTACULAR SUMMER CONTINUES – CASES OF SUNSTROKE ALREADY REPORTED!' Applying myself to the sandwiches, I read first the ads, then the sports page. Apparently, Junek planned to collaborate with her husband Cenek in this year's German Grand Prix race. As I brushed aside some breadcrumbs, my eyes fell on an unsigned article at the bottom of the local page:

NEW CASE FOR MASTERMIND MANETTI

Heeding an anonymous call received late Friday night, the police found a woman murdered in her own home in the Otto-Ludwig-Straße. (For out-of-towners: that's in the west part of our city!) In her late thirties and single, the woman, who lived under ordered circumstances, wasn't previously known by the authorities. But appearances deceive! The police, still reticent, have been able to link her to the kind of activities that in other countries are conducted in the so-called *zone rossi*, also known as the 'Chinese district'. How they've been able to establish this fact in such a short time, mastermind Karla Manetti, our famous inspector at the city's Homicide Squad, prefers not to divulge. 'But murder is murder, no matter what the deceased person did for a living. We won't rest until we've found a credible explanation.' The Inspector urges the person who made the call, perhaps a 'sister' of the dead person, to come forward. 'Many questions are still unanswered.' The number to reach the police is 53970. The unknown caller, most likely a law-abiding lady, can expect the authorities to respect her 'need for anonymity'. The *Tageblatt* joins Inspector Manetti's plea with a request of its own: fellow city-dwellers, let's show ourselves from our best side!

I realised I must take the initiative. Folding my paper, I walked briskly over to Heino. As I entered his basement store, he was putting the finishing touches on three burial wreaths, adorned with wide black silk ribbons and ordered by an elderly lady who, gasping, fanned herself with a feather. The air was thick with molten flowers and stale water. Heino merely nodded, forehead aglitter, as I pointed to the telephone in the corner. Carefully, I stepped over Chérie lying on the floor, vainly flapping her tail, and placed the paper so I could see the article as I dialled the number. I had forgotten the photo of Dora that Wickert had given me at home.

'Homicide.' A typewriter rattled furiously in the background. I mentioned my errand. At the other end, the receiver was put down. A minute passed.

'Inspector Wickert here. With whom am I speaking?'

'Knisch,' I said, lowering my voice. 'Alexander Knisch.'

'Speak up, please. I can't hear you.' The typewriter was still holding its position.

'Knisch, sir.' I cleared my throat. 'This is Alexander Knisch.'

'Keusch? Kirsch? Ah, Mr Knisch! What a – But why – Are you – As – Should – One moment – Please – Pieplack –' Every other word was shot down. 'Hello?' Suddenly the Inspector came through loud and clear. His communicative colleague must have deserted his post. 'Still there? Excellent. Do you wish to make a statement?'

'Statement? Now?'

Wickert suggested I come by in an hour, at 11 a.m., so he could prepare the case. I shot a glance at the clock mounted on the wall behind Heino, and realised that would give me time enough to visit a barber on the way. It might be wise to look respectable. Dabor put his bandaged head through the door, then vanished just as abruptly – proving my point without a word.

'You've been in trouble, too?' Heino turned towards me, keeping his index finger pressed against a half-made bow. I shrugged, sidestepping Chérie, and went upstairs. I would have to tell him about what had caused my black eye and fat lip later.

According to the paper, the police were convinced it was murder. Manetti must have picked up some suspicious scent; now I was sure she wouldn't let go. Clearly, the smartest thing to do was to play along, that is, to show myself from my 'best side' – but preferably to Wickert, whom I was convinced was easier to deal with. Now that Anton had fashioned me an alibi of sorts, I hoped I didn't have anything to fear.

As I walked to the tram, I wondered what would happen to the body and whether to buy a wreath. Probably the police would keep it in the morgue for another few days – until the cause of death had been established conclusively and they were confident the case could be solved. But then what? The same night Dora had told me about Mr Walther's restaurant, she put down her glass and looked at me, curiosity shading into incredulity. 'Love, you said? More than that was needed for me to move here. Just because Jupp was the first, I'm not going to wax sentimental. I'd never be able to return to him.' Twenty metres ahead of me, a tram rattled by. I broke into a run. And now? Having jumped onto the platform, I squeezed inside, shoving my hand through a quivering leather handle. Would the body be buried in Kolberg in spite of everything that had happened there?

Next to me, a sweating man was standing in a collarless shirt so shiny from dirt it seemed made of silk. Between his legs, a sack of potatoes shivered. If he was on his way to the market hall he was a bit late, I mused as the potatoes performed their diminutive kind of thunder. The man had put one hand in his pocket; with the other, he tried to clean his teeth using a toothpick that looked absurdly small in his bulky fist. Four stations later, the tram turned down towards the big square where the police headquarters abut the market hall and the *Stadtbahn* station. The man grabbed his potatoes. But only I got off.

Since they began work on the new underground station a few years ago, chaos has reigned in this part of town. Still, somehow people manage to avoid the potholes in the street, the mountains of rubble, stacks of bricks, and grey, dusty beams of wood piled along the façades. I walked by three women grandly seated on beer crates that had been turned upside-down. Spread out on a piece of cloth were rusty cutlery and a scatter of tie clips gleaming like strings of molten butter in the sun. Next to the women was a chap who must have carried at least twenty pairs of shoes slung around his neck. Surprised, I realised it was the same person who had sold me the much-too-narrow shirt I was wearing. He moved with effort, the shoes seething like seaweed for each step taken.

Cutting through the throng, I passed between an advertising pillar and a pair of motionless constables with moustaches twisted upwards and hands folded on their backs. Then I entered the train station. On a side street behind it, next to the junk shop in which I had found the cigarette case for Dora, is a women's store that offers clothes and shoes in larger sizes, not only to women, and next to it is Kretschmer's barber shop. Exiting on the other side of the train station, almost immediately I spotted the rotating peppermint stick mounted on the façade. The sun quivered like egg yolk in the shop window, but inside it proved dark and cool. Two gentlemen were waiting, their backs turned to a big mirror and their eyes tranquilly attached to another in front of them – that immediately returned their vacant gazes a thousandfold. To judge from their conversation, the men were colleagues at the university a few blocks away. Half an hour later, it was my turn.

As I sank into the soft chair, Erhard Kretschmer covered me in a whirling piece of fabric. Since it made me think of the film I had seen the evening before, I twisted uncomfortably. Here and there, I noticed short, silvery stubble shining on the black cloth. It must be the remains of the previous customer, a seemingly bald professor, who, a quarter of an hour earlier, had pointed to his head and pronounced: 'The standard aesthetic, Kretschmer. Get rid of all useless biology!'

As if reading my thoughts, the barber placed a comforting palm on my shoulder. I barely had time to relax, however, before he seized the hair on the top of my skull, holding it like a trophy while clipping the air with his grotesque instrument. 'Difficult questions of an aesthetic nature appear in a clearer light if they are solved biologically.' I had no idea what he was talking about, but as he exercised his scissors again (impatient, metallic sounds), I hurried to point out I was perfectly content with my aesthetic nature the way it was. As a matter of fact, I added, I was only thinking of getting a shave. Sighing, Mr Kretschmer put his scissors away and walked over to the sink. Rinsing a tangled brush under running water, he whipped up some lazy lather in a bowl, and began, reluctantly, to spread the lukewarm, mint-scented foam across my chin. With one corner of the covering cloth, he removed some froth on my ear. Then he retrieved a razor from a glass filled with alcohol solution and applied it lovingly to a strop that hung from the wall. Content with the sharpness, he poked me on one side of my nose, placing the blade against my right chin.

It didn't take me long to discover that shaving might not be the wisest thing to which to devote oneself after a beating. Clenching my teeth, I suffered quietly. But as the barber moved the razor across my sore cheek, it felt like torture. Tears welled up in my eyes, and I was about to declare that was quite enough, thank you, he wouldn't have to do the other side, when he re-poked my nose tip, this time from the other side, and pulled the razor from my black eye and down. Curiously, the left half of my face hurt less. When, finally, he reached my upper lip, Mr Kretschmer squeezed my nose between thumb and index finger – 'If you don't mind, sir' – and pulled it straight up. Surprisingly hard, with a touch of military drill, he pulled the razor downwards three times exactly. Then, to round things off, he removed the remaining lather with a clean towel, poured shaving water into his hands, and slapped my face with well-administered care.

'Does that solve the problem?' The barber eyed me surreptitiously. Again he reached for his grotesque scissors, clipping the air, and wondered whether he might not . . . No, no, I hastened to thank him, there really was no need. In order to appear convincing, I paid him a few reichspfenning extra and returned to the street with smarting cheeks – as if daubed in winter wind.

The big clock mounted on the station façade showed twenty past eleven as I cut across the square, hurrying towards the red-brick walls in the east. Too late I recalled that Wickert had asked me not to use the main entrance, but to walk along the railway tracks where I would find a side door that would bring me straight to his office. Having explained my errand to an officer at the main entrance, I was instructed to take the stairs and then follow a corridor to room this-or-that. There, a colleague would direct me further. When I found his colleague, an older man with wavy hair and chubby fingers hovering above the keys of a typewriter, he informed me he hadn't seen Inspector Wickert this morning. The officer was just about to lower his fingers again, no doubt performing a military waltz of some kind, when I explained my concern.

'But why didn't you tell me right away?' Kindly, he extended a visitor's form which I signed, surprised and uneasy. Accepting the form with delicate fingers, the officer then asked me to join him. He made an understated but sympathetic gesture; I assumed he must be one of Wickert's assistants. As we walked through a nondescript corridor, the metal tips on his shoes clicked professionally against the linoleum floor. We passed a series of boring doors, then another, until we came to a door that stated 'K. MANETTI, CHIEF INSPECTOR'. Immediately my heart inched up a few notches. This was hardly what I had asked for! Pretending not to notice my discomfort, the officer knocked and waited, studying his nails with newfound interest. After a while there was a mellow 'Yes?'

The door was opened and I saw nothing. Or rather: all I saw was a contour surrounded by a halo of light. Manetti was sitting behind a desk, with her back towards an open window against which Venetian blinds, twisted open, rattled calmly. Because of the streaked lighting, or because the policewoman had just materialised, in the nick of time, her face remained shady and inscrutable.

'Chief Inspector, Mr Knisch. Mr Knisch, Chief Inspector.'

'Knisch?' Manetti seemed to have her thoughts elsewhere. The voice was surprisingly dark.

'Alexander Knisch, Chief Inspector. The case in the Otto-Ludwig-Straße.'

'Ah, yes. Thank you, Pieplack. Pieplack . . .' She stopped her assistant. 'Nobody is to disturb us.'

'As the Chief Inspector wishes.' The door latched shut. I could hear the officer disappearing, like a tap-dancer leaving the stage.

Since I didn't know whether to move forward, I stayed where I was, tense as a tin soldier. 'Wouldn't you like to relax, Mr Knisch?' Manetti pointed to a chair next to the door. I sat down – and immediately got the noonday sun in my eyes. Now I saw even less of the city's supposed mastermind. I may have felt uneasy, with a heart nudging its way into the realm of my throat, but I wasn't yet so senseless from anxiety that I didn't realise this was, of course, the Inspector's intention. The obtrusive sun, playing tricks with my perception, served as a little demonstration of power.

In order not to be blinded, I let my gaze wander. At the far end of the wall hung a sabre with a dusty tassel and a couple of diplomas; closer I could make out a city map with varicoloured pins creating intersecting patterns; and just next to me was a framed photograph. I leaned forward and studied it. To my surprise, I discovered Wickert in the foreground, ten years younger and smiling generously. A few feet behind him were a younger officer and a gawky woman, standing on either side of a figure with bared teeth and fists in cuffs. Perhaps it was the infamous werewolf at the Leine river? If so, the woman holding him under the arm ought to be Manetti – in which case I could understand why she preferred to act but not to be seen. The city's grey eminence was younger than I expected, thirty-five, forty at most, and looked unmistakably southern in appearance. Her complexion was neither quite dark nor quite light, her face grim, with thin lips and marked eyebrows. Eyes watchful but indifferent, nose prominent, she preferred to comb her hair with the severe kind of parting usually favoured by men. But most impressive was the scar: on the right side of her face, an almost vertical line ran from the tip of her nose to the slope of her chin.

'You wish to report something?' Manetti seemed content with her assertion of superiority. Now it was my turn to demonstrate command of the situation. Carefully nipping what remained of the creases on my trousers and crossing my legs, I held up my cigarettes with a querying look. The Inspector waited for me to light up, then added: 'I mean, has something happened?'

I inhaled, trying to combat my desperate heart, and wondered whether I should mention last night's beating. The sun was just as penetrating as before, so when finally I told Manetti what had happened, my voice too quaking for comfort, it felt as if I spoke into a luminous but hardly harmless unknown. Although the words sounded stilted, as though spoken in obsolete novels, the inspector listened attentively. When, eventually, I finished, I added, almost as an afterthought, that I had considered 'the case' and reached the conclusion that . . . Well, it was like this: the woman in the photograph Wickert had given me had been a friend. I wasn't completely sure, of course; after all, the picture was old and grainy. But if it showed the person I thought it did, we had met in the past. Yes, I knew. I should've said so earlier. But better now than never, no? Wilms, Dora Wilms was her name. She used to live in the west part of town. Perhaps the Inspector would like her address?

'Wickert? Photograph?' Manetti considered the information. As she continued to speak, it was in a tone grey as city air, seemingly addressed as much to herself as to me. 'I see. Why, of course. Diels asked to examine the material last Friday, once Pieplack had filled out the report. So you've met Miss Wilms, then?'

Met? I recrossed my legs. As I said, it was a while ago that we used to see each other. Much happens in life; you lose contact; you lose touch. I merely recognised . . . Wait. Did the Inspector mean to imply . . . Had something *happened*? (I'm afraid my surprise didn't seem quite convincing.)

'Enough for the papers to report on it.'

So it had been Dora! That's what I feared. I mentioned the article I had read that morning. The description fitted my friend. But, I assured Manetti, I had nothing to do with her murder.

'I'm claiming nothing of the sort, Mr Knisch. Not yet, at any rate. Allow me to ask you instead . . . In this report here,' she took one of the files she had been consulting, 'there's no mention of how Miss Wilms supported herself. Even if I have one or two ideas about her main source of income, it would . . .'

'Dora used to see gentlemen, if that's what the Inspector is getting at.'

'No secret?'

'Why should it be? We live in a free country.'

For the first time Manetti laughed, with no evident beauty. 'Among the materials seized during our search of her abode was a notebook in which Miss Wilms seems to have jotted down meetings and other matters she wished not to forget. Interesting reading, if a bit cryptic. Until recently, your friend seems to have led a busy life, that much is certain.' She opened the file on the desk and retrieved the notebook. Leafing through its pages in what seemed a random fashion, first this way, then that, reading some words here, deciphering a few scribbles there, Manetti hummed and declared: 'Well, "Kr." stands for Hotel Kreuzer, of course.' I don't think she noticed the sigh of surprise that squeezed past my bumpy heart, but just to make sure I lit another ciga-rette. 'That's in the city centre. Perhaps you've heard of it? Maybe even been there? No? Well, we have. According to the staff, Miss Wilms used to rent rooms by the week. But she doesn't seem to have been around recently. Perhaps she took up a different line of business? No? Nothing you would know about?' When I didn't answer, Manetti continued: 'Clearly, your friend was once a woman in demand. Still, she found time to enjoy herself – visiting restaurants, going to the cinema, that sort of thing. She even seems to have had time to look up a scientific institution here in town that . . .'

At this point in our conversation, I thought it might be

opportune, after all, to demonstrate a certain degree of compliance, so I interrupted Manetti, telling her that, as a matter of fact, come to think of it, I did meet Dora at the cinema. 'As late as last week, actually. At the Apollo,' I explained. 'I work part-time there, as a projectionist.' Extinguishing my cigarette in the rushed manner of somebody about to impart a secret, I added that it had been the first time we had met in months. I had barely recognised Dora. Probably that was why I had forgotten to mention it to Wickert. She had cut her hair unusually short and seemed different somehow, if the Inspector cared about such impressions. More, well, more natural than before. Less . . . How should I put it? Less extravagant, perhaps.

'You mean to say she wore no makeup?' Unimpressed, Manetti continued to leaf through Dora's notebook. 'I see here that in recent years, she saw a certain "AK" regularly. Last winter, however, the meetings seem to have stopped. But on June 29, this past Friday, in other words, she was visited again by "AK" – at "6 p.m.", I gather. Is that not a coincidence, Mr Knisch? I'm wondering who this "AK" might be, when, unexpectedly, you pay us a visit.' Before I had time to decide with what degree of deceit I ought to reply, she continued: 'You shouldn't believe this book's the only thing we've retrieved in your friend's flat, however. Among other matters, we also found an address book. By the telephone. Very suggestive.' I nodded quietly. Or dumbly. 'Under the letter *K*, for example, there are two persons listed. A certain Doctor Karp, and you, Mr Knisch. If you hadn't appeared of your own volition, as you may understand, we would have had to call you in.'

The Inspector's tone was mild and courteous, but I could sense it harden around the edges. Clearly there was no point; I only made things worse by remaining silent. At last, I confessed that, quite frankly, Dora and I had planned to see each other last Friday. But in the event, our meeting had never taken place (gratefully I thought of the bicycle clips stored in the upper drawer at home). It so happened I needed to finish an article. The square, Chérie, Sergeant Vogelsang . . . 'Surely Inspector Wickert mentioned these – I believe you call them extenuating – circumstances?'

Manetti seemed no more impressed than before. 'Allow me to remind you, Mr Knisch, that we're investigating a murder – whatever the Vice Squad might believe, and whatever you might claim. It cannot be ruled out that you're involved in the matter. Personally, I have my opinions. But there are rules to follow, and in police work facts decide, not intuition. For the moment, I'll note that you looked me up on your own initiative. But until further notice, I must ask you not to leave the city. Should it become evident, in the course of our investigation, that you haven't told us everything you know, I won't be able to prevent it from being held against you.' She paused tactfully. 'This city's no provincial village, where everyone knows everything about everybody else. Even here at headquarters, knowledge isn't distributed evenly. Presently, this is considered a murder case. But if it turns out that Miss Wilms died from natural causes,' Manetti laughed coolly, 'and that the case may be connected to what appears once to have been her main source of income, it's far from certain her file will remain here, on my desk. Everything depends on the cause of death – about which the autopsy report soon will inform us.'

Again the Inspector patted the file in front of her. 'Although I understand Inspector Wickert wishes the case to be transferred to the Vice Squad, let me tell you, Mr Knisch: I don't believe it will. Much indicates that my colleague's competence would help us – and naturally, we'd be grateful to profit from it. The Homicide Squad is already overworked as it is, and I believe in a sensible division of labour. But I also believe in principles.' Getting up, Manetti walked round the desk. 'You ought to do something about your face, you know. Those bruises must be hurting. Try children's ointment. It helps.'

The person who stepped out of the light was cool and correct. I saw her lips move thinly, her dark hair shine. But I didn't understand her words until later, long after I had pulled myself out of the slump of a chair in which I was sitting. The Inspector was, in fact, smiling. 'Sometimes new pieces of information emerge. Things you don't remember, insights to which you're suddenly prey. Then it's important the information quickly reaches the hands in which it belongs.' As if to make her point, she extended her right extremity. 'I hope I've expressed myself clearly enough, Mr Knisch. Goodbye.'

Chapter Thirteen

As I emerged from the red-brick building, my heart gradually returned to its proper state, one edgy beat at a time. Sweat ran along my sideburns, down my neck. I wiped myself with a kerchief, then carefully pressed the wet cloth against my black eye. Everything felt soft and sore and foreign. My eyesight wasn't diminished, but Manetti must have been wondering what I'd been up to. Her considerate suggestion regarding the benefits of children's ointment hadn't fooled me, however. Although the city's mastermind still lacked evidence, obviously I was her prime suspect. And from what I could gather, she was now trying to elbow Wickert off the case. What should I do? The last thing I needed was two police officers using me in order to get at each other.

Apprehensive, I cut across the square. The air shivered like hot, invisible jelly, yet the construction workers seemed little perturbed by my state of mind. Tanned like Greeks, they laughed and shouted, well aware that they were performing for a lunchtime audience. Most of the men had removed their clothes from the waist up; some of them displayed tattoos that looked like exotic skin diseases. One worker had just emerged from a basement, carrying buckets full of mortar. He walked steadily but stiltedly, like a puppet, with long arms and stiff neck pressed backwards. Across his chest, an amorous couple were doing their best to cover each other's genitals. On the shoulder of a fellow-worker, who was busy tearing down a maddening tangle of electric cables from a ceiling, a mermaid writhed shyly but knowingly.

Their display made me think of the tattoos Dora and I had inspected at the Foundation for Sexual Research. Karp had claimed they were usually found on sailors and criminals, but sometimes also on people from society's finer strands. Pointing to a coloured poster with six cases set in three rows, all of them culled from the Foundation's circle of acquaintances, Dora's friend informed us that he had once written a dissertation on tattoos from a 'socio-biological' perspective. In it, Karp had argued that it was not the execution but the choice of motif that gave away a person's class.

On the upper part of the poster, an emaciated chest displayed a couple not unlike the one I had just been privy to. Next to it, a lower arm covered with rich, blond hair revealed a figure lying on its side, its hands under its head and bow-legged legs generously parted. And at the bottom of the poster, two men were depicted. One had had his organ tattooed to look as if it had pulled on a slipover. Along the calves, languorous courtesans stretched out – one carrying a wreath above her head, the other a star. Both lifted their hands as if they were propping up the man's pelvis. Displayed on the other picture was an abdomen tattooed in finest Gothic script: '*Nur für Damen.*' Apparently, Karp had met these people while conducting fieldwork in Germany and abroad. Many of them had visited the Foundation; some had even become patients. But he left it to us to decide which persons on the poster came, respectively, from the upper and lower classes.

The most compelling pictures were those in the middle row, which, we inferred, must represent the middle class. Both showed women, and both were cut so that only the tattooed parts were visible. One of the ladies, who seemed younger, had turned her front towards the viewer. Her body design consisted of frilly underwear, with edgings that ran across pelvis and calves. Slitting one's eyes, it actually looked like a piece of clothing – perhaps not the finest sort of *dessous*, but aesthetically aware and carefully executed. The other woman, who seemed older, had been photographed with her back towards the spectator. Tattooed on her posterior were a clever cat arching its back and a taciturn mouse sliding down the crack. The two animals, frozen in supple enmity, were painted on either side of the body parting – which left the scene depicted curiously suspended in mid-action, with a nimbus of danger. According to Dora, it was hard not to imagine that the woman invited friends, or foes, to investigate in which hole the little little mouse planned to hide from its big big pursuer.

As for herself, she sported no tattoos. 'Why defile my body?' she retorted as we stood in front of her closet mirror last Friday. Remembering something I had heard, I had just wondered whether women really thought men with tattoos had 'class'. Dora was helping me put on the high crêpe collar. When she was done, she cupped her hands underneath her breasts, inhaled deeply, almost with relish, and held her breath. Not until she released the air again did she say: 'Tattoos? Class? Pah. There are natives who wear rings in their nipples and plates of finest metal around their neck. That's class, if you ask me. But then people speak of primitive cultures.'

Imitating her pose, I suggested there might be primitive people in Germany, too. Dora looked at me quizzically. On my way over, I explained, I had bicycled past a construction worker who had been lowering sewer pipes into the ground. With tattoos covering his entire body, he wore rings in his nipples which had been connected with five or six chains dangling and glittering in the sun. His friends must have got used to the extravagance, because when I asked the men what time it was, they merely rocked the sewer pipe in place with a bored look. In reply, Dora laid out a skirt for me on the bed, announcing that: first, beauty belonged on the inside of people; second, it could not, there-

fore, be a class issue; and third, as far as she was concerned . . .
But now the bell rang and she was forced to interrupt her lecture.
Calmly she pressed the yellow blouse into my hands, and asked
me to hide in the closet.

The more I thought of it, the more I became convinced the
visitor must have been an acquaintance. Dora didn't seem
surprised by the bell. If it was true, as Manetti had claimed, that
the only entry for Friday had been 'AK 6 p.m.', which surely
designated our meeting, Dora must have been expecting somebody whose visit she didn't need to take note of in order to
remember. I knew of only one person who'd be able to tell who
that mysterious being might be: Felix Karp. Perhaps, at our last
meeting, he had forgotten to mention something that might
explain with whom Dora had been in contact during the last few
months? Or perhaps I had missed something he had said? My
attention hadn't exactly been a hundred per cent last Saturday.
Hung over, I had felt so sluggish that I had even been forced to
invoke poetic licence in order to recollect what had been said.
Yes, Karp would be the right person to talk to. Also, I needed
to find out in what way the Foundation was involved in
Stegemann's private sessions. Who, for instance, was the pimply
youth with the blond hair?

As I entered the market hall, I could see the morning commerce
was dying out. In one corner, two women were collecting spoiled
fruit in their ample aprons. One of them reminded me of my
landlady, so I rushed by with my face turned the other way. But
there I discovered Ivan Britz about to pour crushed ice onto a
wide, almost empty counter. As soon as the ice had gushed out
over the last few fish, slippery and shiny, he evened it out with
crunching palms. Luckily, Ivan was so taken by the drama he
didn't notice me. Aiming for the restaurant at the centre of the
market hall, I forged ahead. At the only table taken, I discerned
two men who devoted themselves to a giant heap of steaming
sauerkraut in the manner typical of Prussian office workers: left
elbow propped on table, fork in right hand, they dug into their
mutual mound with the synchronised swerve of pistons. A woman

with deflated bags for triceps was just serving them tall glasses of frothing beer. But the methodical men continued to eat, not breaking their stride.

Pumping glasses into a bubbly sink, the owner of the establishment, clearly tongue-tied, merely told me 'the lady' would be back. As his wife returned, huffing and puffing and glossy from sweat, she informed me that there was hardly anything left. I raised my head and I noticed that, indeed, most dishes listed on the black slate behind her had been effaced with a sponge leaving a vague but persistent veil. Of one there remained '*with salad*', of another '*pickles*'. I ordered a '*sausage plate with*', wondered whether it'd be possible to add some salad and pickles, and asked for a glass of cider.

The drink turned out to be lukewarm; the slivers of sausage to which I was treated swam in a vinegar solution with the faint but unmistakable look of aquarium water. Saddened by the company, the lettuce had withered; the cucumbers were downright inedible. I finished my meal after a few bites. Instead I acquired a couple of apples, hard as stone, on my way out. Since I had left my paper at Heino's, I also bought the *8-Uhr Abendblatt* from a man with fingers so black they seemed dipped in ink. It annoyed me that he folded the paper before extending it to me, which is why, on the train westbound, I refolded it, this time vertically, in order to mark its passing into my possession. Then, biting into one of the apples, I eyed the ads. Perhaps some 'honest work for an office worker with diploma' would help me cover the remaining rents? Or would the income promised by Schultheiss if one took 'a true German job' at their brewery be enough? Three stations later, I got off. The air was blue as a gas flame, the platform empty.

This time there was another person at the reception, a young woman who looked faintly sick and very emaciated. Wearing a scarf around her neck, she seemed to prefer a great deal of makeup and had eyes the colour of – let me see – fresh lime. Her movements were many, swift, and futile. Despite this astonishing activity, the woman didn't do a terribly good job at being present – one moment she was all business and attention; the next, she disintegrated into a scatter of limbs and motion. Presently, she grabbed the ledger with hands that featured sores on two prominent knuckles. As she noticed my appearance, she pursed her mouth, shoved her hands into her armpits, and attempted, leaning forward, to decipher my script: 'You want . . . You want to visit the museum, Mr . . . Mr What, if I may?' She had perfect, pale irises.

'Actually, I'm looking for Dr Karp.' Finding nowhere to dispose of the carcass of my apple, I put it in my pocket.

'Karp, Dr Karp . . .' It took the receptionist an age to understand of whom I was speaking. 'Ah, Dr Karp!' she exclaimed. 'Of course. He's not here any longer. Sorry to say. No, he's left the Foundation. Of course. Dr Röser has asked all visitors to contact him.' Frowning, she scrutinised my signature. 'I must ask you to write more legibly, sir.'

Not here? Left the Foundation? I was already regretting my visit. 'Would you know where to find him – Dr Karp, I mean?'

Something girlish came over the woman. 'Dr Röser will tell you. In the library. Oh, yes.' Making a note, probably in order to log which section of the Foundation I'd be visiting, she extended her pen with an eloquent gesture.

I signed quickly. Then, thanking her, I hurried up the stairs. As I entered the library, I noticed a gentleman at the big desk, working his way through a stack of documents with an air of mounting irritation, as if he were searching for statements he was convinced were there, but which a cunning editor had had the cheek to print in invisible ink. He seemed familiar in the vague manner of most scholars. His hair was thin, his nose narrow and bird-like in shape, underneath which ensemble a well-tended goatee rested. Celluloid collar, impeccably knotted tie. On his right pinkie, a signet ring gleamed in the lazy summer sun. Behind the visitor, a stout woman was just ascending a ladder on thick but unevenly shaped legs. Reaching the top shelf, she wriggled out a reference book, descended, and limped into an adjacent room. From the same room, Dr Röser now approached – soundlessly, almost hovering, like a jellyfish in water. As he saw me, he applied a Buddhist smile. 'Sir wishes?'

The librarian didn't seem to recognise me. Nonetheless, I decided to be careful. 'How do you do?' Extending my hand, I tried to find a hold in his black eyes. 'I'm looking for some books, sir. Dr Karp was kind enough to recommend the library.'

'You've just been to the museum?' Röser looked at my hand, still extended.

'Last weekend.' Feeling awkward, I pocketed my extremity – only to encounter what remained of my apple. 'Perhaps I ought to speak to him again?'

'I'm sorry to inform you that Karp has left us. He called last Saturday. Rather suddenly, as a matter of fact. Left his post with immediate effect.' The librarian consulted his pocket-watch. 'And what books would you be looking for, if I may ask? I'm in charge of the collection.' I mentioned the only title I could think of in a hurry – the study that Froehlich had published in 1910 of which I possessed a copy at home. 'I see.' Thoughtfully, Röser reinserted his watch into his pocket. 'You'll find the Health Chancellor's books over here. If you'd be so kind as to follow me, sir.' Pulling out a chair at the far end of the desk, he asked me to wait. A moment later, with a gesture that indicated either reserve or discretion, he placed the volume I had mentioned in front of me, twisting it so that it lined up with the edge of the desk. Then he left without another word.

Out of habit, pointless on this sunny day, I reached for the brass strap connected to the green-hooded reading lamp and turned on the light. Karp hadn't said anything about leaving the Foundation. Obviously, it was his decision if he wished to resign. But wasn't it peculiar he had done so immediately after my visit? Had something I had said frightened him? Or perhaps he hadn't told me the whole truth about Dora? Silently, I cursed myself for having had too many beers at the Blue Cellar. If it hadn't been for my majestic headache, I was convinced I would have been able to tell something wasn't right. Irritated, I looked up and noticed that Röser was speaking to the visitor who had been leafing through the documents. Although they kept their voices low, it wasn't difficult to tell they were in better spirits than I. Mentioning something that sounded like 'elevation', but which, considering the circumstances, must have been 'elation', the librarian now informed his guest: 'Aunt Martina won't be back until . . .'

'Very good,' the visitor broke in. 'If she understood what true brotherhood is about, she'd share her results. You're doing the right thing, my friend. Information of this nature oughtn't be restricted.' Straightening his back, he held up a couple of files. The gesture seemed to make Röser uneasy. Reaching for the man's hand, as if to soften his enthusiasm, he directed him away from me – and their conversation returned to its previous level of mumble. A minute passed, then the visitor, not to be subdued on this glorious day, announced: 'That's that, then. I'll be in touch once I've confirmed my results. The triumph shall soon be ours!' As the doors closed behind him, I noticed a few of the documents he had inspected were still lying on the table. Now Röser noticed them, too. Not wishing to seem inquisitive, I returned to my book.

Froehlich's wooden prose didn't allow me to follow the argument for more than a limited stretch at a time. Still, I continued to read and found several things to divert my thoughts. At least half an hour must have passed before I raised my eyes again. I was just about to devote my attention to a case study describing the tragic life of a shop assistant from Halberstadt, when a new visitor entered the library. Discovering whom it was, I quickly returned to the text. Heart sinking sickly, book tilted as a cover, I tried to pretend it wasn't the young man with the biscuit-yellow hair. But my efforts weren't successful. Fortunately, he didn't notice me as he vanished behind the library counter. Nonetheless, to make sure, I allowed a few moments to pass. Then I got up, smoothly as a mimic, and stole past the counter with long, elastic steps. I had to force myself not to break into a run. Yet as soon as I closed the door behind me, my sense of decorum abandoned me, and I took the stairs two at a time.

'Sir, I must ask for a legible . . . Sir . . . Sir!'

Chapter Fourteen

As I emerged into the hot, humid afternoon, my thoughts were in turmoil. Although I hadn't been able to identify Röser's visitor, his voice had sounded curiously like the one I had heard in the dark at the Apollo. But surely my imagination, so carelessly wired, was making the wrong connections? It couldn't very well be Froehlich's former colleague, Horst Hauptstein, could it? What would *he* be doing at the Foundation? Hadn't the Health Chancellor fired him once he had discovered he flaunted a fake doctoral degree? What was Röser up to? Why the 'elation'? And who was the man with the biscuit-yellow hair?

Agitated, I returned home. My questions were many, mad and mutinous. Failing to detect a pattern among them, I understood I needed assistance. Often, when stuck, it helps me to air my concerns in the presence of somebody willing, simply, to listen. Sitting at my desk but getting nowhere, I decided to call on Heino. Yet our neighbourhood's coal and flower merchant turned out to be more interested in expatiating on how delightful it was that he and Boris were partners again. So, towards evening, I decided to take the tram to the Misery. A sphinx, I realised, might be just the interlocutor I needed.

*

The streets north of the city's famous hospital are narrow and dirty, the residential buildings dark and dishevelled. A few blocks away, there's a railway station that connects with the harbours and summer resorts up north, but also with chosen destinations across the water – exotic places carrying names like Trelleborg, Malmö and Stockholm. If one believes the 'soul biologist' about whom I read in the paper a few days ago, while waiting for Anton at the Blue Cellar, the topography of the Swedish capital corresponds to that of the human brain. I don't know how he's been able to reach such an audacious conclusion. But if you performed a similar test on the city in which I live, I mused as the tram continued north and the sky turned a heavenly shade of crimson, odds were it might yield the shape of a scrotal sac. After all, just like the male appendage, my adopted hometown consisted of two weighty but well-defined parts: east and west. Between them, a river ran which even reluctant believers had to admit was as close as one was likely to get, in geography, to the *ductus ejaculatorius* with its rich delta of connecting straits and canals. Also, more oval than round in shape, the two parts were embedded in a moist, fertile surrounding. As if this wasn't enough, I nodded grimly to my reflection in the window, on the outskirts of town a tall steel construction had just been erected, pointing stubbornly to heaven: the new radio tower. Yes, it'd be difficult to find a region more intimate than this.

According to those whose familiarity with our city begins where that of Baedeker ends, there are a dozen red-light districts in town, each with its own profile. North of the Misery, too, there are bars, massage parlours and hotels where customers may stay an hour at most. Yet the particular notoriety of the area rests on the thin shoulders of woodchucks and doll-boys. Before night descends and they head into the city centre, they're posted along the streets surrounding the train station. The nature of a 'doll-boy' is, I imagine, not difficult to tell. Rarely more than ten or twelve years old, they'll accept cigarettes and temporary shelter as payment, too. 'Woodchucks' are women, often older, with physical disadvantages: war injuries, amputated legs or hunchbacks, faces disfigured by fight or fire, knife or acid. Teasing the women for their radical looks, the boys find ever new ways of alluding to the exhibits of the Anatomical Museum, while the women, wearing the indulgent smile of those who've heard it all, point out, index finger tapping wrist, that it's well past bedtime. To which the boys respond, eyelashes aflutter: 'If only', while they try to catch the eyes of the gentlemen walking by.

Otto and One-legged Else blend well into this neighbourhood. They live on a side street several blocks away from the train station, but off and on, one sees red-faced men with chafing collars here, too. They always walk briskly, never glancing sideways, as if they were sporting blinkers the way racehorses do. Perhaps they believe that whatever they don't see won't notice them either? I'm sure they'd prefer to be entirely invisible, if possible. As for me, I could afford to be noticed. Considering my situation, I realised it might in fact be the only thing I could afford at this point. Getting off the tram and turning into the street where my friends live, I heard a melodious whistle. At first I thought it would be one of the woodchucks offering me her amorous services, then that it might be a dollboy. But all I could see was an indistinct shape slipping through a crack between the wooden boards of a hoarding on which a withered ad announced the presence of a mechanic's close by.

I crossed the street and arrived at a gate wide enough for a lorry. One evening last autumn, I had walked Otto here, having taught him how to create, by using the ebony keys alone, that exquisite shiver that makes thrills course along the spine of an audience. In the cool shade of the gate, a boy, aged five or six, was kicking a ball against the wall. It flew away with a dusty thud – and rolled back with a compliant hum. Again and again.

'Otto, Else?' Placing his dirty foot on the ball, doing a diminutive version of a general who has just conquered a hilltop, the boy eyed me carefully. 'Oh, you want me to *show* you, do you?' His new set of teeth had not yet appeared. Pushing his tongue through the crack in the middle, he decided I must be all right, for, without further ado, he kicked his ball and ran after it. When he had covered about twenty metres, he turned round and made a sweeping gesture with his arm. I left the gate and the humid evening returned.

In the first courtyard, all windows were open, the smell of greasy food smearing the stale air. A disembodied hand had just placed the burned remains of three lamb chops on a windowsill. Hoisting himself up from the chair in which he had been lying with a newspaper covering his face, an expectant husband pulled a canny face. From several windows there was the noise of combative children. One seemed the home of a gruff gramophone; another emitted the sound of low, methodical hammering – somebody was just pounding one tack after another into a pliant rubber board. My guide had already dribbled his way into the next courtyard. 'There,' he now shouted, pointing towards the last yard. As I waved, he shrugged and began to dribble his way back again.

Reaching the third courtyard, I noticed two older boys sitting on the banister of a basement staircase. One of them whittled a wooden stick, tense and concentrated. His knife didn't seem particularly sharp; tiny shreds of wood darted this way and that. Having nothing better to do, the other boy pointed nonchalantly across the yard. In the farthest corner, I made out a low building on which a roof of corrugated metal jutted out. At one time, it might have housed a mechanic's workshop. In the comforting shadow by the squat door, next to a table with accompanying chair, sat the only sphinx I know personally.

As I crossed the yard, slivers of sun, reflected and multiplied by the open windows, whirled up meaningless dust in my brain. Frankly, I felt a little foolish. Persuading myself there were worse things to feel, and nothing else to do, I approached Else. I needed answers to my queries, and if I had to wait until the next time I saw her at the Apollo, it might take a while.

My colleague wore a kerchief on her head, hands resting on the rubber wheels. The blanket that usually covers what remains of her legs had ridden up and was now exposing two pale stumps. 'Monday no show.'

'Good evening to you, too, Else.' I stared at her amputations with reluctant fascination. The legs ended just above the knees and had cross-shaped stitches that made me think, incongruously, of Christmas ham. Quietly I wondered whether the stumps were of equal length. And whether it mattered if they weren't.

Else, pretending not to notice, nodded towards the stairs. As I shifted my gaze, she took the opportunity to adjust her blanket. 'Lech and Thaddeus', she informed me, 'report figure red hair on his way. Only Knisch possible.'

One of the boys must have been the shadow that had slipped through the crack of the hoarding. 'In that case,' I replied, 'perhaps you also know why I'm here?'

'Radio scope nothing for old lady.' Prudently, my colleague gripped the brakes. 'What I be of service, Sascha?'

'First of all, I'd like to ask for a few days off.'

'Granted.' Raising one of her hands, as if to bless me, Else waved away a fly. 'Please sit.'

'And second . . .' I saw the insect recede, buzzing, into the shadows gathered underneath the corrugated roof. 'Oh, I didn't know Himmel was your last name.' Printed in capital letters on the door, underneath a crossed-out symbol for what looked like a lorry, was 'E. & O. HIMMEL'.

'No choice.' Names, clearly, weren't enough of a conversation topic for Else.

'And second . . .' I continued, hesitating again. On the opposite side of the courtyard, the boys did their best not to appear curious. Sinking into the chair and searching for cigarettes, I looked for the right angle. 'Second,' I reiterated, fishing out the remains of an apple, 'I'm wondering whether you're aware of what happens at the Apollo when we're not working.' My colleague shrugged but didn't reply. I got rid of my find, then continued my search. Retrieving what I was looking for, I lit up and explained, flicking away the match, that I had happened to visit the cinema the night before. I had merely wanted to fetch my bicycle. But then I thought I might exchange a word with her, and had stepped inside.

'Impossible.' One-legged Else released the brakes.

'I know. You weren't in the projection room. Perhaps in the theatre, I thought, and tried to look for you there. But it was too dark and I couldn't discover you there either. Instead I had a peek at Stegemann's private screening. Not exactly something for movie buffs, is it? If that's supposed to be science . . .'

The door opened and Otto emerged. Smiling as he saw me, he executed a series of swift movements with his balletic fingers, then turned to his mother, who nodded and explained: 'Soon eat, Sascha.' Sitting up, I told her I wasn't hungry – whereupon Else signed to her son, who, shaking his head sadly, returned inside. As soon as the door had closed, my colleague rolled out of the shadows and turned the wheelchair towards me. 'Pity. Now. What Sascha observe?' I began to tell her. 'More?' I continued. 'And?' Suddenly, Else seemed all interest. I cogitated. No, nothing I could think of. Was it so important? Clearly, the film Stegemann had screened was about some testicular disease, no doubt scientifically exciting, that the doctors wished to discuss. 'Perhaps . . .' Interrupting herself, Else again glanced over my shoulder. The window behind me was just being opened. 'Testifortan,' she continued neutrally. 'Contain yohimbe bark from West Africa. Clam shells from Baltic. And much more. Expand blood vessels. Increase lust. Of course potency, too. May be acquired at pharmacy. Sascha not see Froehlich's ads?'

As usual, my colleague had an answer to everything. To the well-organised sound of Otto chopping vegetables, she explained that the Health Chancellor often advertised drugs with a thera-peutic influence on ailing vitality. Because these ads also served the purpose of sexual clarification (poor people had no access to books, but newspapers would always find a way into their hands), they were usually accompanied by illustrations. Apparently, the most widespread of these depicted a male body, sliced in half, in which the different stages of the process were demonstrated with the help of varicoloured arrows and fat exclamation points. Hadn't I noticed the drawings in the paper? I shook my head. I rarely paid much attention to the ads, I confessed, at least ones of that kind. Else continued to describe the process. After a pill had been taken, it took a minute before it dissolved and mixed with the intestinal fluids. That was the first phase. During the next, the drug was assimilated into the blood system, and during the third, the addition of new hormones stimulated the pituitary gland, so that, with blood circulation increasing, important muscle groups thickened and hardened.

'Else, you surprise me.'

'Impossible compliment. Why Sascha think Else called One-legged?'

Extinguishing my cigarette, I pretended not to have heard her. 'Sascha believe Else not know? Even more impossible.' My colleague seemed disappointed. 'Big fire last year of war. Otto and Else saved. But heavy price.' She looked around, perhaps contemplating her current lodgings, then told me she had to have amputated first one leg, then the other. Between these two dates, a year had passed, which had been time enough for the other patients at the Misery to invent a nickname for her. 'Phantom pain,' Else declared, patting her blanket. 'Testifortan only relief. Organism younger, performance better, Else strong again. Price 9.80 reichsmark per package. Fluid form one mark less. But pills for women two marks more. Difficult with salary from Stegemann.'

'Actually, I've met Froehlich,' I said in order to make my colleague think of other, if not more pleasant, things. 'Together with Dora, you know – my friend, who visited me at the Apollo last week. But what does the Health Chancellor have to do with Stegemann's screenings?' Behind us, Otto was now frying onions. The smell, unexpectedly pleasant, wafted through the evening air, a faint trail of parched skin floating behind. I began to regret not having accepted the dinner invitation.

'Froehlich? Nothing.' Turning her chair around, One-legged Else prodded me to push on. Perhaps she didn't like the smell from the kitchen, or else she wanted to continue our conversation some place quiet. Slowly we rolled across the yard. A cloud of flies, hovering in mid-space, performed their habitual evening ritual, approaching a trembling version of deadlock. Else waved her hand; the boys nodded grimly; the flies dispersed. ('Just say the word,' one boy mumbled. 'We'll be over in a flash,' the other seconded, testing the point of his stick.) Then, out of fly-view and earshot, my colleague added with a new edge to her voice: 'But Sascha's friend. This Dora. Time Else explain.'

It was difficult to believe what my colleague now told me. But in the end, I had no choice. Of course I was aware that Stegemann rented out the Apollo to scientific groups. For a long time, he had put the premises at the disposal of non-profit-making organisations devoted to the standard mixture of fun, enlightenment and agitation. In that way, Adolf Koch had been able to use the theatre before he had found a better location on one of the central streets in the city. What I didn't know, however, was that parts of a well-known documentary about the male's relation to his own body had been shot at the Apollo. Nor that, with time, our boss had refined his interests, so that these days he had placed his premises at the exclusive disposal of an association called the 'Brotherhood'. One-legged Else couldn't, or wouldn't, tell me what this club for body culture was up to. But she'd be surprised if it didn't have links to a certain Doctor Hauptstein.

'Hauptstein?' I stopped in my, or rather the wheelchair's, tracks. 'Horst Hauptstein? Are you sure?'

Hushing, Else asked me to push on. As I reluctantly continued, she explained she had met Hauptstein shortly after Stegemann had hired her. He was part of a film crew financed by a scientific-humanitarian foundation, and had wondered whether her son might be interested in participating. The scientist had seen Otto help his incapacitated mother, and although the boy was only in his early teens, he could see he displayed athletic promise. Hauptstein had even claimed 'it would be an honour to show audiences such a genuine German specimen'. Prodded by his mother, who thought it might do her son good to meet other boys his age, Otto had agreed. As for his contribution to the film, however, all Else knew was that her son had been asked to demonstrate exercises meant to strengthen man's sense of self.

I realised my colleague was speaking of the film Dora had mentioned. Barely able to contain myself, I asked her what more she knew. But Else merely shrugged. Otto had only been part of the production for a week. Returning home one night, he had made it clear he didn't wish to continue. 'No more film.'

'Why?'

'Otto say boy engaged by doctor not behave well.' When Else had asked her son to explain what had happened, he had shaken his head, unwilling to say more. His mother could tell the experience pained him, but no matter what she said, or did, he refused to give further details. Turning her head up towards me, Else declared: 'I convinced boy steal money, Sascha. Therefore I emphasise to boss: Otto nevermore.' Neither mother nor child had mentioned the film again. Yet last year, seeing Hauptstein emerge from Stegemann's office, Else hadn't been able to resist confronting the person who so obviously was responsible for her son's malaise.

When she described his appearance – 'thin as shoelace, goatee, military posture' – I stopped in my, or rather the wheelchair's, tracks for the second time that night, halfway across the first courtyard. One-legged Else had just described the visitor at the Foundation's library. So it *had* been Hauptstein who had talked to Osram Röser. 'What did you want from him?' I decided to broach the issue carefully.

'Not me. Otto. Damage costs. What else?' Apparently, my colleague had rolled into Stegemann's office and told his visitor he had exploited the services of a minor. Now that her son was of legal age, he had the right to proper compensation. Stegemann had coughed and squirmed and wondered, in a voice that had seemed to come from a place where he was not, what Mrs Himmel could possibly mean. When Else had repeated her words, this time adding that, as far as she was concerned, taking legal action wasn't unreasonable given the circumstances, our boss, smoothing his clipped moustache, had promised to discuss the matter with his visitor.

But time had passed, and nothing had come of it. Finally, tired of waiting, Else had decided to stay behind one evening when the Apollo was closed for one of Stegemann's private sessions. Hardly had Hauptstein entered the foyer before she cornered him with her wheelchair. Stiff as a pencil, he had maintained that the film in which her son had taken part had been screened only in select cinemas. Moreover, he was forced to inform her that all scenes in which Otto had featured had 'suffered in the busy battle of scissors'. Finally, she must recognise that the public interest in athletic exercises being sadly modest in the aftermath of the war, whatever remained of the footage hadn't been able to command an audience. And in any event (here Hauptstein had made an attempt to squeeze past Else), even if it might be proven that one of the young athletes he had employed had stolen Otto's money, which personally Hauptstein found difficult to believe (another attempt to squeeze by, also unsuccessful), as Mrs Himmel certainly must see, there was nothing for which he could, or should, pay her son. Yet today, he added, lowering his voice conspiratorially, ten years after the war, the public sentiment towards athletics seemed to be changing. 'Madame,' the Doctor had announced proudly, 'our nation is getting healthier.' If Otto agreed to take part in a new venture that he planned, Hauptstein might be able to promise fair recompense.

'Take part in what?' I wasn't sure I liked what I heard.

'Abracadabra.' Still cornered, Hauptstein had tried to explain what he meant by a healthier nation. Increasingly worked up, he had told Else he wished to contribute to a society founded on classical ideals. In it, wise, well-muscled men would rule, surrounded by boys who, for each task they mastered, rose through the ranks. Loosening his celluloid collar, Hauptstein had termed the model 'titanic', since, as he had explained, it relied on the male principles of courage, strength and fortitude. Although it was difficult to tell without proper examination, from what he could see, Otto was a fine sample of a future German – 'perhaps even a cremaster, my lady!'

'A "cremaster"? Are you sure that's the word he used?'

Padding the blanket covering her legs, Else looked offended. 'I know anatomy, Sascha. And name of muscle, too. According to Doctor, ideal society function as rolled-up scrotum. Require strong leader with vision. Thus name.' The Greek city-states had functioned in this manner, Hauptstein had concluded, and there was no reason why such principles couldn't be deployed today, perhaps even on a greater scale. 'He think our city "divided between Sodom in east and Gomorrah in west." Right place for "mobilisation". What Sascha think?'

I didn't think anything. Hauptstein could organise the city's boy gangs any way he wanted to. They couldn't possibly be worse than the nationalists who seemed to be employed on construction sites these days or the storm troopers who had begun to roam the streets. Personally, I preferred to have nothing to do with either group. Lowering my voice, I added that I thought Otto shouldn't either – unless, of course, he liked the sense of brotherhood that the scientist seemed so eager to stimulate.

'Stimulate? Sascha hush. Otto need no brother. And Else . . . Good evening, Mr Latek.'

The man who had been resting with the newspaper spread over his face had just emerged from a door. 'Mrs Himmel, would you believe what I have to put up with?' He held out a bowl with unidentifiable content. 'Since Rosa took the job down at the brewery, nothing's the same. "Emancipation" – is this it?'

Huffing, Else made a swirling sign, and we began our bumpy trip back to Otto. Recalling the fried onion, I admitted I wouldn't mind a bite after all. Then I mustered what courage I had left and asked my colleague what Dora had to do with all of this. And that's when she mentioned the film clip.

Chapter Fifteen

That night, having entered apprehension's uncomfortable labyrinth, I fell asleep late. Restive, I fiddled with the ominous thread offered to me by One-legged Else, trying to determine whether it was a snare or a support. If she was to be believed, while I had been punching tickets last Friday, Dora had got comfortable in the projection room. With her usual candour, my colleague had inquired how the visitor knew me. Dora had laughed and replied she was wrong; we weren't friends in *that* sense. Frankly, she had continued, she was visiting not because of me but because of the screenings. What went on at the Apollo when we weren't open to the public? 'Sascha's "friend"' – twirling her index fingers, Else fashioned quotation marks in the air – 'mention scenes of documentary shot at Apollo. Sascha work there. Friend interested. But call you "Anton" . . .'

'Anton?' I replied, scraping my thumbnail against one of the handles of the wheelchair. The wood, dark and smooth, revealed a crack of interesting pattern. 'Must be a mistake. Lakritz once brought us together. Perhaps she was referring to him?'

Instead of responding, Else placed her palms on her legs, squeezing and re-squeezing them. Quietly she explained that, last winter, cleaning up the mess I had created when I spilled coffee in the projection room, she had replaced the reels at the bottom of the stack with new ones. The soiled cylinders had seemed hopelessly ruined. Yet a few metres of film had turned out to be intact, so Else had cleaned a canister and stored the footage in a filing cabinet we didn't use. During her conversation with Dora, following a premonition, she had tried to dig the reel out.

For the third time that evening, I stopped in the wheelchair's tracks. This time, however, I walked around and squatted in front of my colleague, placing my hands on hers. 'This is very important, Else. What was on the film you gave Dora?'

Although fidgeting, my colleague didn't remove my hands. Instead, she leaned forward with a kind of doleful tenderness, folds fanning out from the corners of her eyes. 'Else sorry. Else not know. Canister imprint *"Foundation for Sexual Research"*. Else wanted to give to Sascha's friend. But not possible because steps in stairway. Else: "Sascha come." Friend: "Once upon time Anton." Else: "Lakritz? In that case, not want to hear."'

'What did you do?'

'Else? Do? Nothing.' But once we had closed that night, she had retrieved the footage. No longer able to give it to Dora, she had decided to return it to its proper owner. As the distance was too far for a wheelchair-bound woman, although still agile, she had asked Otto. And the next day, her son had delivered the material.

'Do you remember to whom he gave it? Or if Dora said something more about that documentary?' I clutched Else's hands. 'Please try to remember. It's important.'

Removing her hands, my colleague replied evenly: 'First answer: doctor at Foundation. Second: no.' Pointing to the former workshop, she then added: 'And now: Otto await dinner.'

The person to whom her son had given the film material must have been Karp. If the footage contained scenes from *Prometheus Unbound*, then, involuntarily, he had suddenly received proof of what Hauptstein was up to. Considering what I had been privy to at Stegemann's private session last Sunday, Dora's friend had, understandably, become worried. Now it no longer surprised me that he had resigned from the Foundation so unexpectedly. Wasn't it likely the film contained incriminating evidence?

As we approached the former workshop, I whispered in One-legged Else's ear: had Dora really not said anything else? Although my colleague shook her head, I persisted. Karp had left his job so abruptly, I explained, that he must have felt threatened – most likely for reasons connected with Dora. Was Else completely sure my friend hadn't passed along any other information, perhaps something concerning a boy she had given birth to? I mentioned the adoption. Personally, I was beginning to suspect that the child for whom Froehlich had found new parents . . .

'Please, Sascha, quiet.' Again, my colleague held up her hands. 'Now Else understand perfectly. Film, friend, cause for visit.' She adjusted the kerchief on her head. 'Only one thing not. Sascha's name really Anton?'

On the tram home that night, I continued to screen my relationship with Dora against the backdrop of a reluctant memory. Finally, I was forced to admit that, after a while, I had begun to feel awkward. It wasn't that I didn't desire her. Our nights were just as rich, our bodies just as curious as always. But I was pained by the fact that Dora didn't use my real name. Couldn't she see that the person in whose attributes I dressed up didn't square with the being I was? The more often we saw each other, the greater difficulty I had to extricate myself from my lie. And a part of me, possibly not the most beautiful, blamed Dora for treating trust so straightforwardly.

Last winter, we met again at the Paris Bar. It must have been in January, because at a memorial service I had attended between Christmas and New Year – for Molly Beese, 'the ace of the skies', who had committed suicide two years earlier – I ran into the woman Anton thought he had seen on that tourist boat. The memorial service was a sorry affair with sullen faces and soiled veils. The woman was standing by the grave, with a person I didn't recognise, while I was shivering with Anton in the last row, under an exasperating umbrella that sprouted vanes in all sorts of directions. We didn't trade a single word, although I was convinced she had recognised me. A week later, I phoned Dora – out of a misplaced sense of revenge, I realise only now. Finally I had decided to tell her my name, to explain what I did for a living, to claim the person I was – the whole, sorry story.

In the event, I didn't get very far. 'Knisch? If you say so.' Dora put away her napkin, while I, tapping a Moslem against the table, produced a smile more wry than wished-for. The mirror behind her back made me curiously self-conscious. 'I suppose that's a name. Although I've never heard it before.' Retrieving an American cigarette from her case, she leaned forward, towards the match I held out. 'Thanks.' Then she padded the velvet seating, surprisingly cheerful. 'You may always sit here, Mr Knisch. If the mirror disturbs you, I mean.'

Once I had switched sides, Dora explained that, early on, she had begun to divide customers into those who told her their name as soon as they entered room 202 and those who, slithering like an eel, helpless but cunning, made one up. The difference between the two groups matched another variation she had observed, one in which she thought Froehlich might be interested. Either, Dora had discovered, customers wanted to see their actions in her mirror or they avoided it as if it were bewitched. 'Some of my guests can't get enough. For them, one mirror is too little. They want to see everything that happens, from as many angles as possible, from the moment they take off their hat until they put it back on. What I do while they get dressed. My shoes or their rear. The drama between the legs. And so on. Others are frightened stiff by the mere thought of a mirror.' Dora rounded off the tip of her cigarette against the edge of the ashtray. 'It happens that a visitor wants me to treat him a little less mildly. As you know, that's not my style. But if he really insists, I suppose I may ask him to take a close look at himself. Most customers prefer to resist, since it increases their pleasure. Those who don't want to, however, those who really can't confront their own gaze, refuse until I get the point.' She laughed quietly.

'It's almost always the same men as the ones who invent their names.'

What did she do then?

'Leave them alone, of course. Why force people? I'd never do that.' Her eyes clouded over. 'Actually, that's not true. I did force a person once. A despicable character, with a voice like sandpaper. Wedding ring on his finger, French accent, a typical diplomat. Incredibly condescending. He behaved as if I had forced him to visit me. I wasn't worth a reichspfennig. At first, I thought he was one of those people who like to provoke. Some do that, you know, just to whine and roll over the moment I begin to talk back. But this one was serious, although he kept smiling the whole time – as if we shared some malicious secret.'

Urging her guest down on his knees, Dora had painted his lips violet, then told him to crawl to the mirror. As the visitor complained, Dora had pressed down a foot on his back, gently but firmly, informing him that she wouldn't release him until he kissed himself in the mirror. She nudged me in the side, laughing. 'Some men are so simple-minded. I really think they may be more interested in each other. Women serve merely as an excuse. Why can't they admit it, instead of creating this tremendous circus? Such feelings are hardly wrong, you know. It's only wrong to exploit people who don't have anything to do with the matter – and quite frankly, who couldn't care less.' She laughed again. 'He whimpered and wrestled all right. His fat belly was wobbling, his face was red as a tomato. I thought he might burst any moment. He was so fantastically furious, and so dreadfully excited, that he could barely contain himself. But eventually he did what I told him. I knew it'd be a matter only of moments before he'd press his snout against the mirror. The imprint looked like a carnation, dark and puckered, as if made by a pig.'

Dora smiled. 'I asked him what he saw. At first, he didn't reply. "You want me to tell you?" I wondered. Still no answer. "You're looking at your *œillet violet*, that's what. And now, please ponder what you just did."' I must have looked uncertain, because she hastened to explain that she was referring to the sonnet Karp had quoted during our visit to the Foundation. 'I told the Frenchman he could help himself while he meditated on his imprint. Personally, I had had enough and wouldn't return for half an hour. By then, I wanted him to have finished his ruminations. And thank me the way pigs do.'

'And how's that?'

'How do you think?' Dora grunted.

I laughed. 'Did you really leave?'

'Of course. But when I returned, he had vanished. The imprint on the mirror was gone, too. Even so, he came back a week later – dressed in a starched shirt and leather coat, no doubt thinking that would help. Types like that always do. They imagine they may "correct" any misunderstanding – with violence, if need be. "Really,"' Dora feigned a whiny voice, "'I'm not the way you think I am.'" She extinguished her cigarette. 'I told him to go see somebody else. Dominique, for example. He likes to deal with people like that. There were no services I could think of offering him. The naked truth? Without lipstick, that pig would never have brought it across his lips.'

A month later, one of the first days in February, I tried again. At long last, I had decided to invite Dora home. A year had passed since we had begun to see each other outside of room 202, and my reservations seemed to me if not immature, at least impractical. If we were to become partners properly, I had to lower my guard. Besides, the city in which I now resided wasn't Vienna, in which people still seemed to live as if in the nineteenth century – spats, frock coats and walrus whiskers for the gents; corsages, lace umbrellas and lorgnettes for the ladies. My new hometown was the birthplace of a modern century, 'the New York of Europe, characterised by social diversity, ethnic tolerance and new gender roles' – at least if you trusted Froehlich in the paper Dora had given me as a souvenir. Perhaps my friend wouldn't have anything against my living in a derelict building in the east, with no central heating, cold water sprinkled with copper flakes, and a toilet shared with a former sergeant?

When I called her, Dora merely replied: 'I've never asked, Anton. But that doesn't mean I'm not interested. Of course I'd love to come.' I gave her my address.

Before she arrived, I tried to fill out the psycho-biological questionnaire Karp had given us. It seemed to me I owed it to the spirit of openness we were about to embrace. Froehlich had begun to collect data pertaining to people's intimate life as far back as the turn of the century, proclaiming, in 1915, that his questionnaire, which he had steadily improved upon, now constituted the safest method of establishing the 'gender aspect' of an individual. The answers received, often long and laborious, are gathered according to statistical principles, and have served as the basis for a series of case studies. Kept in the Foundation's archives, the original material is treated with the utmost confidentiality. Only established scholars may consult the hundreds of questionnaires completed over the years – by people from the nobility, the clergy and the military, but also from the middle class, the proletariat and criminal circles, from red to brown on the political spectrum, and representing all ethnic minorities within the borders of the republic. At present, Froehlich is working through the material, planning, soon, to present the first comprehensive view of man's 'rainbow essence' in his formidable *Geschlechtskunde*.

I managed to fill in name, date of birth, address and present occupation, and also to answer the first forty-some questions before, eyeing through the remaining hundred queries, I was overcome by doubt again. Take question number 44, for example: 'Can you whistle?' Or number 92: 'Do clothes play a special role in your life? Do you prefer a simple or multilayered appearance, tight or loose-fitting garment, high collars or open ones? Do you wear jewellery? Or carry a knife in your pocket? Which is your favourite colour?' Number 133: 'Does it anger you if a person refuses to tell you about his sexual particularities?' Or the last question (Appendix no. 1): 'Tell us an intimate secret – from *a* to *o*!' Such queries demanded either a shrug or a dissertation for an answer. I realised the intention was good. But would the questionnaire really reveal where on the sexual spectrum I'd fit in? Why couldn't you belong to many different places simultaneously? And what might it signify, if anything, that it wasn't Alexander Knisch, registered with the police, but a fictitious Anton, carrying the same last name, who answered the Health Chancellor's questions?

When Dora arrived that February afternoon, wrapped in an elegant lady's coat with a fox boa but dressed as a schoolboy underneath (blazer and trousers, black tie, patent leather shoes with Spanish heels), I explained I had tried to do my homework. I was sure it would be fun to add a nuance or two to Froehlich's palette. Still, I wondered whether the fact that I didn't wear any jewellery, nor carried a knife in my pocket, said something about my drives. Honestly, was my intimate life anybody's business? Lying down and adjusting the pillow under her black, glossy ponytail, Dora explained that, actually, as far as she was concerned, my 'sexual question' did matter to her. And anyway, I had nothing to hide, did I? If she, as a well-known minette, was willing to divulge the particularities of her intimate life, surely I, as an unknown schoolgirl, ought to be able to do the same? Or was I embarrassed to admit why I had visited her at Hotel Kreuzer? Personally Dora found it difficult to believe that I, of all people, felt discomfited by the eternally feminine. That wasn't the Anton she had grown so fond of. 'Besides,' she added, 'Froehlich's a serious scholar. Your answer would never end up in the wrong hands.'

Putting aside the questionnaire, I declared I had no reason to doubt the Health Chancellor's integrity. Nonetheless, it felt a little like handing in homework to one's teacher. Did the data really convey anything dependable about me? These weren't exactly mathematical queries for which there could be only one correct answer. Even if a person lifted the veil prudently covering their love life, in order to be themselves, surely, off and on, they needed to experience moments of perfect blankness? And in any event, my visits to Hotel Kreuzer had taught me more about myself than I thought Froehlich's evaluation would ever do.

181

'Please, Anton. Theory has practical effects, too.'

'But that's exactly my point.' During the protracted hours at room 202, Dora had lowered my psychological speed with dextrous fingers and expert daring, revealing a richness of emotion I hadn't known existed. Contained within me, I discovered, was an entire rainbow. Depending on the light, or the atmosphere, or simply the staged setting, a different person would emerge. Why now limit myself to confessing some tawdry intimacy? The practical side of me seemed infinitely more variegated than my boring theoretical self was ever likely to become. 'Also, I wonder whether a person's drives remain the same for a whole life. One day, dirty violet may be my favourite colour; the next, I prefer loose-fitting clothes. Although I suppose that much is true: I've always been able to whistle.'

'Do you really believe Froehlich sees everything in black and white? That's rather naive, Anton. Remember what Felix told us. It's about the grey sex. And anyway, at times the part may contain the whole.'

Reluctantly, I admitted she might be right. Obviously I could lower my psychological speed and choose a particular facet of my private rainbow in the hope that it would yield the entire marvel of the spectrum. Yes, now that she mentioned it, I suppose I could do that. If she didn't mind, however, I needed time to figure out which one to pick. 'You first, yes?'

Dora brushed her tail to the side. When she looked at me again, her eyes were glassy and distant. 'All right. But just so that you understand it may suffice to tell something you've never told anybody. Sometimes a single story reveals more about you than you could imagine.' She fell silent, then added quietly – more to assure me than herself: 'It has got to do with Froehlich's Appendix, no?'

'You first.'

'Yes, yes, don't be so impatient.' Her shoes dropped to the floor. 'First I need a cigarette. Would you give me one of yours, please?' Lustfully, Dora wriggled her feet. 'You have no idea how painful it is to live up to the expectations of others.' I assumed she was referring to her high heels. Once I had lit us a Moslem each, Dora stressed, cigarette in hand, that the story she was about to tell me was true – '"from *a* to *o*", just like Froehlich wants it.' Inhaling with pleasure, she proceeded to explain that, as a child, she had lived next to a country inn. She and the other kids used to play in the courtyard. One day, they'd spy on the staff; the next, they'd dress up and open their own place, turning stones into potatoes and baking cakes of mud. Almost always, Dora assumed the role of maître d', as she liked to bring customers to their table, conducting cultured conversations and displaying herself. 'And I really mean: displaying myself.'

When, in the morning, the postman came by, Dora bolted for the door. Called 'Uncle Fritz' by the kids, he was unflinchingly courteous. As soon as he had performed his customary bow of deference, the postman presented the day's letters with a delicate gesture, as if they had been sent from a remote empire and might disintegrate after so many years' travelling. At the time, Dora had thought him old, but now she realised he couldn't have been many months over thirty. Uncle Fritz sported thick whiskers that left only his mouth bare; his nose was usually bruised, as if it were being used for purposes other than breathing; and the buttons on his uniform shone like coins. Carrying the mail in a worn leather case, he pulled the bag onto his belly and rummaged around. Sometimes Dora would be allowed to peek into it. But mostly, he rearranged his voice, spreading his hands ominously, and wondered what kind of secrets his magic holder might contain today. Every morning had offered its own special drama.

As Dora grew older, at the age of eleven or twelve, she wanted to return the favour. The feeling continued to grow within her. 'And finally, one day, I did it. As Uncle Fritz rummaged around in his bag, I lifted my dress. Even though I wasn't wearing any underwear – it must have been summer – there couldn't have been much for him, or anyone, to see. But Uncle Fritz turned red as a beet and began to stutter. I made a quick curtsey, took the mail he didn't know what to do with, and closed the door.' Dora suppressed her laughter. 'It felt as if we'd become friends

– trading secrets, you know.' Once she had got over her initial trepidation, she lifted her dress more often. The feeling of beauty was so intense, the sensation of freedom so evident, that she couldn't resist it. But then, one afternoon, there was a knock on the door. Since the mail had already been delivered, Dora's mother opened. It was Uncle Fritz. He had just finished his round, and would like a word with the lady of the house – in private, if possible. As soon as he had left, half an hour later, Dora's mother asked her daughter into the kitchen. Was it true what the postman had reported?

'When I . . .'

'Wait, I'm not done.' Getting up, Dora opened the window and threw out her cigarette. 'Yours are too strong.' Having worked the latch, she retrieved her cigarette case from her coat pocket, then lay down again. The sun, having disentangled itself from the barren branches of some trees, was just about to perform its standard descent behind the buildings on the opposite side of the square. 'For the first time in my life,' she continued, 'I realised I ought to feel ashamed. Both for what I had done and for what I had experienced. I suppose I could accept the first, but the latter seemed to me unjust. It felt as if my nakedness no longer belonged to me. My mother forced me to promise never to do it again, otherwise she'd have to inform my father. As he wasn't particularly understanding, her threat was enough to prevent me from bothering Uncle Fritz again. Instead, I began to raise my dress for the cooks at the tavern . . .'

Smiling – sadly, I thought – at the memory, Dora took the ashtray I handed her. 'Gradually it dawned on me that adults were shocked by nakedness. Probably their reaction gave me a sense of power. But to tell you the truth, I think my performance had more to do with wanting to be appreciated. For what is more difficult to say. Perhaps Froehlich would know. In any event, it was quite enough to sneak into the kitchen, to hide behind the big pots and monstrous pans, and to lift up my dress as soon as someone from the staff happened to pass by. I felt an inexplicable rush of happiness as I did it. Maybe you find that odd?' Dora looked at me. 'No? Well, there was this girl who used to come along. *She* did. Adele was her name. We were about the same size and always borrowed each other's clothes – although Adele was a few years older and later turned out to prefer trousers. When I stood there pressing the hem of my dress under my chin, trying to see what my friend was up to, she was usually already halfway out the back door.'

Dora explained the kitchen staff had smiled and inquired whether she wouldn't want to return in a few years' time, and then give them the adult version of her performance. But there was one cook who wanted her to step forward already now. First Dora had declined. As usual, her friend had vanished and, left alone, she felt uneasy. The cook had a big, bruised face and hairy hands. Yet when he told her he'd give her the entire block of chocolate he used to grate over desserts, she gave in. Smiling complicitly, the cook closed the door to the courtyard, hunched down, and lifted the girl onto his lap. Running his meaty thumb across her lower parts, he mumbled various flustered things. Noticing he smelled foul, Dora was just about to ask for the chocolate when there was a knock on the window. Pressed against the spotty pane was Adele's flat face, and behind her, that of Dora's flushed brother. Immediately, the cook got up and began to shout so that she thought his eyes might burst. What did she think? Such extravagant filth! What a little slut!

Dora looked at me, longer than I expected, then extinguished her cigarette with a pensive twist. 'My mother explained that, this time, she wouldn't be able to help me. My father had to be told.' The smoke trailed erratically in the dim light. 'And that was it, I thought. But to my surprise, my father declared he wouldn't punish me before he had found the appropriate method. For several days, I could hardly sleep. My mother behaved as if I had come down with the plague; Adele was nowhere to be seen. Only my brother treated me nicely. Each night I was allowed to sneak into his room, where he soothed me until I managed to fall asleep. Then, finally, the day of reckoning arrived. After dinner, my father asked my brother to go upstairs. I was left alone with him and my mother. After a while, my mother, too, was told to leave. Putting his hand on a stack of books that had been lying on the table throughout the dinner, my father now informed me he had found a proper method of punishment. I must understand it was for my own good.'

Apparently, Mr Wilms had spent the previous days studying pedagogical literature. Although he wasn't entirely convinced, he had come to understand the most successful method of child rearing involved ordaining a surfeit of the maladjustment that gave the child pleasure – which would turn it into its opposite and produce a 'pedagogical corrective'. Closing the door behind his wife, he asked his daughter to take off her clothes. 'I thought I didn't hear right. But he repeated what he'd said, adding that I needed to experience shame for what I had done. Finally, I stood there in my underwear, crying my heart out. My father crossed his arms and waited silently until I had removed my underwear, too. I was only allowed to keep my shoes on. Having checked something in one of his books, he nodded to himself and ordered me to go outside. Then, repeating it was for my own good, he shut the book and locked the door.'

Dora had never felt so abandoned. Her punishment may have been pedagogically prudent, and fortunately it was summer, but she shivered and cried and had nowhere to turn. Confused, she stumbled across the courtyard, while her parents pretended not to hear their daughter's sobbing. An eternity seemed to pass before the twelve-year-old girl ran out of tears. By then, all lights in the house were out, save for one on the top floor. Exhausted, Dora now recalled the cart in one corner. It was difficult to find, and she stumbled several times – once so badly that she hit her chin against the cobblestones. Running her tongue across her teeth, she could feel that the corner of a front tooth had been chipped off.

'Wonderful pedagogy.'

'Wait, I'm not done. What I wanted to say is – oh, this is difficult.' Dora shifted her weight in the bed, then cleared her throat: 'What I wanted to say is that the darkness made me excited. No, be quiet. It's true. Despite the tears and the blood, my runny nose and weird tooth, I was warm and sad and happy and desperate. All at the same time. And terribly confused. Everything hurt, but everything felt pleasurable, too. Finally, I found the cart, got up, and hid underneath a horse blanket. For the first time in my life, I felt odd all over my body. Kind of prickly, you know. Like when you've had too much soda water.'

With eyes I had never seen before, Dora scrutinised my mouth. 'I've never told this to anyone. You're the first, Anton. Every time I press my tongue against my tooth, I'm reminded of that night. After a while, I got more adventurous and tried to locate where the confusion came from. Running my hands over my body, I gradually realised it must issue from you-know-where. So . . . Well, it's not much of a secret, really: I began to touch myself. But the blanket in which I had wrapped myself reminded me of the cook's hands and soon I stopped. Finally, somehow, I fell asleep.' Dora paused, thinking. 'I was awoken by hands helping me indoors. It was late, closer to morning than to midnight, and I hurt all over. Still, I understood the hands belonged to my brother. My mother only ever did what she thought her husband condoned. My brother was the one who really cared. Once he had put me into his bed, he lay down next to me.' Again she paused. 'He did that later, too. But then it was more difficult to sleep . . .'

Dora's voice trailed off. I could see the white shirt and the wave of her black tie heave and sink tranquilly. She seemed at once infinitely remote and infinitely close. I wondered whether she'd continue. It had felt like it – as if, within her story, there had been another one waiting to be told. But since she remained motionless, and wordless, I realised I had been wrong. Eventually Dora adjusted the pillow under her head. 'That'll do. The rest has nothing to do with Froehlich's Appendix. Come and lie down, Anton. The turn has come for your sexual question.'

Stiffly I got up from my chair. Obviously, there was much I could tell her about – a shameful experience, a forbidden fantasy, a *tic sexuel*. Yet how could a single episode from an entire

187

intimate life possibly . . . 'I won't use thumbscrews, if that's what you think. You may keep your secrets. But a promise is a promise, you know. Besides, don't you think we're beyond pretending by now?' Taking her eyes off the window, Dora smiled and made room on the bed. In retrospect, I suppose it was appropriate that the sun decided to vanish at this moment behind the buildings opposite.

'To you,' I began, searching for a way into the maze that was spreading in front of me, 'I guess I could confess something I've never told anybody.' Lying down, I tried to locate Dora's ear with my mouth. It took me a while – first I found her shoulder, then her neck – then I continued, whispering into her intricate ear: 'Although that's not the same thing. When I think of Froehlich hunched over my answers, glasses polished and pencil sharpened, it feels as if he'd connect a shapeless cloud of dots, creating a contour that doesn't fit me. That questionnaire has the feel of a straitjacket, you know. Also, isn't the "sexual question" just as much about fantasies you don't understand as about experiences you do? No? But what if I wrote *them* down rather than genuine recollections? Who would be able to tell the difference? And please, now that we're beyond pretension, explain to me why one's sexuality should say more about one than other things in life – like what you prefer to laugh at, or your relation to sadness?' Dora's hair smelled of cedar.

'If that's what you're worried about, Anton dear, we might as well trade questionnaires with each other. Do you really think that's the point? That, that . . .' She searched for the right word. 'That this is about you and your *inhibitions*? No, please, stop it.' She removed her ear from the tongue that I had deployed in order to dispel the solemnity of the occasion. 'Your answers serve a purpose, if you haven't figured that out yet. They help Froehlich understand people better – which hopefully will make life a little easier for those who don't have as ordered an existence as you do.' I looked around: rickety bookcase, wobbly desk, discarded mattress. Perhaps Dora was right. 'I wasn't referring to the way you live, you fool. But how things are ordered up here, sweetie.'

Propped on one elbow, she knocked against my forehead. 'Use your imagination.'

Evidently, she wasn't going to let me out of my obligations easily. 'The drawing teacher in my school,' I began, leaving the words suspended in midair, 'a certain Mr Maier . . .' Dora lay down, and I realised I must continue through the gate that, unexpectedly, I discovered led into my personal labyrinth of marvel and mortification. But hardly had I stepped across the threshold, when I realised I wasn't sure in which direction the story might take me. 'Maier was also our athletics teacher,' I tried at first, recovering some ground. 'One of those gentlemen with hard, nervous hands and a head full of Greek ideals. If you couldn't climb the rope or get across the vaulting-horse fast enough, you had to stay after class. According to Mr Maier, a sound soul always mastered its body. Hence an athletic posture was the surest sign of a great spirit. Whoever was weak or clumsy had, in reality, an unhealthy mind. Only discipline might help you overcome your decadent tendencies. If you didn't manage to get across the vaulting-horse on your third attempt, however, you were out – or rather "in", I should say, for then you were ordered to stay behind while your mates . . .'

No, no. Wrong direction. Now I knew. 'One autumn, Mr Maier fell ill and was taken to the hospital or the penitentiary – unclear which. His replacement was a young person by the name of Polster. Polster was Maier's exact opposite. A true bohemian. Calling himself an "*artiste*", he made certain we addressed him only by his surname. "Herr" was something for the petit bourgeoisie, Polster declared. One of my classmates claimed they might have a painting by him on the wall at home – a pale woman, half porcelain, half reverie, who floated among water lilies. Apparently, it was difficult to tell where the vine ended and the arteries began.'

During our first athletics hour, we were allowed to roam about as we pleased. Polster removed his satin jacket and frilled shirt, but kept his worn black beret. Executing a series of spastic movements in his undershirt, he coughed at great, hollow length, then leaned, hands stuck in his pockets, against the vaulting-horse for the rest of the hour. The next day, he explained that physics had nothing to do with metaphysics. Body and soul were different orders of things, like muscles and music. The former was to athletics what the latter was to the fine arts. Only if we exercised our pliant psyche – 'That's your saving grace, boys, for those of you who don't master the Greek' – would we be able to draw what our mind's eye envisioned and discover the true wonders of beauty. 'I'm afraid Polster preferred his prose purple. In order to prove his point, he decided to put us to the test. Who was a physician, who was a metaphysician? Once he had determined to which group we inclined, those who wanted to play basketball might do so, while the others could devote themselves to movement of a different nature. Distributing charcoal and paper – one piece thin as a baking-sheet, the other thick and creamy – Polster urged us to use the latter to draw a human being from memory. Preferably somebody we knew.'

Fischl and Winkler, Mr Maier's favourite pupils, sighed loudly. As for me, the task didn't pose much of a problem. I drew my friend Greta, thinly veiled as a patrician Roman lady, with gleaming bracelets and snakes for braids. With one hand, she daringly raised her toga; with the other, more prudent, she covered her sex. Having placed one foot in front of the other, it looked as if she was about to dance. Most of the boys drew athletes showing off their muscles like so many pounds of stout meat, while the remaining few sketched women in an array of obscene postures. Polster, straight-faced, inspected the results. Some accomplishments he deemed helpless, others hopeless. Fischl's and Winkler's he considered something between swine and soldier. 'As he came to me, twirling his moustache, he remarked that the feet weren't right considering the poise and posture of the body. But otherwise, the result seemed to him acceptable. I had even managed to combine "active" with "passive" aspects.'

Clapping his hands, Polster now explained the purpose of this, the first part of the test. The only pupil who already knew how to draw – 'Sascha with his dynamic lady' – was asked to model.

As the other boys booed, he raised his hands. They shouldn't believe I was given a privilege. Inexpertly, Polster climbed the wall bars by the windows. Incredulous, we saw him unhook one of the curtains, bunching it up under his arm, and then descend. Holding up his booty, he asked me to drape myself in it. 'I was told to sit on the vaulting-horse in the middle of the room. Once Polster had managed to silence my schoolmates, who obviously found all of this uproariously funny, he demanded they take the thin piece of paper and exercise their imagination. Winkler especially, who protested loudly, saying he'd like to provide me with a second curtain so that he didn't have to see me at all, was urged to make an effort. "Imagine Knisch is a woman, with all a woman's attributes." The task wasn't merely to make a reproduction, but to combine freely one's inner vision with one's outer gaze.'

'That sounds like something Froehlich might say.'

'I was mortified. But somehow Polster managed to make the other boys shut up, and finally, believe it or not, everyone was drawing. Personally, I pretended it was raining. But try to sit still while thirty pairs of eyes are trained on you. It's impossible. After a while, the room started to wobble and float, mysteriously set adrift, and I was forced to blink away my tears. The curious thing, though, was that the more watery my eyes became, the less I began to look upon myself from the inside. Losing my sense of time, I began to imagine that the sixty pupils of the class were all mine, like the miniature facets of a fly's eye. I really *was* the entire world. Off and on, I could hear Polster whisper while he moved from one boy to the next, inspecting their stab at artistic immortality. But then I got other things to worry about . . .' Dora shifted her position. 'Suddenly I felt myself stiffening underneath the curtain. It wasn't precisely from lust, nor necessarily from fear. Perhaps the lust was inwardly directed, while the fear was turned outward. I can't tell. But there I sat, in the middle of the gym, and wasn't permitted to move while things happened to my body that I couldn't control.' I cleared my throat. 'I suppose it was a little like for you – but the other way around, if you see what I mean. My first sexual drama was acted out

behind the curtain, with the whole world as my blind witness.'
Satisfied I had reached the centre of my labyrinth, I lay down.

'Was that all?' Dora seemed to have expected me to continue.
When I didn't, she propped herself up on her elbow again. 'Rather
lame, don't you think?'

I explained that it had hardly felt that way to the boy on the
vaulting-horse. Finally, Polster, clapping his hands, had asked me
to dismount and to disrobe. Holding up the drawings one by
one, he proceeded to tell the class what was wrong with each.
On one sketch, the arm's form didn't follow from the body's function; on another, the folds of the dress didn't create the volume
required to endow the figure with a sense of gravity. Quickly he
corrected the mistakes. Obscene drawings were left without
comment. Then he placed the drawings on top of each other,
twisting and turning them until we began to wonder what he
was up to – at which point, well aware of the dramatic effect, he
raised the arrangement above his head, for all of us to see: he
had created a flower. 'Dear colleagues,' Polster now announced,
'what you're witnessing is the sum total of your visions. Please
pay attention: here are all the colours imagined, all the shadings
observed. One fine day, one of you may be able to concentrate
such varying visions into one single image.' Rhetorical pause,
restless boys. 'If so, he'll experience the true wonder of art: irisation.'

'Irisation?'

'It had something to do with the flower-like shape, I think.
Personally, I wasn't convinced the efforts of my schoolmates
justified such grand words. Nor my labour as a model. Still, I
felt oddly at ease. It was as if I had just experienced a revelation.
No, it's true. Although I didn't understand it until much later,
once I realised what I wanted to do in life, intuitively I must
have got Polster's point: art was a way of being yourself as somebody else.'

'So when it's about boys, it's termed art, whereas it's called
pedagogy when it's about girls?' Getting up from the bed, Dora
walked over to my desk. It had got dark. Outside, single snowflakes

whirled aimlessly in the yellow haze of a streetlamp. From below in the square, the impatient rumble of a car could be heard, attempting, and failing, to park. With her back to me, Dora said quietly: 'Sascha . . .'

'Sorry?' Still lying on the bed, I contemplated whether I ought to inform her about the direction I had opted for initially. But did certain recollections matter more just because they hurt more than others? Somewhere far away, wet wheels slithered on slippery cobblestones. Truth be told, I wasn't convinced that . . .

'Sascha . . .' Dora continued as if she hadn't heard me. 'Here, on the questionnaire, it says "Anton". But you just said your teacher called you Sascha. Is that your real name? "Sascha"?' She went over to her coat that I had hung on the back of the door. Suddenly, dreadfully alert, I stuttered that she might be right. But honestly, I had wanted to tell her my real name. No, no. Really. I *was* sorry. Of course I ought to have told her. It was just that the first time we met, I had thought it more prudent to use another name. You never knew what you might get yourself into, did you? And, well, the better we got to know each other, the harder it had turned out to be to rewind time in order to correct a minor discrepancy that anyway didn't . . .

Dora buttoned her coat methodically. 'I thought you were different. But really, you're just like every other man. I'm not here to indulge in make-believe, you know. How could you possibly be honest with me when you're not even honest with yourself?' She adjusted the boa around her neck. 'And that story about iridescence or whatever you called it. Pure fiction, no? You invented it.'

'Don't you trust me?' I replied from the private abyss into which I just discovered I had been decamped.

'No. But I thought I could love you.'

The only other thing Dora said, as I ran after her, almost losing my head as I slipped on the wet stairs, was: 'Stop making a nuisance of yourself. No, please. Stop.' Reaching the ground floor, she turned round. 'And promise not to bother me with

your sexual question again. I don't think I could handle it.'
Then, pushing open the door, she disappeared into the February
night. The impatient car must have been able to park, for as the
door slammed shut, I could hear nothing but silence. And blood
roaring in my ears.

Chapter Sixteen

The morning after my visit to Else, last Tuesday, that is, I enjoyed a cup of bitter black coffee and the day's second cigarette, sitting by the window that faces the square, when I heard a sudden rap of knuckles against the door. Since it could hardly be Anton, or Frau Britz, and since I never receive company this early, at least not without prior warning, I decided to continue enjoying my moment of summery reflection. Mesmerised, I studied the ashes tear themselves off my cigarette in segmented flakes as I extended it through the window. With remarkable buoyancy, they sailed towards the ground, made a salto mortale or two, then a few intricate twists, before they spread, detached, into so much luminous nonsense. Down on the street, a police car was parked with one wheel on the pavement and a puddle of sunspill glittering on its roof.

At last, the knocks ceased. Instead a key was inserted into the lock. I had hardly managed to make the connection between vehicle-on-street and knocks-on-door, when two police officers entered. The older one had blond, wavy hair; the younger sported not only pomade in his hair, but also a severe parting down the middle, made, it seemed, with the blade of a knife. Both were horribly familiar. If I wasn't mistaken, the older officer had escorted me to Manetti, whereas the younger had featured on the framed photo in the Chief Inspector's office.

Now the latter put down the briefcase he had been carrying and announced to nobody, it seemed, in particular: 'Thank you, ma'am. Ma'am, you may go.' As he noticed my bewilderment, he allowed for a grin to defrost parts of his face. The smile had hardly reached his eyes, however, before Mrs Britz squeezed by his colleague at the door, wiping out my curiosity in one rheumatic motion. 'No, thank you, ma'am. That will do, ma'am. I Said. Now. You. May. Go.' Turning to his colleague, the officer made the classical gesture required by the occasion – fingers bunched up and thumb pointing shoulderwards. Carefully tapping Mrs Britz on the shoulder, his colleague repeated the gesture. Then the officer turned his thawing attention to me. Inspecting my bruises, he patted his pockets. As soon as he had located his cigarettes, he made a jerking movement with his jaw, and the smile vanished. 'Alexander Knisch?'

I eased down from the windowsill. 'Who's asking?'

'Diels is asking. Officer Hermann Diels from the Vice Squad. And he's asking: Alexander Knisch?' The officer's nose was stubby, his ears small, the eyes thin as coin slots.

'Surely you must know? My surname's on the door.'

Diels lit his cigarette with efficient hands, then smiled again, albeit not as jovially as before. 'It's for the protocol. We're collaborating with Homicide. Only until we've established what kind of case we're dealing with, I grant you that, but everything must be done according to the book. In other words: it's my duty to inform you that I and Officer Pieplack from Homicide would like to search your flat.' He held up a hand in case I might succumb to the wild notion of protesting. Once he assured himself I harboured no such ideas, he surveyed my flat with an amused look, then explained to his colleague, who was just returning from having seen my landlady to the door: 'The bed and the desk. You may take the rest.'

'But . . .' Thinking better of it, Pieplack shrugged and went over to my bookcase. Once he had inspected its contents, he randomly selected a volume from the upper shelf. It turned out to be *Hands Up!* by Leo Heller. Surprisingly graceful, he leafed through the book, shook it, and let it fall, not quite as gracefully, to the floor. For each book that crashed to the ground in this manner – extended wings, fluttering interior – he sighed quietly. It almost looked as if he didn't appreciate what he'd been asked to do. Having contemplated his colleague's caution, Diels, fixing his cigarette between his teeth, shoved both shirt and jacket sleeves up his forearms, walked over to my bed, and tore off the sheets with a resolve that needed no improvement. Once he had aired my bedlinen, he proceeded to scrutinise my mattress. Satisfied it didn't contain anything but horsehair, he seized the foot of the bed, lifting it straight up, turning it to the wall, and scrutinising its underside, too. For each spring loosened, Diels's hopes seemed to increase. But he didn't find anything of value there, either.

My flat is not particularly big and there are no hiding places – at least no good ones. I was just about to inform my visitors of this, when I realised it hardly mattered. Soon the lodgings would be taken over by my landlady, anyway. (Earlier the same morning, having borrowed money from Anton's wallet, I was able to cover two of the three remaining months I owed, thrusting an envelope into Britz's exclamatory postbox. But now my friend's funds were depleted.) I wouldn't mind hanging on to Heller's book, and to the questionnaire that was still lying in the upper drawer of my desk. Paper clips and pencils might come in handy at some point, I guessed; and Dora's wooden horse, stoically standing on the night table, possessed a certain sentimental value. And one more thing, I suddenly realised. Quickly I walked over to the bookcase and pocketed Dora's cigarette case. Even if it was locked, and thus quite useless, the recollections it contained were too intimate for me to want to share them. As to the rest of my belongings, the police might do with them as they saw fit.

Pieplack eyed me discreetly as I put away the case, then returned to my books. When he had finished – there were twenty-four volumes last time I counted – he proceeded to investigate the Böcklin reproduction on the wall. Diels, for his part, devoted himself to my desk. The older officer finished first and looked on while his younger colleague meticulously emptied drawer upon drawer. Letters, bills and questionnaire were put in a tidy pile on top of the desk, all other items ended up on the floor. As I saw these things pass by, I couldn't understand what had once persuaded me to keep them. A dusty piece of amber containing a dead mosquito? A yellowing article about the city's Health Chancellor from the *Tageblatt*, with a photo of staff and patients proudly posing on the steps of the Foundation? Four, no, five unused postcards from southern France? Utter useless trash. At last, Diels seemed to arrive at the same conclusion. He looked up and, when he discovered that his colleague was about to move on to the kitchen, he raised his voice: 'Not a chance, Pieplack. The kitchen's mine. You take the hallway.'

Fifteen fierce minutes later, the men concluded their search. Returning to the living room, they brushed the dust off each other's shoulders. I almost felt sorry for them. 'You're enjoying yourself, eh, Knisch?' Diels eyed me grimly. Pieplack, for his part, had just discovered Dora's wooden horse. 'You'll see: nothing escapes us. Nothing.' He sat down at the desk again, stuffed the documents into his briefcase, and swept, irritated, the rest off the desk. Fiddling with the horse on the nightstand, his colleague merely nodded, with an air of amused distraction, towards the kitchen chair. Then he located the latch, and the belly fell down. Surprised, he pushed up the lid, pressed the muzzle again, and nodded satisfied as the abdomen, collapsing, performed according to expectation. I assumed that the next time he executed the neat little trick, red-ribboned intestines would gush out.

Reluctantly I sat down on the chair indicated by Pieplack. Diels undid the middle button on his jacket, a hint of belly becoming visible. His shirt was white but wrinkled, his tie thin and startlingly long. Authoritatively, he placed his hands on the desk. Not quite satisfied, he inched them further apart. 'Apparently,' he proclaimed expansively, satisfied he was now in charge of the situation, 'that Wilms woman has a file this thick,' he seized a slate of air between thumb and index finger, 'and if you don't look out, comrade,' now he slapped his palm against the desk, 'you will, too.'

Politely I inquired whether his boss shared his view. 'Inspector Manetti, I mean. Or did Inspector Wickert send you?'

'Manetti?' Diels sampled the word. 'Wickert?' echoed his partner. They looked at each other, after which the younger officer, who seemed in charge, continued: 'This is cosy, Knisch. Books, bed, lots of light . . . Not bad for someone like you. How long have you been the guest of our city?'

'I live here.'

'Ah. He lives here.' He smiled the smile of somebody with nothing better to do. 'No plans to return home?'

'To Vienna?'

'Ha, to Vienna! Did you hear that, Pieplack? To Vienna!' His colleague wanted to say something, but changed his mind. 'So you're Viennese, are you?' Diels's banter ceased. 'I'll be frank with you, Knisch. Don't think you can waltz with us. You're just as Viennese as I'm Turkish. And you've only lived in this city for five years. That hardly makes you a native. Not like me, not even like Pieplack. But regardless of where you're from, the odds are no good. New information has come to light. Oh, yes. In a little while, you'll be joining us down at headquarters, where you'll be asked a few questions. No, there's no need to bring anything along. We'll provide everything you might require – which won't be much, from what I can tell.' He looked around. It was meant as a joke, yet only Diels appeared to appreciate it. 'Before that, however, I thought we ought to have a little chat. Just you and me. And Officer Pieplack here. Between men, you know.' I looked at him. 'Without unnecessary restrictions,' he explained. 'Who knows? Perhaps it'll make it possible for you to stay in our city?' With the expectant look of someone who has just imparted a bit of positive news, he rubbed his hands.

'I'm not sure . . .'

'But you will be, Knisch, oh, you will be!' Again, he brought his palms down on the desk. His partner tried to say something, but Diels silenced him with an effective glance. When he was satisfied he held everyone's attention, he retrieved his wrinkled pack of cigarettes from his pocket. Putting it straight to his mouth, he extracted, slowly and deftly, a cigarette with his lips, then extended the pack towards me. 'No?' Once he had lit up, he lowered his voice in a confidential tone. 'Obviously, there's no reason we shouldn't understand each other. Explore common interests, establish a few mutual benefits. Here, in this relaxed atmosphere.' Fixing his cigarette between index and middle fingers, he turned his hands out and over the desk, almost as if he was about to swim.

'I'm not sure I understand, Constable.'

'Officer, Knisch. Like Pieplack here. But of superior rank.' Holding up his V-shaped fingers, Diels released a satisfying cloud of smoke. 'Still, you're right. No, you're right. We could have been more tactful, couldn't we, Pieplack?' Before his partner had found the appropriate answer, Diels picked a few items off the floor and shoved them, in no particular order, into the drawers. 'But resolve is a principal virtue, and time's in short supply. You must act while you can. That's what Inspector Wickert always says. "You must act while you can." Thus allow me to repeat: it doesn't look good. Oh, no, Mr Knisch. Either you'll be kicked out of our city or you may stay. The question is only where, the question is only how. Without overstating the importance of the police, it might be argued we wield power over your fate.'

Pieplack put down the wooden horse on the windowsill, turning it so that it faced the square. 'But it's the . . .'

'Didn't I say it could wait?' Waving with his cigarette, Diels did his best to close the desk drawers with his other hand. He looked up at me. 'Collaboration's always appreciated, Mr Knisch. That's why I'd like to let you in on a secret. As a small token of my good faith.' He assumed an all-knowing pose. 'You're a suspect in a case that involves certain . . . Well, let's just say: certain sexual habits. Habits that are not typical of the citizens of our country. Habits that are deviations from ordinary ones. In two words: bad habits. In one: vice.' He nodded solemnly. 'It's no secret that such habits tend to end violently. Not always, I grant you that. But it happens, and then the police will get involved. Our task is simple. You might say we correct deviant behaviour. We mend what may be mended, and remove the rest. I and Pieplack here. We're correctors.' Behind me, his colleague grunted. 'Inspector Manetti thinks this is a murder case.' Diels extinguished the cigarette with a brusque thumb. 'An "ordinary" murder, as my partner here calls it.' A last cloud of smoke departed from his lips. 'How I'd like to believe them! One worry less! But I know bad habits when I see them.' He shook his head. 'And if we don't look out, what happened to that Wilms woman will happen again. This is about deviant behaviour. And what would it look like if the city's Vice Squad didn't assume its responsibilities? Allow me to answer, Mr Knisch: vice would multiply. Like lice!'

He sighed. 'It's regrettable. But that's the way it is. Vice is like lice: everywhere. And that's why Inspector Wickert has asked us to act with vigour and valour. "Diels," he explained, "not even mastermind Manetti can deny that Wilms was dressed in a manner that doesn't correspond to respectable habits. Or do you think she was on her way to a sewing circle when death surprised her, made-up and dressed provocatively? In that case, I must disappoint you. After fifteen years on the force, I know how to read the signs. And experience tells me certain traits don't wash out. Bad habits remain bad habits. Once a whore, always a whore, I'm sorry to say."' Diels had whispered the last words with such feeling that I almost believed him.

'I'm grateful for the police's . . . How should I put it? For your concern,' I said defensively. 'But if it's Dora Wilms you're speaking of, she was my friend. And whatever you may think, she didn't deal in "*K. u. K.*" Dora was no "whore".'

'Also, it's the wrong . . .' Pieplack tried again, and failed again.

Zipping up his lips with two pedagogical fingers, Diels informed him: 'One moment, my colleague. Mr Knisch here was just about to tell us something important.' He turned to me again, eyeing me kindly. 'I think we may be getting to the core of the matter. Yes, now's the right moment to show some co-operation, Mr Knisch. Unburden yourself. Come clean.'

'. . . day,' Pieplack managed to add before Diels repeated his gesture, this time as if the zipper had got stuck. Folding his arms, he then smiled winsomely. '"*K. u. K.*" eh? Is that some secret code, perchance? The name of her unknown visitor? Or the last thing she whispered before dying? Mr Knisch,' he leaned forward dramatically, 'would you like to confess?'

'Confess? You mean you're suspecting me? But that's absurd!' I exclaimed. 'Dora was my friend. Besides, I have an alibi. I was at the Apollo. Ask my boss, ask Mr Stegemann.'

'That's just what we did!' For the third time, Diels slapped his triumphant palms against the desk. Behind me, Pieplack sighed for the last time this morning.

When, half an hour later, we arrived at the big red-brick building, the police officers escorted me through seemingly endless linoleum-floored corridors. Finally we reached a door. Pieplack unlocked it with a tired key and heavy face – or perhaps it was the other way around. The space we entered, smelling like a locker room, lacked both windows and ventilation. A sickly neon light fizzled as if about to give up, at any moment, its exhausting fight against the dark. A table was in the middle, and stacked, to one side, a few chairs. With a weary gesture, Pieplack pointed to the latter, then the door latched shut.

I doubted the officers had followed the rules when they detained me; not that it mattered. Neither Diels nor Pieplack seemed surprised by my bruises. Indeed, they were blatantly indifferent. I was convinced they were well versed in the art of backing up queries with sufficient conviction to obtain desired answers. The question was just what kind of truth they expected to extract during the interrogation I was certain would follow. If Stegemann claimed I hadn't shown up for work last Friday, he was lying. I could prove that. What I couldn't prove was that I hadn't been at Dora's place earlier the same afternoon. Luckily, the police still seemed to think she had died late that night. And fortunately, Anton had retrieved my bicycle clips in the nick of time. But not even my friend could erase the incriminating entry in Dora's calendar: 'AK 6p.m.' Perhaps I'd better confess?

I didn't have to ponder my options for long to realise I'd prefer paragraph 168 to being accused of murder. Fate, I thought, certainly had a way of making one warm to the charms of the lesser evil. Dejected, I sat down at the table. The prospects were not good. I had alerted the police myself, reporting that something had happened in the Otto-Ludwig-Straße. Although it had been in my best girl's voice, and only later, when I was safely ensconced at the Apollo, it meant the police could be sure death hadn't occurred later than 9.30 at night. One-legged Else would vouch that I had arrived at the cinema as usual, in time for our first feature at 6p.m. Still, that left an entire hour in the afternoon unaccounted for, when I had claimed I had been sitting with my neighbour on the bench in the square where I live, while Ivan Britz and the bakeresses had performed their callisthenic exercises to the annoyance of the construction workers but to the mad delight of Chérie. If, for some reason, the police began to suspect that death had occurred earlier, and Mr Vogelsang wished to demonstrate just how conscientious a citizen he was, despite mounting senility and a bad pension, I had no way of proving they were wrong.

Gradually, I began to lose my sense of time and space. The room flickered in the greenish light, the walls absorbed every sound. Removed from everything I'd ever known, it felt as if I had been transferred to a dimension that, although folded into the world, belonged to its outside surface – capricious, dangerous, utterly neutral to my plight. It's difficult to say, then, how much time passed before I heard someone approaching. An hour? A light year? But by then, I felt so nauseous I'd have welcomed any interruption. Even soft-spoken, hard-handed police officers seemed to me better than being locked up in nightmarish abstraction. To my consternation, however, my frame of mind managed to shift within the short space of time it took the clumsy key to turn in the lock. At once, my throat filled up with sawdust, my legs turned soft as noodles. My bruises hurt as if I had just acquired them. I didn't know what methods Diels and Pieplack planned to use, but with a paralysing degree of clarity, I realised how little I cared to be informed thereof.

'Mr Knisch, if there's anything you wish to say, it will have to wait. Please sign here. And here.' Dumbfounded, I saw Inspector Manetti enter. Quickly she placed a form on the table, unscrewing a fountain pen.

'Assistant Diels,' I stuttered, signing the form as if automated.

'Is taking liberties to which he's entitled. Thank you. And here. Thank you. Now you may go.' She fanned the form in the air. 'This way, if you will.' Manetti walked me briskly through the corridors. Having passed countless closed doors, she finally pushed one open. It turned out to lead to a stairway. 'You may consider yourself lucky your boss has the qualities of a clown. Justus Stegemann claims you never set foot in the cinema – which made Diels bring you in for interrogation. Left, if I may.' Once we had taken the stairs up two flights, our steps thundering against the metal, we continued along what must have been the same endless corridor, just turned in the other direction. 'Right, please.'

'How can he say that? The whole audience is my witness! Mrs Himmel can corroborate. She was there, too. She saw me!' Confused, I tried to understand what was happening.

'Nobody's disputing her testimony. Not at this point, at any rate.' Manetti stopped in front of a big oak door. 'Your boss thought we were discussing last Sunday, when, I'm told, he arranged a private screening. Inspector Wickert didn't bother to notice the mistake. Diels drew the only available conclusion. It wasn't until Pieplack talked to Mrs Himmel that the mistake was discovered. He tried to point it out, but Diels, having more pressing matters on his mind, pulled rank. I beg your indulgence, Mr Knisch. Still, Vice has not yet taken over the case. As long as we're dealing with murder, I'm in charge.' Manetti eyed me coolly. 'I'm convinced there are things you haven't told us, Mr Knisch.

And I don't believe I'm mistaken when I say they have to do with the death of Dora Wilms.' She pushed down the handle, then added: 'I will only say this once. It's vital you realise the consequences of remaining silent. Otherwise you may be savouring your last hours as a free person.' She opened the door with an almost unearthly calm.

Chapter Seventeen

Last winter, Anton moved, rather suddenly, from Pension Andersen to a place not far from Dora. If I were lucky, he'd still be asleep. As I came out of the police headquarters, I cut across the square, heading towards the *Stadtbahn* station, but was held up by a throng of people outside the entrance. I craned my neck to see what caused the commotion and discovered an Italian ice cream vendor with his back against the wall, surrounded by grinning people nudging each other. Skilfully he scraped cold, shimmering flakes from a fuming ice block into thin paper cones. The customer being served, an elderly lady in a hat, big-eyed the vendor's bottles while small-talking their owner. When, at last, she decided which flavour she preferred, the Italian shook the container ceremoniously, as if it were part of a complicated religious ritual, and poured the precious mixture – which sank, with tardy grace, through the mountain of splintered ice. Pretty soon the concoction would be utterly yellow and utterly sour.

I found it difficult to tear myself away from the sight. Perhaps the drama seemed so saturated now that I was enjoying my last hours in freedom? I had experienced the same bewildering play of tension and beauty permeating my body as I put on Dora's blouse last Friday. That would never happen again, I knew that.

And I doubt there is anything more bitter, anything more sweet, than the exquisite stitch that reminds you of yet another of life's wonders that's about to be lost – every single one just as banal, every single one just as heavenly. A person might go to pieces for less.

Twenty minutes later, I emerged from a station in the west part of town. It felt odd to be in this neighbourhood again. For a brief moment, I wondered whether I ought to walk over to Dora's place, but then I recalled the car that Anton had seen parked outside the building. It must have been Diels and Pieplack. As far as I knew, they might still be keeping watch. A dreamy signal drifted through the air, after which the *Stadtbahn* train continued westwards, towards the lakes and the green areas on the outskirts of town. The people who had descended, dressed in summer clothes and ignorant of my plight, fanned out in various directions. Cutting between two cars, I entered a side street lined with leafy tress. The heat was oppressive and I began to regret that I hadn't bought an ice cream. I was just about to roll up my shirtsleeves when a silver-coloured balloon came floating through the idle air. With its oval shape and trailing string it reminded me of one of the tulip-like drawings that Dora and I had contemplated at the Foundation's museum. Behind the balloon, a boy was running, hand extended, mouth open, and after him, a woman. Catching the string, I returned the balloon to the boy.

'What do you say?' His mother had stopped farther away, with the sun at her back. First she looked at her son, then at me, after which, seemingly perturbed, she brushed a lock of hair behind her ear and uttered what sounded like my name. But I must have been mistaken. Yanking the balloon to make sure there was enough gas left, the boy nodded quickly, offering a cursory 'Thank you' before he returned to his motionless parent.

'That's a nice balloon you've got,' I called, studying his mother. Was it not . . . Impossible to tell. And safest not to ask. If it was the same woman I had seen at the memorial service for Molly Beese, the situation demanded tact. The boy's mother waved neutrally, then took his hand. Perhaps she didn't want to show him she knew me? 'Axel has his birthday today.' Turning to her son, she added, 'Now let's return to the others,' after which they crossed the street – mother, child, balloon. Glued to the soft tarmac, I didn't continue until they had disappeared round the corner. Again I felt that stitch in the region of my heart. I could have sworn . . .

Anton's new lodgings are a few hundred metres from the station, nudged between two new buildings just behind a square. It was no longer lunch hour, but people still ate at the outdoor restaurants. Glasses were brought to mouths, knives and forks sparkled mindlessly in the sun. At one table, a middle-aged man sat placidly, his head leaning backwards and eyes shut. He had placed his naked feet on top of his shoes. Face, neck and what I could see of the chest through his open shirt glistened with chestnut oil. Probably one of Koch's sun worshippers. In the doorway was a waiter, his hands behind his back and an immaculate apron touching his shod feet. He, too, had turned his face towards the sun. A customer caught his attention. Quietly, the waiter made some professional gestures with a corkscrew, before walking over to a woman who, fiddling with her handbag, nonetheless managed to keep one hand extended in the air.

I continued past the restaurant, past a shoemaker, and past a second-hand store. Now I could see 'PENSION LANDAU, 2ND FLOOR' on the tin sign jutting out from a squat building further down the street. Just before I pushed open the door, I glanced at the adjacent shop window. Whoever wanted to, could buy an entire 'hygienic ensemble' at a modest price, including a French razor, an English toothbrush, and a blue-and-white tube of Chlorodont, the famous German toothpaste for which the city's buses have been campaigning since I don't know when.

At a table two flights up, an elderly gentleman sat with his chin pressed against his chest, lips moist. In front of him were hundreds of white beans which he sorted according to some enigmatic principle. At regular intervals, he shoved two, four – no, five beans into what I assumed was a pot. The beans rattled tinnily out of sight. Knocking on the doorframe, I inquired about my friend. 'We certainly have an Anton,' came the answer. 'Two even. But no Lakritz.' The man's eyes were red from booze, his teeth yellow from nicotine. Putting away his pot, he beat his chest as if it contained an alien animal. Having exploded into one of his armpits – infernal, phlegm-packing coughs – he swiped his mouth. 'Are you looking for Anton Knisch or Anton Lueger?'

'I'm sorry?' I didn't find the scene very agreeable.

'Knisch or Lueger?'

'Knisch,' I guessed, taking a step back. What was Anton up to?

'Haven't seen him around today. But you could have a look for yourself.' Again the man exploded into his armpit. When he had wiped his mouth, he jerked his head with a tired motion. 'Room 6. He's usually up late. Probably still asleep.' Then, bending over his beans, he lost all interest in me.

I entered a corridor with creaking floorboards and dustballs retreating with volatile haste. From one of the rooms, there came a low, meticulous snoring; from the others, nothing. Room 6 was all the way down, opposite the bathroom, from which presently a gurgling sound could be heard. I knocked, then tried the handle. Locked. Having knocked a couple more times, I hissed – and now a rusty bed squeaked in reply. Naked feet trotted across the floor; startled, a key came to life in the lock. Then Anton opened in his underwear – the lower part of which was a few sizes too big and in need of a wash. 'Damn, Sascha,' he offered in the charming manner I had come to expect, and returned to his bed. 'Close the door, will you?'

I did as my friend requested, clearing away a few items of clothing, and sat down on the room's only chair. A couple of soundless minutes went by about which there's little to report. 'Hello. Lakritz. Visitors.' Finally, I tugged the lower end of the bed sheet. Anton, turned towards the wall, merely grunted. 'Would it be all right if I opened the window?' The air wasn't exactly pristine. Receiving no reply, I tilted the window open and pulled away the curtain as noisily as possible. But that didn't help, either. Anton merely continued to grunt, now from underneath the pillow he had placed on his head.

Another unreportable while went by. I was just about to kick the bed when, eventually, my friend rolled around, sat up, and, scratching one foot with the other, yawned with relish. 'Trousers, please.' Tired, he pointed with his chin towards the chair I was sitting on. I got up so that he could retrieve them. After Anton had beaten a pair of socks, stiff with dirt, against his knee and located the shirt I had put on the floor, he placed himself in front of the rickety washstand, knees bent and chin extended – as if peering into another, somehow very distant, reality. In front of him hung a small mirror that, from my ignorant perspective, reproduced a sliver of cloudless sky. Spitting carefully into his hands, he ran his fingers through his hair, then stretched his back and yawned again. 'So where's my jacket, Sascha?'

While I waited for Anton to finish brushing his teeth, I told him about Wickert's visit to me and mine to Manetti. 'By the way, did you know the city's "mastermind" is a woman?'

Extricating the brush from his mouth, Anton retorted: 'Karla Manetti? Doesn't everyone?' White foam was forming on his lips.

I shrugged, handing him the towel, and explained that, although the inspector had been polite, she hadn't fooled me. Clearly I was her prime suspect. Then I mentioned that Karp had disappeared, which, considering the situation, seemed to me both sudden and unfortunate; that I had been the witness to a meeting at the Foundation's library I didn't know quite what to think of; and that One-legged Else had told me her son had once been involved in a documentary directed by a former colleague of Froehlich's. Actually, I told Anton about almost everything, including my boss's private screenings and Diels's and Pieplack's search of my flat. I even mentioned the Italian ice cream vendor. The only thing I refrained from dwelling on was my growing suspicion that Dora had had a slip of film in her possession, which she had been given by Karp and which might have something to do with her past. Since Anton had retrieved my bicycle clips, I saw no need to drag my former partner into the case more than necessary. 'With such worries,' I concluded, 'perhaps I may be excused for not remembering to bring your jacket?'

Now we were sitting in the restaurant I had walked by earlier. In the meantime, the well-oiled gentleman had left, the woman with her hand in the air, too. Anton was just polishing his plate with a piece of bread. 'You call those worries?' Wiping his mouth, he waved to get the waiter's attention. 'First coffee, then I akritz will tell you about real worries.'

'I thought your name was Knisch these days.'

'Knisch? Hell, "Knisch" . . . That's nothing. Just a cover. I couldn't come up with anything better, I'm afraid.' He smiled beatifically, partly towards me, partly towards the waiter who just arrived. 'Coffee, please. With cold milk.' Then he put away his napkin. 'It's best if Mr Landau continues to believe I'm a travelling salesman from the Austrian provinces. It won't hurt anyone, Sascha. Would you like anything?' Patting my pockets, I ordered a new pack of cigarettes, then thought there was perhaps a perverse justice in Anton's choice of name. After all, I had used his name for a long time, with neither his knowledge nor his consent.

Unfortunately, nobody Anton had spoken to had known Dora. These days, there were a number of minettes in the city. Most of them worked alone, without 'protectors' who took a percentage of the ladies' income in return for securing their working conditions. Many women also changed their workplace regularly, in order to seek out new challenges or to rid themselves of a persistent past. At times, they didn't even live in the city, but merely visited for a week every month.

'Saleswomen in love?'

The waiter arrived; the waiter left. Stirring sugar into his coffee, Anton ignored my suggestion. When he had mentioned Hotel Kreuzer, however, some women had seemed uneasy. The place was known among insiders, even becoming, recently, notorious. For a long time, it had been used mainly by metatropic ladies and minettes. But now, almost only men lived there. 'The Vice Squad searched the place last weekend. Those who didn't carry their *Kontrollkarte* were taken to police headquarters, where they were asked to explain what they did for a living. The porter, whose line of work was already established, was taken straight into custody.' One woman had told Anton the police had shown an unusual understanding for the plight of the male guests. All of them had been released, whereas many of her colleagues had been forced to pay heavy fines, and some had even been sent to prison. The few women who had been able to produce an identity card had gone looking for a new, or safer, abode. 'I thought it sounded like the hotel was worth visiting, so I went there yesterday.'

Flustered, the waiter returned with the cigarettes he had forgotten. As he departed, my friend asked whether I recalled the coffee shop across the street from the hotel. Sure. Occasionally I'd wait for Dora there. Well, Anton had gone there in order to keep the hotel under surveillance. The place had been empty save for a couple of ladies he happened to know. 'Trade girls, you know.' After a few minutes, he had seen the first person sneak into the hotel, having thrown guilty glances around him. Probably it was an old customer, because he had re-emerged almost immediately. The scene had been repeated a few times. But shortly before night fell, as the coffee shop was closing, new people arrived and didn't return. Unfortunately, because of the dark, it had been impossible to tell who they were, so Anton had bid the ladies goodbye and crossed the street. 'First I spoke to the porter . . .'

'A Russian who solves crossword puzzles? Thin as a shoe string?'

'No, a fat Bavarian, with feet the size of palm leaves. I explained I wanted to visit room 202. That's the right number, isn't it?' I nodded. 'But the porter looked at me as if I was from another planet.' Anton had insisted, explaining he was a good friend of the woman in 202. Eventually the porter had grabbed the ledger, pretending to consult it, and informed him that, no, sorry, the woman had moved. No, she hadn't left her new address. 'For a moment, I thought I ought to ask whether the room was free. But then I realised there was no reason why he shouldn't think I was an old customer. So I left. I could always check out room 202 another time.' As Anton had emerged on the street, a couple of men had stepped out of an adjacent doorway. 'Klaus and Harro, you know.' I must have looked mystified. 'You don't remember? Last Friday, at the Blue Cellar . . .'

'Oh, you mean the boys you picked a fight with?'

'Actually, we were doing business.' Anton frowned. 'Usually they stay up north. That's where their turf is. But lately, their gang has created a lot of trouble downtown. For us aesthetes, I mean.' Although he wavered, I refrained from pressing him. It wasn't my business with whom he wished to trade. 'Perhaps you're not aware of it, Sascha, but the Apollo isn't the only cinema in town.'

'It isn't?' I lit a cigarette.

There were places, Anton informed me, immune to the delicate aspects of language, that screened movies in which the fixtures weren't the most important thing. Personally he thought the aesthetic demands put on these films were just as high as on any other kind, if not higher. After all, they had to build up tension and sustain interest without recourse to something as sham as atmosphere. 'The audience must be seduced by the plot, you know.' Critics claimed the scenes thus created were indistinguishable from one another, and the plot, as far as there was one, knew of only one predictable direction. 'But that's just the point!' Anton exclaimed. 'The audience understands that things always end the same way; *still* it wants to be seduced.' That was possible only if one created the perfect pitch, at once enigmatic and self-evident, with calm, calculated delays, tight squeezes and charming kinks – ending, naturally, with that sudden gush of pleasure that true art alone can give.

'Naturally.'

As long as one thing led to the next, Anton continued, untouched by my ironics, the tension would mount, until finally, no longer able to contain itself, the audience cried for release.

'That way, the film becomes more potent. The final revelation must be teasingly postponed. Yet at the end, the truth is always exposed. The audience knows that, of course, which is why, when the denouement finally comes, the satisfaction is extra-big!' He looked at me, eyes bloodshot and watery. 'You ought to know, Sascha. This is no girlish "risotto" or whatever Polster called it. But true art!'

'Irisation,' I corrected him. To me, it sounded more like pornography. I didn't believe in a truth that came, whole and unharmed, at the end of things, almost like an appendix. Perhaps that was the way in the films of which Anton spoke, but hardly in real life, where the truth was distributed more evenly – somehow suffused with both matter and mind. Slowly, however, I was beginning to understand how my friend made his money. And to what he had devoted himself when he had invited me to southern France a few years ago. 'If you're talking about what I think you are, I'm not ignorant, you know. Perhaps you ought to join up with my boss?' I described the scientific film I had witnessed a few evenings earlier. No, I added, I hadn't stayed to see whether Anton's aesthetic demands were fulfilled.

'Pity. You might have learned something.'

'Thanks, but the triumph of testicles isn't my sort of thing.' I told him what Else had said.

Amused, Anton knitted his hands behind his neck, turning his face towards the sun. 'And she would know, of course.'

It was merely a slogan, I explained. But if Horst Hauptstein got his way, the city would soon be ruled by wise muscle packages surrounded by sylphlike creatures. Apparently, he was trying to organise the street gangs and create a ruling body called the 'Brotherhood'. The boys, having experience from life on the streets, were thought ideally suited to clean up certain places in town in which the air was stained by the odour of perfume and Vaseline. At these refuges, grown-up men were reported to trot around wearing purple socks and patent leather shoes – adorning their dextrous fingers with numerous sparkling rings, painting soft shadows around their eyes, and sporting, for reasons I was loathe to understand, red nostrils. If the Brotherhood didn't take radical measures, supposedly, these 'sisters' would soon become the accepted social type – at which point I gathered the future might be in danger.

'Because testicles appear in pairs,' I continued, 'Hauptstein claims they symbolise the "ideal" friendship between men. That's why the boys patrol the streets two by two. Those who can't, or won't, live up to the Brotherhood's demands are demoted. The more inhibitions, the farther down the social ladder you belong. Women are not even admitted to the lower rungs, but have to remain on the ground. Their task is to give birth to and nurture children. Still, you may sink even deeper than that.'

'Wait, don't say anything. The lowest of the low . . .'

'Are the excluded third. The deviations. The grey sex. And people of that sort belong six feet under ground.'

Anton had heard of the Brotherhood, but had never taken their slogans seriously. Lowering his hands, he turned to face me. Reluctantly, he admitted I might have worries that could compete with his own. 'Hell, Sascha. At last I'm beginning to get a grip on the situation; then you venture out of your closet and stumble across a dead madame. That's damn inconvenient, if I may say so. As if I hadn't enough problems as it is!' He explained that the market had got harder in recent times. It was no longer enough to document waitresses who showed off their red behinds clad merely in adoring aprons, sandals on their feet, and lace tiaras in their hair.

'Was that what you did in the "black box" back at the Shanghai Bar? Documenting the secret life of your staff?'

Anton reached for my cigarettes. What if he had left Vienna because the authorities had begun to show an interest in the films he had shot in the room with the black door behind the pearl drapery? One of our old classmates, Erwin Winkler, had joined the police force, and the first thing he had done once he had nailed his diploma to the wall, was to raid Anton's love emporium. 'Revenge. Pure and simple. Now the bar's run by his mate – Willy Fischl, you know. I gather everything's back the way it used to be when Fischl's farce of a father tried to steady himself by gripping the beer taps.'

Anton admitted that our new hometown might not be the most cultivated capital in the world. But his cineaste studies of skimpy 'pony girls', trained by merry French peasants, had actually enjoyed acclaim among the noble and educated. In recent times, however, the business had fouled. For example, he had invested an entire year's income in a promising film about a stud farm outside the city. But nobody had wanted to see it, since the horses on show weren't trained hard enough – despite the fact that the finest thoroughbred of them all had been a creature so unusual even seasoned Germans ought to have been impressed. Anton swore. Once the taste for the different was awakened, it was difficult to satisfy. The audience's demand for exotic pleasures constantly increased. Those who had located the perverse streak in their souls continued to crave new pleasures however often their hunger was stilled. Riding lessons were no longer enough. If, as a director, one didn't test the limits of one's medium, sooner or later, the theatres would be empty. Anton groaned. He was almost ruined for the second time in only a few years.

'Was that why the police searched the Blue Cellar last winter?'

'Maybe. Rigoberto squealed when he wasn't paid double wages. As both mare and stud, he thought he . . .'

'And why you left Pension Andersen shortly thereafter?'

'Maybe.' Anton squeezed out his cigarette so carelessly it broke in half.

'And why Else turns ruby at the mere mention of your name?'

'Damn, Sascha! I just thought I might use her. She wouldn't have needed to do anything, just sit there and show some leg. There are people who actually appreciate that sort of thing.' Anton made a face as he noticed what he had done to his cigarette. 'But maybe it'll work anyway. I think I've realised where we might shoot the last scene. It'll give the film just the right edge of danger.' Asking for another cigarette, he told me he had used some of his father's more fanciful creations to pay for the tacit assistance of a contact whom Rigoberto had provided. In return, Anton had gained access to certain premises and equipment. But now, somehow, he was no longer able to summon any favours. This was especially irritating, since only the last scene of the new film remained to be shot. Set in a home for war convalescents, it would feature Molly as an adventurous nurse. In order to keep costs down for his white film, Anton had even volunteered to play the doctor himself.

'White?'

'Yes, white.' My friend explained there was a new genre that had gained popularity in recent times, in particular among veterans. The novelty was its supposed veracity. Everyone who had been wounded in the Great War recognised the instruments being used. That created a sense of fraternal bonding, which contributed to the overall aesthetic experience of the film. An oft-repeated scenario included a group of doctors who treated a young wounded soldier. In order for the injury not to get worse accidentally, the patient was tied to his bed, where doctors took turns examining him. Hauptstein was reported to be not uninterested in the genre. Anton had come up with a neat twist to the scenario, which he figured would allow him to corner the market and net him some serious money. 'A field hospital for female soldiers, Sascha! Imagine rows of incapacitated ladies sprawling in their beds, and Molly and me doing the rounds. With your colleague as a war heroine, it'd be a guaranteed success. I told her we'd even conduct "scientific" screenings – just like the ones your boss is doing. That way, everything might be kept close and informative. And I'd be able to avoid hassle from the authorities. But imagine, she would have none of it.'

Imagine. To get off the sordid topic, I wondered whether he knew what the two youths at the Blue Cellar were up to. To me, it looked as if they belonged to Hauptstein's organisation and were patrolling the streets.

'Just what I asked Klaus. "We're keeping things clean," came the answer. But Harro couldn't refrain from asking what I'd been up to at the Kreuzer.' Again he had tried to pull his knife, and if his friend hadn't nodded towards the ladies who had just emerged from the coffee shop across the street, Anton admitted there might have been a fight. I assumed he meant he was still carrying his stiletto.

'What happened?'

'Molly asked if I wanted to share a cab. I'm about to see her now. You've got matches?'

'That's not what I meant.' I handed him the box. 'What happened to Klaus and Harro? Why did they want to know what you . . .'

'I never told them what I had done at the hotel, if that's what you're worrying about.' Lighting up, Anton produced a big, fat ring that trailed placidly through the air. Then, irritated, he exhaled the rest of the smoke in one furious jet. 'For Chrissakes, Sascha, let it be! You've got your alibi, haven't you? Since there's nothing in your madame's flat to point in your direction, I can't see what you're fussing about. Do you remember the red-robed lady on the print in her living room? Well, if I were you, I'd follow her example and keep the lid closed. Who knows what secrets your friend kept?'

'I appreciate your concern,' I said. But as far as I could remember, the lady he was referring to had already lifted the lid, releasing an ominous waft of smoke that had begun to surround her – 'quite like the halo you just set loose.'

Unperturbed, my friend continued, nodding towards my bruises. 'I mean, you've already disturbed *somebody*'s peace of mind. If you don't know who it was, perhaps you ought to watch out? You might be next in line, you know.'

I considered the suggestion. No, I didn't know who had beaten me up. Nor why. If Dora's unknown visitor hadn't found the film clip – I no longer doubted that was what this was all about – he might conclude somebody else had stashed it. In which case it would be wise to take precautions. Probably the visitor had already figured out a third person had been in the flat. 'What do you propose?' I realised I sounded more anxious than I would have wanted. 'That I go up in smoke? Or do you plan to protect me?'

'Protect you? You mean . . .' Anton pulled his fingers through his hair. 'Well, I suppose I could. But only until tomorrow morning. Then I'll need my beauty sleep.' To my surprise, he held out the key to his room. 'And now, you'll have to excuse me. Molly's waiting.'

Chapter Eighteen

I spent the rest of the day in quiet public places and my own boisterous head. I couldn't forget what Else had said. Or what Inspector Manetti had asked me. What did I really know about Dora? Disregarding some private issues of sorrow and verity I thought it would be prudent not to investigate, I decided to make an inventory of the facts firmly in my possession. If nothing else, they might help me answer Anton's query about whose peace I had disturbed.

For example, I knew that my friend's name had been not Dora but Dorothea, not Wilms but Walther – at least for half her life. I knew that she hailed from Kolberg by the Baltic Sea, some three hundred kilometres, as well as thirty years, away from where I was currently lodged in space and time. I knew that, at sixteen years old, she had given birth to a child for whom she would remain the mother merely in spirit. I knew that she . . . I knew that she had decided to stay in the new city and had trained to become a secretary. I knew that quickly, however, she had grown tired of office work – 'Typing and headache, I tell you, that's all it was, typing and headache' – and resolved to make 'faster' money. I knew that she had perfectly straight shoulders and possibly the only hands in the world that could stir my spirits. I knew that, despite her slender, dangerous fingers, she had a talent for simple, reliable gestures. I knew that she never said yes without meaning it. I knew that she . . . That she, when I, that she . . . I knew that she, when I could no longer restrain myself but wailed: 'Dora, I can't,' merely replied: 'You can't what? Of course you can. You're extremely inventive,' and continued her exercises, dedicated and methodical. I knew that the more inventive I became, the more monosyllabic she would become. I knew that . . . I knew that, during the months we didn't see each other, she had decided to cut her hair short, allowing it to return to its pale, original colour. I knew that she used makeup cautiously, even reluctantly, which gave her a manly air – even more so with the short hair. I knew that last Friday she had pretended to visit the Apollo because of the film we were screening, but in reality she had tried to retrieve evidence in a clandestine battle against the Brotherhood. I knew that she . . .

No, there wasn't much I knew – not when, placing palm upon heart, I confessed that these were the facts I knew about Dora Wilms, so help me the Great Whoever. And when, finally, I could no longer avoid sampling some of those private residues of sorrow and verity, I realised the reason why she had asked me to hide in her closet might prove more treacherous than I'd like to think.

After the night in January, when fiction had done so humbly in the service of fact, we didn't see each other for a long time. I wanted to ask Dora, if not to forgive me, then at least to reconsider our partnership – had she only been willing to listen. But she had fled down the stairs, stating curtly, as she had vanished into the winter night, that I could spare myself the trouble. 'Life's a reel you can't rewind. You ought to know that, you know.' Her words had seemed so terse and mad and definitive.

Once I had returned upstairs, hot-faced and cold-footed, I lay awake into the small hours, contemplating the dull task of becoming, again, the person I've been for most of my life. Did I feel remorse, even shame? Frankly speaking? Of course. Pink-eyed and heavy-hearted, I understood I might even feel more than that. Yet love *is* unpredictable. After a few weeks, once I got over the malevolent part of the pain, the part that makes eating difficult and sleeping a hazard, I began to tell myself there was something else. After all, the reason why Dora had left me may not have been the name I had invented, but the person I had been the first few times I had called myself 'Anton'. That night when she had visited my place, I admit I may not have provided her with a full disclosure. But whatever she thought, I hadn't refrained from doing so out of spite. The impressions I had described *could* have been genuine – and that said quite enough, I thought. Wasn't the real problem, rather, that I missed the Fridays at Hotel Kreuzer? I knew that, for Dora, staying there merely meant a way of making money. 'You don't believe I'm here because I enjoy it, do you?' Outside of room 202, she didn't wish to be reminded of her ministrations as a minette. But just because my name wasn't Anton, the reason I had looked her up in the first place didn't simply disappear, did it?

Then I caught myself. Dora was no dupe. She must have understood that the person who had wriggled in her mirror and the one who had played English submarine in her bathtub were different aspects of the same being. Or that the projectionist who mounted newsreels at the Apollo was but another version of the impressionist with pencil in hand. Perhaps she was merely waiting for me to realise this? And act accordingly? I was far from certain. But if so, that might explain why she had deplored the fact I wasn't being honest even to myself. And why she clearly hadn't wanted me to get in touch again. What if I phoned her now, however, no longer pretending to be anyone but my own complicated self? Surely she'd have nothing against that?

As Dora lifted the receiver one sunny but fragile afternoon in early April, she sounded distant. Husky and hesitant, her voice made it evident she felt embarrassed – for my sake, I quickly gathered. Silently I cursed myself. Yet now there was no return. Putting on a brave, if invisible, face, I proceeded to some well-worded, light-hearted banter. And at last, after I had added, in a moment of dejected introspection, 'But in spite of all this, you know, in spite of all of this, I'm constructed mostly of human ingredients,' she laughed – admittedly, a bit sadly. In the wave of delight that now surged through me, I could just about make out Dora's reply. If I wanted to, she said, pronouncing the words as if they were foreign, we could meet the next evening, at the café across the street from the hotel. 'For old times' sake?' I wondered, surprised but elated, eager to discern her reaction between the heavy thumps of my heart. But all I could make out was a dry fizzle of static, then a click. She had hung up.

The next day, snowflakes flurrying in April fashion, I arrived half an hour early – full of mad expectation. Yet somehow more than an hour managed to pass, despite the fact that I was convinced, within moments, really, that the hands of the clock mounted above the counter must be rheumatic. When Dora finally appeared, three quarters of an hour late, I had just decided to get the bill. Now, instead, I asked the waiter if I could see the menu again, while she, having shed her coat, approached, walking between the tables with movements so cool they froze over by the time she reached mine. Dora wore her Amazon dress – tweed jacket and asymmetrical skirt – which gave her a gracious, vaguely aristocratic look. Having not yet cut her hair short, she had pulled it into a ponytail, which made it seem as if she had withdrawn into a hard state of being. In her hand, she was holding her wallet and cigarette case, as well as a folded paper. This would be difficult, I understood, swiftly reviewing a series of possible reactions before I decided to greet her in the strained but hearty manner reserved for moments when goodwill is mixed with guilty conscience.

Once we had ordered, I launched into a monologue about politics, motor sports and film – helter-skelter, without much rhyme or reason, mostly, I fear, in order to convince Dora, and possibly myself, that the world hadn't changed that dramatically since the last time we had seen each other. Did she realise today was Friday the thirteenth? Did she know a bomb had just gone off at the opening of the Milano fair? Had she heard that the Junek couple planned to take part in the German Grand Prix with the same Bugatti 35b with which Elizabeth had ended fifth in last year's race in Sicily? Or that Lya de Putti was playing in *Charlotte Somewhat Crazy*? A stunning performance, if I was permitted an opinion. Speaking of which, I added conspiratorially, Pabst would be filming in Berlin next autumn. Currently he was looking for the female lead. Raising an eyebrow, I declared I might know just the right person . . .

When, eventually, my more level-headed self caught up with the figure who, so recklessly, had rushed ahead, big on words but sparse on grace, Dora opened her cigarette case. While I rummaged around for matches, she explained that, believe it or not, she kept up with what was happening in the world like everyone else. Spreading the newspaper she had brought, she pointed to the headlines. 'ATTENTAT IN MILANO,' one read. 'ENGLAND AND THE QUESTION OF REPARATION' another. 'THE JUNEK COUPLE IN TANDEM' and 'VIENNESE TO FILM NEW PANDORA' a third and fourth, further into the paper. I chewed on my knuckles. 'Maybe you saw this one, too?' Opening the travel section, Dora turned the paper around for me to see. 'DISCOVER THE SECRET CONTINENT OF THE SEXES – IN COPENHAGEN!' a proud headline declared, printed in half-bold script above the main article on the page, some wordy piece regarding the new summer flights between Berlin and Moscow. No, I confessed, I must have missed that one.

I began to read the text, more out of discomfiture at our conversation than an inclination to explore the topic. The article turned out to be surprisingly informative, however. Apparently, Health Chancellor Froehlich planned to found the world's first league for sexual reform next summer. 'A brave charting of an unknown territory,' the paper surmised, urging its 'adventurous readers' to pay a visit to the Danish capital. The purpose of the gathering was to enable sexologists from near and far 'to fraternise, so as to explore the only province of love still unknown to man: the intimate region of the sexes'. I assumed the latter statement had motivated the silly choice of headline. But Dora didn't seem interested in my thoughts on titling policies. Instead she pointed to the photo that illustrated the article, a horizontal oval that contained a lot of stiff characters but little easy interaction. 'Do you recognise these people?'

I leaned forward. The picture wasn't merely elliptical in shape, but also hazy-edged in the manner of old portraits, so that it almost seemed, now that I think about it, to resemble a rheumy eye. Once I had inspected the iris, I realised what Dora meant. If I wasn't mistaken, the picture was an enlargement of a portion of the photo that had illustrated the article from which I had read the morning she took me to visit the Foundation. Hadn't it been a group portrait, I wondered, taken on the stairs leading up to the Foundation on the day of the inauguration?

Dora nodded. 'You should know. I gave you the paper with the original, remember.'

I recalled that, behind the people lined up, inscribed in the arched manner of an eyebrow, we had just about been able to make out Froehlich's famous motto, proclaiming that this was a place 'devoted to love and sorrow'. The employees had worn white coats and holy expressions, while their patients had been dressed in ordinary clothes and desolate looks. Unfortunately, I also remembered that I had said something to the effect that the two groups seemed to represent different football teams: the white-clad ones played for FC Love, the others for Sorrow United. Curtly, Dora had informed me the difference between such affiliations hardly depended on what kind of clothes one wore.

Now, studying the enlargement, I noticed the greyish aura that surrounded the head of the Foundation, who, standing next to his partner, seemed to bask in the glory of the moment. The other people in the portrait had been eliminated, however – or rather: it was still possible to make out, in the smeared area surrounding the centre of attention, one arm and half a face of the persons standing on either side of Froehlich and Gielke, the starched shirt-fronts of those lined up behind them, as well as the forehead of the boy sitting in tailor's position at their feet.

'Do you recognise them?' There was a seriousness to Dora's voice I couldn't interpret.

Why, yes, I thought so. The Health Chancellor wore glasses and laughed invitingly while the wind ruffled his hair. With a scarf draped around his shoulders, Gielke contented himself with a prudish but polished smile. Thanks to the enlargement, I could see that Froehlich held his partner under the arm, whereas Gielke had placed his free hand on the shoulder of the boy in front of the couple. I told Dora I hadn't noticed that the last time we had inspected the picture. The photo was unfocused, the details hard to make out. 'But surely that's the hand of the Health Chancellor emerging from under the arm of Gielke? And that's Gielke's resting, like an epaulet, on the boy's shoulder?'

Dora didn't answer. Instead, she traced the contour of the picture with her finger. 'I believe the editor's trying to illustrate Froehlich's notion that the sexologist's gaze may penetrate into the private spheres of man. As if the Health Chancellor wished to say the vital thing about a person's sexuality is what we behold. As far as our intimate life is concerned, there's more than meets the eye.' She raised her head. 'Isn't that so, Anton – sorry, Sascha?'

Since, at this moment, our beverages arrived with a glassy clatter, I refrained, tactfully, from replying. I'm not sure I know how to describe the feeling that came over me, once the waiter had left and Dora had smoothed out her paper. But I discovered that I recognised everything she did with her hands – and that I missed their deft economy more than ever. Not, however, in the manner that pricks and pains you and prevents you from savouring sleep. And that's what surprised me, before the sensation shaded into something different, something softer, something more like . . . Well, a premonition, perhaps. What I discovered was at once more tepid and more sweet. Suddenly I intuited that I might not love Dora after all, at least not in the way one's supposed to. Rather, I sensed, I might cherish her the way one does a person who's always been present in one's life, somebody who's both more than a friend and less than a partner – in fact, someone quite like . . .

'Do you still have the paper, Sascha?' Dora held up her hand. 'If so, I'd be interested to know who the others were standing next to Froehlich and Gielke – all those people whom the editor seems to believe belong to the blinked-away part of history.' Interrupted in mid-thought, I lit her cigarette. The others in the picture? On the oval photo in the paper, I could only make out sections of the men to the left and right of the Health Chancellor and his partner. Mr Left was present with one arm, whereas Mr Right, turning away from the camera so that only a shoulder could be seen, seemed ready to fuse with the shadows. But at the very front, I saw the pimply forehead of an adolescent.

I recalled that the boy, who had been sitting with fists clenched in his lap, had made us speculate. 'That must be the future heir of the place,' I had ventured – and added, as Dora hadn't deigned to reply: 'He seems to be a bad egg, that one. Just look at those pimples, that back, those fists. He's angry at the entire world!' With two fathers, I had gone on, perhaps that's the way things turn out? 'Enjoying his moment of fame, Froehlich seems oblivious to any parental obligation. And although Gielke has put his hand on the boy's shoulder, he doesn't appear too caring, does he?' It was at this point that Dora had retorted, somewhat snappishly I had thought, that it was about time I considered the sexual question 'soberly'. Then, impersonating a wry mobster, she had pressed the paper into my hands and proposed we visit her friend who worked at the Foundation.

Now, a year later, she rolled her cigarette against the edge of the ashtray, calmly stating that one may not always be aware of what one sees. Since that seemed a promising proposition, I waited for her to continue. But instead Dora asked me to inspect the picture closer. 'Do you see these fingers here?' She pointed. 'They appear to belong to a right hand, don't they? If so, that would mean it can't be Gielke who has placed his hand on the boy's shoulder. It can only be the person to the right here – whoever that is.' I wondered whether it mattered who Mr Right was. 'Maybe, maybe not,' Dora replied, reminding me of what Karp had told us about the various interests of the people working at the Foundation. That certainly was a fascinating topic, I agreed, not terribly convinced. Yet didn't we have more pressing matters to discuss? Folding up the paper, Dora looked at me distantly. 'Like what?'

'Don't you see?' I realised I was disappointed.

'I can't read thoughts.'

Recognising the moment had come, I swallowed whatever pride I had left. 'The first time we went out,' I began, looking for the appropriate words, 'you claimed you disliked people who didn't stand up for who they were. If I understood you correctly, that would be people who disguise themselves.' Dora turned towards the window. I admitted I ought to have told her my real name. But the more times we had met, the more difficult it had become. And then, after that occasion when she had speculated about the letters in my name, it had become downright impossible. No, there was no denying 'Anton' wasn't my real name. Still . . . Dora looked at me, puzzled. 'The *A*, "hard and taut",' I reminded her, 'rising like a mountaintop. The *o*, "soft and pliable", reminiscent of a well. And after that, I couldn't . . .'

'Oh, I see what you're saying.' Dora flicked off some ash. 'You mean it was my fault you didn't tell me the truth.' Again, her movements had taken on that hard quality that made her seem to recede inwardly.

'No, no,' I hastened to explain. But perhaps she might imagine there were people who disguised themselves, yet didn't necessarily think they were lying? People who, on the contrary, thought that, in this way, they'd bring their true selves a little closer? Dora seemed less than convinced. 'Anyway, it's like this,' I said, mustering my remaining courage. 'Last year, during one of my visits to the hotel, you told me you thought it would be nice if we were siblings. That was before you proposed we come down here, to this café – before, you know, before we became partners. But evidently I had seemed so serious you feared you might disappoint me if you broke the spell.'

'So what?' Again, Dora looked out the window.

'Well, I've been thinking about what you said. And I'd like to state,' I declared, 'that I wouldn't be disappointed . . .' The darkness that had eased up to the window must have been peculiarly captivating, because Dora seemed unable to detach herself from it. Nervously I fiddled with my glass, wondering whether it might not be more prudent to ask for the bill. Then I decided it was now or never. 'I wouldn't be disappointed, I mean, if you considered me your . . . You know, if you considered me your brother.'

Slowly Dora turned towards me, her eyes black, plain, simple. 'You can't be serious.'

Ten tongue tied minutes later, I tried to dispel the gloom that had descended upon us by suggesting we go for a walk. If I had known what I know today, I would have acted differently. But last winter, I was still hoping the time spent together would not have been in vain. I could understand she didn't want to see me privately, not after all the disappointments; I could even understand she didn't want to see me professionally, like in old times, on Fridays. But somehow I failed to understand what was wrong with becoming close again – more than friends, yet less than spouses.

As we emerged on the street, the weather was wintry in the dispirited way it tends to be shortly before it turns, once and for all, to spring. The snow had not settled, but the pavement was wet and slippery, the wind sharp and erratic. Dora shoved her gloved hands into her pockets, then began to walk south. I followed. We continued for several blocks without exchanging a word. Now and then, we studied the shop windows, but neither of us said anything. After a while, we reached one of the city's main streets. Hanging in a doorway, an abandoned sign declared: 'NAKED MAN ALONE IS EMANCIPATED!'

'That's easy for him to say,' I joked, nodding towards Adolf Koch's headquarters for Socialist body culture. Dora merely yawned. Gradually and gratefully, the street changed character: the empty shops became less frequent, the peopled housing blocks more dominant. As for of us, we continued in our private spheres, careful not to cross each other's orbit. A few missed intersections later, we turned into a side street, then into another one. Now we were heading north again, back in the direction whence we had come, albeit along a parallel street. There was hardly any traffic and no commerce to speak of. The few streetlights barely managed to illuminate the rim of the naked trees, studded with raindrops, and the odd car roof. A smell of coal and despair hung in the air.

Suddenly, I stumbled in the dark between two streetlights and blurted something about 'the people's cry for light'. I was alluding to Koch's famous slogan, hoping it would cheer up the mood. But Dora merely raised her hands and began, calmly, to walk along a crack that wormed its way between the cobblestones. 'At least I see where I'm putting my feet.' Placing one foot in front of the other, as if she were walking on a tightrope, she advanced carefully but competently. Getting to my feet again, I brushed my knee. 'Try yourself,' Dora said, making a motion with her hand, as if taking off a pince-nez. 'You may borrow my perspective. But you have to see with your own eyes.'

'Thanks,' I said, relieved that at last we seemed to be on the right track. For some reason, I recalled another of Koch's battle cries: 'EVERYBODY SHOULD KNOW NAKEDNESS + SUN + AIR = MORE LIFE!' How could something be 'more' or 'less' life, I wondered to myself, palpating my bruised knee. Surely the world consisted of nothing but singularities, nothing but incomparable persons? As soon as one added them up, one made a mistake that wasn't merely arithmetical in nature. I didn't believe in 'everybody', as Koch seemed to do, but in *each* individual. Those fanatics of nakedness, I thought grimly, assumed they had unique access to life's inner secrets. Through an act as apparently self-evident as shedding their clothes, strangers would relieve themselves of secondary attributes, throw mores and taboos overboard, and congregate in a collective as exulting as insulting, dressed merely in their names. To me, that seemed like a sum that was less than its parts.

I knew what it looked like at the Lunabad on Sundays. The cold water, the sunlamps and the massage boards were at everybody's disposal. The medicine-balls and the Bulgarian yogurt, too. But it was quite enough to hear the slapping sound of flip-flops against wet tiles for this Adamic state to separate people again. As soon as a gentleman appeared, wearing nothing but rubber slippers and silver monocle, the other guests would click their naked heels and make room. That's the way reality looked. Equal to the bones. Oh, sure. Did people really think their social stripes vanished merely because they weren't sporting a single piece of clothing? Why would nakedness be a truer state of a person's being than others?

Dora crossed the street. Limping twenty metres behind, I watched her coat flicker between the trees and parked cars. But did she keep her head high or lowered? High. Lowered. No, high. (Had she thrown herself into a game of hopscotch?) Abruptly I became aware of my boots, squeaking like a caged animal. Putting one shod foot against the other leg's knee, I inspected the sole: the seams had cracked, the metal plate had been lost. Either I must re-sole them or else I had to buy a new pair. I promised myself to have a word with Anton about the matter. As I turned to look across the street again, Dora had vanished. Wherever I looked, I couldn't see her. All I discovered was a gentleman walking towards me, with bright, brisk steps, seemingly involved in a pantomime. Hardly had he noticed me before he lifted his hat, greeting me ceremoniously, and returned to the recalcitrant buttons of his overcoat.

Where had she gone? Should I cross the street or stay on my side? Dora hadn't sneaked across, had she? I turned round. No, just the vigorous gentleman. But this was absurd! Was I mistaken after all? Perhaps she wasn't angry with me for having suggested that we may become siblings, but merely displeased by my allusions to the advantages of nakedness? If so, fine. Koch's set of people certainly seemed preferable to the associations for body culture which only welcomed men of an approved type. At the congregations organised by the city's apostle of Socialist nakedness, at least all sexes and all classes were mixed. Nobody was too young or too old, too dishevelled or too hideous, to be barred from participation. Profession, looks and age; income, political persuasion and religious faith: everybody was welcome. With the help of a little sun and a lot of discipline, inhibitions were shed. People forgot their ailments, regained their confidence, and devoted themselves to the wonders of eurhythmics. Why, that was fantastic! The fact that most of them had tanned faces and underarms but chalk-white bodies obviously played no role. Nor were tattoos, scars or calluses social markers. Of course not. But the drill and the declarations, then? The food rationing and the punishment for young boys who suffered from involuntary erections? Perhaps Adolf Koch didn't exaggerate the function of paradise as an ideal for society. But was a naked body ever only naked, ever only body?

I considered the alternatives. If I returned home, we'd be able to avoid a quarrel, but weren't likely to meet again. If, on the other hand, I went over to Otto-Ludwig-Straße, we might see each other, yet who would be able to prevent the dispute I was sure would ensue? Not much of a choice, I admitted – then it occurred to me: perhaps Dora hadn't returned home, but gone to Hotel Kreuzer? That might be her way of demonstrating that, if we were to begin anew, it could only happen where we met the first time. Why, otherwise, would she have offered to lend me her perspective? Clearly she wanted me to see things from her point of view. No, she didn't need a brother. But if I wanted to, I could remain her sister!

Although it was a daring thought, I found no reason to question its thrust. Instead, irritation left me like a spurned ghost, and I began to walk valiantly, almost victoriously, boots squeaking boldly. Five minutes later, I entered the foyer of the hotel, face flushed and clothes steaming. With a lazy but bemused look, the porter detached himself from his crossword. 'Herr Honig?' he inquired reluctantly. I greeted him energetically, then raced up the stairs, shaking my head. 'Next time, sir. No time for crosswords today!' Gingerly walking along the corridor, I checked my appearance. This was wonderful. A few moments more, then we'd be back where we had begun – in room 202! No more mistakes, no more misunderstandings, only frank desire and delightful dissimulation.

But when I knocked, briskly and expectantly, nobody opened. I tried again. No, nothing. I tried yet again. And again nothing. Despite my insights, I must have been wrong. Hell. Hell. Hell. How could I have been so foolish? And what would I do now – with all my feverish goodwill, all my educated nonsense?

Exhausted, I sank to the floor. My feet felt cold, my limbs stiff and sore. At the same moment as I bent forward to undo my boots, the lights went out. This time, however, I didn't allow myself to be provoked. Instead I took off my coat, disentangled the damp shoelaces, and placed my boots next to me. Legs extended, I tried to wriggle my extremities. The socks were chilly and wet. Yet for each minute that passed, my soles turned softer, and finally I could even feel the cold sweat between my toes. It was a reassuring sensation, not unlike the one experienced when the bathtub is emptied out or a seat is suddenly made available in the tram. Life returns to normal; existence regains its proper dimensions. I got out my cigarettes. A few peaceful minutes and a couple of last, well-intended thoughts, then I'd leave and never bother Dora again. Looking around, I realised it might be nicer to enjoy the dark than to get up and hit the ticking switch every minute. Besides, it might have a soothing effect on my jittery heart. The match flicked, flared, and died.

It wasn't until I extinguished my cigarette a few minutes later that I realised I wasn't alone – and hadn't been since I had knocked on the door. From inside, a muted noise could be heard, as when a body repositions itself. Suddenly the dark, tightening, seemed to breathe. I pricked my ears, yet couldn't make out any other movement. Still, I was certain I wasn't alone. My spine tensed, my ears shrank, my soles turned hot. Then the latch came down and the door opened. Somewhere above me, I could hear Dora speak: 'What's wrong with you? Why can't you use your imagination for better purposes? Not to make up for your blunders, but to help those without the means to?' She paused, then added: 'If only you knew how fed up I am with this place, with the people who come knocking, with the things they want to do. It really has very little to do with *my* sexual question.' She bit her lower lip, about to say something more. Then she changed her mind. 'Trust me,' she added quietly. 'A brother's not what I need.'

That was all. The next time we met was three months later, at the Apollo.

Chapter Nineteen

Towards evening, I returned to Pension Landau. Nobody was around as I reached the second floor. To judge from the musty air that met me as I entered the hallway, the inhabitants were having dinner somewhere secret in the flat (nothing confidential about that night's fare, though: beans and pork). I walked along the corridor, the air getting fresher with each creaking step, and inserted my key under number 6, which was gently glinting in the dark and placed, for some reason, just next to the handle. The window was still open. As I took off my jacket, I became aware of a sound that I've always associated with summer evenings. It's merely a low sort of hiss, or rather a hum, supple and stealthy, barely perceptible, but impossible to ignore once you've picked it up. I doubt one should attach any significance to it. Yet for me, its soft, sad sway is summer's own sonority, and I can listen to it for hours. I've always thought that inside it is a multitude of sounds from which time cannot force life. No, it's true.

Having examined the room – not much of interest, not even in the pockets of Anton's other jacket – I turned the sheets and lay down. From the adjacent room, a giggle untangled itself. A woman said something with muted voice; a man grumbled happily.

I knitted my fingers under my neck, ready to fuse with the soft opacity of summer. After a while, impressions began to transform, willy-nilly, into thoughts. Although Anton had stayed at Landau's for more than half a year by now, there were no personal touches to his room. Wasn't that strange? I knew that, despite his tall tales, he'd never been one to embellish the circumstances of his existence. Yet how could anyone fail to put his mark, however faintly, on how he lived?

During my earlier examination of the room, I had discovered a complete set of toiletries on the shelf above the washstand (wrinkly Chlorodont tube, tangled toothbrush, rusty razor), some dirty clothes thrown pell-mell into a corner, and a locked suitcase underneath the bed. But no pictures on the walls, no documents wedged between mattress and bedframe. And not a single personal item anywhere – save for underneath the chair, where I discovered a pair of white women's boots. I guessed my friend had received them from his father, although I wasn't certain Mr Lakritz was still alive. I remembered Anton's father as a handsome man, with a melancholy baritone and a heart spacious enough for everybody in our neighbourhood – except perhaps people of Friedrich Fischl's sort, who spoke of 'people' as if there was room only for one. Every September, he would resole people's shoes in return for whatever they could manage without: lamb chops wrapped in sticky newspaper, a basket full of vegetables, a wooden horse . . . And every April, anyone who needed new shoelaces got them for free. As for a Mrs Lakritz, however, I never met her. The only time I asked Anton about his mother, he responded, surprisingly tense: 'Not here.' And with that, I understood, one had to content oneself.

My friend was reticent – some people are by birth, others by habit. Already, early on, I realised Anton belonged to the latter category. Over the years, his ability to answer evasively became so developed he almost always made me regret having asked. 'Who knows, who knows,' he'd reply, as usual without the question mark. He didn't do it out of spite, however, he just didn't want anyone to get too close. Most things in his life were 'for women only'. Still, I don't think even they ever became intimate with him in any sense other than the conventional one. When I was young, this saddened me, since I assumed it meant our friendship didn't matter as much to him as it did to me. As I grew older, however, I realised that the consideration Anton demanded from me, without stating it directly, may have saved it. At least he never seemed to have any other friends – only what he referred to as 'company' or 'contacts'. As far as I was concerned, that would have made me feel impoverished. But Anton didn't seem to mind. Nonetheless, even he must be keeping his feelings and confidences somewhere.

The bed squeaked, which made me think of the suitcase. Perhaps I ought to check it? Sitting up, I pulled it out between my legs. Once I had reshaped a coat hanger, the lock was easy to pick. The mechanism clicked a few times, then snapped open. Regrettably, the suitcase didn't contain any great surprises: some clean underwear, a universal picklock of the sort favoured by locksmiths (I guessed that was the way Anton had managed to get inside Dora's), a brown envelope with two fat wads of franc bills and a tacky cherry pip, as well as, strangely, a French study about tattooing. The book, still uncut, had been written by a certain '*Karp, Adele, lic. méd., sous la direction des mssrs Hervé Jacquet, prof. de méd., et Martin Froehlich, dr. méd.*' I was about to close the suitcase again when I pressed my hand against the underwear and found something hard. No, it wasn't what one might expect. Wrapped inside a pair of Anton's underpants was a Valiant stiletto.

Putting everything – well, *almost* everything – back as I had found it, I shoved the suitcase under the bed and adjusted the pillow under my head. Only four days earlier, I had got off my Torpedo three tube stations away from where I now was. It felt like an eternity ago; it *was* an eternity ago. If I hadn't accepted Dora's invitation and cycled across the city, filled with such mad elation, would anything that had happened since really have occurred? Perhaps she'd still be able to conduct a life 'under ordered circumstances', as the *Tageblatt* chose to express it? And

I would have been left in peace, bothered neither by thugs nor by the police – to say nothing of the vexation I was getting to know as my conscience?

No, that was naive. At best, I would have been able to maintain my innocence. (I'm speaking, of course, metaphorically.) Whatever happened at Dora's would have occurred even if I hadn't been hiding in her closet. I might have been able to avoid difficulties of a personal nature, but as far as Dora was concerned, nothing would have changed. She had been in genuine danger – and in that case, what kind of innocence was mine? It sounded more like ignorance. Awkwardly, I realised there were times when one was guilty, even if one hadn't done anything personally.

The fact was I had misunderstood Dora when she had expressed the wish to see me 'under different circumstances'. The fact was she must have ended her life as a minette. The fact was she hadn't been looking for a sibling. The fact was, too, I had taken cover in her closet, however much I wished to pretend otherwise. The very least I could do now, when it might prove to be too late already, was to assume responsibility for my actions – even if that meant the truth about me would come out. I recalled the song I had heard, drifting in from the gramophone in Dora's living room, carrying the unmistakable scent of sexual promise:

> Drive, obscure, I'm in your wicked hands,
> all shrewd ache and furtive glance.
> Drive, obscure, you deny me nothing,
> three years in jail for one thing.

Uncomfortable, I realised the words of the great Rigoberto might come true sooner than I'd prefer.

While I continued to listen to the hot, humming summer, so akin to the dark in Dora's closet, I considered again what I knew. It was depressingly little. Hardly had I managed to articulate my first insight, before I realised it must be made more precise.

Certainly, it was true that Dora had expected me – yet only an hour later than I had assumed: not at five in the afternoon, but at six. I was the one who had got the time wrong, excited that it was once again Friday in the old style. Which immediately produced another insight: however much I wished to believe differently, Dora hadn't expected me to dress up in the manner reserved for room 202. Which is to say: she hadn't been waiting for 'Anton'.

Whom then? Did the doorbell suggest she was now seeing customers at home? If Lakritz was to be believed, the Vice Squad had searched Hotel Kreuzer recently. Still, I found it difficult to believe that Dora had shifted her business to Otto-Ludwig-Straße. She, who insisted that every person needed their privacy, would hardly have been able to enjoy hers had her bedroom been performing double duty as a workspace. It was more likely she had decided to give up her life as minette. If her guest hadn't been a customer, then, I wondered whether that precluded visits from other persons Dora might have known from the hotel – and decided it must. Whoever had pressed the buzzer must be either a friend so close that she felt no need to make a note of the visit or, on the contrary, somebody she couldn't possibly have expected. There was no third option. Against the former alternative spoke the fact that Dora hadn't urged me to return an hour later. Surely she would have done so if she had made arrangements with someone else at 5p.m.? Against the latter spoke the fact that she had shown the visitor into the living room, and even put on a record, while I was getting ready in the closet. Would she have done so if she had been expecting only me?

As soon as I rotated a thought in my mind, it turned out to contain others. Intermittently, however, I had the sensation there was something hovering close by, almost like the shadow of a thought. One moment, it floated next to me; the next, it vanished among other, vaguer forms of motion. But most of the time it seemed just out of reach, spectral and inscrutable, as if it wanted to mislead, no, to spurn, no, to spur me. Something I hadn't thought of, something I must have overseen, was teasing and tantalising me. Lying on Anton's bed in the dark, I grew increasingly frustrated with my own slow-wittedness. It felt as if I was fumbling for a shadow that, in the obvious but evasive way of obscure phenomena, somehow corresponded to myself – to my true self, even. If only I could see clearly for once! One moment, I was convinced there was something moving in the dark, driven but indistinct; the next, I couldn't prevent it from dissolving into . . .

Wait. Did I say 'my true self? Wasn't *that* the expression Dora had used? I thought back. Indeed. When we met at the Apollo, she had said it would be nice to see me again, adding after a pause sated with suggestion: 'your true self'. What if I had been wrong in spite of everything? Suddenly it felt terribly important to hold on to this thought. It yielded only faint light, like the flattened beam underneath a door. Nonetheless I knew I was onto something. I lay motionless in my friend's bed, fearful that the smallest movement might make whom- or whatever was on the other side of the door trip away on teasing toes. Finally it dawned on me: what happened at Dora's *had* to do with 'Anton'. But who said that had to be yours truly? Couldn't it just as well be the person in whose bed I was reclining? After all, Lakritz had admitted he took on a different name after the police raid against Pension Andersen last winter. Hadn't he seemed conspicuously blasé when we met at the Blue Cellar, playing with his glass of beer and smoking jadedly, even falling asleep at one point? I had supposed it was because of what I had told him. To Anton's experienced ears, my story must have seemed routine. Upon reflection, however, I realised his attitude might just as well have been due to the fact that he already knew what I told him. In which case . . . In which case the real question was why *this* Anton had visited Dora!

Heart pounding, thoughts racing, I considered what my friend had told me. At the moment he claimed to be finishing a 'white' film with Molly cast as a nurse. By donating a few of his father's creations to a collector, he had been able to use certain premises and equipment. That person must be Felix Karp. During my and Dora's visit last year, the doctor had explained that, in order to acquire rare items for the museum, he occasionally offered therapeutic services in return. Didn't the book on tattooing that I had found in Anton's suitcase indicate they knew each other? Probably it was through Karp that Anton had first heard of Dora. Or. Wait. No, the other way round. It must have been through Karp that Dora first had heard of Lakritz. Naturally, the name had awakened her suspicions. If she hadn't met Anton personally, there was no way she could have known *I* wasn't hiding behind the name. That must have been why she had visited the Apollo last week: not to see me, but in order to find out whether *I* dealt in white films – and perhaps even was a member of the Brotherhood. Fortunately, Else had sorted things out. And once Dora had realised there was another Anton, one who might even be in competition with Hauptstein, she had invited me home. Or rather: my true self – Sascha.

I wasn't yet able to tell how Lakritz had managed to find out that Dora had something in her possession he might use to black-mail Hauptstein. As far as I remembered, I had never told him about her. Still, the world in which the two of them moved probably was smaller, and a lot less of a mystery, than I imagined. Anton had seemed surprisingly willing to help me retrieve the bicycle clips. Would he have done so merely for my sake? Also, he claimed to have found the clips by the mirror in the hallway. But I was almost convinced only a paper and Dora's keys had been on the table when I raced through the flat, panic mounting in my breast, confusion spreading like fire in my head. Wouldn't I have noticed if they'd been there? Why, yes – as long as they weren't already in Anton's pockets . . .

Again I thought of the movements I had made out, pressing my hot ear against the cool closet door. Unsure whether they belonged to a male or a female, I had decided it was a man if Dora invited the person into the living room, a woman if they went into the kitchen. Since the commotion seemed to come from the kitchen, I had assumed Dora enjoyed female company. Yet it really was impossible to determine the sex of a person merely by way of the sounds they made with their body. Not only was I mistaken about the visitor, but Dora had been in need of help. A few minutes later, as I had thought she was dragging a surprise into the bedroom, it had already been too late. Whoever had placed the lifeless body on the bed had searched the room with impatient hands and hurried motions – first the night table, then the cupboard, and finally the chair on which my clothes were lying. I had surmised it was Dora looking for cigarettes. But it might just as well have been Anton, trying to find the film. Even if he hadn't been able to tell that the clothes on the chair belonged to me, he must have recognised my bicycle clips. Suddenly, he had understood I was seeing Dora. Recalling the name he was using, he must have realised the police would assume the clips belonged to the murderer. And at that point, at the very latest, Anton had stopped looking for the film. In order to protect himself – or me (which, in this case, amounted to the same thing) – he had pocketed my clips and left the flat. A few minutes later, I had stepped out of the closet, expecting a rather different scene.

Not until later the same night, when we had met at the Blue Cellar, did Anton realise I had been hiding among Dora's clothes. That must have been why he had volunteered to search the flat. On Saturday night, having picked Dora's lock, he had pretended to look for my clips, while in reality he had tried to retrieve the film. The only thing he had found, however, was the wooden horse. I still lacked evidence in support of my speculations. And I supposed it was possible that Anton had found what he was looking for. Yet I doubted it. Wasn't it more likely he had concluded the precious film clip was no longer in Dora's flat?

Lying in my friend's bed, I realised that, if I hadn't insisted on becoming the sibling whom I assumed Dora had thought of when she referred to my 'true self', she would have been able to tell me about the real Anton. And if I hadn't remained speechless, as well as near-motionless, in her closet, nothing would have happened to her. My lack of action was more than lamentable, it was close to criminal. Sister or not, I had played the customer when I ought to have become her confidant.

The least I could do now was to try to complete what Dora had set out to do – not using my imagination to project my own wishes and fancies, but in order to help those without the means to. But how? Time passed while I listened to the soft hum of the summer night. Finally, when the light turned a greyish pink and the birds began to stir, I had invented a plan.

Chapter Twenty

As I opened my eyes again, the room was brimming with sunlight. Because of the curtain that just barely covered the window, the light had a flimsy, whipped-up character. From the other side of the wall, two different sorts of snoring penetrated: one fickle, thinning kind of sound and one full-fledged, fervent version. Receding wave and heaving ocean. It must have been the latter that broke over me. Rubbing my eyes, I stretched out and felt surprisingly complete – as if suddenly, ripe with recognition, I was properly part of the world again. My limbs no longer hurt, my muscles no longer tensed. With the exception of a blurry sensation of pain that I located somewhere on my left side, below my heart, I felt re-vindicated – at least from a biological standpoint. To make sure, I ran my hands across my face. No, no bruises, merely crusts and nocturnal gravel clotting the eye pockets.

Shedding the sheet, I shut my eyes anew. The morning sun was only a few hours old, yet it already packed considerable heat. It would be another spectacular summer day. Breathing calmly, I tried to collect myself. If I wanted my plan to succeed, I needed to gather all available resources. Pressing my arms against my body, I made a few flapping motions with my elbows. Slowly I could feel my scrotum scroll up and my penis swell in tiny, clever jerks, which eventually managed to wriggle it out of the humid lair of hair and skin in which it had been resting – before it fell, rather clumsily, to the side. After a discouraging interval, however, while my thoughts trailed and my flopping flagged, it turned upwards with regained confidence, this time bending across the groin with steady pulse beats, before coming again to a quivering kind of rest, hovering diagonally above my belly and almost touching my navel. Now that the turning motion had subsided, instead of swelling, my sex stiffened. Rolling down unaided, one side of the foreskin was momentarily stuck in a painful manner. But then the curly hair that had got involved let go, and the skin, gathered, curled up in the manner of a turtleneck. Subsequently, for each pounding beat that squeezed through this particular part of my anatomy, I hardened – until jerkily, my sex raised itself off my belly and became, well, furiously present.

I stopped flapping my arms. Now that all my attention was devoted to this red and aching thing, I noticed other things as well. For example, that the bulging vessels were thickening so sturdily with blood, from the hirsute root all the way up to the lower rim of the glans, that it positively hurt. Probably the bared hood had already begun to shift in bluish nuances, with whitening patches just above the point where the skin is attached. Tactfully, however, I refrained from verifying this. Nor did I allow myself to be seduced by the dreamy images and movements of considerable daring that now hovered within reach of my consciousness. Instead I concentrated on becoming one with my sex. The morning sun was glowing obliviously, so I'm pretty convinced my experiment would have succeeded, had I not shoved my palms under the small of my back in order to raise my hips into the air. This innocent movement, which solely served to press a little more of myself into the tight sheath that demanded such attention, broke the spell. Suddenly the air went out of me. Flustered and deflated, I witnessed how speedily what might be the most independent-minded part of a man's body transformed itself into a lifeless lump of skin, with some wretched wetness glistening in its shrivelled crack, like a tear-filled, squinting eye.

Bored, I began to look for my underwear. Clearly, full biological 'elevation' was impossible. There was no sex without images or fantasies, memories or dreams – in short: without history. Having attended to various needs in the bathroom, I tripped back into Anton's room. As I discovered myself in the rusty mirror, I inspected my face. What had once been a puffy black eye had turned into a patch of yellow colouration. In the upper corner, there was a green-hued shadow, cast almost as an afterthought, but apart from that, only my lip, still bruised, offered evidence that I had been involved in a fight. I removed a crust that had got stuck in my hair, then combed myself. A few minutes later, polishing my shoes with a section of the curtain, I promised myself to remember what I had just experienced. I retrieved my trousers, which I had placed under the mattress, and put a few things in my pockets. Anton hadn't told me when he'd return, only that I should leave the door unlocked, with the key on the inside. If my suspicions were correct, I needed to be careful: my friend had to be lulled into a sense of security. Scribbling a quick note on a piece of paper, I thanked him for his hospitality. Then I inserted the key into the lock and left.

An hour later, I emerged into the blinding light just south of the cemetery near where I live. Under my feet, the rumbling train continued its light-shy journey through the underworld. On the wasteground where I had been mugged a few nights earlier, Chérie was running in loops, caught up in some self-indulgent fancy. A paper and a blanket were lying in the grass next to the dense foliage. Just as I considered taking the paper, one of the construction workers from the square pushed aside some heavy branches and emerged. As he noticed me, buttoning his fly and drying his hands on his trousers, he muttered: 'You'll see . . .' Kicking half-heartedly in the direction of Chérie, he retrieved his *Völkischer Beobachter* as well as his blanket, and left. I tried to attract the attention of Heino's simple-minded dog, who was now sniffing the bushes. But since she didn't proffer the least sign of recognition, I continued home.

Although it was no more than eight o'clock, work was in full swing. At the construction site next to the coal cellar, men were sawing, hammering and spreading wet concrete onto rusty red bricks. They seemed fewer than usual, but just as full of purpose as ever. Soon the heat would turn oppressive and the tarmac, softening, would begin to stick. At this early hour, however, the day had a pleasant freshness to it, and the workers, still sober, hadn't yet started to foul the air with political profanities. The sun dazzled the windows; a lazy wind stirred the treetops. I entered the bakery, where I bought a vanilla doughnut and some milk. Munching, I thought this was as close as one was likely to get to summer among pastries. The soft, surprisingly elastic bread, the warm, yolky cream, the coarse, crunching sugar . . . Like a greedy god, I devoured an entire season in a few ravenous bites.

Having purchased the *Tageblatt* and cigarettes at the kiosk, I pushed open the door to my building and entered the cool, soothing dark. This time, however, I had no luck. As my eyes adjusted to the light, Mrs Britz emerged from her flat wearing a glorious grin and two pillows that looked more like protuberances than padding. 'Got anything for me then, Knisch? Ivan's ready, you know.' To make sure I'd honour our agreement, she added, with ill-disguised satisfaction, adjusting the carpet beater she had squeezed under her arm like a tennis racket, that she had already informed the neighbourhood of who the new proprietor would be.

'It's only Wednesday today,' I replied serenely, brushing away some sugar crumbs. Inwardly, however, my heart sank at the thought that I had less than two days to come up with the remaining rent owed. A car went by. Then the door shut with a delayed thump.

'Thursday follows Wednesday – and then there's always Friday. But perhaps not in your calendar, Knisch?'

'I count the week like everybody else, Mrs Britz. Thank you, Mrs Britz. Goodbye, Mrs Britz.' My landlady followed me, step by step, up the stairs – first with her eyes, then with her ears.

But I was too far away to hear what she shouted at the very end. It sounded like 'surprise'.

In any event, there can be no better designation for what awaited me when I reached the fourth floor. My door was ajar, and I was just about to open it, curious, when an uproarious thunder unsettled the toilet between my flat and my neighbour's. Presently, the former sergeant at the Potsdam garrison emerged. Holding his pyjama trousers with one hand, Mr Vogelsang carefully patted his sparse hair with the other. I took him under the arm. Reluctantly he leaned against me while shuffling to his flat with bent back and short steps. 'Heading for the front, are we, Knisch?' The few tufts of hair that still framed his head stood straight up, and, in the manner of old men, he hadn't shaved equally conscientiously everywhere. Here and there, bits of toilet paper with rusty patches were attached to his rough skin. I tried to remove them, but Mr Vogelsang withdrew his face and pointed to my door – fingers trembling, and lips, too. 'Mind your own business, Knisch. A cuirassier will bow only to superiors.' Indignantly he added, as if it had anything to do with the matter: 'Next time, you should trick the enemy into coming during daytime. No more manoeuvres in the dark!' Whereupon he hobbled into his flat, locking his door with what seemed to be ten different keys.

Cuirassiers? Enemies? Manoeuvres in the dark? I pushed open the door with my index finger. Diels and Pieplack had hardly left my flat in an irreproachable state, but the mess caused by their search was nothing compared to the mayhem awaiting me now. Everything that had still been standing when the police officers had taken me to their headquarters was lying. At best. Most things were cracked and thrown around, smashed and scattered – glasses, books, cutlery, clothes, shaving equipment . . . Even a dried-up plant that I had kept on the kitchen sink had been uprooted. I stepped over my suitcase lying on the floor with the cast-off leg of a chair inside, and studied what remained of the photomechanical reproduction that had once used to titivate my life (some glossy moonlight shed on dead water).

Contemplating the wreckage, I realised I'd do well to turn on my heels. This was no courtesy call; this was a declaration of war.

Yet my curiosity was awakened. In my combined bed- and living room, the situation looked, if possible, even worse. Sitting down on the three-legged desk chair, I surveyed the battlefield. The floor was covered with book pages, broken pens, crooked coat hangers, and an array of photos in tatters – including, I now saw, that of a young girl in flowery shirt and boa. Here and there, peeking out of the flotsam like the remnants of a shipwreck, were sections of what had once been a bedframe and a bookcase. My mattress had been cut up and was now reclining against the wall with obscenely exposed interior. Buried deep inside the horse-hair was Dora's cigarette case. The two kitchen chairs had been reduced to firewood. What remained of my pillow hovered placidly in the air, a summery version of snowfall. The metal grid of the tiled stove had been ripped out; on the floor were mounds of ash. Black feet had trampled around, trying to get a bearing but losing themselves in a sea of knick-knacks. Being too heavy to demolish, the desk had simply been turned over, the drawers pulled out, their contents discharged. Strangely, Anton's jacket was hanging untouched on the nail that had once supported my Böcklin reproduction. But the contents of the bag he had brought with him were spread generously throughout the room: in one corner, I discovered one of my bicycle clips; in another, the other; and in a third, the yellow blouse. The Trojan horse, too, had managed to survive unscathed. Abandoned on the windowsill, standing on top of a yellowed newspaper, it contemplated the chaos with desolate dignity.

Had Diels and Pieplack returned with some of their colleagues, or possibly storm troopers, last night? The relish of destruction, so in evidence, seemed to suggest as much – in which case there hardly was any point in my reporting the damage. But it might also have been the Brotherhood, I mused. Or possibly even Anton. Perhaps he had concluded that I possessed the film clip and was now hiding it somewhere in my flat? If nothing else, that might explain why my friend had offered me his place last night. While I was sleeping in his bed, he'd be able to search my abode without the risk of being interrupted. In fact, it might also explain why his jacket hadn't been torn to shreds. Anton couldn't very well take it with him, as that would make me suspicious. But that didn't mean the item needed to fare badly. I walked over to the garment and checked its pockets. Half a comb, some fluff and two used matches. Both inner pockets turned out to be empty. Damn. Whoever was behind the chaos had taken Anton's wallet, including the last reichsmarks.

Now I noticed that two windows had been broken and that somebody had shoved an uninhibited foot straight through the kitchen door. Perhaps I ought to save whatever might be saved, pack my suitcase, and leave while there was still time? Not a bad idea. But where should I go? To whom would I turn? Resigning myself to my lot, I began, hesitantly, to clean up. In order to keep further qualms at bay, I trained my thoughts in the general direction of the woman with the child that I had run into on the street the day before. Perhaps I ought to get in touch with her after all? Belatedly, Dora had taught me to stand up for who I was. What if, finally, I were to explain why I had left her three years earlier? Who knew, discussing the sexual question might lead to something after all.

Towards afternoon, the main room was almost presentable again. Having shoved the refuse into one corner, I had got the desk up on its feet again and cleaned the few items of clothing that had survived. Gradually, I realised there had been method to the destruction. As I gathered the printed pages scattered across the floor, I discovered not a single book remained untouched. Every insert had been loosened from its covers and torn apart. I assembled the pages of *Disturbed Ether* and put them aside. Then I collected those pages of the other books that were still intact and arranged them into a neat stack on my desk. While I pondered what to do with the pages, I walked into the kitchen, cleaned the sink, and retrieved my razor and shaving brush. Then I placed my suitcase on the mattress, packing everything that I didn't want to fall into the hands of Frau Britz. When, at last, I was ready, I placed my bicycle clips on top, like two empty pupils, and closed the lid. After that, I took the top sheet of paper from my pile – it turned out to be the title page of *Hands Up!* – and wrote down what I needed to buy if my plan were to succeed.

Because of the devastation, it proved to be more than expected. Having counted my remaining money, I realised it wouldn't be enough to cover both what I had in mind and the last rent owed. The irony didn't escape me. If I wanted to pay Mrs Britz, I was forced to give up my plan. But if I abandoned my plan, I was certain Inspector Manetti would come knocking in a few hours – and then I would have paid my landlady in vain. If, on the other hand, I put the plan into motion, there would be no need for the police to visit me, either now or later – yet nor would I have any money to pay for a flat I'd still be in need of. The choice was simple. I had never intended to spend the rest of my life in Tresckowstraße. If the Brotherhood was conducting illegal experiments, and my best friend somehow was involved, I needed to know. Also, I owed it to Dora to complete what she had set out to do.

When, an hour later, I knocked at Heino's to drop off my suitcase, Boris opened the door. Noticing my yellowing eye and bruised lip, he wondered what had happened. I sat down on the sofa, next to Chérie, who continued to sleep peacefully, with a shivering ribcage that mysteriously moved me. I gave Boris the short version of how, a couple of nights ago, I had been mugged on my way home, cutting across the waste ground. When I had finished, he swore, twisting the fine fins of his moustache, then he sank his grenadier's fist into his grenadier's palm and explained, in broken German, that he knew who it might have been.

'The shadows who jumped me?'

Boris nodded grimly, producing another meaty explosion. The other night, he and Heino had returned home from the Moustache Bar. Walking by the wasteground, they had heard muted sounds and scuffling. When, suddenly, an accordion had rattled to the ground with a drawn-out groan, they realised

Dabor must be in danger. Running towards the commotion, they discovered Wrangel's former captain limply defending himself against three energetic shapes, all of whom had been equipped, it seemed, with iron gloves. Somehow Heino and Boris had managed to get Dabor out of harm's way. But it wasn't until Ivan Britz, who had been on his way to the market hall, had joined the fracas, all muscle and no compunction, that they had got the upper hand. Now two of the construction workers were in custody. Unfortunately, the third shadow had managed to slip away.

I realised Boris might be right. The person I had seen emerge from the bushes earlier the same morning could have been the third shadow. Slapping his palms together, Boris suggested I file a report with the police. It was about time somebody did something. How much longer should those construction workers be allowed to insult the inhabitants of our neighbourhood? I asked him what time it was. Hearing it was already late afternoon, I explained that, as a matter of fact, I was on my way down to the square where the police headquarters were. Yet when I got off the tram twenty minutes later, I didn't head for the red-brick building, but went straight through the train station. At the moment, I wasn't convinced the police would show any greater understanding for either Dabor's or my plight.

The store I had in mind is located next to Kretschmer's barbershop. Two hours later, I returned home having checked all the items on my list. Now I only had to wait for night to fall. Finding nothing better to do, I started to doodle on a piece of paper. After a while, a shape began to repeat itself, half flower, half angel, which somehow pleased me – until I realised what it looked like. In order to rid myself of the suspicion that the sketch might betray some potent portent, I turned it on its head. But that merely made me think of Anton, who, at the Blue Cellar, had proclaimed himself my protector.

Bothered, I re-turned the page and traced the contours with my pen. Slowly the lines repeated themselves, ran into and out of each other, crossed and enhanced one another, until the drawing took on the character of a fatidic palm open for cross-examination or possibly the map of some intricate psychological terrain – as if I wasn't merely diverting myself, but actually trying to produce an accurate representation of the cause of my worries. I recalled the neurologist about whom I had read in the paper while waiting for Anton at the Blue Cellar. According to the Swedish scientist, the topology of the brain, projected onto that of Stockholm, would create a perfect match. If he was right, I wondered what he might make of my current situation, as evidenced by the doodles I had just produced. As far as I could tell, this depiction of my adopted hometown demonstrated none of the enlightened qualities of the Swedish capital.

Seized by a crazy thought, I scribbled an *A* for the Apollo in one of the ovals I had drawn, adding the initial of the street in which Dora lived in the other. These two spots marked the beginning and end of my story so far – or rather, the points between which Dora's and my liaison seemed to unfold. Since their common denominator was Hotel Kreuzer, I jotted down '*Kr*', as well, abbreviating the name the way my friend had in her notebook. If it hadn't been for a certain room at this establishment, it seemed to me unlikely that the luckless events at Dora's would have been connected with what appeared to be going on at the cinema where I worked. Yes, no doubt the establishment had triggered the tragedy. Musing on the two *Kr*'s scribbled in the upper part of the ovals, I tried to recall what Karp, with his thick Pomeranian accent, had termed the muscle responsible for raising the testicles. Then it occurred to me: *der Kremaster*, 'the cremaster' . . .

That did it. This, clearly, was too much. No more projection for Mr Knisch. Having rolled my piece of paper into a ball, I tried to throw it out the window – but managed, merely, to make it drop a few feet away. For all I knew, the capital of Sweden may be reminiscent of the human brain. Yet the city in which I lived couldn't possibly evince any similarity to, to . . . Well, to whatever it was my doodles were supposed to represent. Regardless of what the future might have in store, activated by the latent powers of the past, from now on, I wouldn't rely on speculation to guide me there.

I don't believe it's been pointed out in sexological literature before, not even by Krafft-Ebing or Froehlich, who usually are quite perceptive, so I'm pleased to offer, at this juncture, the following observation: the difference between man and woman is minimal. In truth, it's a matter merely of centimetres. In order to skirt any misunderstanding, I hasten to add that I'm not referring to the length of the particular anatomical part I had just drawn on my piece of paper. Merely the vertical character is the same, and not even that is quite right. No, what I wish to report is, simply, this: the difference between the sexes corresponds to that between shoe heels.

Obviously, this discrepancy may change from one culture to another, but generally it remains somewhere between three and seven centimetres. In virtually all other contexts, such variance would be negligible; in the case of the sexes, however, it has powerful consequences. For example, the higher up a person's heel is placed in relation to their toes, the more dramatic the balance. The wobbly poise created may be counteracted only by a slight shift of one's point of gravity from heel to arch, which in turn makes the calves tighten, the posterior thrust out, and the shoulders straighten. The new curvature acquired by one's spine will emphasise the hips' rolling motion, and the elbows, pushed back, will underscore the breasts. Thus, the higher the heels, the more the wearer will become a woman. In short: the fair sex doesn't exist, it is created.

The shoes I had obtained at the store next to Kretschmer's had heels that were exactly four centimetres high – which, I believe, turned me into an average representative of the opposite sex. I didn't find this realisation disagreeable; likewise, the shiver running through my loins as I got up wasn't of the disappointing kind. Suddenly, I hovered a few centimetres above ground, quite likely the most important ones in my life so far. Balancing capriciously on the front part of my feet, I felt the toes squeeze together, my knees rub against each other. If I were merely a regular woman, what would the ultimate lady look like? Without doubt, the crown of creation, that true wonderwork of verticality, must be a biological sensation who walked on the tip of her toes.

I'm not inexperienced. Naturally I knew that the shift of gravity needed for me to become a member of the fair sex meant that my sense of balance had to shift. As a consequence, I was forced to walk more slowly than usual, with petite steps that tempered, even tampered with, the provocative pose I had assumed. Furthermore, my posture would become more potent but also more exposed, at once strong and helpless. Emphasising my superiority, the heels simultaneously stressed my need for support. Yet what are we not willing to do for art, I reflected equitably, thrusting my chin in the air – and almost twisting my ankle as I was forced, quickly, to sit down.

At Hotel Kreuzer, all I had had to do was to pleat my hair in diminutive bows and make my mouth red and molten. Now the situation required a finer touch, a different sort of class. For the first time in my life, I was about to venture out on my own. When Dora and I had visited the Foundation the first time, Karp had wondered when somebody would be willing to step into the shoes of the opposite sex. Well, here he was; this gentleman was it. If I wished to pass unnoticed, I must apply my makeup with the mature flair expected from a woman of the world. Since Dora was in no position to help me, it took me more than an hour to accomplish the task. By then, a mountain of spotty toilet paper surrounded my aching feet. Yet finally, to my delightful surprise, I was content with the result – even convinced by it. Pressing my lips against the last piece of pristine paper, I scrutinised my creation in the broken mirror propped up on my desk. Pleased, I adjusted the dark wig I had bought. Not even my mother would have recognised me.

Now only a few last attributes remained. A chequered skirt of the kind I had worn when I was still calling myself Anton would have been too girly a garment for the occasion. During my excursion earlier in the afternoon, I had therefore acquired a more suitable piece of clothing. Although it was black and slinky as sin, it was also longer, so that it covered most of my legs. Considering the situation, I strove for a look at once discreet and passionate, with a vague but unmistakable touch of danger. People had to notice me, even be intrigued by my appearance; yet at the same time, nobody should become aware of any deviating traits. The less one thought about my bones and freckles, for instance, the easier it would be for me to accomplish what Dora had set out to do. Thus the cardigan and stockings I chose were black, too. Only my blouse was yellow, but hopefully the black bustier I wore could be traced under its flimsy chiffon. The latter, by the way, I had filled with socks instead of napkins, so as to achieve just the right kind of heft. The buckles of the brassiere strained pleasantly over my shoulders, the colour combination made me think of what the Russian porter used to call me. 'Mr Honig': perhaps I was not a wasp but a bee? Guided by sensations not visible to the naked eye, I'd finally retrieve that obscure item needed to turn bitter suspicions into sweet truth. Considering my heels, I realised that, if need be, I'd be able to sting, too.

Only the handbag I had purchased gave me pause. I quite liked the sleek lustre of its parched leather, but as I unpacked the bag at home, it turned out to be too small for all the things I thought I might need. Contemplating my options, I decided against removing Dora's cigarette case. Although it was locked and thus rather useless, it served eloquently as a token of the female secretiveness to which I aspired. Instead, I determined I could do without the mascara and hairbrush. When removing them turned out not to be enough, I took out my Moslems, too. And this time, I managed to close the bag. Now I only had to decide whether to push it up along my underarm or to sling it across my shoulder and squeeze it to my side. Since I was unsure what a proper lady would do, I thought of Dora. Then I remembered she never used a handbag. Instead I tried to think of my mother and sister, yet I couldn't quite recall what they used to do. Finally, I was reminded of the woman outside the Blue Cellar, the lady whom Konrad had addressed as Dominique, and decided to do things her way – which was, simply, to hold the bag pressed against my chest.

I left shortly before midnight, warm and wobbly, with a mounting sense of independence. My clothes were searing, my blood sang, this was me! For the first time in life, I was not a girl but a lady – admittedly one with that extra *je ne sais quoi*, but nonetheless. With a little luck, I'd be able to procure the evidence needed to reveal the shameful conspiracy Dora must have discovered. Half an hour later, I checked my wig in a shop window and felt my pulse accelerate dramatically – not like earlier, when I had been on my way to Madame with a hard heart pounding hotly in my chest, but swift and sweaty, with a clean sting of fear to it. Then I crossed the street and entered Hotel Kreuzer.

Everything looked like I remembered it: worn-down carpets, dead flower pots, chairs glossy with dirt, grouped around a table on which tourist leaflets were spread in an approximation of a fan. Even the porter's lodge with its peeling oak panelling was the same. Yet instead of a bald head leaning over a crossword, a pair of giant shoe soles rested comfortably on the counter. For a brief moment, I thought it might be the same shoes that had patrolled my flat. Then I recalled the labyrinth into which my propensity for projection had already brought me and discarded the thought. What I needed was not another impasse, but a way out.

Timorously, I pressed my handbag against my chest and took a few careful steps towards the counter. I need not to have worried. The porter had spread a paper across his face, the front page quivering quietly. There was no risk he'd notice me, even less that he'd be able to identify me afterwards, when asked by the police. Although my efforts to disguise myself thus proved unnecessary, I felt relieved. With newfound confidence, I tripped up the stairs, one pointy toe-blade at a time. The hotel seemed evacuated. There were neither voices, nor movement, anywhere. As I reached the second floor, I didn't turn left as usual, but right

– heading straight for the bathroom. A moment of solitary calm would do me good before the denouement.

Standing in front of the bathroom mirror, I shed my shoes and performed some callisthenic exercises. Having got over my initial surge of elation – was there a better designation for the sensation of being elevated four breathtaking centimetres? – I began to appreciate Dora's complaint regarding the pain of having to live up to the expectations of others. Gradually blood re-entered my stiff toes, my calves unclenched in fitful jerks. One flight up, somebody just unleashed a torrent of water. First there was a loud romp, then a brash clatter, after which the agitated water came tumbling down the pipes – much too disorderly, I feared, for the brawl to have a happy end.

I took a towel, surprisingly clean, and pressed it against the sweat that covered my forehead. Retrieving my powder case from my leather bag, I made a few quick improvements. The lips, too, received a hurried smear. I was just about to retract the lipstick into its sheath when I discerned a voice in the corridor, followed by a flat sound that told me the person to whom it belonged had slapped on the light. Now I could hear the voice approaching the bathroom. Ever responsive, I became inspiringly busy, shedding the towel and trying to push my makeup into my pockets – until I realised I had none. Even more troubling, I suddenly recognised I had taken the wrong turn; I was in the men's room. With one frantic motion, I shoved everything off the counter, into my bag.

At the same moment as the door opened, I locked myself in the only available stall. Hunching down with my stocking-clad feet on the toilet seat, I restrained my breath until, at last, I stopped breathing all together. My heart bounced mutely against my ribcage, my throat swelled dangerously. Somebody pulled the handle. 'What the hell?' Yanking it a few more times, the person eventually gave up. Instead, he placed himself in front of the sink and opened his flies. I could hear him shuffle his feet, then there was loud splashing. Whoever it was, he urinated for a long time. At regular intervals, he reshuffled his feet, perhaps in order to avoid spill on the floor. I wasn't even saved from the short, final squirts. Eventually, however, the person closed his flies and began to sing while turning on the taps. When, a few moments later, he dried himself and suddenly fell silent, I realised, to my horror, my shoes were still lying on the floor. A sick, vertiginous minute went by, then the unknown visitor continued to sing:

Oh, la, la, you're in our wicked hands,
all shrewd ache and festive glands . . .

Soon thereafter he left. Pooh. He hadn't discovered my shoes. I was saved.

But for how long? Obviously, I couldn't stay in the men's room one more second. The next visitor wouldn't content himself with the sink and some silly song. Quickly I closed my bag, unlocked the door, and discovered, to my relief, that I must have kicked my shoes under the sink. Saved by disregard. As I bent down to retrieve my footwear, I made another new experience: it seemed it was easier to genuflect dressed in trousers than in skirt. Having wriggled into my shoes, I was once again four decisive centimetres taller, though now I began to doubt they'd get me as far as I hoped. Regretting I hadn't brought any cigarettes – a smoke would certainly calm my nerves – I checked my face in the mirror and was just about to wash my hands, when I noticed the yellow droplets glittering among a host of colourless ones. I decided on a slight adjustment of my wig.

As I emerged, the corridor was dark and empty. From the opposite room, not a single sound could be discerned. Behind the next door, however, I made out mute voices and furniture scraping across the floor. From room 206, nothing. I continued. Nor from 204 either. Somewhere a key was turned. Then, suddenly, I stood in front of the room with which I associated so much in my life: beauty, nerves and deception, obscure drives and clairvoyant fantasies – almost everything, save perhaps for veracity of the naked variety. Yet if I weren't mistaken, whatever had caused the events of the last few weeks to unfold was right here, hidden behind the door of room 202.

Straightening my skirt, which had accidentally ridden up on my hips, I thought about the message I had left for Anton. In it, I had asked him to meet me at the Blue Cellar at 11p.m. at the latest; I claimed to have discovered something revelatory. 'My friend, it's time for the finale.' I was fairly certain, then, that wherever Anton happened to be presently, it wouldn't be at Hotel Kreuzer. Just to make sure, I knocked nonetheless. Then I opened my handbag and retrieved the picklock I had nicked from his suitcase.

Chapter Twenty-One

To my dismay, movements could be heard from inside, then the door opened with a jerk – though not by Anton, as I had feared, but by the man with the biscuit-yellow hair. His shirtsleeves were rolled up and spread across his tanned arms were several tattoos, among them one that depicted a lying male figure with his legs generously parted. He must have expected somebody else, for he opened the door so far that I was offered a full view of the room. The sight didn't necessarily improve my confidence. In the chair in which Dora had used to sit, a male of uncertain age was placed with his feet tied to the front legs and his hands behind his back. Save for an open doctor's coat and a hood that had been pulled over his head, he was naked. Across his pale pelvis, 'Nur für Damen' was tattooed in finest Gothic script.

The patient, obviously in pain, breathed heavily. An inch-wide rubber band had been applied to his left upper arm. Moaning, he rolled his head back and forth on the upper edge of the chair. Unfortunately, the hood made it impossible to say who the person was. On the sofa table were a bifurcating tube, a pocket mirror, a syringe, and what looked like a cine-camera for private use. Some hospital clothes were thrown into a corner, along with a pair of white women's boots. Behind the Chinese screen in the background, I could make out an older man who was just washing his hands.

'I'll be damned.' The blond person eyed me with amused disdain. Correcting his facial expression, he closed the gap of the door. 'What do *you* want?' The crack that remained, palm-wide, was barely enough for thin eyes, pimply nose and full mouth to fit in.

Adjusting the cardigan I was carrying on my shoulders, I pressed my handbag against my chest and took recourse to the lie I had prepared in case my suspicions were proved wrong. 'Good evening,' I said with as much dignity as possible. 'I'm a good friend of Dora's. I happened to be close by, and thought I'd retrieve something she forgot.'

'Dora? Forgot? Friend?' There was movement behind the door.

'Yes, isn't this room 202?' I took a step back to check the number on the door.

With one smooth movement, the man slid out and closed the door behind him. Now I noted he had squeezed a towel inside his waistband. 'Dora?' he repeated. 'Are you two . . . *sisters*?' The tone was softer, without, however, having turned more friendly. Presumably he wished to know what I wanted to fetch, or at least had managed to see during the careless seconds the door had been held open.

'Perhaps,' I said with an oblique smile, pretending not to have noticed anything. 'Dora usually stays in 202. But I can come back another time.'

Mr Yellow Hair studied me. As he finally lifted his eyes from my shoes – I suppose I didn't know on which foot to stand – he crossed his arms. 'Well, what's it going to be, sis?'

'Pardon?' I fidgeted. 'I guess the porter might help me. He's probably woken up by now. Sorry to have disturbed you.' I wobbled over to the stairs while nervously trying to prise open my handbag. My plan was already turning into a big mistake. How could I ever have thought that Anton . . .

'Wait, I'll help you.'

What happened thereafter, I'm loathe to tell. Perhaps I pulled out Lakritz's stiletto, perhaps I began to run down the stairs. The last thing I remember was that the person with the biscuit-yellow hair suddenly was next to me. Then everything turned black.

There wasn't much consciousness involved as I awoke. I recall only a sense of vertigo not of this world. Slithery images, shouting phrases, wicked, stinging pain. None of my thoughts arranged themselves into patterns, words swelled in my mouth. The few sounds I managed to get across my lips took such grotesque proportions they sounded like those made when the speed on a gramophone record is lowered by a thumb brusquely pressed down on the spinning middle. My nose was running, and tattered forms of no consequence swam in my tear-filled eyes. It felt as if I had been stored away deep below reality, and now merely managed to catch sight of unconnected movements, a sick interplay of light and shadow bobbing on the surface above.

How long this state of mind lasted is difficult to say. At one point, I saw the blond man's face close to me. Smiling, he said something that sounded like 'not being moved up'. Since I failed to understand him, however, I wanted him to repeat what he had said. Yet my words turned into wool. Finally he grew tired of my efforts and thrust his hand, simply but brutally, into my mouth. To my surprise, he pulled until he had retrieved a white, wriggling larva, several metres long and covered in wet, white fleece. Curiously, I felt relieved. I realised it must have been this repulsive something that had prevented me from speaking. Yet when I tried to thank him for his help, my throat felt raw and extended. The only thing I managed to do was to explain, with pleading eyes, that I needed time to recover.

Luckily, he seemed to understand. At least he nodded sympathetically where he stood in front of a radiating lamp as big as the sun. Shadows of different sorts drifted across his face in meaningless but beautiful patterns. Then a series of distant knocks rang out, and presently only the stark light bulb could be seen.

I had been left alone. How considerate, I thought. Now I could regain my composure in all leisure. But the light shone with such unusual intensity that I didn't manage to close my eyes. Inside its hard bubble of glass sat a spiral-shaped thread that glowed, even fizzled, with a zeal that seemed positively hazardous. Gradually, I realised it not only looked like a pinned-up insect, but was one. Clearly it was because the larva wriggled with pain that the lamp shone with such febrile light. The more I contemplated the insect, the more it appeared as a copy of the monster that had just been removed from my interior – just a few sizes smaller. Osram, I thought befuddled. Why even give such an organism a name?

That wriggling worm was the last thing I remembered. When I awoke again, I was freezing. The light wasn't as intense and somebody had tied me to a chair. My head thundered, every joint of my body ached. 'Turn it off, Alf. He's coming to.' The voice, foreign and fuzzy, reached me from so far away that, for a brief moment, I thought it might even have been speaking to me from the auditorium at the Apollo. But how should I know? Nonetheless, I promised myself that, should I ever manage to get out of this perverse affair – perhaps by falling asleep; perhaps by simply sleeping myself backwards out of it – I'd appreciate every moment of life, however dismal and flat-deprived. What did it matter to me if it never returned, as long as I had experienced it in all its shimmering multitude, like the oily but pleasantly complicated pattern on a soap bubble? If existence was coated by a veil, I realised it could only be thus: an air bubble kept together by fatty acids, glossy and delicate, the surface tension of which could burst at any second, in order to reveal what everybody, deep down, had known all along: that each transparent moment was but a version of nothingness.

Suddenly I experienced an intense desire to communicate this insight. If it hadn't been for the lights that went out at the same moment, I'm fairly certain I would've been able to develop my thoughts with some *élan*. Yet instead I was interrupted by the fuzzy voice: 'Osram, you said? What do you want from him?

Don't you get it, you deviant? You're in for it. If you don't tell us . . .' This was hardly what I had expected. In order to maintain a modicum of dignity, I shut my eyes and pretended to lose consciousness. But either the person who was hovering in the dark next to me had recourse to a radio scope, or the room wasn't as dark as I thought. My efforts merely led to a slap in my face. I opened my eyes, and received another.

'Now you listen, sicko. We can make life pretty miserable. There's no reason to have patience with a third-classer like you.' The claim seemed to me both preposterous and unsympathetic, and I was just about to point this out, when the voice continued: 'Well, choose yourself.' I nodded as cooperatively as I felt my dignity would allow me. 'The more you tell us, the less painful it'll be. Maybe you'll be spared the treatment the doctor here just received.' The voice had stressed the profession almost ironically. Before I managed to ask why, it went on: 'Do we understand each other? I didn't hear? That's better.' It must have interpreted one of the movements over which I lacked control as an affirmation. Now the voice turned to somebody else in the room. Whoever it was said: 'Remarkable. Apart from the tendency to displacement, I see no signs of hysteria, which typically applies to people of this sort. Perhaps that's because, in spite of the deviant behaviour, his andrine's still in working order. Give him one more shot, but not as big this time. Save the rest for the doctor.'

I felt a needle prick my arm. Then, after a soft, silent minute, my thoughts began to slide apart. Fear vanished, body dissolved, again I became one with a hovering world. The only thing that bothered me was the bell jar that suddenly seemed to have been mounted on my head – either that or my head itself had turned into glass. With a clarity that surpassed everything I'd experienced hitherto, I discovered I could observe my own brain pulsating. The sensation wasn't uninteresting. For example, here and there, the colourless liquid surrounding the grey matter had taken on a violet nuance that made me think of a different kind of head, a meaty sort of helm. Also, in certain folds between the lobes were short bursts of intense sparkle, quite like diminutive thunderbolts. Although I had difficulties getting a grip on what was happening, I gathered this must be the way things looked when you thought about yourself thinking. Both fascinated and nauseous, I determined to follow a chain reaction – mainly as a test, to see if it were possible. Almost immediately, however, with a bewildering kind of ease, it dispersed in thousands of crackling directions, all just as riveting, all just as winding, and I understood that it was too much, at least for my present faculty of judgment, to follow these flittering movements with their tulip-shaped bodies, running in such unexpected directions, almost like . . .

Again the strange, blurry voice sounded – although this time not out of the dark surrounding me, but from inside my own vexing self. In some way, it must have managed to get inside my thoughts! Imploring, it began to pose questions I realised hospitality required me to answer. And it was at this moment that the truly odd thing happened. Hardly had I perceived the voice, before I was seized by inexplicable enthusiasm. Finally I understood contexts that until now had mystified me, and I was delighted to be able to explain them as thoroughly as I was capable of. Applying myself to this task, I accounted for every astonishing detail, even if it was a seemingly insignificant nerve-thread at the far end of a rich tangle of insights. Nothing was unimportant any longer, everything could be turned into significance. The meaning of life was to arrange a multitude of details into a pattern – the more beautiful, the more convincing. If, before, I'd been attentive, I now turned positively creative. Thus the view I had managed to acquire of my own brain slowly but logically transformed itself, assuming the shape of that other kind of head already mentioned. For instance, I grew increasingly convinced that, in actuality, I wore a pale, flesh-coloured helmet, and that my body had acquired the shape of a taut, blood-filled muscle that could think. At the tip of my helmet, the single slit of an eye peered that I needed in order to scrutinise the world in all its simple-minded wealth.

On several occasions, I was asked to keep to the subject, and finally I couldn't refrain from exclaiming that's just what I did! 'Indeed, indeed,' I added more pensively. At last I saw the order of things in all its complicated simplicity. If the voice only knew how obvious the connection was between, say, man's two sexual glands and the east and west parts of our city. Or take the pomade that Olivier Glissant produced for gentlemen and the shoe fat that a 'velocipedist' by the name of Bauer had used in intimate situations. The association between the two things was nothing short of pure poetry! Or if the voice would please consider the relationship between a fantastic shoe at a museum not far from here, the brakes on certain wheelchairs and the handle on a carpet beater that a person I knew deployed when she was smacking pillows. Genial, genial. If it would just understand the magic link connecting these or other seemingly unrelated items, I continued undeterred, I promised the world would reveal itself in all its iridescent splendour! And in any event, I added conspiratorially, I could imagine there was a secret connection between the black eyes of a certain person I had in mind, the spools on a film projector, and the pearl that had been hidden in a shell-shaped cigarette case I happened to have in my possession. I wasn't yet able to determine the exact nature of this connection, but just think of it. Surely it could be the case? 'Osram,' I whispered smartly, raising a delicate eyebrow. 'If you see what I mean . . .'

To my disappointment, the voice paid no particular attention to my insights. Instead, it returned time and again to the same sordid matter. So finally, I felt forced to sharpen my tone. 'Why this constant nagging about Dora and the film, Dora and the film? She no longer exists! She has turned into a woman without qualities. And anyway, her name has nothing to do with Pandora. Or with cinematography. Please understand that. Dora is a cut-out sequence without significance for the true drama. *Cherchez l'homme*, gentlemen. He's your only hope!' Oh, I really talked up a storm. It had been a long time since I had acted with such evident authority, with such sovereign dare. The slightest prodding from the voice inside me caused the most fantastic digressions, one more boldly intelligent than the next, and I conveyed each detail with such studied care that it blossomed like a flower, exposing its rich, intricate interior. My mouth had become a paradise whence issued the most beautiful . . .

Unexpectedly my head began to swirl, as if the ground had just let go, and I experienced difficulties in maintaining my balance. Something wasn't quite right; suddenly the world seemed sick. Presumably I commented upon this unforeseen development, because almost immediately, I was slapped in the face – and then again. Curiously, the slaps multiplied throughout my body, like writhing water coursing through a hose. Why slap somebody who's able to demonstrate such a sister-like desire to cooperate? Again, I was slapped. Now my head began to spin, and I realised it would be safest to concentrate my remaining powers on trying to keep my balance. But only a few seconds of precious relief passed before sickness surged up inside me, and soon I vomited in hard, cramped attacks. The little I had eaten came out in furious spurts, rather like when liquid is disgorged from a syringe, then I wobbled, slithered, and, I presume, lost consciousness.

At one point during my sojourn in the svelte nothingness that followed, somebody must have loosened the ropes and put me on the sofa. For when I came to, trying to patch together colours and forms into something resembling reality, I realised I was lying on my side, studying the pattern of an armrest. My head felt like a pressure-cooker, my mouth was just as desert-dry as when, a few lifetimes earlier, the larva had been pulled out of my mouth. I tried to get up, but my legs caved in. I can't say for how long I was lying there on the floor, a heap of undamaged limbs and broken movement. But at last the feeling of illness faded, so that, exhausted, I was able to sit up with my back propped against the short end of the sofa. No thoughts, no palpitations, no aches.

The film clip, that's what this was about. With a little more imagination than I was able to muster, I might have managed to conjure forth my situation so clearly I would have figured out what was going on. But I'm sad to report my mind's eye wasn't in its most splendid shape, and whatever it might have been able to project on the inside of my forehead wouldn't have been likely to increase my wellbeing. Listlessly I noted that the silk stockings I had bought were torn. My legs were scratched; my kneecaps were covered with blots of blood. Whatever remained of my skirt rested on my hips. The yellow blouse was missing one arm and all the buttons. Now I also noticed that my black bra was hanging out: the shoulder straps had been torn and the socks with which I had stuffed the cups were gone. I put my palm to my temple and realised I had lost my wig, too. Only my handbag, lying in a corner, seemed unharmed.

Slowly I went through my body, part by part. Here was one arm, there the other. There were one, two, three . . . five fingers. There, another five. Good. I realised I could still fill my lungs with air and wriggle my toes. My head was firmly placed on my neck, my neck on my shoulders. Excellent. Since I still felt a bit woozy, however, I shifted my weight carefully as I stretched for my handbag. The pain that shot through me was quite enough to make me understand what had happened. And I can promise it wasn't some little little mouse that had been seeking shelter from its big big pursuer last night. Nausea welled up, and if I had had anything left in my stomach, I'm sure I would have vomited. Instead I shivered cold and bitter – and experienced how my feelings dissociated themselves from my body, tiptoeing away, as if in shame.

When, finally, I managed to gather myself, I dried the tears from my eyes. Eventually, the pain eased so much I could stumble over to the washstand. I cleaned myself as well as the circumstances allowed. Blood-coloured saliva slithered into the enamel bowl, creating rare, veil-shaped patterns. At last I took a look in the mirror hanging next to the door. With the exception of a grandly swollen lip and puffy eyes, I looked better than expected. Admittedly, my appearance wasn't very ladylike, but I seemed exhausted in a fetching, human sort of way. I retrieved my lipstick from my handbag and, leaning against the wall, sank to the floor, realising that one's true self did indeed reside on the inside.

Then I heard a key turn.

To my surprise, Inspector Wickert entered the room – on his toes and with all faculties on alert. Holding a revolver in his hand, he advanced a few steps, then looked around and sighed, with relief, I think, as he returned his weapon to his shoulder holster. Not until he had adjusted his glasses did he realise the room wasn't empty. After some misunderstanding, involving a misplaced smear of lipstick and a kerchief, Wickert managed to help me up onto the sofa. Worried, he inquired whether I could hear him. I frowned. Mouth and throat, although aching, didn't quite belong to the rest of my body. The Inspector offered to get me a glass of water; gratefully, I accepted. Having given an order to somebody in the corridor, he returned his attention to me, careful not to comment on my appearance. 'The situation's under control, Mr Knisch. We've searched the hotel. Incriminating evidence has been secured. I'm glad we found you. We need your help.'

I made a deprecatory gesture, sinking further into the sofa. Immediately Wickert walked over to the window and opened the curtains. As the light hit my eyes, I was forced to make another gesture. 'Oh, perhaps you'd like a little rest before we speak?' He pulled them closed again. 'Hello . . . Knisch . . . Mr Knisch?' I must have sloped to the side, because when I opened my eyes again, the Inspector was trying to place my handbag as a pillow under my head.

'The Brotherhood,' I sighed with effort.

But sliding the bag under my neck, Wickert didn't listen. 'You're in safe hands, Mr Knisch,' he declared, sitting down. 'I just wish I could leave you to your beauty sleep. But action is of the utmost importance. We're about to make a breakthrough.' He retrieved a pencil and his spiralbound writing pad from his pockets, then ran his tongue across his teeth, eyeing me sympathetically. Perhaps I could understand my personal comfort would have to wait at a moment like this? I made a tired gesture, about to return to the lovely nothingness in which I had spent the latter part of the night. 'Mr Knisch?' Wickert prodded me with his pencil. Grimacing, I prised open my eyes. To make certain he had my attention, he adjusted the handbag with slightly more fuss than necessary. I could feel the edge of something hard – presumably the Pandora's Box.

Then, again, the Inspector consulted his pad. The Vice Squad, he informed me, solemnly wetting the tip of his pencil, had kept the Foundation for Sexual Research under surveillance. Evidently, it was an established fact that, over the years, Froehlich had helped many so-called 'sisters'. These activities – there was no need for him to point out they were illegal, was there? – had started long before 'our Einstein of sex' had founded his institute in 1919. Documents the police had been able to secure showed the Doctor had moved to the city from Kolberg by the Baltic Sea. Shortly before the turn of the century, he had opened a clinic in one of the nobler neighbourhoods. There, he had not only tried to come to terms with some of mankind's more unusual expressions. Tracing his notes with his pencil, Wickert pronounced carefully: 'Hermaphrodites, androgynes, transvestites – people of that sort, Mr Knisch. Representatives of the "grey sex".' He looked up, then down again. Yes, I was still alive. 'But Froehlich also accepted pregnant women, whom he claimed were his siblings, and performed illegal abortions.'

The latter activity alone made the Health Chancellor a murderer in the eyes of the law – 'at least as long as certain paragraphs aren't rewritten, Mr Knisch. Which frankly, I doubt they will be.' Pensively tapping his pencil against his pad, then shifting to his dentures, Wickert pointed out that Karla Manetti had chosen to ignore these eugenic activities, probably because she considered them a favour to society. He sighed, admitting that, if required, he might be able to acknowledge her point. Worse, at least from a judicial perspective, was Froehlich's interest in mothers without means. Information had come to light that proved the Health Chancellor didn't merely help young women rid themselves of unwanted burdens, but also had taken several of them under his lab-coated wings. Nine months later, the involuntary victims of his concern had been given away to childless families with considerable assets but no scruples.

At the moment, the Health Chancellor was in Copenhagen with his colleague Kurt Gielke, where, together with the like-minded, they planned to found an international league for sexual reform. Wickert expected them back next weekend. Their absence had offered the Vice Squad a welcome opportunity to take an undisturbed look at their affairs. 'Finally,' he pronounced proudly, 'we've been able to penetrate the Foundation.' Through an inside contact, the police had secured important items of evidence. For instance, they now possessed a complete list of the children who had been given up for adoption, as well as a considerable stack of questionnaires, demonstrating how far sexual corruption had spread in society. Also, with access to the archives, they had been able to uncover the devious methods Froehlich had used to finance his schemes.

Because of investigatory procedure, Wickert was unable to divulge more than that, in several cases, there were prominent members among both patients and adoptive parents. Perhaps I understood these were respectable citizens, who risked losing their reputation if their names were made public? I sank further into the sofa. For a number of years, the Inspector continued unperturbed, these people had been easy prey for Froehlich, who had collected commissions long after a child had acquired its parents. Whence this kind of behaviour came I might guess, of course. No? Well, Wickert explained, leafing through his notes, the Health Chancellor had been able to obtain the lodgings of Adam Hatz, former director of war materials and a person of his sort. He raised his eyes. I got the drift, didn't I? Thanks to Hatz, Froehlich had managed to buy new equipment, including a considerable amount of forbidden literature for purposes of 'enlightenment'. Now I could see where this was going, couldn't I? Wickert added another coat of saliva to his dentures.

'The Brotherhood,' I sighed. The bulky handbag really was uncomfortable.

But instead of helping me, the Inspector declared that Felix Karp had been Froehlich's right hand. 'Their friendship goes back a long way, Mr Knisch. We've been able to determine that both men grew up in Kolberg.' A few years into the new century, shortly after the Health Chancellor had opened his clinic in the west part of town, his childhood friend had looked him up. 'According to Manetti, young Karp had just left nursing school at the Miséricorde. Froehlich decided to employ his friend, and soon gave him responsibility for the adoptions.' Why Karp had let himself get drawn into these sinister activities, Wickert couldn't tell. But he was convinced the men shared medicinal passions. Besides, he suspected the Health Chancellor to have a hold on his friend. Of what nature, the Inspector couldn't, or wouldn't, say. But now he studied me so closely that, despite the handbag, I began to understand.

In conjunction with the opening of the Foundation a decade ago, the adoptions had stopped. 'Yet I assure you the illegal activities continued, albeit furtively.' It was these clandestine activities to which the Vice Squad wished to put an end. Finally Wickert closed his pad. For example, the police had reason to suspect the Foundation had begun to produce so-called sexological films. It had been done earlier, too, although in cruder fashion, and censored scenes still circulated. When asked, an employee had insisted the material was produced for 'pedagogical purposes'. But the Inspector knew better than that. 'Obviously it's pornography, Mr Knisch. What else should it be?' He lowered his voice, as if about to impart a precious secret. 'As you may understand, this is where you become interesting for our investigation. Working at a cinema, you have the required expertise. Also, we've been able to link Dr Karp to Dora Wilms.' He paused delicately. 'If you see what I mean?'

I didn't, but I assumed Wickert would enlighten me. Examining the Foundation's ledger, the police had discovered that Dora had visited Karp a couple of years ago – and almost every day in the last few weeks. Surely she must have told me about these meetings, and perhaps even mentioned details that might help the Vice Squad tighten the net. No? The Inspector informed me the police now possessed data that would astound even the most experienced colleague. The connection between deviant sexuality and criminal activity was well known, of course. Yet what happened at the Foundation had no equivalent that Wickert, though not an expert, was aware of. 'With his supposedly pedagogical films, Karp has been the spider at the centre of a devious net. It's about time we put an end to these activities that use a scientific exterior to cover up a morally rotten interior. In the future, Mr Knisch, there will be no place for . . .'

Seeing my discomfort, Wickert changed his approach. 'It wasn't until tonight that we found out he was hiding here at Hotel Kreuzer.' The Vice Squad had become suspicious when, some time earlier, they had searched a pension in town that had been used as the headquarters of an international 'ring'. Among other things, the police had found several films with women in compromising situations. Also, they had retrieved a sample film that had required medical expertise and access to advanced equipment. 'That's what put us on to Froehlich and his cohorts. The ringleader is an Austrian known by my colleagues not only in Vienna, but also in Paris. He used to deal in horse dressage, but of late, he seems to have moved on to so-called "white films". When we applied pressure, he admitted most of the props came from the Foundation. We offered to lower the charges against him in return for names, and that's when he mentioned Felix Karp.'

Wickert leaned forward. 'Currently we're working on the assumption that Karp set your compatriot up with Wilms, who put her hotel room at his disposal. Why is still unclear. But his name is registered in the guest book downstairs. And not only there.' Smugly, the Inspector prodded me with his writing implement. 'You know, to judge from the ledger at the Foundation, Wilms and the Austrian visited Karp already last Easter . . .'

About to faint again, I wondered whether it wouldn't be opportune, at this point, to tell him it was all madness, utter, blatant madness. None of what he claimed was the slightest bit true! And besides, I knew with whom Dora had visited the Foundation last Easter.

'Yet something went awry.' Not in possession of a radio scope, Wickert continued coolly. 'Your compatriot must have received Karp here at the hotel yesterday. It seems to have been a settlement typical of the criminal world. When we searched the place, we found him tied to a chair. Yes, Mr Knisch. Tied, naked, violated. Dead, in fact. Karp must have lost his head. Fortunately, we could save you. If we had arrived an hour later, I'm not convinced you'd still be alive.'

I managed only a helpless gesture. This time, however, the Inspector seemed little interested in my comfort. To make my point, I slid down the handbag, saliva trickling from the corner of my mouth. But Wickert let me lie there, quite uncomfortable, with one arm squeezed. What should I do? Everything he had said made sense seen from one perspective, but no sense at all seen from another. It was as if the truth of what had happened had been twisted a few precious degrees, turning what might have yielded a convincing pattern into a distorted grimace. Did Wickert really believe I was collaborating with Karp? Or with Anton? We who had been like . . .

'"Brothers", you said, Mr Knisch? Considering this situation, that might not be the most fitting description.' Politely shaking his pencil, the Inspector averted his gaze. I was just about to clarify my point, when suddenly there was a rap on the door. Wickert got up. As he returned, he held a glass of water in his hand. I attempted to rise, grunting more or less believably. 'Mr Knisch', the Inspector stated as I brought the water to my lips and swallowed – first one mouthful of cool liquid, then another. 'When we went through the files confiscated at your home the other day, interesting data emerged. Here.' Again he pulled out his kerchief to dry my lips. 'The questionnaire we retrieved was only half completed. Yet some of what's being described is punishable by German law. And this . . . This . . . This situation' – finally he managed to reinsert the kerchief in his breast pocket

– 'which so eloquently corroborates what your questionnaire leaves unspoken, hardly makes matters better, does it?' Wickert grinned. 'Especially not since the name on your form appears to be the same as that of your murdered compatriot.'

I must have lost consciousness. When I came to, Wickert was pressing my handbag into my arms, regretting that he could offer me no more time to rest. Felix Karp was still on the loose, and until he had been captured, I was in danger. However drugged I had been, I was the only witness to what had happened in room 202. Karp could hardly risk that I might remember acts of a compromising nature. 'You must hide until we've managed to correct the situation. Who knows what Froehlich will do once he returns?' For the last time this morning, Wickert, still grinning, ran his tongue across his dentures.

'You mean . . .'

'Yes, I do, Mr Knisch. The rot is spreading to all levels of society. The Health Chancellor has friends high up in the hierarchies – even at our headquarters. And if we don't . . .' He must have registered my surprise – or realised, mid-sentence, that I was referring to something else. Buttoning his jacket, he quickly added: 'No, no, Mr Knisch, I doubt you'd be able to commit an act of violence this studied. Only an educated physician could have punctured your compatriot's heart with such precision. In other words: Dr Karp.'

I pressed my bag to my breast.

'As we searched the hotel, not only did we find the Austrian dead, we also discovered you unconscious – with a stiletto in hand. Quite a bloody one, at that. I'm convinced the scene was arranged. But I fear Manetti may not see things as favourably. She claims intuition shouldn't be allowed to colour the cool consideration of facts. Thus far she's been right, of course – if you discount the Wilms case . . .' Sensing my disbelief, Wickert explained the autopsy report had just come. It looked as if Dora had died from an aneurysm in her brain. According to the coroner, although usually reserved for cruel cases of epilepsy, such incidents were known to happen to people put under severe pressure. Taking my arm, the Inspector walked me to the door. 'You see, Mr Knisch, we must assume her cause of death was natural. Regrettably, the city's "mastermind" has made her first false assumption. The case will now be transferred to the Vice Squad.'

Opening the door, he added: 'But the danger's not over. Two assistants will now take you home. I give you my word they won't leave until Karp has been captured.' Wickert motioned to Diels and Pieplack, who had been standing outside the door, then turned to me again. 'As you see, we're on your side. Of course it's mere chance that the murdered person and you have the same name.' He gave me a complicitous handshake. 'As long as you look at things from our perspective, Mr Knisch, your questionnaire will be in safe hands.'

Chapter Twenty-Two

For the last few hours, I've been waiting for Manetti to knock on my door. It's become dark, with a touch of cool to it, and she could come any minute now. Rising around noon, I spent a long time cleaning myself, hunched in my zinc tub. While carefully scrubbing every aching part of my body, I tried to convince myself it still belonged to me. Then, satisfied, or rather dissatisfied, that it did, I got dressed and went over to Sergeant Vogelsang. All he could offer me was some old coffee powder, with a faint whiff of roasted bean, and pretzels hard as stone. A belated breakfast followed, since which I've been trying to maintain my balance sitting on my three-legged desk chair.

Soon this flat will no longer belong to me. In a few hours – according to the alarm clock it's now 9.30 in the evening – it'll be transferred into the callused hands of Frau Britz. She'll probably wait until tomorrow to implement the change of ownership, but after that, I'm convinced I won't have a home. The question is where to turn next. Half an hour ago, as I made myself some new coffee, I saw the sun sink behind the trees and tombstones in a blushing haze of filth. My landlady was just beating rugs in the courtyard. Her determined look as she gazed up towards me was more eloquent than any words. Another beautiful evening was turning to dust, I gathered, and went into the living room again. Installing myself on the windowsill, I had a Moslem. Down in the square, a solitary figure – more shape than substance, more shadow than shape – made himself comfortable on the bench. Perhaps it was the third person from the wasteground? Perhaps it was Dabermann? On the roof of the police car parked outside my building, a few slivers of sun still glistened. The ashes from my cigarette whirled thoughtlessly through the evening air. Then, finally, I drew in my head, retrieved my fountain pen, and returned to this account.

When I got up earlier today, I resolved to write down everything that has happened. And everything that hasn't happened. Given Inspector Wickert's account, I had only the fig leaf of my pride left to lose. Since I found nothing else to write on, I decided to use the pages torn from my books. Yet for each sheet I've been moving from the decreasing left stack to the increasing right one in front of me, I've become more uncertain as to what has occurred. My report may not exactly have been improved by the printed sentences on which my gaze has fallen when, occasionally, I've taken a moment to reflect. As a precaution, I turned all pages upside down in order not to be distracted as I wrote in the margins of the text. Still, at times the temptation has proved too great. A few minutes ago, for example, I read a passage from *Hands Up!*, which was followed by one from Froehlich's 1910 study. At first I didn't realise they were pages from different books. But eventually I understood the guns in Heller's novel couldn't have anything to do with the shooting that ensued. Without noticing, I had slipped into one of the Health Chancellor's case studies. Despairing at the incomprehension with which he's been met in life, a shop assistant from Halberstadt just pressed a muzzle to his temple and fired – not once but twice.

I'm convinced I wouldn't have acted the same way as Mr Willibald Grothe. But the preceding pages have demonstrated how hopeless my situation is. By writing, I've recreated a world that seems not to want to know of me. Probably the shop assistant experienced something similar when the first bullet brushed his hairline. Grothe's problem, I believe, was that his surroundings assumed he disguised himself when he dressed up in the clothes of the opposite sex. In reality, he displayed what he considered biology to hide. After all, a person's sex doesn't have much to do with their genitals. Now that I'm about to collect my last impressions, my final hope rests with the insight for which Grothe was never given credit: the truth need not always be naked.

There's much that irritates me in this story – details I don't comprehend, circumstances I can't understand. For a long time, I assumed everything had to be connected in some obscure yet ultimately evident way. The only thing required was that I exercise my intuition. Eventually, the veil of secrecy would be lifted, revealing the reason behind everything. Now I realise I gave in to a false impulse. The urge is great to place one detail next to another, then that next to a third, and once a sufficient number has been reached, to consider their sum the solution to the problem. I doubt reality adds up in this way. The story in which I've become involved probably consists of different plots sliding in and out of each other. At times, one will influence another; more often, there's merely a fleeting relation.

As I placed the two pages I had just read on top of the right stack in front of me, I realised *that* might be the reason why I hadn't been able to figure out the true nature of things. In the same way as the pages torn from the contents of my former library might just as easily be ordered according to some other principle, the elements of this story might. I was reminded of my substitute teacher back home in Vienna. Once Polster had compiled the drawings executed by my classmates, he had turned and twisted them in such a way that the elbow of one sketch became the nose of another and the ear of a third transformed into the eye of a fourth. Eventually, a picture would emerge in which each detail was part of its original context, yet also contributed to the creation of a novel image. Perhaps I ought to do something similar? What if I gathered all the contradictory details of my story and arrange them into a new, more convincing pattern? Only thus, I suspected, would my tale become more than its parts. What it needed was an irisation.

Take Wickert, for example. Last night, vile as it was, I may not have been particularly lucid. But not even the uncomfortable handbag on which my head had rested prevented me from understanding that everything the Inspector said couldn't possibly be true. A scientific institution like the Health Chancellor's was no source of contagion, spreading sexual corruption throughout the city. Karp and Froehlich may have collaborated over the years. If nothing else, the book I found in Anton's suitcase indicated as much. But why not? They're professional brethren. And in any event, the publication had been penned by a Karp whose first name began not with an *F* but an *A*. Even if it happened to be the same person, something I reckoned circumstances allowed me to assume, I doubted he was an offender – or worse, a murderer. I happened to know something to which Wickert didn't seem privy: although he considered himself a member of the male species, Karp couldn't possibly have given me the treatment I received at Hotel Kreuzer. More, I believe, need not be said about *that* matter.

If such a vital detail in the interpretation of what had occurred wasn't correct, there was no reason to assume all others were. The question, however, was to determine which information offered by Wickert needed to be twisted so as to yield a different interpretation of the overall picture – and, of course, whether the Inspector was aware of it. As long as the head of the city's Vice Squad could exploit the situation and close the Foundation, I feared it mattered little to him whether what he claimed turned out to have a sound bearing on veracity. What could offer a better opportunity to shut down the Health Chancellor's institute than the fact that he and Gielke were in Copenhagen? Surely, in such a situation, establishing what truly had happened was no priority? The real question, rather, was why Wickert had placed me in what amounted to house arrest.

I was certain Froehlich's name had been on the slip of paper

Dora had been clutching as she arrived from Kolberg. Presumably Karp, working as a nurse at the Health Chancellor's clinic, let her stay with him. When we visited the Foundation, Dora had told me he was her oldest friend. It was safe to assume, then, that originally he had used his given name of Adele, before earning a French doctor's degree and returning to Germany as Karp, Felix, *dr. méd*. According to Wickert, Dora had visited the Foundation on several occasions over the last few months. The Inspector seemed to think it was because of sexological films. But as far as I could see, even if accurate, that was likely to be only one part of a pattern. Another part, perhaps of a different pattern, was what Karp himself had told me: Dora had begun to wonder what would happen to the boy she had given up for adoption if she were to contact the police. If only I could manage to twist these parts so that they would yield a different picture from the one I had made myself thus far!

I doubt it would have entered Dora's mind to contact the authorities if she had known her child was pampered by parents and spoiled by nannies. The visit to the Apollo hadn't been a courtesy call. Most likely, she had been looking for evidence that might strengthen her suspicions – which ought to imply that the boy to whom she had given birth half a year after arriving from Kolberg had connections with the Brotherhood. Why else her clandestine investigations? Now, Dora didn't know whether she'd be putting her son in even greater danger by contacting the police. Perhaps he had fallen out with his adoptive family and joined one of the gangs Hauptstein was recruiting? But Klaus and Harro weren't old enough to be her child. Who was her boy then? And how had she managed to find him after so many years?

When we met at the Paris Bar the first time, Dora had confessed she didn't want to know who had adopted her son. By cutting her ties to the past, she claimed it would be easier to start a new life. She must have heard about or seen her child in a different context, then, perhaps by chance, and suddenly realised that . . . No. Wait. Now I know who it must be! Strange that I haven't thought of it before. How blind I've been! But the boy in the photo that accompanied the newspaper article we had read – couldn't it be him, sitting stiffly in tailor's pose in front of Froehlich and Gielke?

I got up and went looking for the copy of the *Tageblatt* Dora had given me. Finally, after having rummaged around for a considerable time, I found it underneath the Trojan horse. Spreading the paper in front of me, I studied the picture we had mused on last spring, the same morning we visited the Foundation and this affair had had its sad beginning. There was Froehlich with tousled hair and tremendous grin; there was his partner with flamboyant scarf and discreet smile. And there were Mssrs Left and Right. Now I could see that, to the left of the Health Chancellor, Karp stood smartly, whereas to the right of Gielke, Osram Röser posed fatly. The former looked into the camera with a faint twinkle retiring to the corners of his eyes; the latter had turned his face to the side, so that only the side of his face, pale as dough, met the viewer. And there, sitting on the lowest stair, in front of patients and employees alike, was a twelve- or thirteen-year-old boy with pimply face, fists clenched in his lap, and a back as straight as a plank.

It wasn't difficult to tell who he was today, ten years later. The hair was the same, the apprehensive eyes and the athletic build as well. Mr Yellow Hair. Dora had given birth to her child in 1907. If the boy had reached puberty when this group portrait was taken at the inauguration of the Foundation in 1919 – acne and anger seemed to indicate as much – he must be twenty-odd years old by now. That appeared about right. Perhaps Dora had begun to suspect who he was the first time we had discussed the photo? And tried to find out during the months before we saw his forehead on the cut-out last spring? And I had called him 'the heir of the place', even a 'corrupt soul'! Small wonder she had turned silent. Inspecting the portrait, I could now see Dora's suspicion had been right: it wasn't Gielke's hand that rested on the boy's shoulder, it was Röser's. I assumed that meant he was the homeless boy the librarian had taken into his custody, the one who today was working as his assistant. When we visited the

Foundation, Röser's aide had been on his break. Perhaps nothing would have happened if Dora had met him then. But this way, she felt compelled to probe further, in order to calm her mounting suspicions. What was the name of the assistant again? Albert, no, Alfred, no, Alf something. Alf . . . Alf Kinkel. Heavens. 'AK.' What if *he* had visited Dora last Friday?

In that case, it was hardly surprising she hadn't contacted the police. Or that she had agreed to treat me as her sister when I had arrived an hour too early. Dora must have realised she had made double appointments – perhaps the initials confused her – and the best way to get rid of me had been to acquiesce to whatever whim had struck my fancy. But only if she was paid properly, so that I'd understand that the sisterhood we were about to re-establish was of a temporary nature. She was no longer a minette, and I was no longer a customer. Yes, last Friday, Dora was visited by two 'AK's. When the doorbell rang a second time, she had no choice but to shove me into the closet and open the front door. To judge from the pie prepared in the kitchen, she had planned to celebrate. However, she and Kinkel must have got into a fight. If Röser's assistant had the background I suspected he did, he would have defended himself against any suggestions of a relationship. For someone who believed in the triumph of the testicles, Dora's truth must have been too hard to accept. Perhaps he taunted and provoked his mother, who, already pressured, suffered from an aneurysm? It was impossible to tell. But if so, it was as good as murder.

As I twisted the details of what might have happened, I understood there were two, if not three, patterns involved in this story. The first concerned Dora and her son. The second involved Hauptstein's attempts to organise the city's gangs in order to increase the potency of roughly half of Germany's population. And the third, most likely, had to do with Anton's films. Since it attracted unwanted attention to their own affairs, the Brotherhood must have felt threatened by my friend's attempt to shoot a white movie. Karp had explained that Froehlich's opponents were trying to secure the means with which to extract a hundred per cent pure andrine from male glands. The film to which I had been privy during Stegemann's session suggested they were onto a method. A few days later, when I visited the Foundation's library, I had witnessed Hauptstein and Röser exchange files. It must have been the Health Chancellor's studies on the subject. Why else the hurry? Froehlich was expected back next weekend, and with the police breathing down their necks, the Brotherhood couldn't risk losing time now that they were so close to the solution.

Although the patterns related to each other, there was no single configuration. Still, I could see there was something like a focal point: the Foundation for Sexual Research. The more I considered the unpleasant things that had happened, the clearer it seemed to me they were related to the 'apostle of semen' Karp had elucidated at the museum. Hauptstein was using the Foundation's resources behind the back of Froehlich, in order to prepare for a society based on ancient ideals. Yet to judge from what had occurred last night, something must still be threatening his plans – and *that* could only be the film clip. Most likely, it contained footage that exposed the activities of the Brotherhood for what they were: criminal. But what more precisely? Else had told me that, one day, Otto had declared he didn't want to continue his acting. When she had wondered why, he had explained another boy had treated him 'badly'. That must have been Alf Kinkel. And now, fearing it might destroy his plans for the future, Hauptstein fought to prevent the truth of what his assistant had done from coming out.

Inspired by my revelations, Anton had rented room 202 to shoot the concluding scene of his film. When Klaus and Harro had discovered what he was up to, they had reported to Hauptstein, who must have thought Lakritz was onto the missing film. I no longer doubted the person I had seen hunched over the washstand had been the leader of the Brotherhood. Together with Kinkel, Hauptstein had overpowered Anton and searched the room. Not finding the film, they had tried to force a confession out of my friend. But he hadn't been able to provide them with a satisfactory answer. And why would he? Worried that Anton might incriminate them, the Brotherhood had had no choice but to kill him. Which meant . . . Which meant that Dora hadn't hidden the film at Hotel Kreuzer after all. Where then? Where it had been all along, of course. In her own flat.

Anton hadn't found it during his nocturnal visit to the Otto-Ludwig-Straße. But then, he hadn't had much time. If I managed to get hold of the clip, I'd be able not only to prove my own innocence, but also to take revenge for my friend's death. Although retrieving it would be a triumph of sorts, actually, the shrewd thing to do, I reflected, would be to make sure the clip was still hidden at Dora's flat and then place another anonymous call to the police. In this way, I'd not be implicated more than necessary. The film would prove what Hauptstein and Kinkel had been up to, and sooner or later the police would understand the same thing had happened to Anton. 'AK' would turn out to stand for Dora's son – her murderer, if not in person then in spirit – and I'd be left in peace. Furthermore, there was that object Anton had noticed in Dora's kitchen which, I reckoned, it might be prudent to take care of.

But instead, I'm locked up in a flat that soon won't belong to me, protected by a police force that, whether it knows it or not, is shielding murderers from further harm.

Does that mean the Vice Squad is collaborating with the Brotherhood? I doubt it. Still, even if Wickert isn't actively assisting Hauptstein, he's furthering his cause. By pronouncing Dora dead of natural causes, the Inspector has been able to throw Manetti's sense of judgment into enough doubt to allow him to take over the case – which would suit the Brotherhood only too well. The sole kink remaining is the film clip. Anton couldn't say where it was, so Hauptstein killed him. Then I came along, all sixth sense but zero reason, and unexpectedly, he was offered another chance. Unfortunately I was drugged so strongly I lost it entirely. Later, after Hauptstein and his people had cleared out, Wickert arrived at the hotel, interpreting what had happened in just the way the Brotherhood hoped.

Supposedly, the officers downstairs are here to protect me. But I realise now there might be a different explanation. Since I'm locked up, I won't be able to interfere with Wickert's investigation. Manetti may coolly and logically deduce that I murdered Anton and come to arrest me. In this manner, Wickert will solve his case and get us both out of his way. The evidence is staggering, and no judge in the world will . . .

Wait. The door just slammed shut downstairs. Now I can hear steps ascending the stairs. Soon Manetti will knock on my door. And this time, there really is no way out.

Chapter Twenty-Three

Much has happened since I interrupted my account and tied a torn silk stocking around these loose book pages. Now it's already Sunday night, July 8, 1928, almost two days after there was a heavy knock on my door – and Ivan Britz entered, limping. At first I didn't believe my eyes. Repeatedly he had to inform me he brought no inspector in tow. Manetti? Karla Manetti? Ivan had no unfinished business with the city's mastermind. Still, if she planned to come by, he wouldn't mind trading a few words. 'Comrade,' he groaned, putting down the pillows he had been carrying, 'it's criminal to live like this!'

Returning out into the stairway, Ivan was about to describe the situation to his mother, who was still waiting on the ground floor, gaze trained upwards, through the slit created by the winding banister, when I shoved him into the flat again. I had just realised there might be a way out after all. Quickly I showed the flat's new inhabitant around, offering him all my worldly possessions, albeit unsorted, in return for his help. But it wasn't until I pointed out that I'd even be prepared to give Ivan my last reichsmark, including Anton's jacket and half a pack of Moslems, that he ceased to shake his head. Dubious, he crossed his arms. '"Help", you said. In what struggle?' I explained, and a series of shakes later, Ivan steadied his shorn skull. 'It sounds unnatural. But I suppose it's for a good cause.' He frowned. 'Just as long as we don't have to set eyes on each other again, all right?'

That's how, shortly after midnight, I was able to leave what had amounted to my home for the last three years without being noticed by the police. Dressed in Ivan Britz's raincoat, soiled and stinking of fish, I had tied the two pillows he had brought with him around my waist, so as to fill out the rubberised cover. Sunk to the level of my eyebrows was a fishmonger's straw hat. In order to seem purposeful, I carried a bundle of paper under my arm. Dressed as a man, I had no difficulties in passing unnoticed. The assistants merely saw a gouty worker on his way to the marketplace. One of them looked as if he were prepared to crank down the side window and ask about labour conditions. But discovering that the fishmonger aimed for a black Torpedo leaning against the façade, his colleague placed a quick hand on his shoulder. As for me, I placed my bundle on the back of my bicycle. A minute went by, then the punctured back tyre echoed carelessly between the houses as I rolled across the cobblestones, around the corner, down towards the Stock Exchange and the big square.

Dora's street was empty as I turned into it half an hour later, clinking and clattering. To make the trip more comfortable, I had tied the pillows to the saddle once I was out of sight of my protectors. Still, it was a relief to get off the wobbly vehicle. There was no police car parked outside Dora's building, no cigarette glowing in the dark underneath the *Stadtbahn* tracks. Even so, to be safe, I refrained from turning on the lights. As I ascended the stairs, two steps at a time, I wondered what would happen to my friend's flat. Personally, I was without a place to live, and perhaps it'd be possible to . . . I didn't have time to complete my thought before I reached the third floor and discovered the police's seal had been broken. At this point, at the least, I ought to have become suspicious. But I was too excited about getting out of the trap that Wickert had set to devote more than fleeting attention to the matter. Quietly I slid in and closed the door behind me.

The air was thick and fusty, with a sucrose tang to it, as if it had begun to decompose. Nonetheless I experienced something close to serenity. For so long, I had been stumbling around in a dark full of fantasies and disreputable activities. Malice, pleasure and secrecy seemed, wilfully, to have traded places. Yet finally, having twisted the events and explanations of the last weeks, a solution had revealed itself that even I, making so much of dissimulation, could support. A sweet thrill coursed through my body, not unlike a muscle gradually tensing. I checked my pockets for cigarettes – but found only Dora's locked cigarette case. Removing the stinking raincoat, I untied my boots and continued on naked soles through the corridor. The wicker mat tickled pleasantly, there was a hum in my blood. I knew I was on the right track.

While I had been scribbling my account along the margins of torn pages earlier the same day, I had had more than one occasion to ponder what Dora had expressed not in loud words but in silent deeds. And at long last, it had dawned on me where she must have hidden what everyone seemed to be looking for. It hadn't been in room 202 at Hotel Kreuzer after all, but right here, in the Otto-Ludwig-Straße. The Trojan horse that Anton had retrieved was not it, however. Dora's wooden animal did indeed contain something she didn't want to display publicly. Yet the frayed ribbon stored in its abdominal cavity was not her secret but Dorothea Walther's. What love was to one, sorrow was to the other. In her own manner, Dora had tried to make up for Dorothea's wrongdoing. Never again would she confuse heart and hormones. The last thing she must have expected was that a person calling himself Anton would force her to reconsider. No, that was probably the second-to-last thing. The last thing she had expected must have been that he wouldn't understand her.

The living room was streaked by the sloping light of streetlamps falling in through the window – just enough for me to see where to put my feet. A *Stadtbahn* train roared by. Once its fastidious thunder had receded, I walked across the room, to the reproduction hanging above the gramophone. The last time I had pondered the woman robed in red had been a week ago, when I had put down one bill after another on the coffee table, while Dora had assumed the same mien as the secretive lady. Where would she have hidden the film clip if not behind this woman's back? Unceremoniously, I stepped up to the picture.

'Good evening, Mr Knisch.'

The reproduction came crashing to the floor. As I turned around, empty-handed and faint-headed, I could just about make out a shape seated in the chair to the right of the window, next to a floor lamp. 'I suppose this is what you're looking for?' The person held up a shiny object which, in the jerky light of a new *Stadtbahn* train, this time heading in the opposite direction, could be seen only a single frame at a time. Despite the unnerving row of the carriages, it wasn't difficult to distinguish the voice. 'Why don't you have a seat?'

I considered my options. When, finally, I realised I had none left, I lost all remaining willpower, all remaining hope, and sank into a chair, drained and deflated, as if I'd never be able to get up again. There. The last chance to help Dora and to clear my name had just disappeared. A ghostly hand reached for the floor lamp. I could hear the chain of metal studs rattle against the pod. Then there was a click, and light yellowed the dark. It was Inspector Manetti.

I think I should insert an empty space here in order to register my shock.

If I had devoted more than a brief thought to the broken seal at the door, I might have been able to guess somebody was in the flat – Inspector Wickert, for example, Alf Kinkel, or even Horst Hauptstein. But Karla Manetti? Now I didn't know what to think. Or to say. I made a well-known gesture, hoping she'd appreciate my situation. Yes, that's right. That was my towel. I was giving up.

'Spare me the drama, Mr Knisch.' The Inspector's voice was silken but steady, with a touch of something I couldn't help interpreting as amusement. Struggling, I sat up. Perhaps she cared to explain what she meant? Otherwise, I didn't know whether . . .

'I can see you have no reason to trust the police. But this time you may rest assured. If you cooperate, you'll get what you want.' Manetti smiled noncommittally. 'We don't have much time, however, so let's determine the background to your visit, shall we, Mr Knisch?'

When I didn't reply, she continued. 'This sad affair began in the spring 1907, when a pregnant girl knocked at Martin Froehlich's door. I assume you know of whom I'm speaking? Good. At the time, the girl was sixteen years old and called herself Dorothea Walther. She had a childhood friend, who worked as a nurse at the Doctor's clinic. Let's call this friend Karp, shall we? Dr Felix Karp.' Again, I nodded wearily. 'After consulting with Froehlich, the girl was given the advice not to have an abortion. She was already in her third month, and the Doctor couldn't rule out fateful consequences. If she had told him who the father was, he might have offered a different diagnosis. But she maintained the person responsible had been a cook at the family's inn, so he advised her to sit out the remaining time and then give the child up for adoption. Karp promised to take care of the girl, while Froehlich agreed to secure her child a dependable future.'

I muttered something about having already arranged those details into a pattern. In this particular case, my source of information had been Karp himself, who . . .

'Ah, yes,' Manetti broke in, 'the evasive Dr Karp, who hasn't been seen since Miss Wilms died last Friday – except by you, of course.'

I explained that I may have suffered from a hangover, and that accordingly, my visit to the Foundation last Saturday had felt like a bad dream. But the knowledge I had acquired was faultless; my attempt at irisation proved as much. If the Inspector wanted to, I could explain everything. In order to instil vigour into my assertion, I expounded on the person who first had called herself Dorothea, then Dora. And this time, I didn't keep anything of personal importance back. 'There you have it,' I finally sighed.

'That's it. The naked truth. And if that's not enough, Inspector, I don't know what is.'

Manetti had listened patiently. Yet when I finished, she merely acknowledged: 'It all sounds very revealing, Mr Knisch. But I think a few details still need to be accounted for, don't you? And they might yield a different picture than the one you just proposed. Or do you disagree?' I shrugged and patted my pockets for cigarettes. All I found, however, was the locked cigarette case. 'Take the parents of Miss Walther's boy, for instance.' According to Manetti, Froehlich had contacted a childless couple he had acquainted in conjunction with a court case. The Health Chancellor's Hippocratic oath prevented him from divulging who it was. 'But many years have passed, and today the adoptive parents are dead. Are you familiar with the name of Adam Hatz?'

'Of course.' At least if the Inspector was thinking of the former director of war materials. Wasn't he the one who had donated one of the buildings in which the Foundation for Sexual Research now resided?

'Indeed. "This place consecrated to love and sorrow", as Hatz put it in his will. Froehlich met him in connection with the affair at the Potsdam garrisons. Hatz was accused of "unmanly" activities as well as of corruption of highly placed officers. From what I gather, the former accusation was groundless, the latter perhaps not so. In order to demonstrate his standing, the court asked Hatz to prove his virility. A curious demand, if you think about it, which apparently he was able to fulfil only by having a child.'

Slowly I began to understand what Manetti was getting at. And how wrong I had been. My irisation hadn't been complete. Now I knew who Dora's son was. And it wasn't Alf Kinkel.

Before I managed to utter the boy's name, however, the Inspector continued. 'Since Hatz felt the need, though not necessarily the drive, to make his wife pregnant, the couple chose to adopt. Thus Froehlich was able to solve two problems with one stroke. At the same time as he helped Adam Hatz display his virility, he found new parents for Miss Walther's child.' According to

Manetti, Dora's boy was raised in a home characterised by Prussian virtues – which, among other things, meant he saw his parents only sporadically. 'Fortunately, he had a Polish nanny, who took care of him as if she were his mother. The older the boy got, however, the more evident his hereditary traits became.' Manetti wasn't thinking, primarily, of the fact that the Hatzes had been swarthy, chubby and short, like so many people of Galician origin, whereas their child had seemed blatantly 'Nordic' in appearance: blond hair, steel-grey eyes, and so on. The decisive differences were of an inner nature. Young Mr Hatz demonstrated un-mistakable signs of aloofness. He spoke rarely, preferably not at all, and seemed blissfully oblivious to the demands of people around him, electing to live in a world of his own making, surrounded by sounds and tones only he was able to hear.

'We'll never know what happened. But in August 1918, the Hatz's residence was ravished by fire. The gutter press claimed it was a gruesome form of suicide committed by a desperate Galician, who wasn't ashamed of taking his close and dear ones with him in his personal disaster. They even spoke of an "Unhinged Prometheus". I'm less sure. What do you think, Mr Knisch? Perhaps it was arson, perhaps merely a fatal mistake? The only thing proved by the investigation, conducted jointly by us and the insurance company, was that somebody had been playing with matches. We weren't even able to determine conclu-sively how many people died in the fire. Since nobody contacted the authorities, however, I should think it safe to assume the entire family, nanny included, perished. If anyone managed to get out alive, the physical injuries must have been punishing.'

Thumbing Dora's cigarette case, I wondered when Manetti would get to what she really wanted. 'This is where our mutual concerns intersect,' she now declared, as if she had been radio-scoping my thoughts. 'I'm not interested in what Froehlich did twenty years ago. Nor in what you're up to today, Mr Knisch. Only the Vice Squad bothers with paragraph 168. Still, I won't walk around with my hands primly placed behind my back, while others are doing their dextrous best to reinterpret the law.'

'But . . .'

Manetti waved away my objections. 'The matter's simple, Mr Knisch.' She pressed her fingertips against each other. 'Only if you cooperate will I be able to prevent Gunnar Wickert from proving that you killed Anton Josef Lakritz.' I flinched. 'My colleague claims he found you resting on a sofa at Hotel Kreuzer. Supposedly you were holding a stiletto in your hand. In the room next door, your compatriot was sitting naked save for a doctor's coat. I regret to have to inform you he wasn't only stabbed in the heart, but also had been submitted to certain acts before he died. Need I add they're forbidden by paragraph 175?' Manetti studied me, not unsympathetically. 'Wickert's charge is serious, Mr Knisch, and if you don't oblige, I'll be forced to take you in. Regrettably, you don't have much time to make up your mind. Diels will soon realise you've left. I have ordered Pieplack to make him stay, but he can't pull rank. As you may understand,' the Inspector lowered her hands, 'it would be helpful if we solved our mutual problem before they join us.'

I knew better than to open my mouth.

Evidently, the Vice Squad had been keeping Anton under surveillance. 'As long as his contributions to cinematography were passed around in private circles, Wickert couldn't interfere. But then Lakritz began to borrow props from Froehlich's museum. Soon, less scrupulous cinemas in town were screening films in which equipment and machinery were demonstrated that had no obvious pedagogical purpose. Somebody at the Foundation must have given your friend access to the collections.'

'Karp,' I suggested quietly.

'The Doctor probably thought Lakritz produced scientific films. And now, having resigned from his job, he has disappeared, ashamed of this collaboration . . .' Curiously, Manetti shook her head but smiled. 'Last winter, during one of its annual drives to clean up our city, the Vice Squad searched a night club called the Blue Cellar – a rather tumultuous affair, I gather, which led to Inspector Wickert, dressed as a civilian, having his teeth knocked out. But there were positive side effects to the investigation, too. One of the persons detained turned out to be a former partner of Lakritz's, a singer of German-Latvian descent. In order not to be charged, she decided to settle an old score. That's how my colleague was tipped off about what happened at the Foundation on certain nights, when the museum was illuminated by artificial light and shadows moved behind the curtains. Shortly thereafter, the Vice Squad searched the pension where your friend was staying. Incriminating material was seized, but Lakritz managed to escape. Since then, he's been swallowed up by the ground.'

I coughed. 'A place called . . .' I coughed again. 'A place called Pension Landau might have ingested him.' Wearily I understood how events, seemingly unconnected, had influenced each other. 'It's not far from here. He was using a different name, though.' I told Manetti which.

'That would make sense. According to the porter at Hotel Kreuzer, an "Anton Knisch" rented room 202 last night. Referring to some kind of code – "K. u. K.", I believe – Wickert claimed that was proof enough the two of you were collaborating. Obviously he was mistaken. Lakritz was preparing to shoot a scene at a convalescent home when he was surprised. If his assistant, an African woman, hadn't alerted the police, we wouldn't have known anything. Wickert headed straight for the hotel.'

Getting up, Manetti looked out of the window. A minute went by, then a train approached on the elevated *Stadtbahn* tracks. As it reached us, it shuddered, slowed down, and glided, with a shrieking noise, into the platform. From the station half a block away, there were several signals. The odd door slid open and one or two late passengers hurried down the stairs. Once the train had left the station again, vanishing in the far distance, the Inspector cleared her throat. 'I suppose you'd like to keep certain things under cover, Mr Knisch.'

'Like most people, Inspector.' Twisting the item in my hands, I realised we might be getting to the final denouement, after all.

'Good. I, on the other hand, would like to solve a murder. If our two concerns were connected, we might be able to resolve this situation in a manner that could prove mutually beneficial.' Manetti turned towards the picture I had dropped, shoving together the shards of broken glass with her foot. 'Let's assume neither you nor I can say who visited Miss Wilms last Friday. We might know better, of course. But as far as I can tell, there's no way to prove the matter. What we're left with is our imagination. Yet imagination, too, is worthy of consideration, wouldn't you agree?' She straightened up. 'Take yourself, for instance. You claim you were working on an article on Friday afternoon, sitting in the square where you live. Shortly before six, you left for the Apollo on your bicycle. Your colleague, Mrs Himmel, has corroborated that you arrived in time for the first screening. So obviously, you can't be the unknown "AK". And it could hardly be Adele Karp, could it, seeing that it's been years since she changed her life, including her first name?'

When I still didn't reply, the Inspector smiled thinly. 'If that's the case, Mr Knisch, mustn't we assume it was Lakritz who had an appointment with Miss Wilms last Friday – although not under his real name, but the one you just told me he was using at his pension? You and I may know better, of course . . .' Manetti paused. She seemed to be thinking through the ramifications of her reasoning. I could almost hear the smooth spin of cog wheels clicking into one another. 'Yet something must have happened that made Lakritz lose his bearings. Perhaps he threatened her in a fit of panic? Or maybe he overreacted when she didn't offer him the services expected? The only thing we may tell for sure is that his actions caused a sudden aneurysm with fatal consequences.' The words hung in the air. 'Yes,' the Inspector finally added, having pondered her line of argument and decided it might hold. She sat down again. 'Yes, we must assume the person who died was Dora Wilms and not her visitor, since the latter would presuppose a switch of identities – and that's impossible in the case of Lakritz. It would make sense only if the visitor were a member of the opposite sex, like Felix Karp. Given that the venerable Doctor has disappeared, however, that means the sole person who may tell us what happened at your friend's place – your compatriot – is dead.'

I began to see why Manetti was considered a mastermind. The solution she had just proposed was keener, bolder, infinitely more imaginative than my botched attempt at irisation. In this way, what had happened – or, for that matter, what hadn't happened – in the Otto-Ludwig-Straße need not be divulged. Wickert wouldn't be able to invoke paragraph 168, and I was relieved from the burden of explaining what I had been up to in Dora's closet.

'The only possible obstruction to this rendition of events,' Manetti said, 'is this.' She held up a metal object. I could see it was the same object Anton had noticed in Dora's kitchen. 'We found it when we searched the flat. The visitor must have brought it. You'd almost think it's a spatula, no? As far as I'm aware, however, only Doctor Karp suffered from epilepsy.' The object shone ominously. 'So, since we've agreed Karp couldn't be the "AK" in question, we must assume this obscure object is – well, no, not an olisbos, but, well, perhaps a modern cake-slice?' Manetti smiled, a little less thinly. 'Tell me, might it be one of the reasons you're here, Mr Knisch?'

I shrugged.

'Please, take it. Whatever it is, it merely complicates the scene I just sketched.' She nodded towards the broken glass. 'I understand the slice is not the only reason you're here, however. May I inquire why you found the Rossetti reproduction so interesting?' Again, I shrugged. 'Indeed, it *is* prudent to remain silent, Mr Knisch. But allow me to remind you that silence is a complicated matter. It cuts both ways.' Her smile disappeared. 'Take the anonymous call we received last Friday night, for example. What has been bothering me isn't so much what was said, but what wasn't said. Why didn't the caller give us her name? At first, I assumed Miss Wilms had only one visitor. But wouldn't it make more sense if our caller was already in the flat when the visitor rang the bell? That would explain why Wilms rested so peacefully on her bed, wouldn't it? I doubt Lakritz would have bothered to carry her body into the bedroom. No, once he had departed, our anonymous caller, sneaking out from wherever she was hiding, tended to the dead.'

My restive fingers must have fiddled with the cigarette case more than I was aware of, for Manetti eyed them curiously. 'Please go ahead, Mr Knisch. I'm not bothered by smoke.'

'Thanks,' I said, holding up the case. 'But it's locked.'

'In any event,' the Inspector resumed, 'there's another reason to believe a third person was in the flat. Actually, it's the strongest one. I kept thinking Wilms's visitor came for something he assumed to be in her possession. But then it occurred to me it might be the other way round. What if he hadn't *departed*, but *arrived* with something?' Manetti crossed her legs. 'In that case, logic demands that whatever this *je ne sais quoi* was, it must have been in the flat when we searched it – as long as there wasn't a third person, that is, who took it once the visitor had left. In short: our anonymous caller.' She paused delicately. 'You see, Mr Knisch, there's more to silence than one might think.'

Clearing my throat, I agreed that Manetti's reasoning seemed flawless, at least as long as one accepted the premises – which, however, as she herself admitted, remained based on speculation. How could she prove the pattern created was correct?

'Oh, I suppose it would be pleasing to establish the identity of our anonymous caller, but I doubt it would solve our problem. No, let's merely assume *you* know her. And let's assume, furthermore, that you happen to have in your possession the secret she took with her. For me, that would be enough. If my feeling is correct that you didn't come tonight merely to retrieve what I just gave you, but also to hide something, perhaps behind the back of the red-robed lady here,' she nodded towards the reproduction, 'that might suffice.'

There was no longer any point. The moment had come. Reluctantly, I extended Dora's cigarette case. 'Thanks, but . . .' Manetti studied the object. 'Ah, I get it. A Pandora's box. How appropriate. Let's see what evils it contains.' She tried to prise open the two halves.

'You need a key,' I informed her. 'Unfortunately, I don't have one.'

'I'm sure this will do.' The Inspector took the obscure object she had put on the table. Inserting it between the two halves, she twisted. It was a match made, if not in heaven, at least in a laboratory. Promptly there was a crack, after which the case opened. 'Just what I thought. Have you had time to look at it?' I shook my head, unsure whether it was the right answer. Manetti closed the case. 'If my suspicions are correct, uncoiled, this roll of film will prove to contain incriminating scenes. I understand they are from an operation performed on a boy whose andrine was removed erroneously, instead of his gynecine. I take it the surgeon can be identified. It's not like in the films that Stegemann shows these days.'

Stegemann? Did she know about my boss's screenings?

'Your colleague was quite cooperative when Pieplack spoke to her. They're from the same country, you know. Mrs Himmel claims you visited the other night, telling her about the scientific films screened outside your regular programme. She also informed Pieplack that, after a visit by Miss Wilms the other week, she had asked her son to return a spoiled film reel to its proper owner.' Manetti looked at me. 'I imagine these sticky frames are from that reel. If we're lucky, they'll be enough to charge the surgeon. Whether they'll be enough to indict his assistants, too, remains to be seen.' She handed me the metal object. 'But if there's to be a chance, I need your cooperation, Mr Knisch. I must ask you to exercise that talent you're using when you're not working part-time as Apollo's projectionist.'

I beg her pardon?

'Your imagination, Mr Knisch. What else?' Coolly, Manetti put the cigarette case in her pocket. 'I need an account of what has happened. And what hasn't happened. In return, I promise that the person we've chosen to refer to as Felix Karp will be left alone. Incidentally,' she added, patting her coat pocket, 'the same applies to the boy on this film – wherever, whoever, he happens to be today.' She got up. 'Yes, let's assume you really saw Doctor Karp last Saturday. Let's assume he told you about Dorothea Walther. And let's assume he resigned with immediate effect, before he simply went up in smoke.'

Since Manetti, smiling ambiguously, had stopped asking me questions, I chose to exercise my right to remain silent. Then, recalling the bundle of paper I had left on my bicycle downstairs, I admitted I might already have attempted to do what she suggested. But after our nightly conversation, as far as I could gather, my failed irisation would only be misleading.

'Misleading?' Manetti seemed amused. 'You know, Doctor Froehlich would argue that deviations, too, have a certain merit . . .' Noticing my incredulity, she added: 'Mr Knisch, I'm afraid I'll have to ask you to offer your perspective – deviant or not. With a little luck, it may suffice to bring this case to court.' The Inspector smiled pertly. 'Let's consider it your contribution to forbidden literature.'

As we parted, the sky was just clearing. Soon the sun would rise above the rooftops. When, half an hour later, I reached the square where I live – sorry, where I used to live – I noticed the police car in front of my building had left. I threw a scatter of gravel at Heino's kitchen window. A minute went by, then Boris opened, flattening his sprightly moustache with muscular fingers. While I rubbed off the worst of the fish reek at the kitchen sink, he told me the men who had attacked Dabor had confessed. Working at the construction site next to Heino's, they had mugged people and burgled over a dozen homes in the neighbourhood. Boris poured a glass of vodka, then added he wouldn't be surprised if they were also responsible for turning my flat into a battlefield. Thinking the landlady's son had already moved in, those nationalists must have tried to even the political score. I dried myself with a towel and explained that, as far as I was concerned, it didn't really matter. The flat belonged to the Britzes now. Having downed the vodka in one greedy gulp, I then installed myself on the kitchen sofa. The sun, rosy but hazy, had just risen above the neighbouring building. Chérie wagged her tail, but didn't move. Soon we both fell asleep, and at least in my case, it amounted to a deep, dreamless sleep.

I was awoken at lunchtime by a rough tongue exploring my face. When Heino had managed to brush aside his inquisitive poodle, he announced that he and Boris had decided to visit Heino's mother. Perhaps I wouldn't mind looking after the business while they were gone? The turnover was best during the weekends, when people had time to pay dead or dear ones their courtesy, and now that it looked like they were partners again, Heino needed the extra income. I nodded. Once they had left, I filled Chérie's bowl, carried it into the courtyard, and closed the door as soon as I had managed to lure the dog out. Then I prepared a hot bath and soaked in the searing water until the fish stench disappeared completely, my fingertips turning white in the process and my toes wrinkly as raisins.

That Saturday afternoon, between the odd rose and funeral wreath sold, I made arrangements for Anton's final resting place at the cemetery behind my former home. I also managed to fix my Torpedo. It was pure, unadulterated joy to grease the chain and pump up the wheels, to polish the mudguards and oil the wooden handles. I even adjusted the saddle, so that it would no longer creak. Just as I was about to close the shop for the day, the phone rang – five lengthy clatters before I picked up. Names don't matter, but for simplicity's sake, I shall refer to the person at the other end of the line as Felix Karp.

Having handed in his resignation, he had travelled to Copenhagen to sort out a 'personal matter' with the Health Chancellor. As I thought I could hear him pause to light a cigarette, I took the opportunity to tell him what had happened since we had last seen each other. When finally I had finished, he inhaled deeply and asked whether he could still count on my silence. Of course, I retorted, if this affair had taught me anything, it was the precious cost of just that. Then I inquired whether he had any use for the object Manetti had given me. A cake-slice? No, Karp didn't need one. After that, we sat with the receiver pressed to our ears, listening to each other breathing. What could be said had been said. We both knew this might be the last time we'd hear from each other. Karp was looking forward to a new life; I, having no other option, planned to enjoy my old one. Finally, rolling the tip of his cigarette against the edge of an ashtray, he asked me one last favour.

Now it's already Sunday night, and I'm almost done with my irisation. I fear it may remain a bit oblique, but I trust clear eyes will see the point of that. As I carried my bicycle upstairs this morning, onto the pavement, I could sense the air was stale and humid. Half an hour later, there was brash, bumpy thunder, and now the rain is pouring down. After weeks of 'spectacular' summer, the sky finally cracked open. At regular intervals, the square is illuminated by jittery lightning, as if some higher power were nervously fiddling with the switch. When I brought the last bucket of flowers downstairs, I discovered not a single drop had hit the threshold. The rain was a massive curtain half a metre from the façade, tight and streaming. I shut my eyes, feeling the fine spread of humidity across my face, and thought I might see a different world when I opened them again. But all I saw was Chérie, drenched and dejected. Giving in, I let Heino's pitiful dog inside, and when her master called to let me know he and Boris would be late, I told him about the havoc wreaked by the rain. Dirty water was running down the stairs, creating brown puddles around pots and buckets. Heino asked me to put rags in front of the door and pray for the best.

A few minutes ago, I did the former. Now I'll lock up, hide the key under Chérie's bowl, and do the latter. Then I'll put this bundle of paper in an envelope and send it to Manetti. After that, there's only the object I promised Karp I'd deliver before I'm free to do as I wish. I've just put on Ivan Britz's raincoat. The clips already grace my ankles, and Dora's wooden horse is in the suitcase on the back of my bicycle. Soon the bouncy wheels of my black Torpedo shall carry us humming across wet tarmac, away from love and shame and sorrow, all the way to the neighbourhood beyond the Misery.

Appendix

After close interrogation, it has emerged that Alexander Knisch, thirty-five years old today and registered at the Otto-Ludwig-Straße 1, was standing in the closet of said flat on the last Friday in June, 1928. Holding his fists clenched, he claims to have been shutting his eyes violently. Finally, however, he felt forced to give in to his 'obscure drives' (Knisch's words) and leave his 'involuntary paradise' (ditto). As he emerged, he opened his eyes and saw Dr Felix Karp lying dead on the bed.

Shortly thereafter, Dora Wilms entered the room. She informed him that Karp had paid her a visit, during which he had suffered an epileptic attack. Half an hour later, Knisch was dressed in his own clothes, while Wilms had traded hers for those of the dead doctor. Since she planned to catch the train to Copenhagen, she hurriedly extended her cigarette case to her accomplice. According to Knisch, she said: 'Promise me not to open it the way you did with your sister's diary. Before I've found out what's going on, I don't want the contents to be known to anyone.' Putting the key in her pocket, she added: 'And for heaven's sake, Sascha, don't tell anyone I'm alive.'

When Knisch asked her what he was supposed to tell the police, she merely replied: 'Just say Felix told you about my boy.

If they ask when, claim you visited him at the Foundation. Or better: pretend you're doing it tomorrow. That way, nobody will think it's Felix rather than me who's dead.' She nudged her accomplice into the stairway. 'Now, please go.'

In connection with the successful investigation of the Foundation for Sexual Research in May of last year, data emerged that resulted in the final closure of the case. Unfortunately, it has not been possible to trace the whereabouts of Miss Wilms. As I suspected already during the summer of 1928, this is due, in no small measure, to the fact that Chief Inspector Karla Manetti kept important information to herself. But sooner or later, the naked truth will prevail. Finally, Horst Hauptstein, the man behind Testifortan Plus, may be vindicated. The fact that he died while still in jail, and thus is unable to experience this moment of triumph, is hardly reason enough not to balance the scales of justice.

The data secured in conjunction with said investigation will serve as evidence in the charge of grave misconduct that shall now be made against Manetti. During our search of her offices, the attached manuscript was found. I have had the far from agreeable task of undoing the stocking used as a string and of evaluating the contents. The best that can be said about the account is that it has an imaginative, at times almost floral character. When Knisch was taken into custody, he denied all knowledge of the text. After certain measures were taken, however, he corroborated scenes reproduced above. There is reason to believe, then, that Knisch suffers from a serious defect of the sexual instinct. There is also reason to assume his 'obscure drives' have, in reality, been directeds towards a Hebrew from Vienna. The questionnaire confiscated during our search of his former lodgings strengthens this impression. Evidently, the formula '*K. u. K*', that is, 'Knisch and Knisch', signals a far from ideal friendship between men.

Nonetheless, the flimsy suggestions scattered across nearly every page of this manuscript, are not – I repeat: *are not* – supported by hard evidence. In addition, judgments concerning certain citizens border on defamation. Dr Osram Röser, for instance, who meritoriously runs the Institute for Biological Culture, is above suspicion. The same applies to Mr Alf Kinkel, Röser's old assistant and comrade from the early years of the struggle. And it goes without saying that Inspector Diels at the Section for Political Security merely acted in accordance with the law. What better proof is there of the integrity of these fine gentlemen than the former Health Chancellor's cowardly flight abroad?

For these reasons alone, it is my conviction that Karla Manetti should not be allowed to refer to Knisch's speculations when her case is brought before the court. Deviant literature of this nature must be forbidden, and thereafter face the same fate as the Hatz residency so many years ago – or for that matter Froehlich's library last spring. In one word: fire. Just as in the case of the treatment of one's own body, literature cannot be the individual's solitary responsibility. Words are like clothes: nobody is free to choose them at the expense of his surroundings. What will happen to men of Knisch's sort, I am certain the future will show.

Dr Gunnar Wickert
Department of Criminal Medicine
January 1934